PRAISE FOR
BACKSTAGE PASS

"Olivia Cunning's erotic romance debut is phenomenal. The chemistry between Myrna and Brian is palpable, and their sexual encounters page searing… Cunning has me hooked on The Sinners and I cannot wait to follow their journey with the next book, *Rock Hard.*"

—Love Romance Passion

"Superb sexual chemistry… a very strong, well-put together story… This is not your average erotica romance; it's oh SO much better. This series is going to be a big hit with readers who like strong stories, hot sex, and a wild ride to their happily ever after!"

—Sia McKye's Thoughts Over Coffee

"These guys are so sensual, sexual, and yummy… Each member of the band is unique. You can't help but fall in love with them all."

—Night Owl Romance, Reviewer Top Pick

"A wonderful debut novel by a talented new contemporary writer… I am a huge fan of Maya Banks' Sweet series… Well, ladies and gentlemen, I believe I've found its equal!… I wanted to start this book over the second I hit 'the end.'"

—Yummy Men and Kick Ass Chicks

Rock
HARD

OLIVIA
CUNNING

sourcebooks
casablanca

Published by Sourcebooks Casablanca, an imprint of Sourcebooks, Inc.
P.O. Box 4410, Naperville, Illinois 60567-4410
(630) 961-3900
FAX: (630) 961-2168
www.sourcebooks.com

Library of Congress Cataloging-in-Publication Data

Cunning, Olivia.
  Rock hard : sinners on tour / by Olivia Cunning.
     p. cm.
  1. Rock musicians—Fiction. I. Title.
  PS3603.U6635R63 2011
  813'.6—dc22

                              2010043655

                    Printed and bound in Canada
                    WC 10 9 8 7 6 5 4 3 2 1

Dedicated to the memory of Kurt Cobain
whose talent and ingenuity
inspired a generation of musicians,
stirred the hearts and souls
of innumerable fans,
and convinced me that
"a mosquito, my libido"
are magnificent lyrics.

Chapter 1

JESSICA WAS THE HAPPIEST woman on the planet. Life could not have been more perfect. She snuck up behind Sed, wrapped her arms around his neck, and kissed his ear. "Hey, baby, guess what?"

"What?" he said absently.

She peeked around his shoulder to find him scowling at a stack of invoices.

"I got in!"

His scowl deepened in confusion. "You got in? Got in what?"

She pulled the acceptance letter from her back pocket and snapped it open in front of him. This would wipe the scowl from his gorgeous face.

While he read, she gazed at her recently acquired engagement ring. After all her hard work in school, her dreams were finally becoming a reality. Having a hunky rising-star rock vocalist as her fiancé was the frosting on her Pop Tart.

"Law school?" His deep voice rumbled through his back against her chest.

"Yeah. Isn't it great? I'm so excited. We have to go out and celebrate." She kissed his temple and squeezed him. "I'll go put on a skirt. We'll go sightseeing. I want you to make love to me on a crowded street. Maybe Rodeo Drive. Or Hollywood Boulevard. What do you think?"

"I can't afford to put you through law school, Jess. I can't even afford to fix the transmission in the fuckin' tour bus." He tossed her acceptance letter on his stack of invoices.

"Don't worry." She pulled out a second letter. Her financial aid award letter. "Scholarships, grants, waivers. I only have to come up with $3,000 a semester."

Sed shoved his chair away from the table and went to open the banged-up refrigerator. Finding it empty, he closed it again. "I don't have $3,000, Jessica."

He didn't get it. This was her dream. He was encouraged to pursue his. Why wasn't she? Even though Sed's band, Sinners, would probably never make it as big as their front man envisioned, she believed in him. Was it so much to ask that he believed in her, too?

"I don't expect you to pay for it, Sed. I'll find a way. I just want you to be happy for me. Congratulate me. Something. This is the most important thing that's ever happened to me."

He leaned back against the counter and crossed his arms over his chest. For a second, she was struck by how attractive he was. Those broad shoulders, bulging muscles, narrow hips. Black hair, blue eyes. A face that belonged in movies. And then he opened his mouth. "I'm the most important thing that's ever happened to you. And *you* aren't going."

"What do you mean I'm not going?"

"You're not going to law school. You'll be far too busy keeping me entertained in the bedroom. When that gets boring, you'll pop out five or six kids and take care of them while I tour with the band and make us all rich and famous."

That was his big scheme for her life? Was he fucking kidding her? "I've dreamt of being a lawyer since I was a little girl, Sedric. I *am* going to law school. And you're not telling me how to live my life."

"If you want to be my wife, you're not going. I forbid it."

She stared at him in disbelief. "You did *not* just say that."

"Yeah, I did."

"Then I don't want to be your wife."

He scoffed, looking amused. "You don't mean that."

That cocksure attitude of his—the one that had attracted her to him in the first place—made her grit her teeth. She yanked the ring off her finger and flung it at him. It hit him in the chest and he caught it against his body with his hand.

"There! Go hock that cheap piece of shit, fix your precious tour bus, and make yourself famous with your stupid band, you asshole."

He stared at her in disbelief.

"We're through, Sed."

His blue eyes widened. "You're breaking up with me?" For the first time in their four months together, Jessica saw a dent in his armor of self-assurance. "No one has ever broken up with me. Ever."

Fuckin' A, he totally missed the point. "What did you expect? That I'd be happy as your little toy?"

His cocky grin returned. "Well, aren't you? You never complain in the bedroom."

She had no complaints in the bedroom. Their bodies were made for each other. Their sexual appetites perfectly in sync. It was everything else that didn't work between them. "I'm leaving, Sed."

She hesitated. This was his last chance to make things right between them. All he had to do was admit he was wrong to try to control her life. Wrong to think of her as an object instead of a person. A person he supposedly loved enough to be his wife.

She waited. Wanting him. God, she always wanted him. As overbearing and arrogant as he was, she wanted him. She did not, however, need him.

"I don't think you will." He chuckled. "You're not strong enough to leave me."

Jessica snatched her acceptance letter off the table and proved him wrong.

Chapter 2

JESSICA'S CONFIDENT SMILE FADED as the grade on her final paper burned its ugly red image onto her retina.

F.

An F?

She gulped air.

An F! Failure. Failurino. Failurocity. Failtacular. Failpendous. Epic… fail.

The note scrawled beneath Jessica's inconceivable grade read, *Perhaps next time you will consider completing your paper as assigned, Ms. Chase.*

"Check it out," the guy seated next to her said. He leaned way into her personal space and tapped his paper with the back of his fingertips. "The Ice Queen gave me an A minus. What did you get, Wonder Brain? The Pulitzer prize for best final paper evah?"

Jessica hurriedly stuffed her failing (*failing?*) paper into her leather folio. "They don't give Pulitzers for that."

"Duh. That was a joke. So, are you tired of rejecting me yet?"

She climbed from her chair, her knees shaky. An F? How? *How?* There had to be some mistake.

She headed toward the podium at the front of the room where Dr. Ellington stood. Ellington always looked perfectly put together. Her sleek blonde hair, cut in an ear-length bob, swayed slightly as she placed papers into her briefcase. Her trim navy blue skirt suit was worth more than Jessica's car. Ellington might have been considered pretty if she didn't look so shrewd. And intimidating.

Jessica gripped her portfolio tighter.

Someone grabbed Jessica's arm. She turned to find the guy with the A minus looking down at her hopefully. Handsome and neat in his blue Polo shirt and Dockers, he raked a hand through his sandy brown hair. "Join me for coffee?"

"No, thank you."

"A movie? Dinner?"

"No, uhh…" Her eyebrows drew together. "What's your name again?"

His pretty-boy face fell. "Doug. I've sat next to you for four months and you don't remember my name?"

Well, lots of guys sat next to her. She couldn't be expected to remember their names when she had zero interest in them.

"Sorry. Doug. I can't talk right now. I need to speak to Dr. Ellington about something important."

"I'll wait for you."

"Not interested."

"Of course not. You're never interested in anyone. You only date assholes, am I right?"

Her ex-fiancé's image flittered through her mind's eye. Sedric Lionheart definitely qualified as an asshole. But they'd split two years ago, so she no longer dated assholes. Or anyone, for that matter. "What kind of question is that?"

"Nice, smart, and beautiful." He ticked his words off on three fingers. "The recipe for a woman who only dates assholes."

Jessica's eyes narrowed. "Then why do I keep turning *you* down?"

Doug winced and covered his heart with one hand. "Ouch. The beauty has claws." He chuckled. "I'll meet you outside."

"Seriously, Doug, don't bother."

"I'll wait."

She shook his hand off her arm and continued to the podium.

When Jessica stopped in front of Dr. Ellington, the woman smiled like a snake in bronze lipstick.

"Do you have a moment, professor? I'd like to talk to you about my grade."

"Nothing to talk about, Chase."

"I don't understand how you could have…" Jessica swallowed and forced the next word out. "…*failed* me. My paper is good." She straightened her spine, grasping for self-confidence she didn't feel. "Excellent."

Ellington shrugged. "Maybe, but as I clearly indicated, you didn't follow directions."

That wasn't true. *Exactly.* "I dissected the assigned case. Reviewed all the court documents. The associated literature. Tackled the defense's position and the plaintiff's. Evaluated the verdict and the effects the case had on future cases."

"You also determined that the defense took the wrong position and proceeded to rebuild the case in some egotistical attempt to prove you could win."

Egotistical? Jessica opened her mouth. Closed it again. Took a gasping breath. "But the defense lost because they approached the case from the wrong standpoint. If they'd have followed my strategy—"

"Ms. Chase, you are a second year law student. Do you really think you can win a case that professional lawyers couldn't?"

"Yes, actually, I do. If you'd take another look—"

Dr. Ellington lifted a hand to silence her. "The grade stands, Chase. You need a serious attitude adjustment." She smiled coldly. "Have a nice summer."

Jessica caught her arm. "Wait. I'll rewrite it. Take out every reference to my alternate strategy."

"You should have done it right the first time." Ellington brushed her hand aside. "Your pack of male admirers is waiting for you." She nodded toward the door. "Maybe they can help you with your little problem."

Jessica glanced over her shoulder at the six or seven guys watching her from the doorway. What did they have to do with anything? She covered her forehead with one hand, fighting tears.

"Oh, don't cry, pretty little Jessica." Ellington gave her a pitying pout. "You wouldn't want to make my day now, would you?" She scraped her briefcase off the podium and turned. She stopped abruptly so she didn't careen into the Dean of Students, Dr. Taylor, who had just entered the door behind her.

Taylor kind of looked like Perry Mason, except, well, *old*. "Can I see you in my office for a few minutes?"

Ellington stiffened, lowered her head, and nodded.

Taylor then turned his attention to Jessica. "You look upset, Jessica. Everything okay?"

No, everything was decidedly *not* okay. She glanced at Dr. Ellington, somehow feeling it was wrong to complain about the woman's grading practices to her boss. Maybe Jessica had deserved to fail. She hadn't followed the assignment's directions. Instead, she'd tried to impress her professor with her brilliant strategy. She'd obviously failed at that.

"Everything's fine," Jessica croaked.

"If you'd like to discuss something with me in private, my door is always open."

Kind of him to offer, she thought. She glanced up at him to find him staring at her chest. He licked his lips as his eyes drifted up her throat and then back to her breasts. "Yes, my door is always open for you, Jessica Chase."

Ellington grabbed his arm. "Let's go have that meeting now."

Dr. Taylor grinned. "Oh yes, our meeting." He touched Jessica's cheek. "Have a nice summer."

Before Jessica could flinch away from his touch, he turned and strode toward the door with Ellington on his heels.

Jessica shuffled out of the building, the chattering of her

following classmates background noise. She'd probably have to retake Ellington's class next year. As a third-year student. The ultimate humiliation for the head of the class. Or she had been at the top of the class. Now? She was probably at the bottom.

As she stepped out of the building, she gazed up at Southern California's hazy blue sky. The sun shone in complete contrast to the storm clouding her perspective.

"Jess!" Her roommate, Beth, also a law student, grabbed her in an enthusiastic hug. "Last day of classes. Ready to go celebrate?"

Jessica's one female friend. The only person she had ever allowed herself to depend on. If it hadn't been for Beth's support, she'd probably still be crying herself to sleep over Sed every night. Jessica clung to Beth, fighting tears. Beth tugged her away and looked down at her, cupping her cheek gently.

"Oh no, something's wrong. We need chocolate ice cream. Stat!"

Later, with a carton of chocolate ice cream between them on Jessica's bed, Beth responded to the situation with appropriate best friend angst. "I read that paper. That was an A paper. An A *plus* paper. Ellington has it out for you or something. You should go to Dr. Taylor. Tell him what happened. Maybe he can help."

Jessica shoveled another spoon of ice cream into her mouth, feeling marginally better with each gulp. "That guy is sleazy. All he does is stare at my breasts."

"Everyone stares at your breasts, Jess."

"I'm also the only student he knows by name."

"You really don't get it, do you?"

"Get what?"

"You're gorgeous. You have guys falling all over themselves to be with you, yet you turn them all down. And how long has it been since you've had sex?"

"You know I haven't since—"

"You dumped that stupid prick you were engaged to."

Jessica nodded. She didn't understand why Sed still plagued her.

"Are you ever going to get over him?"

"I am over him." She hated his fucking guts. Mostly because she missed him so much.

"Whatever, sweetie. Just who do you think wiped your tears every night for six months?"

"But I don't cry over him anymore."

Beth gave her a pitying look. "I know. I'm sorry I brought him up." She slurped ice cream from her spoon. "Did you find a job yet?"

"No." Which worried her. All the paying positions she'd tried to line up for the summer had fallen through. She could have her choice of unpaid internships, but she needed money and the job market sucked. "I've got to make at least $8,000 extra this summer. One of my scholarships was only renewable for two years. I have to replace that money somehow."

"Just take out some loans."

"I refuse to be in debt. You've seen my mother's situation. I'll never follow her path to financial ruin. Required to have a man to take care of me. No self-respect." Jessica shoveled several spoonfuls of ice cream into her mouth at the thought of her mother.

"I don't think it's quite the same, Jess. You're paying for an education. What was she paying for?"

Jessica rolled her eyes. "Breast implants. Nose job. Tanning. Body wraps. Lingerie. Things to land herself a rich husband."

Beth chuckled. "Yet she married four losers."

"Five, if you count the current loser."

"See, no comparison. Just take out a loan and spend the summer on the beach."

Jessica smiled. "You're a bad influence, Beth."

"The only way you'll make that kind of cash in three months is illegally." Beth got a reflective look on her face. "Or…"

"Why don't I like the sound of that 'or'?"

"My cousin, Aggie, works at a strip club called Paradise Found in Las Vegas."

"A strip club? What does that have to do with me?"

"She makes a fortune, Jessica. With your looks and that body, you'll have men throwing money at you by the handful."

"No way in hell, Beth."

"Why not? You were a natural when we took that pole dancing fitness class. The instructor said you should go pro. And I know you had fun. You liked it."

Pole dancing was fun and she had liked it. Loved it, actually.

"Don't you think exotic dancing will hurt my chances for respectable employment as a defense attorney?"

"Nope. Not really. Just use a stage name. No one will know."

"Uh, duh, Beth, employment history is searchable under your social security number."

"No one is going to care if you worked in a club while you were in college. Stop making excuses. Admit it. It's a good idea."

"It's not gonna happen. Just drop it."

"So I guess that means you're staying with your mother and stepfather this summer." Beth snorted with amusement. "That should be fun. How's Ed?"

As a rule, Jessica tried not to think of her stepfather, Ed. The way he always stared at her with his protruding eyes. Accidentally touched her and rubbed up against her. Picked the bathroom door lock to catch her in the shower. Watched her sleep. Used her toothbrush "by mistake." One time she'd caught him jacking off in her closet with her panties wrapped around his pathetic cock. Jessica shuddered. Ed was a good enough reason to avoid going home, but her mother's inevitable "blame Jessica for my darling hubby's weakness" position was too much to bear.

Jessica covered her churning stomach with one hand.

There was nothing wrong with exotic dancing, really. Perfectly legal. Great money. Potentially empowering. Maybe it was time for her physical gifts to give her something besides anxiety.

"Paradise Found, huh? Do you have Aggie's number?"

Chapter 3

IN THE DIMLY LIT bedroom of Sinners' tour bus, Sed gazed down at the bombshell blonde. She pressed her unnaturally firm breast into his arm, a coy smile on her hot pink lips.

"But Sed, the show's sold out." She pouted and placed a presumptuous hand on his belly. "Don't you have some extra tickets?" When he didn't respond, her hand drifted toward the low waistband of his jeans.

These chicks were all the same.

"I might." Sed rubbed his jaw. He needed to shave before they headed to the club for his lead guitarist's bachelor party. He had a few minutes, though.

"Can I have them?"

"Depends. What will you give me in return?"

Her hand gripped his waistband and she jerked him toward her. "I'll suck you off."

They never offered to do his laundry.

Sed fished several condoms out of his pocket and examined them. "I've got cherry or piña colada flavored."

"A condom?" She wrinkled her too-perfect-to-be-God-given nose at him. As hot as she was, with her bleached hair, bronze tan, and long pink fingernails, she radiated fake.

"I don't know where your mouth's been."

She shrugged and grabbed a condom out of his hand. "Whatever."

She opened the fly of his pants and freed his half-hard dick from its confines. By the time she unrolled the condom over his cock, he was rock hard.

"I wasn't expecting you to be so big," she said in awe.

"Afraid you can't take it?" he said, grinning crookedly.

"No, I think I want you to fuck me."

"You *think?*"

She grabbed the base of his shaft and encircled its head with her bright pink lips. Overly plump lips. What did they call that shit they injected into them? Collagen?

At times like these, he missed Jessica. Jessica had been real.

The blonde on her knees drew Sed into the warm recess of her mouth, sucking gently. He closed his eyes, picturing Jessica's face while Fake-n-bake sucked him. He placed a hand on the top of her head, finding her hair sticky with hair spray. He didn't even know this chick's name. She'd accosted him outside the tour bus only ten minutes ago, when he'd been backing Myrna's '57 Thunderbird off the trailer. Myrna was a sweetheart for letting them borrow her car to take her man to a strip club. Any other bride-to-be would have told them to walk.

The blonde pulled back, allowing Sed's cock to spring free of her mouth. The fact that he could think indicated she couldn't keep his interest. Few women did. He opened his eyes to find her staring up at him.

"Okay, now I know I want you to fuck me," she said.

Sed checked the time on the clock radio beside the queen-sized bed. "I don't have time. The guys are gonna want to leave in half an hour."

"I don't care if you hurry."

She climbed to her feet and peeled her tank top over her head. She wasn't wearing a bra. Didn't need to. Her tits were firmer than the cantaloupes they resembled. He cupped them in his hands and squeezed. They looked good, but should be softer and yield to the palms of his hands. He pushed them together and released them, watching them settle back into place with minimal movement.

"Like I said, I only have half an hour," he said.

"I don't need foreplay."

He honestly didn't think he could get off with this chick. It could take hours.

"Hold on." He opened the bedroom door. "Eric!" he called to the band's drummer.

Eric stuck his head out of the bathroom. His hair was already fashioned into spikes along the center, short on one side, long on the other. The lock of hair that trailed down the side of his neck was currently dyed crimson red. Half of Eric's lean face was covered with shaving cream; the other half, clean-shaven. He was practically ready to go, which meant Sed needed to hurry. The guys would be waiting for him and he wanted Brian's last night as a bachelor to be memorable.

"What?" Eric asked.

"Are there any more groupies around? This chick wants me to fuck her."

"Dude, we're leaving soon. Just tell her no."

"You don't want to watch us?"

"No time." Eric tapped his watch with the handle of his razor. "Come on. We have to hurry."

The blonde leaned against Sed's back, her arm wrapping around his waist. Her hand encircled his dick.

He should just tell her no, like Eric said, but he had this hard-on to contend with now. No sense in jacking off when he had warm and willing flesh at his disposal. "Thanks, Eric. For nothing."

Eric shrugged and disappeared into the bathroom. Sed stepped back into the bedroom and closed the door. A compromise. He turned to look at the blonde and found she'd become naked.

"I'll fuck you for like fifteen minutes," he said, "but then you'll have to suck me off with some enthusiasm."

"You can't come in fifteen minutes?"

"With one chick? No." Unless it was Jessica. He'd never had a problem finding satisfaction before he'd met her, but since she left him…

"All right. If you don't come in fifteen minutes, I'll suck you off. With enthusiasm," she said, finger quoting "enthusiasm."

He kicked off his pants and wrapped his hands around her narrow waist. "Are you wet?"

She grinned at him. "Fuck yeah, I'm wet."

He lifted her off the floor by her waist. "Then slide it in."

She wrapped her long legs around his waist and reached between them to guide his cock into her body. His hands moved to her ass. He tilted her hips and drove himself deeper. She gasped, her head falling back. "Ah, Sed."

He stepped closer to the bed. "Lean back."

She clung to his shoulders and leaned away from him.

"Farther," he instructed.

"I'll fall."

"That's the idea."

She slowly leaned back, obviously not trusting him. As she lost her balance, she tumbled back on the bed, landing on her shoulders, her back bent. He followed her as she fell and drove his cock deep.

"Oh God," she cried. "Sed! Yes, ram me hard."

At least she was a screamer.

He sandwiched her pelvis between his hands, holding her steady as he thrust down into her and ground his hips. He pulled back and growled as he thrust into her again. Typically, chicks loved it when he growled. He did it when he sang onstage, so it reminded them who was fucking them. This one was no exception.

"Yes, Sed! Yes! Oh God, your voice is so sexy." She played with her nipples, stroking and plucking at them as she gasped in delight.

Sed used his hands to encourage her to rotate her hips, while he continued to thrust hard and grind deep. She screamed when an orgasm gripped her. Her body quaked and strained against his as her spasmodically clenching pussy sucked greedily at his dick. He grabbed her around the waist and slid her farther up the bed, so that her crotch rested even with the end of the mattress. She relaxed, apparently thinking he was finished with her. Her fifteen minutes were far from over.

He turned her onto her side and straddled one of her legs at the edge of the bed. Taking her from the side, he thrust into her, rotating his hips to stimulate her clit.

"Ah, Sed, you're an absolute god."

He found her to be boring, actually. He glanced at the clock, wondering if she'd notice if he cut her time short. Maybe if he closed his eyes and thought of someone else…

No good. Jessica actually moved, participated, knew how to please him. She was the one who'd gotten him addicted to sex in the first place. This girl (whatever her name was) didn't even try to satisfy him.

When she screamed with a second orgasm, he turned her flat on her back and slid her further up the mattress. Why should he work so hard to please her when she was just lying there taking it?

He settled between her thighs, his thrusts easy and even. Missionary position brought them face-to-face, but it was easier on his body. She looked up into his eyes. Hers were brown and glazed with pleasure. Jessica's were jade green, surrounded with thick lashes.

Fake-n-bake lifted her head to kiss him, but Sed pressed his forehead into her shoulder to prevent their lips from meeting. He hadn't kissed a woman in almost two years. He certainly didn't want to get personal with this chick.

She ran her hands up his back and he shuddered, gasping softly. She'd discovered his most sensitive erogenous zone, but either she didn't notice his reaction or didn't care. She clung to his shoulders, vocalizing her pleasure in the back of her throat.

After a few minutes, he said, "I think it's time for you to suck me. I've got to leave soon."

She sighed. "All right. Can you take off the condom though?"

"No." He pulled out and rolled next to her.

"I'm afraid I'll suck it down my throat."

He chuckled. "I don't think that will be a problem." He sighed when she sucked him deep. She wasn't too bad at this. A bit timid. "Suck it hard," he said. "Harder. Yeah, that's it."

He usually fought orgasm for as long as he could, but in this case, he concentrated on coming as quickly as possible. When he let go, it was far from satisfying, but at least it was over.

She grinned up at him. "How was that?"

"Tolerable." He climbed from the bed and removed the condom, tying a knot in the open end and tossing it in the wastebasket.

"You're an asshole."

He found his pants and put them on. "Yeah. So. Is that a problem?"

She laughed. "Not for me. Can I have my tickets?"

"I'll see if Jake has one." Jake, one of their long-time roadies, usually distributed tickets and backstage passes to women he thought might interest the band. He had an eye for good pussy.

"One?" she said, pouting annoyingly.

"Yeah, one."

"What about my boyfriend?"

Sed lifted an eyebrow at her. "Do you really think he's gonna want to come to my show if he knows how you got his ticket?"

"Of course. He's a huge fan of yours. He'll be excited to put his junk where yours has been." She scrunched her hair with both hands, eyeing herself in the mirror over the dresser. "Two?"

Sed tugged a black T-shirt over his head and rubbed a hand over the soft stubble of his short hair. "Uhhhh… No. You're lucky to get one."

When he left the room, she was getting dressed and scowling.

Eric accosted Sed in the corridor. "Everyone is waiting for you."

"Just let me shave. And tell Jake to give that girl a ticket for tomorrow night's show so she'll get lost."

"I don't think he has any left. We're opening for Exodus End. Not the headliner."

"Then ask Dare for one. He'll share." Dare was Exodus End's lead guitarist. He was also the older brother of Sed's rhythm guitarist, Trey. Sed and Dare went way back. Sorta. "Come on, man. I'd do it myself, but I need to shave. You're ready."

Eric sighed loudly and turned to exit the tour bus, muttering something under his breath about a fucking errand boy.

Sed hurried through his shave. He'd nearly finished when Myrna, soon-to-be Mrs. Brian Sinclair, came to stand in the doorway. She leaned against the doorframe and watched him carefully draw the razor up under his chin. She wore a trim tweed skirt, purple camisole, and two-inch heels. Strands of auburn hair had come loose from the knot at the base of her neck to curl against her lovely heart-shaped face. Now here was a classy and beautiful woman. Someone Sed could respect. He totally understood why Brian had to tumble her into bed every couple of hours. She had an untouchable quality that heightened a man's sense of challenge. Too bad she only had eyes for his lead guitarist. Sed's every attempt to seduce her had met with failure.

"Promise me you'll bring him home safe, Sed," Myrna said.

He grinned at her. "I promise. He might be too drunk to walk, but he'll be safe."

Brian appeared in the doorway next to Myrna. He wrapped an arm around her waist and nuzzled her neck. "I think I'd rather skip the bachelor party," he murmured. "Celebrate the end of bachelorhood in the bedroom with you."

Sed rolled his eyes. "You can't have a bachelor party with your fiancée, you dumbass."

The couple in the doorway stared into each other's eyes as if they were the only two people on Earth. Sed didn't know whether to be jealous or repulsed.

"I love you," Brian murmured.

Myrna touched Brian's jaw. "I love you."

"You sure?"

"One hundred percent."

Brian smiled like a lunatic and kissed her. "I love you."

"I love you," she whispered, her fingers stealing into his shoulder-length black hair. Only inches separated their mouths as they continued to lose themselves to their closeness, completely in tune with one another.

"Knock it off, you two," Sed demanded. "You're giving me diabetes."

"Tomorrow I get to call you Mrs. Sinclair," Brian said to Myrna, ignoring Sed.

"What do I get to call you?"

"My Personal Sex God."

She chuckled. "That's a given."

Trey, Brian's best friend and the band's rhythm guitarist, wriggled between the couple's bodies. "Isn't there some sort of rule against the bride and groom seeing each other before the wedding?" He covered Myrna's eyes with one hand and Brian's with the other. "No peeking."

Brian punched him in the ribs.

Trey clutched his midsection with both arms. "Did you see that, Myrna?"

Myrna brushed Trey's hair from his face and kissed him on the forehead. "Poor baby."

Trey hugged Myrna's waist and rested his head on her shoulder. "Hold me." He gazed up at her with one emerald green eye. His over-long black bangs concealed the other. Everyone knew his innocent looks were entirely fabricated, but Myrna didn't seem to care. She wrapped an arm around him and rubbed his back.

"Get off her," Brian insisted, shoving Trey into the corridor.

"We going?" Jace, bassist and token platinum blond of the group, asked. He maintained a growth of dark beard stubble to toughen up his look, but it was his cold, chocolate-brown eyes that prevented most people from fixating on how fucking adorable he was.

"Just waiting on Sed," Trey said. "Where'd Eric go?"

"He's hunting Jake," Sed told him.

Brian had Myrna pinned to his body now, kissing her like he was trying to permanently meld his mouth to hers. Slowly inching her conservative skirt up her thighs, he rubbed her ass and ground his pelvis against hers. They were already enjoying themselves more than Sed had not ten minutes ago. Didn't seem fair.

"Trey, do something about your friend," Sed insisted.

Trey grabbed Brian by the top of the ear and pulled him viciously from Myrna's embrace. "Save it for the honeymoon, stud."

Brian leaned over to ease the pull on his ear. "Ow, ow, ow, ow. Okay!"

Fake-n-bake wandered out of the bedroom, fully dressed now. "Are you guys going out? Can I come with?"

"No," the four band mates said in unison.

Eric stomped up the front bus stairs. "Here," he said, thrusting a ticket at the blonde girl. "Enjoy." He squeezed his lithe form between his band mates to stare at Sed, who was wiping the last traces of shaving cream onto a towel. "Don't ask me to be your errand boy again, Lionheart."

Sed chuckled. "You know you'll do what I ask, Eric. No one else indulges your bizarre fetishes."

Eric glanced behind him at the other guys. "Yeah, well, maybe I'm tired of watching you get laid."

Trey and Brian burst out laughing. "Yeah right, Eric," Trey said. "You ready, Sed?"

"Let's go."

Brian kissed Myrna good-bye. "You can come with us."

"To a strip club?" Her eyebrows shot up in question. "No, thanks. I can get some work done on my band groupie project while you're gone. You have a good time with the guys."

He backed up a step. "I love you."

"I love you too. Now go!"

He turned reluctantly and shuffled after the other guys.

"Don't worry, Myrna. I'll keep an eye on him," Sed assured her.

"Thanks. And could you do me another favor?"

"Anything."

Myrna tilted her head pointedly at Fake-n-bake, who was watching this all transpire as if it were on Pay-Per-View.

Sed took the blonde by one elbow and directed her toward the front of the bus. "Come on, time for you to leave."

There was a loud *thunk* on the side of the bus. "I love you, Myrna!" Brian called from outside.

Sed shook his head. "God, I can't believe he acts like that when he's sober."

Myrna chuckled. "Stay safe. Which club are you going to? In case I need to find you."

He released the blonde's elbow and stepped close to Myrna, using his height and breadth to its greatest advantage. "Are you being a nag or a drag, Professor Sex?"

She stood her ground, lifting an eyebrow of annoyance at him. "Which club, Sed?"

He chuckled. He loved a chick he couldn't intimidate. "Paradise Found."

Chapter 4

SED HELD OPEN THE chrome-plated swinging door for Brian and slapped him on the back as he passed. Brian winced, though Sed couldn't tell if it was from being knocked around or because he'd caught his first glimpse of topless women. Even the cocktail waitresses treated them to full frontal nudity. Very nice.

"Sed, honestly. This bachelor party is unnecessary." Brian paused on the threshold and raked a hand through his black hair. Tonight, he wore it like he did onstage—lightly gelled and sticking out at odd angles. Thank God he'd gone without his guyliner. "I'd rather just go back to the tour bus and spend the evening with Myrna."

Sed rolled his eyes and shook his head. "Dude, after tomorrow, you're going to be saddled with her for life. For *life*. She a great chick and all, but that's a very long time. Enjoy your last night as a bachelor. Trey, do something about this guy." Sed looked behind Brian. Trey had been there a moment ago.

No Trey now, just their bassist, Jace.

"Where'd Trey go? What's a bachelor party without the best man?"

Jace jerked his bleached-blond head toward the bar three doors down.

Sed glanced at the sign over the door and rubbed a hand over his face. "A gay bar? When is he gonna decide if he likes dick or pussy?"

"I think the problem is he likes both," Eric said.

"A lot," Brian added.

"Equally," Jace said.

"Don't worry," Eric said. "It shouldn't take him long to pick up some tail."

Sed sighed. He worried about the members of his band. Brian was the most normal of the batch and he was acting like a total wuss now that he was getting married. "Well, Brian, it's your call."

"Fine, we'll stay. If you promise not to buy me a lap dance."

"Dude, Myrna won't find out. Who's gonna tell her?"

"I'm sure Myrna would be cool with it. I'm just not interested."

Eric grabbed Brian by the arm and urged him further into the club. "You need to loosen up, Mr. Stuffy von Stickinthemud."

Sed followed them to the bar. He ordered a whiskey on the rocks and scanned the various stages, looking for the stripper he found most attractive. Two blondes on the center stage worked the pole together, caressing and kissing each other whenever their dancing brought their bodies together. "That is hot," Sed said. They'd make a nice Sed sandwich. He wondered if he could convince them to work *his* pole together. He downed his whiskey and thumped his glass of ice on the bar for a refill.

"That is hotter." Jace nodded at the leather-clad, black-haired woman brandishing a whip on the left-hand stage. His entire body jerked with excitement every time her whip cracked.

Brian took his beer and headed for the stage on the far right side of the room. The most sedate of the three stages featured a strawberry blonde in white silk, lace, and feathers. A wide, silk scarf concealed her eyes and accentuated her femininity. Though she couldn't possibly see where she was going, she had her moves down perfectly and had no problem maintaining her mesmerizing, sensual dance without falling off the stage. Ah, well, it figured Brian would go for the sweet meat. Not that Sed minded, he had a soft spot for strawberry blondes. Jessica's hair had been strawb… Christ, why couldn't he stop thinking about her? The bitch had left him two frickin' years ago.

All the tables near the stage were full. Brian scanned the room for an empty seat, but Eric took his arm and directed him to a table in front of the stage. Six college-aged men looked well settled there, but Sed knew Eric wouldn't take no for an answer one way or another. Sipping his whiskey, Sed followed his friends.

"Hey, dudes, my buddy is getting married tomorrow," Eric said to the young guys. "How about you all get lost so we can sit here?"

One of the clean-cut guys said, "I feel for your friend, really, but we were here first."

Sed had to give the kid credit. Sed and his band mates didn't look like guys you should fuck with. Tattoos. Piercings. Chains. Jet black hair, with the exception of Jace and his bleached spikes. Denim and leather. They'd probably fit in better at a biker bar.

Tall and muscular, Sed was the largest and most intimidating of the group. He moved to stand beside Eric as back-up. He'd rather have these guys frightened into giving Eric his way. Sed didn't want to fight them, but he knew it wouldn't take much to move Eric to blows.

"I think you should reconsider." Sed glared down at the guys around the table.

Eric flexed his long fingers and cracked his knuckles.

"Christ, Eric, don't get us all arrested again." Brian massaged his forehead as if in great distress. "I mean you can only have so many deadly assault charges on your record before they keep you in the slammer for good. You know?"

Wide-eyed, the college-aged guys grabbed their drinks and moved to a table near the back of the room.

Sed smiled at Brian. "Smooth, Master Sinclair."

Brian shrugged and sat at the table. He took a sip of his beer. Sed sat to Brian's right. Eric to his left. Jace had vanished somewhere. Probably blowing a couple thousand bucks on the dominatrix on the other side of the room. Sed tossed his whiskey down his throat and signaled a cocktail waitress for another refill. Brian sipped his beer and glanced up at the dancer crawling across the stage toward them. He choked.

"Fuck me," Eric said, his eyes on the stripper as well. "Isn't that…"

Sed glanced at the beautiful woman, now lying at the front of the stage with her hair dangling over the edge, her backed arched and her perfect, naked breasts jutting into the air.

"Jessica."

Sed jumped to his feet. He shrugged off his leather jacket and tossed it over her body. Her *naked* body. Jessica. *His* Jessica was naked. *Naked.* In front of all these men.

When he pulled her off the stage, she gasped in surprise. He cocooned her against his chest, protecting her from lustful gazes.

A wall of bouncers surrounded them immediately. "No touching the dancers," one of the mountains of flesh said.

Jessica struggled in Sed's arms, but he wasn't about to let her go. Wasn't about to let these men gawk at her body.

"Sed." Brian grabbed his upper arm. "Let her go."

Jessica gasped. "Sed?" She rubbed her face against his shoulder to push the silk scarf from her eyes. It fell down around her nose and mouth. Her eyes widened. Those jade-green eyes. The ones that haunted him day and night. How was it possible that she'd become even more beautiful since he'd last seen her?

He lowered his head to kiss her, his heart swelling so full he thought it might suffocate him. It didn't matter that the scarf separated their mouths. He remembered the taste of her lips all too well.

A thick forearm wrapped around Sed's throat from behind, jerking his head back. He planted his boots firmly on the floor to prevent himself from tipping backward.

With her shoulder, Jessica nudged the scarf down to her neck. God, her lips. So full and inviting. He needed to kiss her again. Never stop kissing her.

"Put me down, Sed."

Her soft voice—just as he remembered it. The way she said his name squeezed his insides. So long since he'd heard it. Too long. He bit his lip. He didn't know if the bouncer's grip or his heart trying to force its way out of his mouth caused the greater ache in his throat.

"Let go of his throat, you fucking cretin," Eric bellowed. "He's a professional singer."

"I don't give a shit who—"

Eric punched the bouncer holding Sed and his grip loosened. It tightened further a moment later. Sed winced. Several bouncers grabbed Eric and forcefully escorted him away from the front of the stage.

"Get your fucking hands off me," Eric protested.

"Go quietly or we'll call the cops." Even with the throbbing music playing through the club, Sed heard several fists connect with flesh.

"Motherfuckers!" Was that Jace? More fists connected with flesh. The door slammed shut.

Jessica squirmed in Sed's arms. He had no doubt that if her hands were free she'd be slapping the shit out of him.

Brian sighed loudly beside him. "Well, I guess I've got to kick some ass now. Can't let my boys down." He moved out of Sed's peripheral vision toward the exit.

The door opened again. "What the fuck is going on?" Trey yelled into the club.

"Bellaway," Jessica shouted to the guy behind Sed. "I know this guy. I'm fine. Seriously, don't injure his throat." She looked into Sed's eyes. "Put me down, Sed. Now."

Sed tried to shake his head, but couldn't move his neck.

After a long moment, the arm around Sed's throat loosened.

The bouncer stepped away.

Sed swallowed. His throat burned, but he refused to release Jessica. Refused.

"What are you doing here?" he asked her angrily, except his usual baritone growl came out raspy.

"Put me down, Sed." Her nostrils flared in that way that always turned him on. There was nothing on Earth sexier than this woman when she was pissed off. Lucky for him, she had one hell of a temper.

"Answer my question and I'll put you down."

"Isn't it obvious?" Her eyebrows arched as she gazed up at him. "I'm dancing."

"I thought you were going to law school. Wasn't that your excuse for walking out on me?"

"That isn't why I left and you know it. Besides, law school isn't free. I've got to make money somehow. Now put me down. I answered your question."

"If you needed money, you should have asked." He set her on her feet and reached for his wallet. He pulled out a wad of cash and held it out to her. "Here. There's a couple thousand bucks here. I can get you more. Whatever you need."

"I don't want your money, Sed."

"Why, because I'm just giving it to you? Fine. What do you charge for an hour of your time? A couple hundred? I'll buy you for the night. Or the week."

Smack! She slapped him so hard he tasted blood. He winced, tonguing the cut on the inside of his cheek.

"I fucking hate you," she spat, her eyes narrowed dangerously. She stalked off, dropping his coat on the floor. Her perfect bare ass was the last thing he saw as she stormed out of his life. Again.

Chapter 5

JESSICA BURST INTO THE dressing room backstage, startling several of the girls who worked the next set. She plopped down on the stool in front of her mirror, pulled the silk scarf from her neck and lowered her face into her hands.

Of all the strip clubs in the world, Sed had to show up in hers.

Don't let him get to you. You're over him. Remember?

Someone dropped a robe around her shoulders. She glanced up at Beth's cousin, Agatha, the black-haired dominatrix who worked the south stage.

"You okay, kitten?"

Jessica nodded and wiped at a stray tear with the back of her hand. "Yeah, I just didn't expect to see a man from my past. That's all."

"That guy who pulled you offstage?"

"Yeah. I was engaged to him once."

"He told me to give you this." Aggie dropped a fat stack of cash onto Jessica's dressing table.

"Oh my God, that ass! Do you see why I couldn't marry him?" She looked up at Aggie, beseeching her for understanding.

"Uh no, actually, I don't. The guy is hotter than Phoenix in July. Absolutely gorgeous. That big, hard body. And that sweet, handsome face that completely contrasts with his 'who gives a shit what you think' aura. Growl." She bared her teeth, ruby red lips curling.

Aggie's ever-expressive face made Jessica smile. Just a little.

"You got all that from talking to him for twenty seconds?"

"Hey, you work in this business for very long and you get to know men. If he's carrying around that kind of cash, I'm guessing your eye candy is rich, too. Booyah!" Aggie thrust a fist in the air.

"No. No, *booyah*. He's not only rich, he's famous, which means his ego is larger than Alaska."

Aggie's brows drew together. "Famous?"

"Lead singer of Sinners. The band."

"I think I've heard of them. Rock music?"

"Hard rock. And you missed his most notorious 'quality.'" She finger quoted. "He has an insatiable appetite for sex. You can't get him out of bed long enough to have a decent conversation with him."

Aggie laughed, blue eyes twinkling. "I'm liking him more and more, doll."

"You're welcome to him."

Aggie's eyes wandered toward the ceiling as her expression turned thoughtful. "I don't think he'd be fun to dominate. I would probably just tick him off."

"I'm sure."

Jessica's gaze moved to the dressing table and the thousands of dollars sitting on its surface, mocking her. It would take her weeks to earn that kind of money, and Sed just tossed it around like it was a pittance. To him, it was. The bastard. Flaunting his wealth. Thinking it made him superior.

Jessica shook her head in annoyance, jumped to her feet, and scooped the money off the dressing table. Sliding her arms into the robe sleeves, she rushed out of the dressing room. She ran through the club with her robe flapping behind her and burst through the front doors, looking for signs of Sedric Lionheart. Apparently, he was long gone.

"Damn that man," she muttered under her breath.

She'd just have to hunt him down and shove his unwanted money in his face. He always did this. Treated her like she couldn't take care of herself. Like she needed Mr. Ego Trip to look after her. He'd never learn. Stupid asshole.

Someone needed to teach the guy a lesson.

Chapter 6

SED ENTERED THE TOUR bus first, his bruised and bloodied band mates behind him. Myrna sat at the small square dining table working at her laptop computer. She glanced up and her pretty hazel eyes widened in surprise.

Sed massaged his scalp. *Fuck, what a night.* Topped off with telling Myrna he'd broken his promise and failed to keep Brian safe.

"What are you guys doing back so early?" Myrna asked. "I thought you'd be out until dawn."

Sed blew out his cheeks as he tried to think of the right words. "I have to apologize to you, Myrna."

Her brow furrowed and she glanced behind Sed to Eric. Her eyes widened. "Oh my God, Eric. What happened?"

She jumped from the bench seat and pushed Sed aside. Easing Eric onto the cream-colored leather couch, she inspected the bleeding gash over his left eye. She turned, hurriedly wet a dish towel in the small stainless steel sink, and moved to dab at the blood running down the side of Eric's strong jaw. Eric winced, but smiled with pleasure as she fussed over him.

"Were you in an accident? Wait…" She looked at Sed. "Why are you apologizing to me, Sed? You didn't wreck my car, did you?"

He opened his mouth to explain, but she lifted a hand to stop him.

"You know what? It doesn't matter. It's just a car. At least you're all right. Where's Brian?" She glanced at Trey, who was searching the freezer for ice. And then Jace, who was trying to realign his jaw by shifting it back and forth with his horribly swollen and bloodied hand. "Where's Brian?" she repeated, a panicked edge to her voice.

"Brian's safe. We weren't in an accident, Myrna." Sed cleared his throat. It hurt to talk. How in the hell was he going to sing tomorrow?

"Then what happened?" She headed for the bus exit, anxiety marring her lovely face. "Brian?"

Brian stepped around the corner wearing Sed's mirrored sunglasses. "Hey, sweetheart. How was your evening? Did you get a lot of work done?"

Sed chuckled and shook his head. He'd wondered why Brian had wanted to borrow his shades. Like Myrna wouldn't notice his two black eyes at the altar tomorrow.

Myrna flew into Brian's arms. He winced in pain, but she had her face pressed against his neck, so didn't see his expression. "You scared me," she said. "I thought you were hurt."

Brian wrapped his arms around her and kissed the top of her head. "I'm okay."

Sed glanced at Trey, who was now holding a towel full of ice to the back of his head. "You need to call your brother." They were opening for his brother's band the next evening. Or they were supposed to. They weren't fit to perform now.

"I've had enough ass whippings for one day, thank you very much," Trey said. "You call him."

Myrna removed Brian's sunglasses and looked up at him. He avoided her gaze. "You've been fighting?"

"Wait, wait. I can explain."

She shoved him hard in the shoulder. "Am I marrying a seventh grader? I can't believe this."

She spun on her heel and stalked toward the bedroom at the back of the bus.

"Myrna." Brian started after her.

"Do *not* talk to me." She pushed Sed aside. "You were supposed to make sure he got home safely," she spat at Sed.

"Myrna," Sed said, but she brushed past him and entered the bedroom. The slam of the door echoed through the entire bus.

Brian rushed down the hallway and knocked. "Myrna? Sweetheart…"

"You should let her cool down," Sed advised.

"Go away!" she yelled from inside the bedroom.

There was a *thunk* as something hit the other side of the door.

Brian opened it, sidestepped an airborne high-heeled shoe, and closed himself in the room with the angry tigress. There was a whole lot of high-pitched yelling for several minutes, and Brian's lower pitched voice, calm and consoling. The rest of the band sat quietly nursing their injuries.

"What are we going to do about the concert tomorrow?" Eric asked. "Can you sing, Sed?"

He shrugged. "I don't know. My throat is bothering me. I can call Dare if you want, Trey."

"They won't have time to find a replacement to open for them. We might as well wait until morning and see how we feel," Trey said. "God, my head hurts. Do we have any aspirin?"

One of the bouncers had whacked Trey in the back of the head with an aluminum bat. By the time Sed had entered the fray, it had been over. He hadn't even gotten to throw a punch.

"Do you need to see a doctor? You blacked out for a couple of minutes."

"My head's harder than a bat. I don't think it's even bleeding." Trey fingered the goose egg on the back of his head and examined his fingertips for signs of blood. "I do need an aspirin though."

Sed retrieved a bottle from the tiny bathroom near the bedroom. The sound of Myrna calling Brian's name in ecstasy had already replaced the angry yelling.

Sed grinned and nodded toward the thin bedroom door as he handed a bottle of aspirin to Trey. "I guess they made up."

Trey chuckled. "Who can stay mad at Brian?" He swallowed several pills and passed the bottle to Eric.

"I'm glad they made up," Eric said, holding the dish towel to the gash above his eyebrow. "I'd have felt terrible if she called off the wedding."

"You should feel terrible," Jace said, his voice quiet, his brown-eyed gaze focused downward. "You started the whole thing."

"Well, I didn't ask for your help, little man, now did I?" Eric said.

Jace pursed his lips and nodded slightly. He left the bus without a word. Outside his Harley roared to life and the motorcycle's rumble faded into the distance.

"Why do you always torment him, Eric?" Sed asked.

Eric shrugged.

"He didn't hesitate to jump into your fight when you were outnumbered."

Eric rubbed a hand over his pursed lips and then squeezed his cleft chin between his thumb and forefinger. "Yeah, I know. It's just… He's not Jon, you know?"

Thank God for small favors. Sed knew that Eric and their previous bassist, Jon, had been close friends, but the guy had been bad news. They were much better off with Jace in the band.

Trey licked at the blood at the corner of his mouth. "Did you see the way Jace fought? I've never seen him fight before. I was like, holy shit. He pounded the crap out of three bouncers all by himself. I'm pretty sure *little man* could kick your ass if he wanted to, Eric."

"Shut up, Trey." Eric scowled.

Trey shrugged and glanced up at Sed, who stood leaning against the back of the booth. "So what are you going to do about Jessica?"

Sed's heart skipped a beat at the mention of her name. "Nothing. Obviously."

"Obviously?" Trey turned over his towel of ice, pressed it to the back of his head, and winced. "You pulled her offstage at a strip club. There's no obviously about that."

"I was just... surprised. I don't give a shit what she does with her life."

"Uh-huh." Trey sounded almost as convinced as Sed felt.

Chapter 7

JESSICA'S HEART SANK. "FIRED? You can't fire me over this. I didn't do anything wrong."

Roy, the club owner, cleared his throat, refusing to look at her. He reminded Jessica of a bloated Elvis, minus The King's good looks. Men should not wear white spandex or sequins—separately or in combination. Especially not hairy, overweight men. "Have you seen the condition of my bouncers? Your friends—"

"They aren't my friends."

"Then why are you protecting them?"

Jessica shook her head, her eyes wide with feigned innocence. "I'm not."

"By the time the cops got here last night, they were long gone. If you're not protecting them, tell me their names and where to find them, so I can press charges."

"I don't know them."

"I don't believe you." He considered her for a long moment. "Clear out your dressing table, Feather. I don't want to see you in my club again."

"But I need this job." She'd only been working for three weeks. She didn't have enough saved up for school yet. Not by a long shot. "It's just for the summer."

"Sorry, babe. I don't need your kind of trouble. You're beautiful and sexy, but I've got a long line of applicants who want your job and they don't bring their thugs into my club."

"They're not thugs."

"I thought you didn't know them."

"I don't."

He slid an envelope across his desk toward her. "Your pay."

She snatched the envelope off the desk and stormed from Roy's office.

Sed never ceased to fuck up her life.

Jessica burst into the dressing room and tossed all of her crap into a bag. She almost ran into Aggie on her way out. The black-haired beauty grabbed her by both arms to steady her.

"Hey, kitten, what's the rush?"

"Roy just *fired* me." She needed to get out of the place. Her throat ached with unshed tears and she didn't want anyone to know how upset she was. It was just a stupid job. Just another *failure*.

"What? How could he fire you? You're already a local favorite."

"This is all Sed's fault," she said. "When I see him, I'm going to rip him a new asshole."

"I think he's already got a corner on the asshole market, sugar."

Jessica tried not to smile. Failed at that, too.

"You said he was in the band Sinners, right?" Aggie asked.

"Yeah, so?"

"So they're opening for Exodus End tonight at Mandalay Bay."

"How do you know that?"

Aggie shrugged. "I saw a flyer tacked up somewhere."

"Perfect," Jessica said, starting to feel marginally better. "Now I can tell him where he can stuff his money. Better yet, I can *show* him where he can stuff his money."

"If you happen to run into that blond guy who was with them last night… the fine-looking one with the tight little ass… and the hard bod… and that face… and those…" Aggie's hands clenched and she shuddered in undisguised delight.

Blond? Jessica's brow furrowed. "Do you mean Jace Seymour?"

"Jace." Aggie smiled, her ruby red lips parting to reveal a perfect set of teeth. "Tell him I still owe him a dance. He paid, but ran off to fight bouncers before I could treat him to my special brand of pain."

Jessica chuckled. "Soft spot for him, Aggie? It's not like you to worry about pocketing some easy cash."

Aggie winked. "Maybe."

"I'll try to remember to give him your message when I go kick Sed's ass." Her hands clenched into fists. Sedric Lionheart would regret getting her fired. Oh yes, he would.

Chapter 8

SED TOOK A LONG draw from his beer and gazed down at the picture in the palm of his hand. Jessica had given it to him a couple of years ago. He remembered that smile. Doubted she'd ever share it with him again. She fuckin' hated his guts. So why was he sitting in the dark, staring at her picture, and drinking by himself again? Tradition, he supposed.

He set her picture beside his beer can and opened the journal he used to write songs. He couldn't concentrate well enough to write actual lyrics, but words kept popping into his head. He pictured them, but mostly he felt them. He scrawled words on separate lines with blank spaces between so he could add phrases later.

Eyes of jade. A heart betrayed.

Anguish. Languish.

Pain. Insane.

Heart of stone. Alone.

Alone.

He took a ragged breath.

Alone.

The song would come later. He didn't want to forget the feelings, though. He closed the journal, stuck it back in its hiding place under the bench seat cushion and picked up Jessica's picture, fingering its worn edges.

The bedroom door at the back of the tour bus opened, and then the bathroom door slid shut. Sed tossed the picture on the table and took another sip of his beer. A few minutes later, a gentle hand touched his shoulder.

"Are you out here by yourself again?" Myrna asked.

Sed glanced up at her. "I couldn't sleep."

"Can I sit?"

When he shrugged, she slid into the bench across the table from him.

"I'm sorry I didn't take better care of Brian last night," he said.

"He told me what happened and I don't blame you. He's the idiot who got involved." Myrna picked up Jessica's picture and examined it. "She's stunning, Sed. Is this Jessica?"

She glanced up at him and he nodded.

"How are you doing?" she asked.

She handed the picture to him and he slid it into his pocket with the crummy engagement ring Jessica had flung at him one devastating afternoon two years before.

"Me?" He shrugged. "By the time I got out there, everyone was fleeing the scene. I didn't even get to throw a punch. I just grabbed Trey off the sidewalk, stuffed him in the car with Brian, and we took off."

"I meant how are you doing after seeing Jessica?"

His heart stuttered every time her name was mentioned. This time was no exception. He shrugged. "It's no big deal. She still hates me. I still hate her."

Myrna ducked her head, but not before he saw her knowing grin. "I see. So you aren't going to go back to see her?"

"Why would I?"

Myrna shrugged. "Because you're a glutton for punishment. And… you still love her."

"No, I—"

"Has she always been an exotic dancer?"

"What?"

"Well, I assumed since you went ballistic when you saw her stripping—"

"I didn't go ballistic. I lost my cool." He pinched his thumb and forefinger together. "A little."

"Uh huh. But you reacted. So was it because you didn't expect to see her, or because you didn't expect to see her dancing nude for strangers?"

Sed chuckled. Dr. Myrna Evans, human sexuality professor, always tried to get in everyone's psychology. "That's the last place on Earth I'd ever expect to see Jessica. She's the independent feminist type. The way you are, I guess you'd say. So yeah, I was stunned. That's why I pulled her off the stage. Not because I actually cared that she was shaking her tits at dozens of sleazy jackasses."

His beer can crinkled in his fist.

"There's nothing wrong with having these feelings, Sed."

"You sound like a shrink."

She cringed. "I thought it might help to talk about it."

"No, it doesn't help. I was finally over her and then… this."

"You're over her?" She laughed at him. "I don't think so, Sed. Who do you think you're talking to here?"

A busybody who is too smart for her own good. But he couldn't say that aloud so he changed the subject. "You're still marrying Brian tomorrow, aren't you?"

Her brow furrowed. "Of course, why wouldn't I?"

"You were *pissed* when you found out he'd been fighting."

"Just because you're mad at someone doesn't mean you stop loving them."

Sed nodded. "I guess." He reached across the table and squeezed her hand. "Myr, I'm glad Brian found you. You're exactly what he needs, but if he ever mistreats you, he'll be answering to me."

"And me!" Eric called from his bunk.

"No fucking privacy around here," Sed grumbled.

"If you want to have one last legal affair before you're permanently saddled with Master Sinclair, there's room in my bunk," Eric called.

"Do you want me to hit him for you, Myr?" Sed stood up from the table.

"I got it," Trey said. He leaned off the top bunk and there was a loud *thunk* in the bunk beneath.

"Ow!" Eric yelled.

Myrna climbed from the bench and gave Sed a warm hug. "Good night, Sed."

He hugged her back. It felt wonderful to hold a woman without any sexual expectations.

She released him and returned to the bedroom.

Myrna was a good woman. Sed envied Brian.

It used to be the other way around.

Back before Jessica hated him.

Maybe he *should* go see her.

Nah. She'd probably kick him in the nuts.

Chapter 9

How was it possible for two people to look *that* happy getting married by an Elvis impersonator in a drive-through? Brian had pulled into the first chapel they'd found. There wasn't time for a long ceremony. They all had to be onstage in a couple of hours.

Sed grinned as Myrna and Brian recited their vows and exchanged rings. The size of Myrna's rock put Jessica's cheap piece of shit to shame, but Sed was very conscious of the discarded ring's weight in his hip pocket as Brian slid a platinum band on Myrna's finger.

They'd put the top down on Myrna's pink convertible '57 Thunderbird coupe. Brian sat on the back of the front seat with Myrna on his lap. Trey, the best man, sat in the middle beside the happy couple. Sed sat on the passenger side as their second witness. He supposed that made him the maid of honor. Always a bridesmaid…

"I now pronounce you husband and, uh, wife," the Elvis justice of the peace said. "I say, uh, you may kiss your beautiful bride."

Brian kissed Myrna deeply. She clung to his shoulders, the Vegas sunshine making her auburn hair glow like fire. She looked absolutely stunning in her white gown. Sed wondered if they'd even make it back to the tour bus before Brian had it off her.

Eric, who sat behind Jace on the motorcycle next to the car, cheered.

"Congratulations." Sed reached behind Trey to pat Brian on the shoulder.

The couple continued to kiss. And kiss. And kiss. Tug at each other's clothes. Kiss some more.

"You guys," Trey protested. "You're making Jace blush."

The newlyweds drew apart and stared into each other's eyes, both of Brian's surrounded by dark purple bruises. "God, I love you," Brian murmured. He kissed her again, before drawing away to stare at her with the stupidest grin on his face. She smiled just as stupidly, love shining in her eyes.

Sed had had that. Once.

But no longer.

Stupid Jessica. Sed crossed his arms over his chest, trying his damnedest to be happy for Brian, no matter how miserable the occasion made him feel.

"Are we going to sit here all day?" Trey asked.

"You act like we're ordering burgers and fries," Brian said, glaring at Trey.

"Well, what do you expect? We are in a drive-through. Hey, Elvis!" Trey called at the window. "Can we get ketchup with that?"

"One marriage license is all you shall receive from The King. Move along, folks," Elvis said, his accent evaporating. "We've got a line today."

They slid down into the white leather bench seat and Myrna shifted to sit on Trey's lap so Brian could drive back to the tour bus.

As they peeled out of the lot, Myrna toyed with Trey's hair. "How's your head, sweetie?"

"Hurts like a sonuvabitch."

"You need to go to the hospital and get checked out," Myrna said. "You look pale." Using her fingertips, she tested his forehead for fever.

"That's how the best man always looks when his best friend gets shackled with a ball and chain."

"Ball and chain?" She poked him in the ribs and scooted over to Sed's lap. Sed wrapped an arm around her back. "Sed doesn't insult me."

"Not to your face," Trey murmured. He leaned back and closed his eyes.

Myrna was right. Trey didn't look well. At all.

Myrna's mouth dropped open and she turned her head to glare at Sed. "What did you say about me?"

"I'd never say anything bad about you, Myrna." He shrugged. "Well, except you have bad taste in men."

She grabbed his chin between her thumb and forefinger. "Don't be insulting my husband."

"Yeah," Brian said, an ear-to-ear grin plastered to his face, "don't be insulting her husband." He wrapped his right hand around her ankle beneath her plain white wedding gown. At the top of the steering wheel, the wide platinum band on his left ring finger caught the afternoon sunshine. Sed stared at it. That symbol of together forever.

Forever.

"Eh, I'm just jealous," Sed said quietly. He hugged Myrna affectionately and she placed a kiss on his temple.

"I hope you find happiness, Sed," she said. "I really do."

Only one woman could make him happy. And it just so happened that she despised him.

But he could never despise her. He hoped the money he'd given her at the club had been enough to help her out. If only Sinners' third album had gone platinum a few months earlier. He could have afforded to buy her a nice ring and put her through law school. Then she'd have never left him in the first place.

Chapter 10

OUTSIDE MANDALAY BAY'S EVENTS Center, Jessica tapped a security guard on the shoulder. "Excuse me, can you tell me where I can find Sed Lionheart?"

The gigantic, bearded man turned to look at her, but didn't answer her question.

"He's the lead singer of Sinners. Sedric Lionheart," she said, enunciating the syllables of his name slowly. "They're playing here tonight."

"Stay behind the barrier." The security guard pushed his sunglasses further up his nose with an index finger.

"I need to give him something. It's important."

"Stay behind the barrier."

"I *am* behind the barrier. Does he come out this way after the show?"

"Look, lady, I have no clue. My instructions were to make all the fans stay behind the barrier."

"I'm not a fan. I'm a friend."

"Sure."

An attractive thirty-something woman appeared beside the security guard. She wore a well-tailored navy skirt suit and held a clipboard. With her hair twisted into a conservative knot, she looked more out of place than a professional wrestler in a ballet.

"Are you Jessica?" the woman asked.

Jessica's brow furrowed. "How do you know my name?"

"I saw a picture of you once. I'm Myrna Evans, I mean, Sinclair.

Myrna Sinclair. Brian's… wife." Her expression wavered between disbelief and elation as she dropped this bombshell.

Jessica's eyes widened in surprise. "Brian's wife? When did Brian get married?"

The woman checked her watch. The ginormous diamond on her left ring finger sparkled in the streetlights. "About five hours ago. So, why are you here? I'm pretty sure Sed doesn't want to see you."

Jessica got a mother hen-ish vibe from this Myrna woman. Sed's protector? Why would Sed need protection? The jackass could take care of himself just fine.

"He gave me a big chunk of cash yesterday. I came to return it."

"Why are you returning it?"

"I don't want his money. He's always doing this to me. Screwing up my life and then trying to fix everything. I don't need him to fix everything. I can take care of myself, you know?" Jessica's eyebrows shot up. When Myrna didn't reply, her face fell. "You don't know, do you?"

"Sed is a protector type personality," Myrna said. "That's who he is. He tries to fix everything for everyone." She smiled. "He's really sweet, actually."

"I don't think we're talking about the same Sed. Sedric Lionheart. Tall guy. Broad shoulders. Blue eyes. Short black hair. Body befitting a Greek god. Sings. La la la la."

Myrna chuckled. "You don't think Sed is sweet?"

"No. He's a pompous ass who can't keep his nose out of people's business."

"Because if someone he cares about gets hurt, he feels personally responsible. It's his way of showing he cares."

The congregating crowd outside the barrier cheered unexpectedly. The members of the band Exodus End emerged from their tour bus and headed for the building. Amongst them, Jessica recognized Trey's older brother, Dare Mills. She hadn't seen Dare for ages. She doubted if he'd even remember who she was.

"It's noisy out here," Myrna shouted. "Do you want to go talk on the bus?" Myrna pointed to the black and silver tour bus parked behind her.

Jessica's stomach plummeted to her feet at the idea of seeing Sed again. Of being trapped in the bus where she couldn't easily flee. "How about I just give the money to you and you give it to him?" She reached into her purse.

"I think you should tell him why you don't want it. I don't think he understands you were insulted by his gift. It would be a good lesson for him."

Jessica gaped at Myrna. How did this woman know Sed's money insulted her?

"Yeah, I get it. Independent woman meets protector-type man and personalities clash. I bet your love affair is smoking hot, though." Myrna laughed.

Jessica blushed. They had once had a smoking hot love affair. And it had never fizzled out. Just exploded.

"Charlie, can you help Jessica over the barrier?"

The security guard grabbed Jessica around the waist and hauled her over the metal barrier fence.

"I'm a mess." Jessica rubbed her hands over her hair. She knew she looked like crap. It was fitting. She'd had a craptacular day. As if getting fired wasn't bad enough, she hadn't had enough money to pay for her rented room. Roy had deducted bouncer *medical* expenses from her wages, the jackass. Since there was no way in hell she'd ever use Sed's money to pay her rent, she'd spent most of the day packing her belongings into her piece of shit Nissan Sentra. Apparently her landlord preferred to rent her room to someone with *actual* money. As for sleep… What was that? When she'd tried to catch a nap in her car, some bicycle cop had pounded on her window and lectured her on how quickly the temperature inside a car could rise to deadly levels. Like she was an idiot or something.

Why did she care how she looked anyway? She didn't have anyone to impress and she was in a foul mood.

Jessica tucked her long, wavy hair behind her ears and followed Myrna to the tour bus.

"Jessica? Is that you?"

She paused and glanced up at Darren Mills, Exodus End's lead guitarist. He was even better looking than his younger brother, Trey, if that was possible. They both had the same dreamy green eyes, but Dare had a stronger jaw that was covered with a sexy shadow of beard growth. Dare's long black hair, straight and shiny, was the envy of shampoo models the world over.

Jessica smiled at him, blushing slightly. It was hard to be inconspicuous when people kept recognizing her. Her plan to drop the loot and get the hell out of Dodge was not going as anticipated. "Hey, Dare. Yeah, it's me."

"I thought you dumped Sed. Are you guys back together?"

Jessica shook her head vigorously. "No chance."

"Yo, Dare, get a move on! We're on in thirty minutes," Exodus End's drummer, Steve Aimes, called from the back door of the venue.

Dare tossed his head in acknowledgement and then glanced down at Jessica. "I've got to go get warmed up for our set," he said. "It was good to see you."

"Yeah, I'm glad you stopped to say hi. Break a leg," she said, and punched him gently in the arm.

"Thanks." He turned and jogged toward the venue.

Jessica glanced at Myrna, who was following Dare's perfect leather-clad ass with her eyes. "You know him?"

"That's Dare," Jessica said. "Trey's older brother."

"So that's Dare. Mmmmm. And I thought Trey was sexy."

Jessica chuckled. "What about Brian? Weren't you recently married to him?"

"He'll have my undivided attention soon enough." Myrna turned to enter the bus. "Besides, getting married didn't make me blind."

Jessica followed Myrna up the bus stairs and entered the main room behind the driver's seat. For a moment, Jessica thought they were in the wrong bus. Sinners lived in a state of constant filth, but the interior of the bus was spotless without even the obligatory stack of dirty clothes to mar its cleanliness. Next to the wall that blocked the driver's seat from view was a comfortable-looking leather sofa in soft beige. Across from the sofa were two matching captain's chairs. A large-screen TV was anchored above the chairs with a video game console and stereo system situated nearby. Further in, a small kitchen filled one wall and on the opposite side stood a square dining table with booth seating. Close, but comfortable.

"What happened to this place?" Jessica asked.

Myrna continued to the small square table near the sleeping area, which consisted of two sets of curtained bunks stacked on either side of the corridor.

"Huh?" Myrna glanced over her shoulder.

"The bus. It's clean."

"Uh, one too many loogies between the toes and I made the guys clean it up. I couldn't live in that disgusting mess."

"Impressive." Jessica couldn't get the "guys" to do anything when she'd briefly toured with them over two years ago. And they'd been less famous then. Less full of themselves.

"Have a seat," Myrna offered. "Would you like something to drink?"

"Thanks. That would be nice." Jessica slid into the booth, her back facing the exit, and looked around the bus. On second glance, this wasn't the same bus they'd had when she'd toured with them. This one was much nicer. It even had a pair of doors that led to other rooms near the back.

"What would you like?" Myrna asked.

"Aren't my choices beer, beer, or beer? Sinners' only food group." Jessica chuckled.

"No alcohol on this bus," Myrna said. "If you want a beer, you'll have to brave the other bus, which we've monikered the pigsty bus. The roadies keep to that one mostly. We have bottled water. Juice: orange, apple, cranberry or grape. And Trey's new addiction, black cherry Kool-Aid."

"Water is fine."

Myrna retrieved two bottles of water from the fridge and sat across the table from Jessica in the booth. Jessica took a long drink.

"Brian told me you were going to law school," Myrna said.

Jessica's eyes widened. Why would that even come up in conversation? "Yeah, that's right."

"So why are you working as a stripper?"

Was this woman direct or what? Sheesh! No wonder the guys obeyed her commands. She probably intimidated the hell out of them.

"I'm pretty sure that's none of your business."

Myrna shrugged. "I suppose not." She chuckled. "I guess Sed was right about you."

Jessica's brow furrowed. "What did Sed say about me?" She knew she shouldn't care, but her heart could scarcely beat in her constricted chest.

Myrna shook her head nonchalantly and took a drink of her water. "Nothing."

"I needed the money is all. Why did Sed say I was dancing?"

"You needed money."

"Doesn't matter anyway. Because of that cocky idiot, I got fired."

"Sorry to hear that. Are you looking for another job?"

"I dunno. I couldn't afford to pay my rent, so I got evicted. I'll probably just go to my mother's. You know, I've had a very crappy twenty-four hours. It all started the second Sed touched me."

Jessica hesitated. She'd forgotten that Myrna seemed to actually *like* Sed. "Sorry to unload on you. You don't even know me."

Myrna smiled kindly. "I don't mind. You know, I've been thinking of hiring an assistant to help me with my research project."

"Your research project?"

"That's why I'm touring with Sinners. I'm doing psychology research on their groupies. I'm trying to determine what it is about rock stars that makes certain women promiscuous."

Did she really need to do formal research to figure that out?

"I wondered why you were walking around looking like one of my law professors."

Myrna chuckled. "Actually, I dress like this because I know it turns Brian on. Don't tell him I told you that." Myrna winked at her. "Anyway, are you interested in the job?"

"Me?"

"I'm offering á job. You need a job. Makes sense to me. I assume you're an intelligent person if you're going to law school. How are your grades?"

"Almost straight A's." Except that failing term paper in Ellington's class. But now was not the time to start hyperventilating over a bad grade. Something wasn't right here. Jessica didn't even know this woman and she just offers her a job out of the blue? "What's the catch?"

"No catch. The stipend will be ten thousand dollars if you see the project to its end."

Jessica's jaw dropped. "Ten *thousand* dollars? How long is this project?"

"About two more months. A lot of the burden of data collection and entry will be put on you. I couldn't keep up before, and now I seem to be a newlywed." She grinned. "How did that happen?"

Jessica chuckled. "Congratulations, by the way. Brian is a prize catch."

"Thanks. I think so." Myrna smiled dreamily, radiating happiness.

Jessica had had that once. Stupid Sed and his ridiculous ultimatums.

"So what do you say?" Myrna asked.

"Can I get an advance so I can find a new apartment?"

"You'll be touring with the band, Jessica. You don't need an apartment."

Her bubble of relief and happiness ruptured.

"I can't tour with the band. Sed—"

"What about Sed?"

Why did Jessica feel like this woman was manipulating her and planning her demise? "We can't get along."

"This is a professional relationship, Jessica, not a personal one. Besides, you'll be working for me. You can ignore Sed entirely."

Jessica didn't think it was humanly possible to ignore Sed. Sed was... Sed was... well, *Sed*. She sighed aloud. "I..."

"Do you have a better option?"

Jessica shook her head. "I'm really grateful for this offer, Myrna. I just don't think I can be around Sed for two months."

"Why not? Do you still care about him?" Myrna asked.

"No!" Jessica said, a little too fast and a lot too loud.

"Then what's the problem?"

"No problem. I gratefully accept the job. Thank you, Myrna. You saved my life." Or potentially ruined it.

"Awesome. I hope you can start tonight. I'm leaving on my honeymoon in about..." She checked her watch. "...ten minutes."

Well, what did Jessica have to lose? Except her sanity and already pulverized self-respect. "Um, okay. Sounds good. Just show me what to do."

Myrna was explaining how to enter her huge backlog of data into a spreadsheet when the crowd outside the bus erupted in cheers. Jessica's heart raced. The members of Sinners were probably headed this way right now. How would Sed react to her joining his band on tour? How would she stand being so close to him for two months? Living quarters on a tour bus were... intimate.

Brian climbed the stairs and entered the bus. He didn't even notice Jessica. He went straight to Myrna, drew her against his sweaty body, and kissed her hungrily. "Are you ready to go?"

"Everything's packed," she murmured. "I just need to explain a few more things to my new assistant before we head out."

"Assistant?" Brian's eyes, surrounded by purple bruises and a thick rim of black eyeliner, settled on Jessica. "Jessica?" he said breathlessly. "What the *fuck* are you doing here?"

His hostility surprised her. Brian was such a nice guy. She wondered why he was so pissed to see her.

"Hey, Brian," she said, offering a single wave. "Long time no see."

"Sed's on his way. You'd better leave before he sees you."

Myrna ran a hand up Brian's sweat-drenched T-shirt. "She's staying for a couple of months. I just hired her as my assistant."

Brian looked down at her incredulously. "You did *what*? Are you insane?"

Myrna smiled and shook her head. "Trust me, m'kay?" she murmured, dropping a kiss at the corner of his mouth. "Besides, with an assistant's help, I'll have more time for us." Her hand clenched, gripping his T-shirt at the waist.

He stared at her as if in total awe. "God, yes, you definitely need an assistant. I love you."

"I love you," Myrna returned.

Jessica averted her gaze. So much mushiness was sickening to watch.

"Did you reserve a nice suite?" Brian's fingers clutched the fabric of Myrna's suit jacket as if trying to control the urge to rip it from her body.

"Uh-huh. At the Venetian. One with a jet tub."

His breath caught. "Nice. Mmm, I love you. Did I tell you that today?"

"Only a million times." She smiled. "Please, continue."

He kissed her again. "I love you," he murmured against her lips, before drawing away.

"Five minutes and I'll be ready to leave," she said. "I promise to hurry. I can't wait to get you alone."

"I'll go wash off my stage makeup."

"Leave it for now," Myrna murmured. "I want to love both of you tonight. I'll start with the rock star and work my way to that regular guy hiding under that makeup somewhere."

He grinned. "I'm glad you didn't see our show tonight, then. We sucked. Sed couldn't hit his high notes. Jace's hand is so swollen he can barely play. Trey kept having to sit down with dizzy spells. I couldn't concentrate because all I could think about was you. At least Eric kept the beat." He scratched his head behind his ear. "Well, most of the time."

"I'm sure it wasn't that bad," Myrna said.

"Yeah, it was pretty bad, but I honestly don't care at the moment. Hurry. I need to devour you."

"Me first." Myrna kissed him and then turned her attention to the computer again. She was decidedly distracted as she explained the rest of the data entry to Jessica. Luckily, entering the data wasn't difficult. Just time consuming.

"Just work on this for the next couple of days," Myrna said. "We'll be back on Monday to hit the road again and you can help me with the groupie interviews."

Groupie interviews? Now that did *not* sound like fun, but she'd be an idiot to turn down this job. "Okay. I can handle this. Do you want me to work on anything else?"

"Probably, but I can't form a coherent thought right now. It will wait a couple of days."

There was a commotion outside the bus. Several sets of feet marched up the front steps. The chorus of feminine giggles could only mean one thing. Jessica reached for a stack of Myrna's raw data so she could look as busy as possible when Sed turned up. She would do her damnedest to ignore him.

"Will you two get out of here?" Sed said to Brian and Myrna. "The bedroom is mine tonight."

Speak of the devil.

Jessica couldn't stop her body from tensing involuntarily, but she didn't take her eyes off her work.

"Sed, don't chase off my new assistant while I'm gone. I need her," Myrna said.

"New assist—"

Jessica glanced up at Sed and smiled her impersonal smile. "Hello." Could he see that her hands were shaking as they hovered over the laptop's keyboard?

Sed gaped at her. Her gaze traced the beads of sweat running down the side of his face. Oh God. Eyegasm. Why did he have to be so fucking attractive, anyway? The bastard.

"What?" Sed sputtered, his mouth opening and closing like a goldfish.

Brian fled the bus, but Myrna didn't abandon Jessica. She grabbed Sed's arm to gain his attention. "Your little stunt got her fired."

He slowly dragged his gaze from Jessica to Myrna, who was almost a foot shorter than he was, but somehow standing as his equal.

"What?" he said again.

"She needed a job and a place to stay, so I hired her to help me with my research. You *will not* harass her."

Sed scowled. "Why would I harass her? I don't give a shit about her." He glanced at Jessica and then Myrna again. "You hired her? What do you mean you *hired* her?"

"Sed," one of the three women who'd followed him on the bus complained. "Are we going to party, or what?"

"Yeah, shut up," he bellowed at the attractive strawberry blonde. "I'll be with you in a minute."

The woman didn't even bat an eyelash at his rudeness. Jessica bit her lip to keep from scolding him. It wasn't her business. Sed was free to do whatever he wanted with this woman. Correction. These *women*. Three of them. The heat of anger rose up Jessica's throat. Why did his trio of willing flesh irk her so much?

Myrna said calmly, "She is my employee, Sed. I expect you to treat her with the same respect you treat me."

"Myrna, are you coming?" Brian yelled from outside the bus.

"I've got to go." Myrna planted a chaste kiss on one of Sed's cheeks and patted the opposite one. "Behave. Do you hear me?"

"Whatever," he said. "This is bullshit, Myrna. You should have consulted—"

"Pretend I don't exist," Jessica said. "I'll do the same for you."

Jessica went back to her data entry, trying to ignore the girl who had plastered herself to Sed's back and ran her hand up and down over his crotch. Jessica couldn't help but notice the growing bulge in his pants. She crossed her legs. No, not because she knew what that bulge could do to her. The bench-seat just wasn't very comfortable. Uh, yeah…

"Sounds like a plan," Sed said gruffly. He took the young woman's hand from his crotch and tugged her toward one of the doors at the back of the bus. The bedroom, Jessica presumed. "Follow me, ladies," he said to the other two girls. The door opened and closed behind the four of them.

Jessica suppressed the urge to punch something. She hadn't slept with anyone since they'd broken up. She wondered how many hours he'd waited before fucking one of his groupies. Or three of them.

God, she wanted to break something. Preferably his face.

Eric stomped up the bus stairs. "Where's Sed? Did he start without me?"

Jessica glanced up from the blurry computer screen. "How the fuck should I know?" she growled, her face aching from the tension in her expression.

Eric gaped at her. "Jessica?"

"Yeah, guilty."

Her mood had gone from foul to horrendous. The copious giggling coming from the bedroom did not improve her disposition.

Eric slid into the booth across from her and whispered, "Does Sed know you're here?"

"Uh, yeah. He had to pass here to take his little sluts back there." She pointed at the offensive bedroom door.

"My God, Sed, you're absolutely perfect," a muffled voice came through the door.

"Can you always hear everything that goes on in that bedroom?" Jessica asked.

"Pretty much," Eric said. "You think Sed and his groupies are loud, wait until Brian and Myrna get back from their honeymoon. She makes this sound in the back her throat. It's like... gah, instant boner."

"I'm moving to the pigsty bus," Jessica said, rising from the bench. She closed the laptop and scooped the stack of papers on top.

"I wouldn't do that if I were you," Eric said. "The place is toxic to sensible females."

"Is Jace over there, by any chance? A friend of mine wanted me to give him a message."

Eric scowled, an uncharacteristic look of guilt on his ruggedly handsome face. "Not sure where Jace went off to."

Sed's deep groan carried through the door. "Suck it harder," he demanded. "Yeah, harder. Harder. That's better."

Jessica rushed down the hall and threw open the bedroom door. It banged against the wall. Sed stood just inside the doorway entirely naked, save the cherry-red condom on his cock. His three girls were in various states of undress. One was on her knees in front of him, sucking his shaft down her throat. A second knelt behind him flicking her tongue over God-only-knew-what. The third girl ran her hands up and down the hard muscles of his chest and abdomen as if she was inspecting The Statue of David for flaws.

Sed gazed at Jessica through half-closed eyes, a sardonic smile on his handsome face. "Can I help you?"

With an angry growl, Jessica grabbed the girl sucking Sed's cock by the hair and yanked her down to the floor. Sed's yelp of pain seemed well deserved. And the girl? Jessica wanted to kill her. "Get away from him, you fucking slut," Jessica spat.

Jessica narrowly avoided a kick to the head and tossed the screaming young woman into the hall by her hair.

"Cat fight," Eric announced excitedly, nudging the ejected female further down the hall.

Jessica spun around, prepared to fight off the next Sed-fondler, but he had taken each spare girl by an arm and escorted them from the room. The young women looked confused as he pushed them out into the hall. Eric caught them against his body.

"Awww, Sed," Eric said. "I wanted to watch them pull each other's hair."

Sed closed the door in Eric's face, shutting himself and Jessica in the bedroom.

Alone.

Together.

Jessica swallowed hard and glanced up at him, startled by his nearness. How had she ended up here? She'd been on her way to leave the bus and then...

He continued to watch her, waiting for her to say something.

"I hate you," was the best she could come up with.

"I hate you more."

"It is not possible to hate anyone as much as I hate you." She tried to open the door, but he lifted a hand against the frame and held it closed.

"If you hate me, why are you fighting off my entertainment for the evening?"

Good question.

"Because." She couldn't drag her gaze from his bright blue eyes. Why was he looking at her like that? Like he actually gave a shit what she had to say. It had never mattered to him in the past.

"Because?"

"Because I… hate you," she whispered.

His sardonic grin returned. "I can see that." He lowered his head and brushed his lips against hers. His feather-light kiss lasted less than a second but her heart thundered in her chest. Her knees went weak. The entire core of her body tensed with need. His tongue brushed her upper lip as he drew away.

He stared down at her for her reaction.

Oh my…

She snapped back to her senses. How *dare* he kiss her? She shoved him, her hands pressing against the warm flesh of his naked chest.

Big mistake. His skin burned hers with awareness.

She had to get out here, before… Before she…

When she reached for the doorknob, he grabbed her wrist.

"I wish I'd never met you," he said.

"Well, I wish you'd never been born!"

He drew her body against his and covered her mouth with a searing kiss.

Oh my, my, my…

She groaned. Her bones turned to jelly. His large hands splayed over her back to keep her from sinking to the floor as he laid her senses to waste. This man. She really did hate him. That's why it was so maddening to *want* him so completely. No matter how hard she tried, she couldn't get him out from under her skin.

His fingers unhooked her bra through her thin T-shirt. Hands sliding up her sides, he broke his kiss long enough to strip both garments from her body in one smooth motion. She made a sound of protest in the back of her throat, but it was lost in his mouth as he lowered his head and kissed her senseless again.

He tugged her closer so that her naked breasts pressed against his chest. His erection brushed against her lower belly, just above the waistband of her low-cut jeans. She tensed and then melted against him. Her arms moved around his hard body to draw him closer, her hands sliding up his smooth back.

He gasped into her mouth. She knew his back was one of his erogenous zones. When her fingers reached his shoulders, she drew her fingernails downward, raking them over his skin. He shuddered violently and tore his mouth from hers. He stared down at her, seeking her willingness. If she didn't want this to happen, she knew this would be her last chance to say no. This man was a beast in bed. Once he got going, she'd have no opportunity to—

He grabbed her around the waist, turned and tossed her on the bed. Before she could reorient herself, he'd unfastened her pants and had stripped them, her panties, and sandals from her body all at once.

"Sed?"

He grabbed her thighs and spread her legs wide. She didn't resist. She didn't want him to make love to her. She wanted him to fuck her, and he was of the same mind.

She reached down, took his thick cock in one hand and directed it to her wet, eager body.

He made a sound of primal longing, which drove straight through her, and then slid deeper with one penetrating thrust.

Sed. Oh, Sed.

He filled her as only he could.

Slowly withdrew.

Oh my…

Thrust hard and deep.

Oh my…

Rotated his hips.

Oh my…God!

Her back arched off the bed and she moved up onto her elbows to keep herself in that glorious position. He held her bent legs up and wide open with his forearms. His feet on the floor, he leaned his weight into her to force himself deeper. He rotated his hips again, grinding against her. Jessica's head fell back and she cried out.

"Yeah," he gasped and slowly pulled back. "You want me, don't you?"

He had no idea.

She shuddered and spread her legs further. Wanting him deeper. *Deeper. Please. Inside. Oh… Sed. Fill me. I'm so empty without you.*

He shifted his arms to hold her position. He thrust into her again and ground his pubic bone into her throbbing clit. Withdrew. Ground into her. Withdrew. Ground into her. *God, yes, Sed. Take me deep.* Her vocalizations grew louder with each thrust as he drove her closer and closer to orgasm.

"Sed. Sed!"

His breath hitched in his throat with each thrust, causing goose bumps to rise over every inch of her body.

"Jessica," he whispered.

She lifted her head to look at him. He was watching her. Their eyes met and he ducked his head, but not before she saw the pain in his gaze. Before she could contemplate what it meant, his gyrating thrusts sent her over the edge. She screamed, her body tensing as ripples of pleasure coursed through her.

As she trembled in the aftermath, Sed moved her further up the mattress and joined her on the bed. He drew her legs closer together now and switched from deep, gyrating thrusts to hard, fast strokes.

She lifted a hand to caress his face. He captured her wrist and pinned it to the bed near her head.

He didn't want her to touch him? Fine. She could tell he just wanted to blow his load as quickly as possible. He'd probably throw her out in the hallway with his groupie sluts when he finished with her. Hell, he hadn't even respected her enough to change into a new condom before thrusting into her body. He was still wearing the same one that little whore had sucked in her disgusting mouth.

Jessica swallowed the lump in her throat and rocked her hips side to side to bring Sed to his peak quickly. She knew how to make him come. She hadn't forgotten all the tricks she'd mastered to satisfy him. To make him hers. She squeezed him inside her, tighter, tighter, tighter, and then relaxed, before repeating her clenching and releasing.

He gasped, his thrusts faster but not as deep. "Jessica," he whispered. "Oh, Jessica. Yes, baby. Squeeze me. I need it. Ungh."

She loved to watch him let go. To witness that moment when he lost all control and spent himself inside her, his face contorted in ecstasy. But this time, as he shuddered against her and cried out in triumph, she kept her eyes tightly closed. She didn't want to lose herself to him again. Hated how he made her feel—weak, needy, dependent. She hated everything about him, except the way he pleasured her body.

When his tremors stilled, he collapsed on top of her, cocooning her in his arms. He pressed a kiss to her temple, but she didn't want his feigned tenderness. The jerk! She squirmed to get away. He lifted his head to look down at her.

"You can get off me now," she said between clenched teeth.

A muscle above his left eye twitched. He pulled out and rolled off her, settling beside her on his side. He kissed her shoulder and rested a hand on her naked belly, releasing a sigh of contentment. She brushed his hand aside, rolled off the bed, and reached for her clothes.

She drew her panties up her thighs. "I'm glad we got that out of our systems."

He rolled onto his back and covered his eyes with his forearm. "Yeah."

She dressed quickly, not bothering with her bra or sandals. She needed to get away. Quickly. She couldn't let him see how wounded she was. Not when she knew how indifferent he felt. How many dozens of women had he fucked the same way he'd just fucked her? She didn't want to know.

She left the bedroom, closing the door quietly behind her. She burst into the tiny bathroom and locked herself inside. Caught off guard by the wrenching pain in her chest, she sucked a raged breath into her lungs.

Sed meant nothing to her. Nothing. She was over him. And she hated him. She hated him so much. She pounded the flimsy wall with her fist. Hated him… hated…

She bit her lip, trying to stop its trembling. No good. She lowered her face into her hands and let the tears fall, struggling to keep her sobs as quiet as possible.

He had never experienced this kind of hurt. Just once she'd like to take him down a notch. Make him suffer, like she suffered. Make him pay for his callous disregard for other people's feelings. And it wasn't just her. How many other women had he used and discarded?

"Payback is a motherfucker," she murmured under her breath, tears dripping from her chin. "Let's see how you like being used, Playboy."

Chapter 11

When Jessica closed the door behind her, Sed moved his arm from his face and stared up at the ceiling, trying to get his emotions under control. It was hard enough to keep his thoughts off the woman when she was hundreds, sometimes thousands, of miles away. But now? With her this close? How would he survive? And how could Myrna do this to him? He'd thought she understood how hard this was for him. She probably thought she was doing him a favor.

The door opened and Sed lifted his head from the pillow for one happy millisecond thinking Jessica had returned.

Eric peeked in. "Are you finished?"

"Unfortunately." If he'd known she'd be gone in a heartbeat, he would have made it last longer. Sed peeled the condom from his dick and disposed of it. He rolled off the mattress and slid into a pair of gym shorts.

"You can join us, Sed," said one of the three girls he'd brought on the bus.

"No, thanks." He pushed past the girl and into the hall.

She shrugged and grabbed Eric by the shirt, tugging him into the bedroom.

"Are you okay, dude?" Eric asked Sed with genuine concern in his vivid blue eyes.

"Yeah, I'm gonna catch a nap."

Eric's brow furrowed. "The other two girls headed for the pigsty bus with the roadies." His girl was yanking on his arm now, but he held on to the doorframe. "I think Trey's partying over there and Dare will probably show up later."

It would be nice to hang out with Dare; Sed hadn't seen him in a while, but he shook his head. The last thing he felt like doing was socializing. "I'm tired. You have fun."

Eric released the doorframe and let the girl pull him inside the bedroom. He kicked the door shut.

Sed climbed into the bottom bunk next to the bathroom and pulled the curtain closed. He punched his pillow a few times, settled into a comfortable position and closed his eyes. His mind was too full to sleep, but at least he could hide reasonably well in the curtained bunk.

Soft crying sounds came from the other side of the thin wall near his head. Someone sniffed their nose. Toilet paper unrolled. A nose blown delicately. Who was crying in the bathroom? Not one of the groupies. Eric had said they'd gone to the other bus.

Jessica?

His heart stuttered.

Maybe she did care about him.

But she'd jetted from the bed the instant he'd tried to be tender with her. Was she so disgusted with their lovemaking that she was in tears? What else could it be?

Sed slid out of the bunk and knocked on the bathroom door.

"Oc-occupied," Jessica called.

"Are you crying?"

She hesitated. "Of course not."

He leaned his forearm against the doorframe, his hand clenched into a fist. "Are you almost finished? I need to use the facilities."

"Yeah, just a minute."

Water splashed into the tiny sink. He heard her sniff her nose again, and then she slid the door open. She had her head ducked down as she tried to brush past him. He poked her in the ribs and she glared up at him. Just as he'd suspected. Her eyes and nose were red and puffy.

"You were so crying."

"Just leave me alone, Sed. You're the last person on Earth I want to see right now."

She was the only person on Earth he wanted to see. Ever.

He let her pass and entered the bathroom, closing the door quietly. He didn't really need to use the bathroom. He'd just wanted to be near her. Even if she did spout her hatred at him. Hatred was better than nothing. Hatred he could deal with. He couldn't deal with nothing. He'd tried to deal with nothing for two years. It never went away. Just sat there inside his chest as a big empty hole.

Sed flushed the unused toilet and washed his hands. He opened the door and stood in the doorway. Jessica's shoulder dominated his attention as she sat at the dining room table booting up Myrna's laptop. He needed an excuse to be in the dining area. Any excuse. His stomach rumbled on cue.

He found some shrimp scampi and pasta primavera in the refrigerator. Leftovers from the feast Myrna had made for Trey the same day she'd agreed to marry Brian. Had it really only been three days ago?

Sed glanced over his shoulder and caught Jessica staring at his naked back reflectively.

When her eyes met his, she jerked and rapidly keyed several numbers into her spreadsheet.

"Are you hungry?"

"A little," she admitted quietly.

When he placed a plate of warmed-over food on the table beside the computer, she glanced up from her work and smiled. His heart skipped a beat.

"Thanks," she murmured.

Her gaze dropped to his bare chest. Her tongue darted out between her lips. She shook her head slightly and then focused her attention on her food.

"This smells awesome," she said. "Did you make it?"

"If by make it, you mean heat it up, yeah. But Myrna cooked it. She has a soft spot for Trey's stomach." He chuckled. "All our stomachs benefit from that helpless puppy look of his."

She laughed. "I don't think there's a woman on Earth who can say no to that look."

"Quite a few men can't say no to it either."

She smiled. A genuine smile that softened her features and lit her eyes. Sed's breath caught. God, he'd missed that smile. And those lips. Against his.

"Is Trey still batting for both teams?" she asked.

"Unless something's changed since yesterday."

He dug a couple of forks out of a drawer, handed one to Jessica, and settled into the booth across from her with his plate.

She took a cautious bite. "Delicious!" Jessica slurped noodles into her mouth and shoveled in several shrimp. She gave him an enthusiastic thumbs up.

He chuckled. "Are you hungry?" Typically, she was the slowest eater on the planet. Or she used to be. Maybe she'd changed. The idea unsettled him.

"I forgot to eat today."

"How do you forget to eat?"

"Between getting fired, evicted, cussed out by a cop, and then hunting you down, it sort of slipped my mind. Which reminds me." She heaved her massive purse from the table and pulled out a familiar stack of cash. "I don't want this."

When he didn't accept the money, she dropped it on the table.

"You'd rather be evicted than take money from me?"

"Yes."

He would never understand her. Never. It wasn't as if he couldn't afford to take care of her. He wanted to do it. It gave him satisfaction to provide for the people important to him, but she'd never allow him that simple pleasure. The things he gave her—his ring, his money, his heart—obviously weren't good enough for her.

As soon as the cash was out of her possession, the tension left her expression and she sat up straighter. She took a deep breath and said, "Myrna said I should tell you that I felt insulted by your gift."

She met his eyes briefly, her cheeks pink.

"Insulted?" He tugged on his earlobe. "Why would it insult you? I was just trying to help. It's not a big deal."

"It's a big deal to me. I want to make it on my own. I need that."

"But why struggle with money? I can give—"

She lifted her palm in his direction. "I didn't bring it up to start an argument. I don't want your money. End of story. I'm doing fine without your help."

And that bothered him. Made him feel less of a man. Especially when she rubbed it in his face like that. "Well, I'm sorry I got you fired, then," he lied.

She shrugged. "I hated that job anyway."

His heart swelled and he smiled broadly.

"What are you smiling about?" she asked, pointing at him with her fork.

"Nothing." His smile widened further.

She grinned. "Your dimples are showing, Sedric."

He flushed.

"And you're blushing."

He scowled. "I'm not."

"Don't stop. It's adorable."

He lifted an eyebrow at her. "Sedric Lionheart is not adorable."

"But you are. Adorable, I mean. When your dimples show and you blush."

It was impossible not to grin and blush when she said things like that. While he was basking in her compliment, she stole a piece of shrimp from his plate.

"Are you trying to distract me so you can steal my food?"

"Maybe." She stole another shrimp and popped it into her mouth.

"Hey."

She laughed and poked another shrimp with her fork. He caught her fork with his before she could lift her prize to her open mouth. Was she flirting with him? And teasing him? Hadn't she just told him she didn't want to have anything to do with him? He would never understand her. He didn't know why he bothered trying.

"If you want my food, you should ask," he said.

"Can I have one of your shrimp?" She looked into his eyes expectantly. He couldn't refuse her anything when she looked at him like that.

He picked up one of his few remaining shrimp and offered it to her. She leaned across the table and drew his fingers into her mouth. When her tongue brushed his fingertips, his dick stirred in his shorts, ready and willing to take on anything Jessica had in mind. When it came to this woman, that part of his anatomy didn't give a flying fuck what was going on in his head or his heart.

Jessica leaned back and chewed with her eyes closed in bliss.

And that would be why. The woman was too damned sexy for her own good.

"It's soooo good," she murmured.

Sed's mouth went dry.

Her bare foot brushed his under the table. His toes curled. He expected her to move away immediately, but instead she rubbed her big toe against his instep. His stomach clenched with need. Cock throbbed incessantly. Did she realize what she was doing to him?

"Are you going to finish that?" she asked.

He shoved his plate in her direction. "I need a drink." *And a cold, cold shower.* He slid out of the booth and opened the refrigerator. Why had Myrna insisted they move all the beer to the other bus? He didn't feel like going over there and getting one, so he reached for a bottle of water. When a hand settled against the small of his back, he froze.

"Is there anything good to drink in there?" Jessica asked, peeking around his body.

The fruity scent of her shampoo assailed him and his eyes drifted closed. What had she asked him?

Oh yeah. Drink.

"All the alcohol's on the other bus."

Jessica reached in the refrigerator and retrieved a bottle of orange juice. She pressed the container against his belly and he danced sideways. "Cold!"

She laughed and tried to move around him, but he caught her around the waist and turned her to face him. She opened her bottle of juice and took a long drink, looking unconcerned by his nearness.

"What is this you're doing?"

She gazed up at him with those remarkable jade-green eyes of hers. "What do you mean?"

"This. This flirting."

"Do you want me to stop?"

"That depends on its purpose. If you're doing it to mess with my head, then yes, stop, please, it's torture. But if you're trying to work me into a frenzy so I can't keep my hands off you—"

"The second one."

His heart stuttered.

She took another sip of her juice. "Drink?" she offered, tipping the bottle toward him.

Juice sloshed out of the bottle and splashed against his chest. It trickled down the center of his belly and disappeared into the waistband of his shorts. "Whoops." She leaned forward and licked the juice from his skin, working her way down his body.

He wished his brain worked better when his dick was hard. What had turned her from cold to hot in less than half an hour?

"I thought you said you hated me," he said.

She stood straight again and leaned closer, her hand pressing against the tent in his shorts. He drew a sharp breath through his teeth.

"I still hate you," she said. "That doesn't seem to stop me from wanting you, though."

"So, this is just about—"

"Sex, Sedric. Nothing more."

Could he have a purely sexual relationship with Jessica? He had no problem having that kind of relationships with dozens of other women, so why was he hesitating with her? Because she was different.

She could hurt him.

She did hurt him.

Just looking at her hurt. When he couldn't see her, it hurt. When he thought about her, it hurt. When he tried not to think about her, it hurt. But which hurt more, being with her or being without her?

The entire time his internal battle raged, she just stared up at him, waiting for him to make the next move. His hand trembled as he lifted it to cup her jaw. His thumb brushed across her lips. Should he kiss her? She wouldn't realize that he hadn't kissed another woman since he'd fallen in love with her. Maybe his body had cheated, but his heart never had.

Her eyes drifted closed as he lowered his head. He hesitated, a hair's breadth between their lips. Something told him he'd regret this tomorrow, but now seemed more important. He traced the contour of her lush upper lip with his tongue. She sighed, trembling, as her lips parted. His tongue probed deeper, running along the ridge of her teeth, the roof of her mouth, and then stroked the surface of her tongue. She groaned and squeezed his hard-on through his shorts.

He shuddered and kissed her deeply, a ripple of delight streaking down his spine. He drew the tang of orange juice from her mouth into his, kissing her until her unique flavor greeted his tongue. That's what he wanted. *Her* taste. God, he'd missed it so much. He couldn't get enough. She groaned into his mouth.

The bottle of orange juice slipped from her hand. It hit the floor with a *thunk* and tipped onto its side, its contents glugging out and spreading across the linoleum.

Jessica pulled away. "Oh crap."

She bent to retrieve the half-empty bottle, put it on the table, and reached for a dish towel. He spooned up against her back, his hand running up her belly under her shirt.

"Leave it."

"It will just take me a second to clean it up."

"I'll go kick Eric out of the bedroom."

She shook her head. "That's not necessary. Go grab a blanket and spread it over the sofa. I've got something for you."

There wasn't much privacy in the living room area. Someone could enter the bus at any moment, but maybe that's what she wanted. Fine with him.

While Jessica cleaned up her mess, Sed yanked the blankets from his bunk and spread them over the sofa.

"Are you sure you don't want me to kick Eric out of the bedroom?" Sed asked.

"I'm sure."

She approached him slowly, looking deeply into his eyes. When she paused before him, he reached for her, but she placed a hand on his chest and shook her head at him. "No touching the dancer."

"Huh?"

She pushed his shorts down over his hips, drawing them down his legs as she squatted in front of him. He lifted one foot and then the other. She tossed his shorts aside, leaving him completely naked.

She ran her hands up his thighs, hips, belly, and chest as she stood again. Craving her attention, his cock twitched.

"Have a seat," she said breathlessly.

He sat on the sofa and reached to pull her down to join him. She took a step backward. "No touching the dancer."

"Jess—"

"Shh."

He dropped his hands and watched her walk over to the stereo system. After some fumbling, she turned it on and a song from Sinners' latest CD came from the speakers.

"This is my favorite band." Jessica smiled at him over her shoulder. "The lead singer is gorgeous. Listen to that voice. Mmmmm." She rolled her eyes with undisguised delight.

"I hear he's hung like a horse."

Jessica's gaze dropped to his jutting cock and she licked her lips. "Horses are jealous."

He laughed.

His smile faded when her hips started to sway to the music.

She ran her hands over the luscious curve of her ass and bent forward, her long strawberry blonde hair brushing the floor in front of her. She rocked her hips back and forth, and though she was still clothed, he couldn't draw his attention from the sweet spot between her thighs. She stood, flipping her glorious hair over her back as she ground her hips and squatted down to the floor before standing again. She turned to face him, still gyrating her hips. Her hands moved to the fly of her pants.

She unfastened the button and inched the zipper down, dancing for him seductively. Her hands ran up her sides, revealing the skin of her flat belly as she eased her shirt upward.

"Take it off," he murmured.

"Take what off?"

"I want to see your tits."

She pushed her shirt higher, teasing him with the vision of the under curves of her full breasts. She turned around, revealing an expanse of her sexy lower back, and peeled her shirt off over her head. He loved the way her thick, wavy hair brushed over the skin of her back as she continued to sway her hips. He imagined his fingers tangled in those silky, flowing locks, pulling her head back so he could suck on her collarbone, her throat, her jaw, her ear, her…

She tossed her shirt at him. It hit him in the chest and slid down to cover his lap. She turned to face him, her hands cupping her naked breasts. Her pink nipples protruded from between her fingers. He wanted to draw his tongue over them. Make them hard like he was hard. Draw shudders from her body. Deep sighs from her throat.

She danced closer. He reached for her and she paused.

"No touching the dancer."

"This is torture, Jessica."

She pouted. "I thought you'd like it."

"I do like it. I like it too much. It's driving me crazy."

She smiled. "I'm not finished yet."

She pulled her shirt from his lap. When the fabric brushed over his most sensitive flesh, he drew a sharp breath through his teeth. She stood on the sofa, one foot on either side of his hips and squatted in front of him so his face was between her breasts. He turned his head and tugged her nipple into his mouth, sucking it rapidly to a hardened point. She gasped and jerked away.

"No touching the—"

"You didn't say anything about sucking on the dancer," he murmured, and tugged her nipple back into his mouth. She cupped his face and shifted his mouth to her other breast.

"Why can't you behave?" she whispered, shuddering as his tongue flicked over her pebbled flesh.

He leaned back and looked up at her. "Do you want me to behave?"

She chuckled. "Not really."

She pulled away and turned to face the other direction, rubbing her ass and the rough fabric of her jeans over his engorged cock. He grabbed her hips, but she slapped his hands away and moved off the couch again.

While she danced in front of him, she stroked her nipples in hypnotic circles, making them even more erect.

Sed gripped the blanket to keep himself from jumping her. God, he wanted her. Desperately. Had never wanted anything more.

She slid one hand down her belly and into the open fly of her pants. Her hand disappeared into her jeans and her head fell back in ecstasy. She stroked herself for a moment, pushed her hand deeper, groaned and then pulled her hand from her pants. She slid her slick fingers into her mouth.

Sed grabbed his dick. He couldn't take much more of this.

Jessica pushed her pants down her hips, revealing the narrow strip of pubic hair that directed his attention to the juncture of her thighs. She turned, facing the opposite wall, and bent forward as she slid her jeans down her legs.

He groaned as she revealed the secrets between her thighs. She kicked her jeans aside and parted the swollen flesh between her thighs.

"I'm wet for you, Sed. Can you see it?"

"Yeah, I see it. I want to taste it."

A finger disappeared inside her velvety flesh. She plunged it into her body once, twice, and then pulled it free. His entire body jerked.

She moved toward him and slid her finger to his mouth. A hint of her taste teased his tongue.

"How's that?" She watched him with her lips parted as he sucked at her finger.

"Not nearly enough."

She climbed onto the couch with him again, and put a foot on the back of the sofa near his shoulder. The scent of her excitement drove him crazy. He had to thrust into her. Had to. He would die if he didn't possess her soon.

Jessica gyrated her hips in his face, and he grabbed her ass, holding her so he could lap at her juices hungrily. Her hips stilled. Panting, she held onto his head, her fingertips digging into his scalp. Her thighs began to tremble.

He smiled and leaned back. "Are you finished dancing?"

She glanced down at him. "Uh, sorry. No, not yet. Do you want to wear a condom?"

She was giving him an option? "Are you still on the pill?"

"Yeah. Have you been safe?"

"Always. You?"

"Yes."

"Then, no, I don't want to wear one."

She grinned. "Good."

She *trusted* him? She had every reason to—he'd never lie about something that important—but did her trust mean that she... Even though she *said* that she hated him, maybe she still...*cared* about him. Oh God, please, let that be what her trust meant.

Sed released his hold on Jessica and she struggled to regain her balance. She turned her back on him again, returning to her lap dance, but this time, instead of her rough jeans, her slick, warm slit rubbed against his dick. She reached between her thighs and directed the head of his cock inside her.

Just the head.

"Ahh," he gasped, fighting the urge to thrust up into her. She wasn't done teasing him yet, and he was very much enjoying her attempts to drive him entirely insane. It had been so long since he'd had any sexual contact without a condom, he forgot how good a woman felt without one. And it was Jessica's warm flesh teasing him. *Jessica.*

She continued to rub up against him, sometimes he dipped a scant inch inside her moist heat, sometimes she squeezed his punished shaft between the cheeks of her ass, but she never took him deep inside. Never gave him what he craved.

The CD ended with a click. She climbed from his lap and turned to face him. Straddling his hips, she leaned close, her breath tickling his ear. Her hair brushed his chest and his flesh quivered in delight.

"I want you inside me," she whispered into his ear. "Deep, deep inside me."

"Yes," he gasped.

"Do you want me, Sed?"

"God, yes."

"Only me? No one else?"

"Yes, only you." Did anyone else exist?

She grabbed his chin roughly and stared into his eyes. "I still hate you."

His chest constricted. Hope withered. "I know," he panted, pressure building behind his eyes as he fought his stupid emotions.

"And knowing that, you still want me?"

He nodded. God help him. "Yes, I still want you."

She smiled coldly and he wondered where his sweet, tender Jessica had gone. "Then fill me, Sed. Take what you want."

He groaned in torment. He grabbed his dick and rubbed at her clit with his free hand as he guided himself into her little piece of heaven. Oh, she was wet. Slick. Hot. His head fell back against the back of the sofa as she sank down, taking him deep at last. Submerging him within her.

"Jessica," he gasped. "Ah God, you feel so good."

"Touch the dancer as much as you want now."

He squeezed her breasts and then lowered both hands to hold her ass as she rode him with an increasing tempo.

"Best pole dance I've ever had," he whispered.

She looked down at him. "That was a lap dance, silly."

"Feels like you're dancing up and down my pole to me."

She laughed. "It's a two-fer."

He trailed his fingers up her spine lightly and she shuddered. "You're so beautiful." *I love you with everything that I am.* But he couldn't tell her that. She hated him. Hated him, but still fucked him like no one else could. This would be enough.

For now.

Maybe someday she'd let him touch her heart again. He ran two fingers down her breastbone. In here. Her heart thudded against his fingertips, reminding him that she was here. In the flesh. This wasn't a dream. His woman. His heart. Was back. He'd never let her go again.

She squeezed him within her body and his breath caught. Thoughts scattered.

She lowered her head and kissed him deeply as she continued to rise and fall. As her excitement built, she began to vocalize her pleasure into his mouth. A spasm gripped her body as an orgasm caught her. She pulled her mouth from his and cried out, her head tilting back in ecstasy.

Faster now as she sought a second release. Still multi-orgasmic. Still perfect. Still the only woman who could satisfy him.

He watched her, loving how she knew exactly how to get off on him. He could just lean back and enjoy it. Let her take him to heights he never experienced with any other woman. Sed shifted his hips slightly so her clit ground against his pubic bone with each downward thrust.

"Yeah, Sed," she whispered, gyrating her hips as she rode him now, grinding herself against him.

She moved faster. Faster. Her body convulsed, and she shuddered against him. "Sed, oh God. Sed!"

She paused for several seconds to catch her breath and then started rising and falling over him again. He let his head fall against the back of the sofa and closed his eyes, trying to think of something other than her perfect pussy massaging him in warm, velvety bliss. He couldn't think at all though. Could only feel. Hear. Smell. He gasped each time their bodies came together, every molecule of his body aware of her. Immersed in her.

She tightened her vaginal muscles around him again. She knew exactly how to bring him quickly to his peak. But he didn't want it to end. Not yet. *Not yet, Jessica. Make it last.*

She squeezed him tighter.

He groaned. Okay, yes, now. "Jess. Jess? I can't hold back if you do that."

She kissed his neck, her nose brushing against his ear. "Come with me, baby. I'm getting close again. Look at me. You'll know when."

He lifted his head and opened his eyes. The added stimulation of watching her face drove him closer to the edge. It really was Jessica. He wasn't imagining her. She was here. And he was inside her. Inside her. Inside.

She stared into his eyes as she continued to ride him.

She bit her lip, her breath hitching. Her fingers, resting on his shoulders, curled painfully into his flesh. Her head tilted back as she moved faster. Faster. Squeezing him inside. Grinding against him. Squeezing.

Ah God, he couldn't hold on any longer. The urgency had built beyond his limit.

Hurry, Jessica, hurry.

Her cries grew louder and higher pitched as she worked them both to release. Squeezing him inside, squeezing, relaxing. Squeezing, squeezing.

He had to come. Can't... Can't hold back. Jess. Jess.

She stopped moving as her hips buckled. "Now, Sed. Now."

He lifted his hips from the sofa, driving into her, and let go.

Exploded. Deep spasms gripped the base of his cock. His seed spurted into her body. And she took it. Took his cum. Inside her. Ah God, he was inside her. Part of her.

His Jessica. His.

They shuddered and strained against each other. Gasping. Crying out. Whimpering. When their bodies stopped quaking, she collapsed against his chest.

Jessica wrapped her arms around his neck and snuggled against him, still shuddering sporadically. His arms circled her back as he drew her nearer.

A smattering of applause erupted in the dining area. "That was beautiful, guys. Really," Eric said.

Sed grabbed the edges of the blanket beneath him and wrapped them around Jessica's back. He glared at Eric, who sat at the dining table eating what was left of Trey's cherry pie with his fingers. "Get the fuck out of here."

Jessica's entire body shook uncontrollably against him. Concerned, Sed leaned back to look at her face and found her laughing.

"He's right. That was beautiful. You are one hell of a good lay, Mister Lionheart."

She kissed him and lifted her hips to separate their bodies. Sed grunted in protest. He loved being buried in her warmth and would have stayed there forever if she'd allow it. She settled sideways on his lap and leaned against his chest, letting him hold her. She didn't rush away like the last time. Let him hold her. Let him. He kissed her temple and snuggled her close. How had he lived a single day without her? She was as essential to his life as air.

"So I guess this means you two are back together," Eric said.

"Yeah," Sed murmured, not caring that his dimples were showing as he grinned.

"No," Jessica corrected.

He glanced down at her. "No?"

"Just sex, Sed."

His arms tightened around her. "Yeah, that's what I meant. Just sex."

He'd take anything she was willing to give. His heart would just have to get used to that sinking ache inside until he could win her back.

Chapter 12

JESSICA LISTENED TO SED's heartbeat beneath her ear. She didn't think he was feeling much for her. She couldn't hurt him yet and that was okay. He'd eventually get tired of her using him like a piece of meat.

And what a delectable slab of prime rib he was.

God, she'd forgotten how perfectly their bodies responded to each other. She hoped it took a while to exact her revenge, because she was very much enjoying this little game.

"You want to go somewhere?" he asked.

A shiver raced down her spine at the sound of his deep voice. She looked up at him. "Like now? It's late."

"Isn't Las Vegas the city that never sleeps?"

"I think that's New York."

"Right. This is Sin City." He grinned wickedly and combed his fingers through her hair as his gaze caressed her face. "I thought you might like to take a walk down the strip with me." His eyebrows lifted suggestively.

Her breath caught. "Sightseeing?"

"Maybe a little." His gaze locked with hers and he grinned that sexy grin that made her body throb. "When our eyes are open."

Her heart raced out of control. She hadn't toured a city with Sed in over two years. The possibilities for public encounters in Las Vegas were endless. "I have a skirt in my car."

She squirmed off his lap, scooped her clothes off the floor, and headed for the small bathroom near the back of the bus.

Eric wolf-whistled as she darted past him in the nude. She stuck her tongue out at him before shutting herself in the bathroom. She cleaned up in the sink and hurriedly dressed in her jeans and T-shirt.

There was a knock at the door. "I'm coming in," Sed called.

Sed squeezed into the tiny bathroom and turned on the sink tap. She backed into the nook between the toilet and the shower. The man completely dominated the small room. He completely dominated everything. Jessica knew he couldn't help it, but it still irked her. Since he'd become famous, his influence spread beyond his personal sphere, which made him more infuriating. She felt like a washed out shadow whenever she was near him. Except when she was fucking him. Only then did she feel his equal.

"You're glowering at me." He was looking at her reflection in the mirror as he washed traces of their joining from his body.

"No, I'm not."

"Yeah, you are. What did I do wrong now?"

"Nothing you can help." She moved to stand behind him and ran her hands up the contoured muscles of his belly and chest. "You've been working out."

"Just some free weights and lots of push-ups, pull-ups, sit-ups."

"All those ups are really paying off. Sexier than ever."

She rested her cheek against his back and inhaled the unique scent of his skin. Like everything else about this man, it never failed to turn her on.

"Maybe we should go sightseeing tomorrow," he said, covering her hand with his. "We should get a hotel room for the night. There's no privacy here. I want to be alone with you."

"How about we tour a few places, get a room when we get tired, and then continue our tour tomorrow?"

He looked at her over his shoulder and smiled. "You always were brilliant."

She kissed his shoulder and moved around him to exit the bathroom. "I'll be back soon."

Jessica left the bus and hurried to the parking garage where she'd left her car. From her trunk, she grabbed a suitcase of clothes and the bag that contained her cosmetics and personal necessities, and then hurried back.

Sinners' fans had cleared out, and with them, the security guards. No problems getting around the barrier this time.

She found Sed leaning against the bus. His wide-brimmed hat was tilted low over his brow, his pretty blue eyes hidden behind a pair of dark sunglasses. He wore black leather pants, a white T-shirt, and a long leather duster.

"It's pretty warm out here for a coat," Jessica said, an eyebrow lifted at him.

"I'm willing to suffer for style."

She laughed. He reached for her suitcase, but she sidestepped him before he could take it from her. "I've got it."

He sighed and followed her onto the bus empty-handed.

Eric wasn't the only band member on the bus now. Trey rested on the sofa, watching TV with his sultry emerald-green eyes more closed than opened. He glanced up when Jessica walked past.

"Jessica?" he said incredulously.

"Hey, Trey. How have you been?"

"I've been better," he said quietly. "Head is killing me."

"Do you need me to take you to the hospital?" Sed asked. "That dickhead bouncer really whacked you a good one."

"I'm all right," Trey insisted. "I just need quiet. The other bus is too noisy. I feel a little better already."

Jessica bent to kiss Trey's cheek. "You sure, sweetie? We can take you to the E.R." She ran a finger down his lightly freckled nose.

"I'm good. I just need to rest. Quietly."

"Eric will keep an eye on him," Sed said.

"Eric? You're kidding, right?" Jessica said.

"Well, Brian's not here and Jace keeps taking off, so who else is there?"

"Dare? He is his brother."

"Guys, I said I was fine. Just shut up, get the fuck out of here and leave me alone."

Jessica and Sed looked down at Trey. "He's fine," they said in unison.

"I'll go change clothes now." Jessica carried the suitcase to the back bedroom and knocked on the door. A moment later, Eric opened it.

He wore nothing but a pair of black boxer briefs and a smile. She tried to keep her eyes from drifting down to where the sexy V of his hipbones disappeared into his underwear, but failed.

"Yes, you can join us." He pulled Jessica into the room by the arm. The girl on the bed covered herself with the heavy red comforter, but not before Jessica saw the huge vibrator she was plunging into her body. Eric still liked to watch, apparently.

"I need to change clothes," Jessica said.

Eric nodded in agreement, settling both long-fingered hands on his hips, drawing her attention again to where it did not belong. This man was all cord and muscle. And in those low slung boxer briefs, one hundred percent distraction.

"Without you in attendance." Jessica nodded toward the door.

"Hey, I was here first."

"The only thing you should be watching right now is Trey. I'm worried about him."

Eric's teasing expression turned serious. "What's wrong with Trey?"

"Brian said Trey was dizzy on stage tonight. And now, he's lying around with a headache. I think he's hurt pretty badly. Sed and I tried to talk him into going to the hospital, but he insists he's okay."

Eric grabbed his pants off the floor and hopped into them. "I'll take care of him."

He left the bedroom.

The girl on the bed growled in frustration. "What does a girl have to do to get laid around here?" She dropped the industrial-sized vibrator on the floor, climbed from the bed and searched for her clothes.

Jessica tossed her ancient hard-shell suitcase on the bed and popped it open. "It's not usually this crazy around here."

"Hey, aren't you that bitch who yanked Margo's hair for sucking Sed?"

Jessica riffled through her suitcase until she found the flowing skirt and form-fitting top she sought. A little wrinkly, but it would do. "You might as well spread the word. Sed's mine for the next two months. I won't put up with any of you slutty groupies touching him."

The young woman slid into her lilac-colored thong and matching tiny bra. "I think that's his decision, not yours."

"He likes it when I'm possessive. Run along now." Jessica removed her T-shirt and contemplated if she should wear a bra. The twisted styling of her top's bodice had plenty of support and it had a single tie around the neck. Her straps would show and she had no idea where she'd packed her strapless bra. Deciding against *any* undergarments, she slipped the green form-fitting top over her head.

The other girl had finished dressing and left the room, slamming the door soundly behind her. Jessica shrugged and changed into her bold-patterned, loose skirt. She topped off the outfit with three-inch strappy sandals, several bangles, and an anklet. She was putting on her make-up when Sed entered the room.

"What's taking you so long?"

"Almost ready." She applied tinted lip-gloss with her little finger.

"Always worth the wait. Damn, you look hot."

She grinned at him. "You're the one who looks hot. Are you sure you want to wear that coat?"

He winked at her. "I'm sure."

She fluffed her hair with her hands and checked her reflection in the mirror before approaching him in the doorway. "Let's go."

He grabbed her hand and dragged her through the bus. They passed Eric sitting on the couch with Trey's head resting on his thigh. Eric pressed a finger to his lips. Trey was fast asleep.

"We'll be back sometime tomorrow," Sed whispered.

Eric winked at them as they hurried past. Jessica stumbled down the steep bus steps, but Sed caught her before she fell flat on her face.

"Slow down," she complained. "I can't keep up with you in these heels."

"I'll carry you." He scooped her into his arms and smiled down at her. "Where to first?"

"I've already seen all the casinos. You pick."

Still carrying her, he cut across the parking lot, headed toward the wide sidewalk along the Vegas strip. His long strides covered ground quickly.

"Wanna go see the fountain at the Bellagio?" he asked.

She'd hoped he'd make that request. She loved the giant fountain. With its water jets choreographed to music, it was a moving work of art. Romantic. She knew from experience that it was lonesome to watch it alone. But tonight, she wasn't alone.

"I'd like that. Can you put me down, please?"

He paused and lowered his head to kiss her. She wrapped her arms around his neck and kissed him in return. When they drew apart, he set her on her feet and took her hand.

"Let me know if you get tired," he said, as they started up the sidewalk. At the far southern end of the strip, the crowds were relatively thin. They'd make good time for the first few blocks.

"It's only about a mile and a half to the fountain." She loved to walk along the strip, look at the extravagant casinos, and watch the menagerie of ever changing people. "

"A mile and a half is a long way in those shoes."

"If you weren't so tall, I wouldn't have to wear them."

He wrapped an arm around her back, his fingers pressing into her waist. "It's times like these I wish I was shorter like Jace. We'd be more height compatible then."

Height compatibility did have distinct advantages, but so did the strength of a big man. She admired the wide cut of his shoulders for a long moment before the name Jace sank into her addled thoughts.

"Damn. Speaking of Jace, I'm supposed to give him a message from a friend of mine. I keep forgetting."

Sed fished a cell phone out of his pocket. "Do you want to call him?"

Jessica shook her head. "I'll tell him tomorrow. I don't think Aggie is working tonight anyway."

"Aggie?"

"She's a dancer at the club I used to work for."

"Dominatrix chick with long black hair?" Sed pointed to his head. He also had black hair, though he kept it very short—like a military recruit.

"How'd you know?"

He laughed. "Lucky guess. A thousand bucks says Jace already picked up your message in person."

Jessica grinned. "Don't expect him to be able to move for a couple of days then. When's your next show?"

"Not until Tuesday. We're heading to Phoenix."

"We'll have to go sightseeing together there, as well."

His hand flattened over her belly as he drew her closer to his side. "We'll go sightseeing in any city you want. Let's catch a cab. I don't want you to wear yourself out with all this walking."

Was he thinking of her comfort or her sexual stamina? It didn't matter to her either way. She smiled. "Okay."

Inside the cab, he took her hand. When had he gotten so affectionate? Tender kissing. Holding hands. He'd never been like this when they'd been engaged.

"So how's school going?" he asked, a little too nonchalantly.

Her heart skipped a beat. Why did he want to know? He'd never wanted her to go in the first place.

"It's all right. I do have this one professor who hates my guts and won't give me a break."

"Why would anyone hate your guts?"

Jessica shrugged. "She just doesn't like me. She *failed*…" Jessica cringed. "She failed me on my final paper. Totally has it in for me. That's what Beth thinks."

"She's probably jealous of your gorgeous legs." He slid her skirt up to reveal her thigh. A little further to expose her mound. His fingers brushed over the curls he found there.

Jessica tugged her skirt down and rolled her eyes at him. "Give me a break."

"And who's Beth?"

Jessica smiled. She hoped Beth was having a nice summer. "My roommate."

"You have a roommate?"

She couldn't figure out why he looked so astonished. "Why wouldn't I?"

He shrugged. "Too proud to split the rent."

She scowled at him.

He scratched behind his ear. "Forget I said that."

"I'm not too *proud* to split the rent. Splitting the rent is fine."

"You're yelling."

Of course she was yelling. Why wouldn't she be? "No, I don't want someone to take care of me like I'm incompetent and boss me around and tell me how to live my life, but—"

He covered her mouth with one hand. "You're still yelling."

She slapped his hand away. "Let me finish."

"Don't be mad."

"Don't tell me how to feel."

He pulled her onto his lap and sank a hand into her hair to tilt her head back. His mouth claimed hers. She stiffened and tried to twist away, but his free arm tightened around her body and pinned her against his chest. He kissed her until she was clinging to his shoulders like a drowning kitten.

He drew away and looked down at her with a self-satisfied grin. "That's better."

God, she hated him sometimes. She gulped several deep, calming breaths. She needed to get a grip and quickly. He was turning her game against her and playing by his own rules. She had to regain control of this situation before she lost herself to him.

"You're so sexy when you're pissed," he whispered into her ear. "I couldn't help myself. I had to kiss you."

She slapped his chest. "You're such a jerk."

"I know." He cupped her jaw and brushed his thumb over her cheek. "Forgive me?"

No, but she could pretend. Her hands slid down his hard chest. "Kiss me again."

He hesitated, looking leery of her intentions.

"Sed, please," she whispered breathlessly. "I want you." That wasn't a lie. She did want him. She also wanted to beat the crap out of him.

He leaned forward in the seat and claimed her mouth, his tongue brushing her lip tentatively. Her hands moved around his body beneath his coat. She slid her fingers up under his shirt, stroking the smooth skin of his back.

He shuddered and tore his mouth from hers. "If you keep that up, I'm going to offend our cab driver by fucking you right here."

"Do you want me?"

His tugged her closer. "Always."

She squirmed in his lap, his cock growing hard against her hip. Yeah, that's the condition she wanted to keep him in. His hand moved under her skirt and up the inside of her thigh. She opened her legs for him. He hesitated, but when she spread her legs further, he took her cue and plunged two thick fingers into her swollen pussy. She shuddered and rocked against his hand, driving his fingers deeper.

"You wanna come right here, baby?" he murmured. "I'll take you there."

His thumb brushed against her throbbing clit and she sucked in a deep breath. Damn, she'd forgotten how sexy it was to do this kind of thing in public.

Unexpectedly, his fingers withdrew and he removed his hand from beneath her skirt. Confused, Jessica followed Sed's glare to the front seat. Their driver had lifted his butt out of the seat so he could see what they were doing through the rearview mirror. He wasn't watching the road at all. When he noticed they were staring at him, he cleared his throat and settled back down in his seat. "The Bellagio, right?"

Sed nodded curtly.

The cab driver did a U-turn near the end of the Vegas strip so he could drop them off in front of The Bellagio. The final sounds of the song accompanying the fountains faded as they stepped out of the car.

"I think we missed it," Sed commented.

"It starts over every fifteen minutes at night. What time is it?"

"Almost midnight, I think."

"I hope we didn't miss the last show." She took his hand and led him through the crowds. She rounded the edge of the semi-circular man-made lake that housed the fountain and headed toward the hotel.

He laughed. "Where are you going? I thought we were going to watch the fountain before we found a room."

"If we go around to this side we can see the Eiffel Tower at the Paris Hotel across the street. It's beautiful when it's all lit up at night."

Sed glanced over his shoulder. "Oh, wow. You're right. Spectacular." He hesitated. "So do you come here often?"

"Yeah. I love this fountain. Especially at night."

"With another guy?"

She paused and glared up at him. "Is that any of your business? You can't tell me you haven't been banging every girl who will spread her legs for you."

He bit his lip. "You're right. It's none of my business. I'm just glad I'm here with you now."

He drew her against his body and lowered his head to kiss her again. It was as if he were starved for her mouth. He never used to kiss her this much. Not that she minded. Just… why?

She clung to the hard muscles of his chest beneath his soft cotton T-shirt. Thinking about what was soon to come made her thighs quake. He broke the kiss and gazed down at her in the low light. They kept the area around the fountain dim so the streetlights didn't compete with the fountain lights. That was good, because they'd need the cover of darkness.

He bent his head and whispered in her ear, "Are you ready for me?"

"Yeah. Hot, swollen, and dripping wet." As if he hadn't felt it for himself in the back of the cab.

He growled. Her nipples tightened.

He led her to a sparsely populated expanse of the thick concrete fence surrounding the fountain. She stepped onto the short ledge and found it difficult to gain the leverage required to stand on her own. Sed moved directly behind her and wrapped his arms around her waist to assist her. His long coat enveloped the sides of her body, cocooning her in his warmth. His scent, mixed with the heady aroma of leather, engulfed her. The sound of his pants unzipping made her belly quiver in anticipation.

"Lift your skirt for me, baby," he whispered. "You won't believe how hard I am until you feel this inside you."

"Show me." She carefully lifted her skirt in the back, but not the front, so anyone who happened to notice them wouldn't see what was going on under Sed's black leather duster. They'd look like any couple cuddled against each other watching the fountain.

He leaned forward, his rock hard cock seeking entrance into her body. When his gentle probing found her eager opening, she bit her lip and pressed back against him. He filled her slowly, his growl of torment making her nipples tighten. Jessica stepped off the ledge, taking him deep. They gasped in unison. He stepped forward, pinning her against the smooth stone railing, and drove himself deeper still. *Ah, God.*

The lights in the fountain flashed on as water spewed into the air and the gentle music swelled in the background. The water swayed in perfect synchrony to the song, the beat maintained by lights flashing beneath the surface of the water.

Jessica rose onto her toes and then rocked back on her heels again. Sed couldn't thrust into her, like she wanted. Only her limited movements allowed any stimulation between their joined bodies.

"This is a beautiful song," Sed whispered.

"Yeah." She forced her eyes open to watch the arcing water, moving in time with the music. "Celine Dion."

"Yeah." He sang the romantic lyrics into her ear, two octaves lower than the famous diva. The sound of his incredible voice in her ear, singing words that would make any girl's heart melt, was almost as spectacular as having his cock buried inside of her in public. Almost.

"I'm surprised you know the words to this song," she whispered, hoping she looked inconspicuous as she climbed back up on the concrete railing in front of her and slid up his cock.

"Near. Far. Wherever…" he sang quietly.

She stepped off the barrier again, driving him deep. He leaned forward, pressing deeper.

"Ah, Sed," she whispered.

"…heart will go on." He paused in his singing. "God, Jessica. This is too much."

"Do you want to stop?"

His hand slid up under her top, his strong fingers caressing the bare skin of her belly. "No. It just makes me want to throw you in that water and tear into you like an animal."

She grinned. "I'd like that."

She leaned over the banister, drawing him out of her slightly. He leaned back and then took a step forward, thrusting deep into her. She bit her lip, stifling a groan.

Jessica caught movement out of the corner of her eye. One of a pair of young men pointed at her and whispered something to his friend. The second guy's eyes opened wide and he whispered something back.

"I think those guys over there are watching us," Jessica murmured.

Sed wrapped his arms around her, drawing her against him. "Do you think they can tell what we're doing?"

"If they can see my face, I'm sure they've figured it out. You feel so good inside me. I can't hide my pleasure."

"I want to see your face."

"When the song ends we'll find a room."

They watched the fountain's performance, sometimes standing still, sometimes moving together and apart, never finding a tempo, but always in tune with the sensuality between their bodies. He continued to sing into her ear. Every nerve ending in her body came alive, tingling with excitement. Nothing existed on Earth but Sed's body, his intoxicating voice, and the gushing water of the fountain.

The song ended and the water fell still with a gentle splash. The area around the fountain went dark. Using the darkness as cover, Sed thrust into her vigorously, his tongue lavishing a pleasure point behind her ear, his breath stirring the fine hairs along her neck. His hands massaged her breasts, rubbing her nipples against the fabric of her shirt until she thought she'd go mad. Her back arched as her body trembled with release. She came so hard her legs gave out on her. She clung to the railing, biting her lip to keep from crying out.

The street lamps around the fountain flickered on. Sed pulled out and quickly shoved his rigid cock into his pants, while she rearranged her skirt.

She took his hand, her face flushed. "Let's go find a room."

"Let's go to the Eiffel Tower." He nodded in the direction of the brilliant white lights engulfing the pointed tower across the street.

"I think it closes at 12:30."

"Then we'd better hurry."

Her pussy throbbed with renewed excitement as her mind raced through possibilities. She trotted after him toward the pedestrian bridge at the end of the street, giggling at his enthusiasm. About halfway across the bridge, he deposited her on his shoulder and took off at a run. She laughed and let him carry her, holding her skirt down over her thighs so passersby didn't get an unexpected view of her bare ass. He didn't set her down until they reached the entrance of the Eiffel Tower replica at the Paris Hotel and Casino.

"We're getting ready to close," the attendant told them. "It would be better to wait until tomorrow. If you go now, you'll just have to turn around and come right back down."

"That's fine." Sed handed a hundred dollar bill to the young man and took the escalator to the elevator entrance, ignoring the photographer who wanted to take their picture.

They were the only ones waiting to go up, though when the elevator opened, at least a dozen people got off to leave. After the car cleared of tourists, Sed tugged Jessica into the glass-walled elevator. He pushed the up button and when the door closed, he backed her up against the wall. She pretended his proximity didn't affect her.

"The view on the way up is spectacular," she said, but she wasn't admiring the view outside. The scenery inside the car held a grander appeal. She reached up and removed Sed's sunglasses so she could look into his sky-blue eyes. She tucked his shades into his pocket, never taking her eyes from his. His eyes glazed over with desire as he stared down at her.

"Let me out of my pants," he urged. "I need to be buried inside you again."

She unfastened his pants and his cock sprang free.

Sed grabbed her thigh and lifted her leg to his waist before guiding himself into her body. He groaned as he thrust up into her. He took her hard and fast, grinding into her and grunting his enthusiasm with each penetrating thrust.

The rapid raising of the elevator car made Jessica unsteady. She gripped his shoulders and leaned her back against the railing so she didn't lose her balance as she strained against him. One of his hands stroked her naked thigh, the other tangled in her hair. He pulled her head back and sucked on her throat.

The car began to slow as it neared the top.

Sed sighed remorsefully and pulled out, tucking his abused cock into his pants again.

When the elevator door slid open, they were standing innocently side-by-side holding hands. Sed guided her around the crowd of people waiting to get on the elevator and led her to the observation deck. A few people stood gazing out of the tower at the bright lights of the strip below, but most waited at the elevator to leave the closing attraction. Sed pulled Jessica to a deserted corner and shielded her body from the thinning crowd with his body.

"You know I can't control myself around you," he said.

She was counting on it.

His hands moved under her skirt, massaging the globes of her bare ass. He lowered his head to kiss her. He thrust his tongue into her mouth and she sucked it deep. He pulled her closer, grinding her pelvic bone against his—crushing his cock between their bodies. His fingertips ran down the crack of her ass until he found the puckered flesh he sought and dipped the tip of his ring finger inside her. She jerked and tugged her mouth away from his.

"I want to swallow you," she whispered. "We need to find a room immediately."

He glanced over his shoulder and looked around. There was no one there but the two of them. His hands moved to her hips and eased her down. She peeked around his body to ensure herself that no one was nearby and then crouched down in front of him. A cool breeze fluttered under her skirt and drew her attention to the hot ache between her thighs. Why was it always like this with him? He made her so wet and needy. Another reason to hate him.

And want him.

Sed's hands gripped the wire cage surrounding the observation deck as she freed his cock from his pants and drew him deep into her throat.

His head fell back, his hat tumbling to the ground as he groaned in that primeval way that made her pussy clench. She clutched the leather encasing his muscular thighs as she sucked him, drawing her head back and then taking him deep into her throat again. She bobbed her head faster, sucked harder, knowing he needed release.

"Ah, Jessica. Ah, yeah. That's perfect. Everything you do to me. Perfect."

"Excuse me, sir. The observation deck is closed now," a hesitant voice said behind them.

Jessica paused, her heart racing in her chest. Public engagements always excited her, but getting caught? Not so much.

Sed glanced at the female attendant over his shoulder. "I'll give you a thousand dollars if you forget I'm up here for twenty minutes."

"Oh. My. God," she said, her pitch and volume increasing with each word. "Sed Lionheart. I'm your biggest fan!"

Jessica released his cock from her mouth and stood up. Sed let go of the wire fencing to wrap an arm around her, drawing her against his chest and poking her in the belly with his erection.

"We're kind of busy," Jessica told the star-struck young woman.

Her gaze moved from Sed's face to Jessica's. "I thought you were alone," she murmured. Her eyes widened in sudden realization. "Oh. You can't do that here. The deck is closed. You have to go down now."

"I was going down," Jessica told her.

Sed tossed his head back and laughed, his arm tightening around Jessica's body. Jessica's hand slipped between their bodies and wrapped around his cock. He jerked, his breath catching in his throat. Poor guy was about to explode. Her hand shifted to his balls, finding them hot and full. He shuddered.

"Sweetie, I'll autograph something for you if you just disappear for about twenty minutes," Sed said hoarsely.

"I saw your concert tonight," the girl said, her gaze stuck to Sed like superglue. "How's your throat?"

"Still a little sore, but it will get better. So, Eiffel Tower Girl, do we have a deal? Leave us alone for a few?"

"Yeah, I'll pretend like I didn't see you for twenty minutes or so, but I want your shirt."

"You've got it."

"And a thousand dollars."

"Fine."

"Like, right now."

Sed shrugged off his long leather coat, allowing it to fall to the ground, and pulled his shirt over his head. He threw it at her. The young woman caught it, cradled it against her chest, and lowered her face into the fabric to inhale his scent. She sighed, her eyelids fluttering in bliss.

Jessica's nostrils flared.

"I'll pay you later," Sed promised. "Go away now."

The attendant nodded and disappeared around the corner.

"I really hate your fans sometimes." Jessica noticed they were entirely alone now. All the other tourists had left.

"If someone else had caught us, we'd have to leave."

"Good point."

He untied the string at the back of her neck and pushed down her bodice to expose her breasts. "I've been wanting to do that since we left the bus."

He lowered his head and sucked her breast into his mouth, his tongue working against her rigid nipple. Her free hand moved to the soft, short hair on the back of his head, while her other hand slowly stroked the length of his cock.

He released her aching breast from his mouth. "Grab hold of the fence behind you."

The fence? What did he have in mind? She lifted her hands over her head and held onto the thick chain-link wire fencing with both hands. "Like this?"

"Yeah. Hold on tight." He gripped her hips and lifted her feet off the ground. He stretched her body out in front of him, settling his hips between her legs.

"Can you hold on like that?" he asked.

"For a little while."

"Let me know when your arms get tired."

He surged forward, filling her with one deep thrust.

Her back arched involuntarily. "Ah, God, Sed."

He supported most of her weight with one hand under her lower back, the other under her hips. She wrapped her legs around his hips and gripped the fencing tightly as he thrust into her.

"Lean back," he whispered.

She walked her hands down the fence several rungs. When she opened her eyes, the Las Vegas strip came into view upside down. Below, she saw headlights of countless cars, an ambulance flashing red and blue lights in the distance, and the spectacular casinos lit in all their glory. Despite the view, she couldn't keep her eyes open. He felt too good to think of anything but his thick cock filling her, receding, filling her again. In this glorious, yet acrobatic, position, he rubbed against her G-spot with each penetrating thrust. Her arms began to tremble with fatigue, but she didn't want him to stop just yet. She was so close.

"Sed," she called. "Fuck me hard. I wanna come. I wanna…"

He thrust into her harder, his fingers digging into her flesh as he pounded against her.

"Oh. Oh. Oh, yes," her vocalizations grew louder and more needy with each thrust. Her excitement and pleasure built and built and built.

Her entire body convulsed as she came. He almost dropped her and had to strengthen his hold as she screamed into the night. She shuddered violently as ripples of pleasure spread from her pulsating core, down her thighs, and up her belly and back. He refused to relent. Kept pounding into her—harder, harder, oh God, yes, harder—until another orgasm shook her and another. She knew she was chanting his name at the top of her lungs, but couldn't stop. As her fourth orgasm pulsated through her, he thrust deep and held still, waiting for her to regain her bearings. When her body relaxed, Sed squatted and lowered her feet to the ground.

"You okay?"

She released the fencing with one hand and rubbed her face.

She laughed, somewhat maniacally. "You could say that. Wow, that was…"

"…amazing." He pulled out with a wince. "Can you stand? I don't think I can hold you that way much longer. I'm getting tired. I guess I need to work out more."

Most guys couldn't hold her like that for fifteen seconds, much less fifteen minutes. She used the fencing to pull herself to her feet. He stood before her and cupped her face, kissing her tenderly. He stroked the bare skin of her upper arms. "Turn around."

She never minded him bossing her around at times like these. She trusted his sexual inventiveness far more than her own.

She turned to face the Vegas strip. He moved behind her and pushed her skirt up around her waist. Gripping her hips, he entered her again, this time from behind. He had to bend his knees to penetrate her, because even in three-inch heels, she wasn't tall enough to accommodate his height. He caressed her buttocks and belly as he thrust into her slowly and rhythmically. As he had yet to come, she knew he had to be dying, yet he still considered her pleasure first, building her back to the pinnacle methodically.

It was time for her to regain control.

She bent forward slightly, changing the point of friction between their bodies.

He groaned. She rotated her hips, and bent further still, squeezing his cock tightly within her body.

"Jessica, that feels…"

"…amazing."

"Yeah." His breathing became sporadic as his thrusts quickened. *That's better. Lose yourself.* She bent further, her hair brushing the ground in front of her now. Squeezed harder. Relaxed. Squeezed. "Uhn. Uhn." He punctuated each thrust with groans and gasps.

Come hard, Sed. She clenched her vaginal muscles even tighter to increase his stimulation. *Think of nothing but me.* She slowly straightened her back, changing their point of friction again. When she stood completely upright, she slowly bent forward again.

His strokes became rapid and shallow, his breathing chaotic, his groans low and primal. His hands gripped her hipbones, trying to hold her still as he continued to pound into her. Faster. Faster. Harder. Oh, yes. He thrust deep and then paused.

"Hold still, hold still," he pleaded. He took several deep breaths and then began to move more slowly. Deeper. Gyrating to increase her pleasure.

She grinned. There was nothing better than a lover who held back for as long as possible. She put her hands on her knees and rotated her hips to the left and then to the right, grinding him inside her. And there was nothing more fun than trying to make him come.

"Jess. Jess."

She rotated her hips to the left again. With a primal growl, he grabbed her hair and pulled her upright. He lunged forward and pressed her body against the fence, thrusting into her vigorously, repeating incoherent words into her ear.

He grabbed the fence with both hands. Metal rattled loudly as he strained against her and shuddered violently as he let go inside her at last.

"Fuck. Fuck. Fuck," he shouted. "Oh God, Jess. Jess…"

There was nothing sexier than when this man, who was always in command, completely lost control.

His body sagged against hers, crushing her into the fencing. She allowed him to catch his breath for several minutes before she complained.

"Sed, I can't breathe."

"Sorry, sorry," he panted. "I don't think I can pull out yet. Give me a minute." His lips brushed against her hair at the side of her head. He leaned away from her slightly, giving her just enough room to take a decent breath, but kept himself buried inside her.

"You have to leave now," the Eiffel Tower attendant said from behind them.

Sed sighed and pulled away with a stuttering gasp. He tucked his slackening cock into his pants while Jessica straightened her skirt and pulled her top up to cover her breasts. She tied the strings behind her neck. Sed retrieved his leather coat from the ground and slid into it.

His naked chest and stomach, which showed between the sides of his duster, drew Jessica's appreciative attention. Yummy.

Sed located his hat and crammed it onto his head. Walking unsteadily, he dug his wallet out of his pocket and fished out multiple hundred-dollar bills. He handed them to the young woman.

"Thanks for your discretion," he said. "Worth every penny."

She flushed and shook her head. "Keep it. I don't want your money. I do want your autograph." She handed him a black marker and the shirt he'd given her earlier.

Sed signed the stretched fabric against his thigh and handed the shirt back to her.

"And can I have a hug, too?" she asked, smiling hopefully.

Sed glanced at Jessica for approval. She knew he had to indulge his fans on occasion, so she shrugged.

He attempted a weak, one-armed embrace, but Eiffel Tower Fangirl wouldn't settle for that. She wrapped both arms around his waist and rubbed her face against his shoulder. The young woman trembled from head to foot and continued to cling to him long after he'd dropped his arm.

Jessica tapped Fangirl on the shoulder. Not because that pang in her chest was jealousy: no, she just knew that Sed was exhausted and ready to head back to the hotel. "You're done," Jessica insisted. "We're leaving now."

Fangirl's head swiveled slowly and she glared pure hatred at Jessica. Jessica wouldn't have been surprised if the petite brunette started spewing split pea soup in her face.

"No one asked you, *Jessica*."

Jessica's eyes widened.

"Yes, I know who you are. You're the stupid bitch who broke Sed's—"

Sed covered the young woman's mouth with one hand and chuckled uneasily. "I've got to go now."

He pulled free of Fangirl's embrace, took Jessica's hand, and stumbled toward the elevator. Once they were inside and on their way down, Sed leaned against the wall.

"How did she know my name?" Jessica asked.

He shrugged. "Probably read it in a tabloid or something. Don't worry about it."

How could she not worry about it? Some demon-possessed fan girl knew her by name and probably had it in for her. Jessica fiddled with the bracelets on her wrists. She wondered how many other Sedric Lionheart fans thought she was a stupid bitch. Because *Sed* could obviously do no wrong. And why did she care anyway? She knew what a self-centered jerk he was, even if every other person on the planet was clueless.

Sed wrapped an arm around her shoulders and tugged her closer. "I can't wait to get you to a nice, comfortable bed," he murmured. "Nothing but missionary position for the next several days."

She smiled and snuggled closer, her hand resting on the warm skin of his belly. Yes, that was what she needed to focus on. Their sex-only relationship. Not these unfounded feelings of hurt over Sed's ridiculous fans. Who cared what they thought of her? "Missionary? I'll believe that when I see it."

Sed kissed her on the forehead. "You know what I hate about you?"

She scowled, some strange emotion stealing her breath. "What?"

"You know me too well."

"You know what I hate about *you*?"

"What?"

"Everything."

"Oh yeah?"

She nodded.

He chuckled. "Baby, if that's how you show your hatred, I can't wait to see how you show you care."

Chapter 13

SED ACCEPTED THE SET of keycards from the clerk at the Bellagio Hotel's check-in desk. He took Jessica's hand, his heart already drumming with anticipation, and headed for the elevator. Whatever little game she was playing with him, he was more than happy to participate. That h-word did a number on his heart every time she said it, even if he didn't believe she really meant it, but he had no doubt he'd win her back. She was slipping already.

His cell phone rang, startling him. So few people had his private number. Who would be calling him at one o'clock in the morning? He retrieved his phone from his pocket and checked the number on the incoming-call screen. Eric?

"Yeah?" Sed answered.

"Hate to bother you," Eric said. "I didn't know who else to call."

"What's wrong?" Sed covered his free ear with his hand and started walking toward the exit for better reception.

"They just checked Trey into Intensive Care and I can't get ahold of Brian. Trey keeps asking for him, but I guess Brian turned off his phone."

"What? Why is Trey in the hospital?"

"He had a seizure right after you left, so I called an ambulance. They did an MRI and he has a subdural hema-something-or-other. They have to drill through his skull to, oh I don't know, fix it. Can you find Brian? Dare is freaking out and scaring the hell out of Trey. Trey could really use Brian's levelheadedness right about now."

"I'll find Brian. I mean how hard can it be? I have no idea where he is and there are only a million hotel rooms in this city."

Jessica grabbed his arm. "He and Myrna are at the Venetian. A suite with a Jacuzzi tub."

"Jessica says he's at the Venetian. Is Trey going to be okay?"

"The doctor said he has a fair chance of recovery if they can decrease the pressure on his brain in the next few hours."

"If?" Sed ran a hand over his face. "Jesus Christ. This is all my fault."

"Sed, that's bullshit. It's all that bouncer's fault. You shouldn't bash people in the back of the head with an aluminum bat."

Sed glanced down at Jessica who was trotting beside him and staring up at him anxiously.

"If I hadn't reacted the way I did when I saw…" He avoided looking at Jessica and opened the door to the nearest cab. "Can you take me to the Venetian?" he asked the cab driver.

"Sure thing, mate."

Jessica climbed into the cab and Sed slid in next to her.

"I'm off to find Brian at his hotel. You try calling the front desk. I'll call you back soon."

Eric sighed in relief. "Thanks, Sed."

Sed ended the call.

"What's going on?" Jessica took his hand firmly in hers.

He shook off her grasp. He should have been there for Trey, not fucking Jessica along the Vegas strip. If he'd never seen her in the first place, they'd have never been in a bar fight and Trey wouldn't be in this life-threatening position. "Trey's in the hospital. I've got to find Brian."

"What's wrong with Trey?"

"He had a seizure. Something about brain swelling. I don't know. Eric didn't explain it very well." He leaned forward to talk to the driver. "We don't want to sightsee, dude. Hurry up, okay? It's an emergency." He reached for his wallet and tossed several hundred-dollar bills into the front seat.

The cab driver hit the gas, whipping around stalled traffic without hesitation. Soon, they pulled up to the Venetian hotel's entrance and drew to a stop.

Sed handed another hundred to the driver. "Can you stay here and hold the cab for me?"

"My pleasure, mate." He turned on the "off duty" sign and put the cab in park.

"What can I do to help?" Jessica asked.

"Stay here. You'll just slow me down."

She looked hurt, but nodded in agreement. Sed hopped out of the cab and raced into the opulent lobby. He hurried to the check-in counter to find the night clerk immersed in a heated debate with someone on the phone.

"I can't ring someone's room at this hour, sir. I understand that it's an emergency, but the guest in question has a do not disturb under *any* circumstances ord—" The clerk flushed beneath his olive complexion. "No sir, my head is not permanently inserted in my ass."

Sed jerked the phone receiver out of the clerk's hand. "Eric?"

"Who is this?" someone said on the other end of the line.

"It's Sed."

"This is Dare. Will you punch that stupid fuck of a desk clerk in the face for me?"

"If he doesn't call Brian, then yes, I'll punch him in the face for you. And again for me. And three times for Trey."

"Sir, you need to calm down," the desk clerk said, while repeatedly pushing a button to call for security.

Jessica appeared at Sed's elbow. She took the phone out of his hand and handed it to the desk clerk. "Jean Carlo," she greeted the attractive Roman-looking guy.

How the hell did she know him? Had she gone out with this stupid jackass? Watched the fountain with him? Let him put his hands on her? Screwed him? Had she liked it? Begged for more? Sed clenched both fists so he wouldn't reach across the desk and strangle the fucker.

The desk clerk's eyes widened with recognition and he smiled fondly at Jessica. "Feather. Lovely to see you."

Feather?

"I'm sorry my friend is a little out of hand," she said.

"A little? Did you see what he did? He just yanked the phone—"

"I'm sure he's sorry." Jessica looked up at Sed pointedly.

It was obvious that he'd get nowhere with his current tactics, besides tossed out of the hotel on his ass.

"Yeah, I'm sorry," Sed said. "A guest in this hotel has a friend who's in the hospital. He might die. Do you understand? I need to speak to Brian Sinclair. Trust me, he wants to know about this."

"You are the one who doesn't understand. Mister Sinclair is a celebrity, and—"

"I know he's a celebrity. He's in my fucking band. Jesus—"

Jessica covered Sed's mouth with her hand.

Security had arrived. "Is this guy causing a problem, Jean Carlo?"

Jessica stared deeply into Jean Carlo's eyes and shook her head pointedly. He mimicked her motion. "Just a misunderstanding," Jean Carlo said to the security guards.

The four large men stepped to the side of the desk, keeping a close eye on Sed, who happened to be wearing leather pants, a duster, and no shirt. He supposed he did look even more suspicious than usual.

Jessica crooked a finger at Jean Carlo and leaned close to him. Sed's body tensed. As if he hadn't wanted to punch this dumb fuck in the face enough already.

The way-too-handsome clerk smiled while Jessica whispered into his ear. He scrawled something on a piece of paper and handed it to her.

She kissed his cheek and leaned away.

"I'll see you at the club tomorrow night, Feather," Jean Carlo said. "It's payday." He wiggled his eyebrows suggestively.

Sed's knuckles cracked under the strain of his clenching fists.

"Oh, I'm sorry, sweetie," Jessica said. "I got fired. I thought you knew."

Jean Carlo scowled, his slim dark brows drawing together. "Fired? Well, where are you working now?"

"Nowhere at the moment, but I'll let you know if I start dancing again."

Jessica grabbed Sed's sleeve and led him away from the desk.

"Wait, he still didn't call Brian."

"Shh," Jessica demanded. She pulled him behind a pillar and handed him the slip of paper the clerk had given her. "This is Brian's room number. Jean Carlo can't call their room, but we can go up and knock on the door. And if we get into trouble, he did *not* help us. Got it?"

"Don't you need a guest key to get on the elevator?"

She handed him a plastic card. "Any more questions?"

"Did he really call you Feather?"

Her nose wrinkled, making him want to kiss its adorable tip. "My stripper stage name. Any other questions?"

"Did you fuck that guy?" He jerked a thumb in the direction of the front desk.

"None of your business."

Maybe. But he still wanted to kill him. "Let's go get Brian now."

Within minutes, they were standing outside Brian's hotel suite. Sed knocked loudly. No answer.

"You don't think they've gone out, do you?" Jessica asked.

"Highly unlikely," Sed said. "He's with Myrna on his honeymoon. If anything, he's passed out from exhaustion." He knocked again, more loudly this time. "Brian," he shouted. "Open the door."

There was a loud *thunk* on the other side of the door. A moment later, Brian yanked it open. He had a sheet bunched around his naked hips. His entire body was drenched in sweat and his shoulder-length black hair stuck to his damp face and neck.

"This better be important."

"Is that Sed?" Myrna appeared behind Brian, cinching a bathrobe around her waist.

"And Jessica," Brian grumbled.

While Brian scowled at this discovery, Myrna grinned. "You two should consider getting your own room. We're using every square inch of ours."

Sed didn't know how to break the news other than just blurting it. "It's Trey. He had a seizure and he's in the ICU at the hospital. He keeps asking for you, Brian, so Eric sent me to find you."

"Trey?" Brian said, dumbstruck.

Myrna's knowing grin faded. "It's his head injury, isn't it?"

"Yeah, he has a subdur- hema...um..."

"A subdural hematoma?" Myrna winced. "Are they draining it?"

"Yeah, I guess," Sed said. "I don't really know."

"I'll find Brian some clothes and we'll be right out," Myrna promised.

Myrna tugged Brian inside and closed the door.

Sed leaned against the wall heavily. "Thanks, Jessica. I couldn't have done this without you."

She smiled and nodded. "I feel kind of responsible for the entire thing."

"Why? It's my fault."

She shook her head. "You should call Eric and let them know we found Brian."

He dialed Eric, who answered on the first ring.

"Did you find him?"

"Yeah, we'll be on our way in a few minutes. Which hospital?"

Eric relayed the hospital's location. The hotel suite door opened and Brian emerged, still pulling his shirt over his head. Myrna closed the door behind them, stumbling against the wall as she tried to walk and put on her shoes at the same time.

"Lead the way," Myrna said.

When they were all on the elevator, Myrna leaned against Brian and brushed the hair from his face. "He'll be fine, sweetheart."

"What's a subdural whatever-you-call-it?" Sed asked Myrna, who seemed to understand what was going on.

"It's when a person bleeds under the membrane that covers their brain. The blood has nowhere to go, so it just keeps building up and pressing on the brain. That's what causes injury, so they've got to drain the blood before…" She averted her gaze. "His brain is probably fine."

"Probably?" Brian asked, his voice cracking.

Myrna kissed Brian's jaw. "We'll know more when we get to the hospital, but he's been walking around with this injury for over a day. The blood took a long while to accumulate, so he can't be hemorrhaging much."

"Goddamned Eric starting fights," Brian said. "And you," he said, his intense brown eyes swiveling to focus on Sed. "If you'd think with your head instead of your cock on occasion, this would have never happened." His gaze moved to Jessica. "And why are you here anyway?"

"She helped me find you," Sed said. "Why didn't you tell anyone where you were going and then shut off your fucking cell phone?"

Brian leaned heavily against the back of the elevator car and pressed on his temples with both hands. "I don't know. I'm stupid. I was only thinking about myself."

"Brian—" Jessica started.

"Don't speak to me. You have no idea what kind of damage you left behind when you walked out on Sed."

Jessica's eyes widened and she glanced at Sed in disbelief.

Great. Just what he needed: Jessica to know she was his greatest weakness.

"Brian, I know you're upset, sweetheart, but—" Myrna began.

"Don't you dare side with them."

"I'm not siding with anyone. I know you're upset and I don't want you to say something you'll regret."

"Why would I regret telling the truth? You fucked him up big time when you left him, Jessica. He hurts everyone around him without regard for anything but his fucking libido."

Sed couldn't argue. He'd hurt Brian more than anyone, because, as a romantic, Brian was the easiest to hurt. Sed had seduced every one of Brian's girlfriends with the exception of Myrna. He'd have slept with Myrna too, if she'd allowed it.

"I suppose you're fucking her now." Brian pointed at Jessica, who flinched.

Sed and Jessica avoided each other's gazes.

"God! You're such an idiot!" Brian reached over and slapped Sed alongside the head. "She's just going to destroy you again, man. You have the shortest memory of anyone I know."

Sed knew Jessica would destroy him. He knew it, but he loved her anyway. He'd always loved her. He'd never stopped loving her, and he'd still love her after she knifed him in the heart again. Even now she was setting him up to knock him down and he honestly didn't care. Whatever she had in mind couldn't be worse than living without her.

Unless she planned on leaving him again.

His gaze swiveled to the object of his obsession, who was pointedly staring at the floor in front of her. She wouldn't do that again, would she? God, he wouldn't survive if he had to watch her walk away from him again.

The cab sat waiting for them outside the hotel. Sed slid into the front seat with the driver, leaving Brian, Myrna and Jessica to climb into the back. All the way to the hospital, the interior of the cab remained silent. Sed stared out the windshield, wondering how he could possibly fix this mess. He'd do anything to make it better. But really, what could he do? He wasn't a doctor. He didn't have any influence over the functioning of a hospital. He had to try to do something, though. Sitting back and letting things happen was never on his agenda.

The cab driver dropped them off in front of the emergency room. The front desk directed them to Trey's room upstairs in the ICU. There, they found Eric pacing the hall.

Eric seized Brian in a bear hug. "Oh good, oh good, you made it."

Brian pulled away and glanced into the nearest door. "Is he in there?"

"Yeah. Dare's with him. All my pacing was making Trey nervous, so he told me to get lost."

Brian grabbed Myrna's hand and pulled her into the room. Jessica stayed behind in the hallway with Eric, while Sed followed the newlyweds. They found Dare sitting on the edge of Trey's bed, talking to him in hushed tones.

Trey glanced up when Brian came into his line of sight. He smiled brightly and then his gaze shifted to Myrna. He bit his lip and scowled. "I'm sorry I interrupted your honeymoon. I'm such a pussy." Trey spoke with a slurred voice. He concentrated on swallowing and then blinked slowly.

"This is more important," Brian said.

Myrna nodded in agreement.

"Didn't I see you with Jessica earlier this evening?" Dare asked Myrna. "Is this your wife?" he asked Brian.

"Yeah. Myrna, this is Trey's older brother, Darren," Brian said.

"Dare," Dare corrected and extended his hand to Myrna, who shook it.

"Can I borrow you for a moment?" Myrna said, tugging Dare from the edge of the bed by his hand.

"Uh, sure. Okay."

Sed watched Myrna lead Dare out into the hall, thinking her request strange. Brian took the spot on the edge of the bed recently vacated by Trey's older brother.

Trey glanced up at Sed. "They bothered you, too. Sheesh, I'm a regular pain in the ass, aren't I?"

Sed shook his head. "What did they tell you?" *Please say you're going to be all right, Trey. Please.*

"Tore a vein or something in my head." He pointed to a spot several inches behind his left ear. "They have to drill a hole and suck the blood out. It's not as bad as it sounds. The MRI didn't show much blood in there. Just a little hole in a vein. Shouldn't be too hard to f-fix..." His eyes drifted out of focus.

Brian reached for the call button, but Trey grabbed his arm and shook his head slightly.

"I'm all right," he insisted. "I just can't think so good."

"Well, nothing unusual about that," Brian said.

Trey smiled his typical, infectious grin.

"Isn't it dangerous to drill a hole in someone's head?" Sed asked.

"If they don't, I'll die." Trey covered his eyes with one hand. His throat convulsed as he swallowed hard.

"You're not going to die, Trey," Brian said. "If you do, I'll kill you."

Trey chuckled. Sed realized he was probably making Trey feel worse, but he didn't want to leave. He needed to see Trey moving, breathing, joking around. That way he could convince himself that Trey would be okay and that helpless feeling in Sed's gut would ease.

"Did you tell the doctor the last thing you need is another hole in your head?" Brian touched the holes in Trey's left ear, which usually had rings and studs in them, but apparently all of his jewelry had been removed. "Tongue pierced, eyebrow twice, nose, two in your lip, five in your ears."

Trey moved his hand from his eyes. He looked more alert than he had a moment ago. "Might as well make it an even dozen." He laughed and then winced, his right eyebrow twitching slightly. He glanced at Sed. "You look like you're at my funeral."

"What can I do for you, Trey?" Sed asked. "Anything. I'll do anything."

"Smile."

Sed tried, but it made his chest constrict in agony.

Brian's gaze focused on Sed's bare torso. "Did you lose your shirt at the casino, or what?"

Sed glanced down at his chest. "Uh, I gave it to a fan."

"You lose more shirts that way," Brian said.

Trey laughed.

Sed smiled. Trey was going to be okay. He had to be.

Myrna came back into the room. She approached the bed and leaned over Trey. Her fingers gently brushed the long strands of black hair from his forehead and she kissed his brow.

"There will be a fresh cherry pie waiting for you when you come home," Myrna said.

"Awesome!"

"When do you get to come home?" Sed asked.

"Tomorrow, I hope. I fuckin' hate hospitals."

"Do you really think they're going to let you out of here that quickly? After *brain* surgery? Get a clue, man."

"Brain surgery? It's nothing that serious. I don't have a tumor. They're just sucking out some blood. No big deal. A hotel maid could do it." He made a sucking sound and pantomimed vacuuming the side of his head.

Sed shook his head at him. "No big deal, huh?" Five minutes ago the guy was freaking out. What was different? He noticed Trey was clinging to the front pocket of Brian's jeans with two fingers. Ah, Brian. Trey's rock. Sed was doubly glad he'd retrieved him.

"If it was a big deal," Brian said, "don't you think they'd have already started operating?"

"They're waiting for a brain surgeon," Myrna said. "A good one. Dare said their father called her personally."

Why hadn't Sed thought of that? Trey's father, Dr. George Mills, was a renowned plastic surgeon in Beverly Hills. Of course, Dr. Mills would have connections and get Trey the best possible care.

"He'll need a good one. Doc Mills knows his son doesn't have any spare brain cells to sacrifice," Brian said, punching Trey in the shoulder.

Trey scowled at Brian. "Why did I want you here again?"

"To ruin my good time, apparently. You can't imagine the incredible things Myrna was doing to me when Sed interrupted."

"Fine, then. Leave."

"Before seeing your new haircut? Wouldn't miss that for anything, buddy."

"Haircut?" Trey glanced around nervously. "What haircut?"

Brian grinned down at him. "You know they're going to have to shave off all your hair before they start drilling holes through your thick skull."

Trey's eyes widened. He glanced at Myrna for verification. She nodded slightly. "It will grow back, sweetie."

"Fuck that." Trey tried to get out of the hospital bed.

Sed grabbed him by both shoulders and shoved him back, pinning him to the mattress with sheer force. "You aren't going anywhere, Mills. Don't make me sit on you."

Dare entered the room. "They said the doctor should be here soon. She's on her way upstairs now."

Sed caught sight of Jessica peeking in the doorway, gnawing on the end of her index finger. He considered calling her in to join them, but knew Brian would probably just upset her again. Sed winked at her. Her eyes widened as if she'd been caught doing something wrong and she disappeared back in the corridor.

"Dare," Trey whined in his protect-me-big-brother voice, "Brian says they're going to shave my head."

"Well, duh, Trey. I think that's pretty standard." Dare lifted an eyebrow at Sed. "Why are you abusing my brother?"

It took Sed a second to realize he was still pressing Trey down against the hospital bed with both hands. He released Trey's shoulders and stood straight. "Because he was trying to get out of bed."

Dare's green eyes shifted to his little brother. "Why were you trying to get out of bed, dipshit?"

"They're going to shave my head!"

Dare chuckled and tousled Trey's hair affectionately. "Is that really your biggest concern?"

"Do you think I want to look like a total douche?" He lifted a hand in Sed's direction. "Like him?"

"Hey," Sed protested. Yes, he kept his hair very short. But he didn't look like a total douche. Did he?

"No offense, Sed," Trey added.

Sed ran a hand over the soft fuzz on his scalp and eyed the long bangs covering one of Trey's eyes. He'd never pull off an emo hairstyle like Trey's anyway. Too much maintenance.

"You'll wish you had that much hair when they're finished with you," Brian said. "Cue balls will be jealous of your shiny dome."

Trey covered his head with both hands. "Shut up."

A nurse nudged her way through the congregated friends. "You all have to leave. I need to prep him for surgery now."

Trey eyed the razor in the nurse's collection of frightening implements and started to climb out of bed again. Sed widened his stance, prepared to force him back down if necessary.

"If you move from that bed, Terrance, I'll tell Mom why the

last pool boy quit," Dare threatened. "She and Dad are on their way, you know."

Trey's eyes widened and his entire body sank into the bed. "Don't call me Terrance," he muttered.

Brian chuckled. "Deflowering virgins again, Trey?"

"He liked it." Trey's ornery grin made an appearance. "And I really liked it, but I don't want my *mother* to know that." He glared at his brother. "I have a bunch of shit on you too, you know."

Dare chuckled and an ornerier version of Trey's grin spread across his face. "She'll never believe you. Mom thinks I'm her angelic son."

Brian burst out laughing. Sed didn't know Dare well enough to understand what had Brian in hysterics. He could only imagine what acts of debauchery the lead guitarist of Exodus End might pursue.

The nurse squeezed around Sed to stand next to the bed. "I need to get this done."

Trey turned on the charm. "Yeah, you guys get out of here. We have some shaving to do." He lifted an eyebrow at her suggestively. The nurse dropped her gaze and blushed.

Sed wondered if Trey would actually be able to talk her out of shaving his head. Surely not. The woman was a professional.

Sed grabbed Trey's hand in a firm handshake and patted him vigorously on the shoulder. "We'll see you on the other side."

Trey paled, his nose freckles appearing in stark contrast to his light skin.

Sed supposed he shouldn't have reminded Trey what was about to happen. He should just keep his mouth shut and defer to Brian, who was an expert at placating Trey.

Myrna kissed Trey affectionately right on the mouth. "Cherry pie *and* cherry cobbler when you get home."

"Now you're talkin'," Trey said.

Sed grinned. Midwestern women and their way of trying to feed their love to people. Perfectly fine by him. The woman could cook her ass off. A skill Jessica had not quite mastered.

Jessica.

Shit. He'd just left her out in the hallway all by herself. She was going to be pissed. And he wasn't sure why that thought excited him.

Sed found Jessica leaning against the wall outside Trey's door. Eric stood beside her. She had her head resting against his muscular upper arm and he was stroking her long, wavy hair with one hand. Sed buried a spike of inappropriate jealousy. He knew Eric wouldn't make a move on his woman. Eric valued his life too much.

"Sorry I left you out here by yourself for so long," Sed said to Jessica.

Eric cleared his throat loudly.

"It's okay. Eric was keeping me company."

"You could've come inside."

She shook her head slightly. "I didn't want to upset anyone."

Sed drew his brows together. "Like who?"

"Brian."

Sed shrugged. "Eh, he'll get over it."

"I wouldn't be so sure about that," Eric said.

"Why does he hate me so much, anyway?"

Sed loathed the look of hurt in her eyes, but was glad he wasn't its direct source.

"No idea." Like he was going to tell her he'd seduced Brian's girlfriends to make himself feel better about his own lonely, miserable existence. Uh, yeah. That was *sure* to win her back.

Eric sent Sed a disapproving stare, shook his head, and then pushed off the wall. "I'm going to go see Trey."

Jessica turned into Sed's bare chest and wrapped her arms around his waist beneath his leather duster. "Trey's going to be okay, isn't he?" Her voice sounded small, igniting his need to protect.

He pressed his lips to the top of her head. "He'll be fine. I guarantee it," he murmured against her silky hair.

The elevator at the end of the hallway dinged, and repetitive squeaking advanced toward them. Jace slid around a corner and raced in their direction. Sed hadn't known the dude could move so fast. Winded, Jace skidded to a stop in front of Sed.

"Just got. Eric's. Message." He gulped several breaths of air. "Trey?"

"They're prepping him for surgery right now." Sed nodded toward the open door to his left.

"Surgery?"

Eric came out of the room, followed by the rest of Trey's visitors.

"Took you long enough." Eric reached over and peeled something off the side of Jace's neck. "What is this? Wax? What have you been up to, little man?"

Jace flushed. "Can I see Trey?"

"We got kicked out," Brian said. "We're supposed to wait in the waiting area until he's out of surgery." He nodded toward the lounge area near the elevators.

"Surgery?" Jace repeated. Typically a master of hiding his emotions, Jace looked like someone had punched him in the stomach, knocked him flat on his ass, and then pissed on his forehead. "I can't let him go into surgery without seeing him."

He didn't wait for permission. He just barreled right into Trey's room. "What the... You can't be in that bad of shape if you can do *that*."

Sed turned his head toward the open door. *Do what?*

Dare suddenly jetted across the hall and grabbed a tiny woman, who was dressed in green scrubs, in an enthusiastic embrace. He lifted her off the floor and bounced her up and down in his arms. "Dr. Angelo. Thanks for rushing here so quickly."

She smiled. "My pleasure, Darren."

Sed had the urge to demand the woman's credentials before she went mucking around with Trey's brain. As hard as it was for Sed, he knew he had to stand back and not interfere.

"You okay?" Jessica asked.

Sed nodded. She kissed the center of his bare chest tenderly, her fingers splayed over his rib cage. His heart thrummed against her lips.

Eyes on Jessica, Brian made a sound of frustration and stalked off toward the waiting area with Myrna on his heels. What the fuck was he so pissed about?

Dr. Angelo entered her patient's room.

"Dr. Angelo!" Trey's voice carried into the hall.

"Why haven't you shaved his head yet?" Dr. Angelo said sternly. "And who are you? You have to leave."

"S- Sorry." Jace came out into the hallway, his face red.

The doctor's sudden, no-nonsense attitude made Sed feel a hell of a lot better. He smiled and took Jessica's hand. "Trey is going to be fine," he said as they walked toward the waiting area.

"Of course he is."

"Let's go, little man." Eric grabbed Jace in a headlock and hauled ass down the corridor.

When they entered the waiting room, Brian turned his back on the group and wiped his damp face on the hem of his T-shirt. Sed had never seen Brian cry and they had been through some seriously horrible shit together. Brian's earlier nonchalance, his teasing, had all been an act for Trey's benefit. Sed's heart sank. If the levelheaded one of the group had come undone, things were pretty bad.

Myrna took her husband's head between her hands, her fingertips curled behind his ears, and pressed her forehead against his. She murmured to him, "He'll be fine, sweetheart. You have to believe that."

"But what if he's not?" His voice cracked.

"Don't let yourself *think* that way."

Good advice. Sed just wished it was easier to follow.

Brian took a deep breath and crushed Myrna's body against his chest.

Jessica placed a timid hand on Sed's belly and he looked down at her.

"Are you sure you're okay?" she asked.

Why did she keep asking him that? Since when did she give a shit how he felt? And, no, he wasn't okay. He didn't know what to do. There was nothing he could do. He wanted to climb the sterile, white walls just to occupy himself.

"I'm here for you," she whispered, her jade-green eyes watery with tears.

If ever a woman had said the right thing at exactly the right moment, that was it.

Whatever it took to make her love him, he'd do it. To hell with what Brian or anyone else thought. He refused to give up on her this time. She would be his again. And not just in body. That would never be enough for him and he knew it.

Sed drew Jessica against his chest, hugging her close. She hesitated and then her arms stole around his body beneath his leather duster. Her small hands splayed over his bare back and she snuggled close to his chest. His heart throbbed beneath her ear—so full he thought it might burst inside his chest.

Dare entered the waiting room. "Okay, which one of you started that fight so I know who to destroy if Trey doesn't make it through this in perfect health?"

All eyes turned to Eric, who blanched. "Me? What about Sed? He's the one who pulled Jessica off the stage and got the bouncers all riled up."

Sed nodded. "He's right. I started it."

Dare sank into a chair with a heavy sigh and rested his forehead in both hands. "It had to be the big guy," he murmured. "One more reason to pray the little pain in my ass makes it through this."

Chapter 14

JESSICA STARTED AWAKE AND lifted her head from Sed's shoulder. When had she dozed off? Sed's hand squeezed her wrist until she grabbed his fingers to alleviate the pressure. "Ow." She glared up at him and decided he didn't realize he was hurting her. She followed his troubled gaze to the doorway. Dr. Angelo stood at the threshold.

Jessica sat up straight in the uncomfortable chair and gaped at the splatter of blood on the right sleeve of the doctor's surgical gown. Trey's? She forced her attention to the woman's face.

Looking weary but not defeated, Dr. Angelo pulled her surgical mask down around her neck. "Trey made it through the surgery."

"Thank God," Dare said.

He grabbed the nearest person, who happened to be Jace, in a bone-crushing hug. Jace winced in pain and offered Dare an awkward pat on the back.

"But there were a few complications."

Jessica held her breath. Sed's hand tightened on her wrist again.

"I removed the clot, drained the excess blood, and cauterized the damaged vessels, but Trey was in worse shape than his MRI indicated. Apparently, his seizure caused a secondary hemorrhage and increased the pressure on his brain far more rapidly than we predicted."

Dare hauled himself out of his chair. "But he's okay. Right? He's okay?"

"He will live. I have no doubt about that. They've taken him to recovery. He's still unconscious. In serious but stable condition."

Dr. Angelo lowered her gaze before straightening her shoulders and meeting Dare's eyes again. "I'd like to say he's going to be back to normal in no time, kiddo, and I'm hopeful that he will be—he's young and strong—but we can't know for sure until he wakes up. The swelling on his brain might have caused permanent damage. Brain injuries are… tricky."

Jessica took Sed's free hand and offered a comforting squeeze. She knew he felt responsible for causing the bar fight. He always tried to take responsibility for everything—as if it was his life's mission to carry everyone's burden on those broad shoulders. That's what Myrna had been trying to tell her back on the tour bus. Maybe he didn't try to take care of her because he thought she was incompetent and weak. Maybe he tried to take care of her because…

No. She'd made her decision about him and she was going to stick to it. Sed Lionheart was poison. An addictive poison, but not someone she needed in her life permanently. Just someone she needed between her thighs on a regular basis.

"When can we see him?" Sed asked.

The doctor glanced at him and shook her head. "He needs uninterrupted rest for several hours. He's heavily sedated, so he won't wake for a while anyway. Why don't you all go get some sleep and come back in the morning? We'll know more by then."

"Someone needs to stay here in case he wakes up," Dare said. "I'm not going to leave him here by himself."

"I'm staying too," Jace said.

"So am I," said Brian.

Dr. Angelo smiled. "I'm glad he has so many people who care about him. He's going to need you all during recovery, but you aren't going to do him any good if you're sleep deprived."

"Why don't we take turns staying with him?" Myrna said. "Split the time into four hour blocks. When he wakes up, a phone call will get all of us here quickly."

Jessica had to admire Myrna. She had this group of egos eating out of the palm of her hand.

"I'm staying first," Dare said.

"I'll stay with him," Jace said. "I'm wide awake."

"Me too," Eric said.

"Okay, Brian and I will come back around..." Myrna checked her watch. "Eight a.m."

"Then Sed and I will come at noon," Jessica said. It earned her a glare from Brian, who obviously despised her on a visceral level, but Sed squeezed her hand.

"Sounds good," Myrna said, elbowing her husband in the ribs.

Dr. Angelo smiled. "They'll bring him back to the ICU after his anesthesia wears off. I do have high hopes for his full recovery. There was some slight bruising to his brain tissue, but I didn't see any necrosis. That's a good sign." The doctor gave Dare a gentle hug. "Take heart, kiddo," she whispered.

Dare nodded. Dr. Angelo cupped his cheek, her mouth set in a grim line, and then left.

Jessica stood and pulled Sed to his feet. "Let's go to the hotel and get some sleep. You look zombified."

Sed nodded slightly.

Brian refused to look at either of them. He clasped hands with Dare, Jace, and Eric, but turned his back on Sed and grabbed Myrna's elbow. He directed his wife from the room. Over her shoulder, Myrna mouthed to Sed, "I'll talk to him," just before she disappeared from sight.

"Brian is pissed as hell," Eric said unnecessarily.

All four men glanced at Jessica.

Jessica's heart dropped. "Yeah, I know. It's all my fault. I should just stay away." She released Sed's hand and crossed her arms over her chest.

Why did they all hate her so much? What had she ever done to them? She could understand if Sed hated her for leaving, but why the rest of the guys? It made no sense.

Sed headed for the exit and Jessica followed him against her better judgment. Waiting near the elevator, Myrna had her arms around Brian, talking into his ear in a hushed tone. Jessica wished they'd already left. Brian seemed to be the source of everyone's animosity toward her, but now wasn't the time to confront him.

"I know," Brian said to Myrna. "I just can't deal with it on top of everything else."

Myrna leaned away and cradled Brian's face in her hands. "We'll sort it out when Trey's better."

He nodded and she kissed him tenderly.

Sed shifted Jessica behind his back as they approached. Annoyed, Jessica scratched her head behind her ear. Did he think they'd forget she was there if they couldn't see her?

"Hey," Sed said quietly.

"Hey," Brian answered.

"I know you blame me for this—"

"Wrong."

Sed hesitated. "Then what's with the cold shoulder?"

"You really have to ask?"

Jessica couldn't stay quiet any longer. She moved to stand beside Sed. "Our relationship is none of your business, Brian. So why don't you just butt out?"

"Normally, I'd agree," he said, "but he doesn't think straight when you're around, so someone has to try to bring him to his senses." He grabbed Sed by his coat lapel. "Tell me, Sed, what was the happiest moment of your life?"

Sed glanced at Jessica nervously. "Don't do this now, man."

"Just answer the question."

"You already know the answer. You were there."

"Myrna was wondering."

Myrna grimaced. She obviously didn't want to be caught up in the middle of this.

"Post-Gazette Pavilion, Pittsburgh, Pennsylvania," Sed whispered.

Jessica's heart froze in her chest. It was the happiest moment of her life too.

"I asked Jessica to marry me, on my knees in front of thousands of fans." Sed smiled, both dimples showing. "She said yes."

"But she didn't mean it," Brian said.

"I did too mean it!" Jessica sputtered.

"Uh-huh," Brian said. "Did you still mean it when you threw your engagement ring at him and left without a backward glance? What was it? Three weeks later?" He looked at Sed again. "And when was the hardest moment of your life, Sed?"

Sed swallowed. A muscle in his jaw flexed as he clenched his teeth. "That would be *now*, you fucking prick."

Brian gaped at him, and then his eyes narrowed. "Bullshit." He shoved him against the elevator doors. "You're still trying to protect her? After everything she put you through?"

"Don't start this, Brian. I'm not in the mood to take it." Sed straightened and shoved Brian back.

The elevator door opened and Sed stepped inside.

Myrna pushed her husband into the elevator and grabbed Jessica's arm. "We'll meet you at the bottom. You two have a little talk. Or slug it out. Whatever."

"How could you take her back?" Brian yelled at Sed. "Do you realize how much shit you put me through while you were trying to get over her?"

"Is it my fault your chicks like to fuck me better than they do you?"

Brian threw a punch. It connected with Sed's jaw with a loud *crack*. Sed stumbled against the back of the elevator car.

Jessica tried to wriggle free of Myrna's hold, but Myrna refused to release her.

Sed's hands balled into fists and he advanced on Brian, who took another swing at him. The elevator doors slid shut.

Jessica turned to glare at Myrna. "Are you an idiot? They'll kill each other."

"They're guys. This will get it out of their systems."

Jessica jerked away from her and pressed the elevator's down button repeatedly.

"And now that I've got you alone, I have to ask," Myrna said, "what in the hell are you thinking?"

Jessica glanced at the normally calm woman, who now crackled with electric fury.

Myrna continued, "Brian is taking this out on Sed, who doesn't deserve it, because he doesn't feel like he can confront you. I don't have his reservations."

"What? Are you going to hit me?"

Myrna's tense expression relaxed and she chuckled. "Of course not. I just want you to think about Sed instead of yourself. You can't use him like this, Jessica. His heart can't take it."

Jessica didn't like the accusatory tone of her voice. And how did Myrna know Jessica was just using him? Was she that transparent? "For your information, we have a mutual agreement."

"You mutually agreed that you could screw him over? I don't believe that."

"We mutually agreed that I could screw him. Period. He uses women for sex all the time. I don't see how this is any different."

"Then you're stupid."

Stupid?

The other elevator car opened and, fuming, Jessica stepped inside. Myrna followed her.

"He's a grown man, Myrna. He can take care of himself. You and your overly intense husband need to mind your own business."

"Maybe the two of you deserve each other," Myrna said under

her breath. "Just try not to hurt him too much. I know he pretends to be tough and all Don Juan Casanova, but he has the most delicate heart I've ever seen in a man."

Jessica laughed. "Then apparently you don't know him very well."

Myrna shook her head at her. "And apparently you don't know him at all."

Jessica scowled and crossed her arms over her chest. What was this woman talking about? How could she not know him? *Hello.* She'd almost married the man.

When the elevator door opened, they found Brian and Sed laughing with a pair of security guards. Disheveled, bloody, and bruised, the two band mates seemed better off for their elevator brawl.

Myrna hugged Brian from behind and he held her hands against his abdomen.

"Feel better?" Myrna kissed the back of his shoulder.

"Yeah. Let's go get some sleep."

"Or we can finish what we were doing when Sed interrupted."

"What about Trey?"

"You know Trey would want you satisfied. We'll catch some sleep in there somewhere," she promised.

He grinned crookedly. "Later, Sed."

"Later."

Neither of the newlyweds gave Jessica so much as a second glance when they walked away. Not that she cared. Screw them!

"Are you ready?" Sed asked.

Her eyes swiveled to his weary face. "You aren't dumping me?"

"I can't dump you if we aren't seriously dating. There's an unoccupied suite at the Bellagio. Seems a shame to waste it."

"You're okay with all this?" she asked. "With our purely sexual relationship?"

"Why wouldn't I be?"

"Myrna said—"

"What does Myrna know about me? Nothing."

Jessica nodded in agreement, but a niggling doubt teased her subconscious.

They caught a cab to the hotel. Jessica's exhaustion evaporated the moment Sed pulled her into his lap in the taxi's backseat and claimed her mouth in a hungry kiss. She tasted blood on his lips. When he pulled away to gaze at her, she dabbed at the corner of his mouth with her fingertips.

"Did Brian hurt you?"

"Not too badly," he murmured.

"Were you holding back?"

He shook his head. "That would be an insult."

She chuckled. "Guys are so weird. How can best friends come to blows and then all is forgiven the minute it's over?"

"Less talking," he murmured and kissed her again. His hand slid up her thigh beneath her skirt and her body tensed. Her hand moved down his firm belly to the crotch of his pants. She was surprised to find nothing stirred below his belt. He pulled away and moved her body to sit beside him. She looked up at him in question. She'd never known Sed to be even slightly unprepared for a sexual encounter.

"Sorry," he said wearily. "I keep thinking about Trey. And I'm really tired. Could we just sleep when we get back to the room? I'm just not in the mood. You know?"

Maybe that was the truth. Or maybe Brian had made him question their frivolous relationship. Maybe Sed had changed his mind about wanting her. That shouldn't make her chest ache, but it did.

"Of course," she said. "I'm not really in the mood either. We could both use some sleep."

He pulled his cell phone from his pocket and checked it for messages.

Jessica watched him fiddle with the device obsessively, concerned by the furrow creasing his brow. She took his hand. "The doctor said Trey has a really good chance of recovering fully."

He nodded. "I hope he hurries up about it. I can hardly breathe." He rubbed the center of his chest as if to loosen a knot that had formed there.

The most delicate heart I've ever seen in a man. Myrna's words filtered through Jessica's thoughts.

She brought Sed's wrist to her lips and planted a gentle kiss on the pulse point just under his thumb.

"Thanks for staying with me at the hospital," he murmured, looking out the taxi window.

She smiled to herself, knowing how hard it was for him to thank her for something like that. Maybe he had overcome his innate asshole-ed-ness. "No problem."

At the hotel, they wandered through the nearly empty casino, their steps punctuated by the whirring sounds of slot machines. In the elevator, Sed leaned heavily against the interior wall and closed his eyes as it rose to their floor. Jessica had to shake him awake when they reached their destination. Literally asleep on his feet. Apparently, he hadn't decided she was chopped liver and really was exhausted.

Sed used one of the plastic keycards to open the door. Jessica stepped inside and glanced around, breathless in awe. Their suite had a marble entryway and rich mocha and taupe decor. On the other side of the expansive living area, a king-sized bed overlooked the Vegas strip through a wide floor-to-ceiling window.

Sed put out the "Do Not Disturb" sign while Jessica went to the window to stare at the lights below. The fountain now rested, but in the morning she'd be able to watch the water dance from above. "What a spectacular view!"

Sed followed her, but instead of joining her beside the window, he collapsed face down on the bed. "Will you call the front desk and extend our stay another day? I'm sleeping late. Unless someone calls about Trey."

She turned to gaze at him. His face was smashed against the mattress, his eyes already closed.

"Sure."

The hotel was happy to accommodate her request, and by the time she returned to Sed's side, he was snoring quietly. Poor guy looked incredibly uncomfortable. Taking pity on him, she removed his boots and socks. He groaned in protest when she made him stand so she could take off his coat. His pants followed, and once naked, she tucked his gorgeous body into bed.

"Thanks," he murmured, almost asleep again. "Your turn to get naked, beautiful."

He kept his eyes cracked open long enough to watch her remove her clothes and jewelry. He held the covers open and she slid into bed beside him. He'd always been a cuddler, and she didn't mind when he spooned up against her back and draped an arm and leg over her body. He kissed the back of her head and sighed.

"I've missed this," he whispered.

"Me too," she admitted.

She lay there for a long while after he'd fallen asleep, his warm breath tickling her ear. As much as she tried to convince herself that all she wanted from him was amazing sex, she knew she was slipping back into old patterns. Tomorrow she'd be more careful with her heart, but tonight she'd let him hold her while he slept and pretend he still loved her. Which of course he didn't.

Chapter 15

THE RIFF OF SINNERS' "Twisted" drew Jessica from a deep sleep. Sed groaned beside her and tugged her body closer to his chest. Limbs and bedclothes tangled their bodies together. Again the riff intruded upon the room's silence.

What?

Sed's arm shot toward the nightstand. He answered his cell phone.

"Trey?" he said, his voice raspy with sleep.

Jessica kicked herself free of the sheets and sat up beside him, instantly wide awake.

"We're leaving now," Sed said into the phone and ended the call.

"Is he okay?"

"He's not quite awake yet, but he's starting to stir. Get dressed."

Jessica slipped into her wrinkly clothes from the night before. Oh yay, a day without panties. Sed had a similar problem.

"I don't have a shirt." But he looked damned fine in those leather pants without one.

"We could stop by the tour bus and change clothes," Jessica said.

"No time." He shrugged into his black leather duster and reached for his boots.

At least he gave her a moment to use the bathroom before rushing her out of the room and into the nearest cab outside the hotel. She was surprised by how bright it was outside.

"What time is it?" she asked Sed, thinking there must be a law against starting the day with no caffeine.

He glanced at the screen on his cell phone. "Almost noon."

"Noon? Jeez, I slept like a rock."

He smiled at her. "Me too. I can't remember the last time I slept that good. Months? Two years, maybe?" He ran a hand over his shorn hair and found the roof of the cab incredibly interesting. "You hungry? We missed breakfast."

"I'm okay. Seeing Trey is more important."

Sed grinned and lifted her hand to his lips. "Brian was all excited when he called. Something about Trey flinching."

In the ICU, they found Brian and Myrna at Trey's bedside. Dare slept in a chair at the end of the bed. Jessica doubted he'd left his brother's presence since the night before. Rumpled clothes, tangled hair, and a growth of beard shadow on his strong jaw, Dare looked about as scruffy as Jessica felt.

Myrna chuckled at something Brian said. She patted Trey's hand. "If you don't wake up soon, sugar, Brian's going to tell me all your dirty little secrets."

The black staples that ran along the left side of Trey's scalp in a semi-circle stood in stark contrast to his unnaturally pale skin. Jessica noticed that only a single wide strip of his hair had been shaved along the left side of his head. How had he managed to get away with not having his entire head shaved? Oh wait. This was Trey. That explained it.

Jessica glanced at Trey's monitor. As far as she could tell, his ECG, heart rate, and breathing rate looked normal. The tube up his nose did not.

"I don't think even Brian knows all of Trey's dirty little secrets," Sed said. "How's he doing? Brian said he was waking up."

Brian scratched the back of his neck. "I got a little over-excited."

Myrna smiled a greeting at Sed. "When Brian told me how Trey lost his virginity, he flinched. That's the only response we've gotten."

Sed cringed. "No wonder he flinched. Sheesh, Brian, give the guy a break. He just had brain surgery."

Jessica's curiosity stirred. "How did Trey lose his virginity?"

"Let's just say he's been with an older woman," Sed said.

"Much older," Brian added.

"There's nothing wrong with older women," Myrna said defensively. She patted Trey's hand again. "Besides, it's sorta sweet that his grandmother's best friend helped him out."

Brian and Sed shuddered in unison.

"I'm sorry I asked," Jessica murmured.

Sed glanced at Dare, who would need a chiropractor after sleeping in a chair in such a position. "Is Dare dead or what?"

"He keeps passing out from exhaustion, but he won't leave," Myrna said. "His band couldn't get him to leave. His parents couldn't get him to leave. Even the doctor and nurses couldn't talk any sense into him. The only one who will get him out of that chair is Trey."

"Trey, you selfish prick," Sed called to him. "Wake up. Look what you're doing to your brother. He's a train wreck."

Trey's eyebrow twitched.

"See, I told you he's trying to wake up," Brian said. "Aren't you, buddy? How about we tell everyone about New Year's Eve three years ago? I still don't think the police report had all the details right."

Dare sat up in the chair, instantly alert. "Is he awake?"

"No. He just twitched a little," Myrna said.

Dare darted across the room and grabbed Trey's shoulders firmly. "Terrance, can you hear me in there? Wake up! Terrance!"

"Fuckin' quit calling me Terrance," Trey mumbled, his voice slurred but coherent. "You know how much I hate that name."

"Thank God," Dare whispered. His head dropped against Trey's shoulder, his body trembling uncontrollably.

"Are you crying? Jesus Christ, Dare. Who replaced my big brother with this pussy?" Trey placed a hand on the back of Dare's head and offered him a weak, yet comforting, pat.

"How do you feel?" Brian asked.

Myrna pushed the call button to alert the nurses. Her smile was infectious. Even though Jessica felt like an outsider, she smiled too. Sed just stood there, looking dumbstruck.

"I am feeling no pain." Trey grinned his irresistible smile. "Good drugs."

A physician's assistant entered the room. "Is our guitar hero finally awake?"

Dare lifted his head, wiped his eyes with the heels of his hands and looked down at his baby brother with a most serious expression. "If you ever scare me like that again, I will fuck you up beyond recognition."

Trey grinned at him. "I will try to keep the brain injuries to a minimum, boss."

Dare planted a big wet kiss on Trey's forehead. "I'd better call Mom and Dad. They went downstairs for some food."

The physician's assistant asked Trey a series of questions and wrote his responses on a paper affixed to a clipboard. His full name. What day it was. Who the president was. The last thing he remembered. The PA smiled and blushed each time he answered. Besides thinking it was a day earlier, Trey didn't seem confused at all. Jessica took that as a good sign.

"My turn to ask you a question," Trey said to the attractive brunette.

She paused in mid-scribe. "What?"

"When will you give me my sponge bath?"

She giggled and slapped his shoulder. "Mr. Mills." She glanced around the room with a blush staining her cheeks. "That's an LPN's job."

"Call me Trey. And I wasn't assuming it was part of your job."

She shook her head at him. "Is he always like this?" she asked Brian.

It would have taken a pressure washer to remove the grin from Brian's face. "Yep."

The PA tugged the covers off Trey's feet. "Can you wiggle your toes?"

Trey scowled as he concentrated on moving his toes. His movement was sluggish at best.

"That's okay," the PA told him. "Try to make a fist."

His fingers curled inward slowly, but his hand never completely closed. Everyone in the room held their breath.

"I can't," he said breathlessly, allowing his fingers to relax again.

"You just woke up. I'm sure you'll get full mobility back with time. Keep working at it. You just have to retrain your brain to move your fingers," the PA said.

"Retrain my fingers?" His incredulous gaze moved to Brian. His breath hitched. "What?"

"I'm sure your fingers will be fine," Brian said. "It's okay."

"How is this okay?" Trey flexed his fingers slightly. "I can't play guitar like this."

The PA took his hand and squeezed it. "Don't panic, Trey. Give yourself time to recover. You just woke up."

He pulled his hand away from her and rolled onto his side, presenting his back to everyone. "I don't want to see anyone right now."

"Trey." Brian touched his friend's shoulder.

"Go away," he said. "I fucking mean it!"

"Why don't you all give him some time to himself?" the PA said, herding the group toward the door.

"I really don't think we should leave him alone right now," Jessica said. Her heart was breaking for him. What must he be feeling? And Brian? And Sed? She was just an unwanted band accessory. They had a huge stake in him getting better. Watching a friend struggle was bad enough, but if this physical problem turned out to be something permanent, it could affect their entire livelihood as musicians.

The PA had somehow corralled them into the hall.

Jessica glanced up at Sed, who hadn't said a word since Trey opened his eyes. He looked like a mule had kicked him in the gut. "Are you okay?"

He shook his head slightly.

Dare lowered his phone and grabbed Sed's arm as they were ushered past him. "You're not smiling. Why have we stopped smiling?"

Sed shook his head again.

"Trey's having some mobility problems," Jessica informed Dare. "Nothing serious."

What would happen to Sinners if Trey couldn't play guitar? They wouldn't abandon him, would they? As she watched the emotions play across Sed's face, she had to admit she wasn't sure.

Chapter 16

SED STARED OUT A window in the waiting room, not really seeing the cars in the parking lot far below. His mind was full, his heart empty. Jessica placed a hand in the center of his back and leaned her head against his upper arm.

He glanced down at her, unable to express his gratitude. She'd sat with him for hours and had even made a trip to the gift shop to buy him a hospital logo T-shirt and a cup of coffee. He wasn't sure why she hadn't left him there on his own to stew. Brian, Myrna, Trey's parents, and even Dare had eventually left when Trey continued to refuse any company. But Sed couldn't desert his duty. He'd just wait Trey out. How long could it take?

"Go talk to him," Jessica said.

"He doesn't want to see anyone."

"Since when do you do what people want?"

"Since never."

"Exactly." She squeezed his arm. "Go talk to him. It will make you feel better."

"I don't know what to say to him."

"You'll think of something."

She was right. As usual. He turned away from the windows, kissed her brow, and then headed down the hall toward Trey's room. Sed entered the open door and peeked around the corner. Trey's bed was fixed in an upright position. The tube that had been up his nose was now gone. Progress. Trey repeatedly tried to pick up a spoon from the tray in front of him, his tongue worrying his lip. Despite his extreme concentration, he ultimately failed to grasp the utensil.

Sed took several steps back and knocked on the wall. "Are you decent, man? I'm coming in." When Sed entered the room again, Trey was staring fixedly at the far wall, his hands buried beneath the covers.

"I *said* I want to be left alone."

"You know I never do what people tell me to do." With a loud screeching sound, Sed dragged a chair across the tile floor to the side of the bed and sat.

"Sed, I honestly don't—"

"Those staples in your head look bad ass. You should keep them permanently."

Trey ran his hand over the shaved side of his head, his slightly curved index finger brushing over the arc of black staples. "I don't know. I don't think this haircut is me."

Sed chuckled. "Looks more like Eric's style." Sed dropped his gaze to meet Trey's eyes. "I've been thinking."

"Always a bad thing."

Trey lowered his arm to rest on the bed beside him. Sed forced himself not to fixate on Trey's fingers, which he continually bent and straightened in sequence. He was trying his best, God love him, but Sed didn't see any thirty-second notes in his immediate future. And the band was on tour. They needed him. Now. Not in a month. Not in six months. Now.

Trey tucked his hand under the covers again and Sed forced his attention to his scowling face.

"I want you to concentrate on getting better. Don't worry about the band," Sed said. "We'll wait for you to recover. Cancel tour dates. Put the new album on hold. Whatever is necessary. I haven't talked to the guys, but I know they feel the same way."

"Jesus, Sed, I've been awake three hours and you're already deciding if you're going to kick me out of the band?"

"That's not what I meant. I just…" God, he was bad at this serious discussion bullshit. "I don't want you to feel any pressure. Well, yes, some pressure. You'd better work your ass off to get better because we need you, but otherwise, don't worry. We'll wait."

"You really suck at pep talks."

"Yeah, I know. Fuck." Sed took a deep breath. "Did I make you feel worse? I'm sorry, man."

Trey shook his head slightly. "Nah. How long do you think they'll keep me in this place?"

"Are you bored?"

"Fuck yeah, I'm bored. And I'm dying for a cherry sucker."

Sed grinned. Something he could do to help. Even if it was minor. "One cherry sucker coming up. Then you have to get some rest, because tomorrow everyone is going to be all over you."

He smiled slightly. "You're probably right."

"You know I am." Sed stood to leave.

"Sed?"

"Yeah, buddy?"

"What am I going to do if I don't get better?" Trey asked in a small voice.

Sed paused, his heart rising to his throat. "Don't talk like that, man. You *are* going to get better."

"Guitar. The band. That's all I have. All I know. I don't know how to do anything else."

"You don't have to know how to do anything else. We aren't going anywhere, okay?"

Trey lowered his gaze and nodded. "Is Brian still here?"

"No, he left a while ago. Do you want me to call him?"

Trey shook his head. "No. He has Myrna now."

Sed didn't know how to deal with someone this depressed. It just wasn't in his skill set. "I'm going to go get you that sucker now." Maybe that would help.

He wasn't sure if Trey even heard him. His eyes had drifted out of focus.

Sed headed for the elevator in search of some place that would sell him a cherry sucker. The gift shop was closed. The cafeteria didn't sell candy. He found a vending machine that sold Life Savers and used all his change to buy as many rolls as possible. On his way back to Trey's floor, he called Eric. "Hey, are you coming in to the hospital soon?"

"I thought Trey didn't want to see anyone."

"Do we care? He's majorly bummed. Bring some cherry suckers with you. He's going through withdrawal."

"Will do. How's he doing? I talked to him, but it's hard to tell on the phone."

"Better, I think. He looks good. The staples in his head look hard-core. The fans will love that. You know about his hands, don't you?"

"Yeah, Brian told me. I'll be there in a few with his lollipops. Jace is fuckin' missing again. I swear I'm going to kick his ass when I see him. Doesn't he know I need a ride?"

"You *could* call a cab."

"I guess. Dave wants to come visit too. Do you think Trey would be okay with that?"

"I don't know. He needs someone to cheer him up." Their soundboard operator wasn't known for his amazing sense of humor, but he was a good guy.

"I'm on it. Later."

Sed ended the call and headed to Trey's room with his meager offering of Life Savers. Five flavors? There was no guarantee any of them were cherry.

Sed walked in without knocking. "I couldn't find any cherry suckers, but…"

Trey had his pretty brunette physician's assistant in his arms, kissing her as if there was no tomorrow.

"Whoa! Pardon me." Sed spun on his heel to leave, but the PA brushed passed him and ran from the room, fleeing for her life apparently. Sed glanced over his shoulder at Trey, who looked rather pleased with himself.

"Even crippled, I still got it." He smoothed his eyebrow with the side of his finger.

Sed didn't like his use of the word crippled, but didn't know what to say. "Uh. I hope these Life Savers will tide you over until Eric gets here with your suckers."

"Eric's coming?"

"Yeah. He's bringing Dave."

"Cool. Why don't you call Jake and have him round up some groupies for me?"

Sed's brow crinkled with confusion. "Huh?"

Trey unwrapped a roll of Life Savers, flicking candies off one at a time with his thumb until he came to a red one. He popped the red one in his mouth. It took some concentration for him to use his hands, but he was already doing better than he had been even a half hour ago. What had changed? Sed decided he was pissed instead of feeling sorry for himself.

"I told you I was bored," Trey said. "Some group sex should take care of that."

"Where is this coming from?"

"Well, you've got Jessica back now and Brian is fuckin' *married*, so that leaves more pussy for me and Eric, right?"

"Trey—"

"Where is Jessica, anyway? Gonna take her out and play along the Vegas strip like you did last night? Did she give you some? I bet she did. I'd take that over a subdural hema-fuckin-toma any day."

Trey started flinging all of his non-cherry Life Savers across the room. Some of them hit the wall and shattered, spreading candy confetti across the floor.

"Can I come in?" Jessica asked from the doorway.

"Speaking of your good piece of ass. I guess she got lonely. Probably wants to give you some right now."

Sed didn't know how to react. This wasn't like Trey at all. When he was a teenager, yeah, Trey had been like this. Chip on his shoulder. The world out to get him. But he'd been content for the past decade.

"Come on in, sweetheart," Sed called to Jessica. "Help me keep Trey company."

"Are you sure?" Jessica asked, stepping through the doorway but not venturing any deeper into the room.

He was more than sure. Maybe she could calm Trey down where he had so utterly failed.

"By all means," Trey said, "join the party. I'm currently waiting for a surprise enema as a punishment for sucking contraband Life Savers. Pull up a chair. Should be fun to watch my continued misery."

"Trey, what the fuck is wrong with you?" Sed asked.

"I don't know, Sed. Maybe I have brain damage or something." He poked himself in the head much harder than necessary.

Sed winced. Where was Brian? Brian would know how to handle him.

Jessica came further into the room and perched on the edge of Trey's bed. "What's the matter, sweetie?" She traced his eyebrow with her thumb, leaning close so only inches separated their noses. Jade green eyes stared into emerald green. Had it been any other guy on the planet, Sed might have been jealous, but this was Trey. He had no interest in another guy's woman. He could get what he wanted from an infinite variety of *available* ass.

"Don't baby me," Trey grumbled at Jessica.

"I'm not babying you. I'm concerned about you. You don't really think you're going to be stuck in the hospital forever, do you?"

He crossed his arms over his chest, bunching his hospital gown across his shoulders. "Maybe."

"Youse wants me and Sed ta bust ya outta dis joint?"

Trey grinned, watching her from the corner of his eye. "Maybe."

"Sed," Jessica whispered.

"What?"

"Start tying bed sheets together." She stood and crossed the room to press on the window with both hands. "I'll work on getting this open."

"We're on the fifteenth floor," he reminded her.

"So it will take a lot of sheets. Raid the supply closet." She glanced at Trey. "You aren't afraid of heights, are you?"

Trey grinned and shook his head at her.

"Good." She looked down at the ground far below. "I'm not sure we can get enough sheets. That's a loooooong way down. Maybe we should make a parachute instead. How do you feel about base jumping?"

"Uh, no." Trey chuckled, his scowl completely gone. "I think I prefer being stuck in this hellhole over attempting your brilliant escape plans."

"If you want to survive," Sed murmured in all seriousness.

Trey and Jessica exchanged glances and burst out laughing.

"Oh jeez," Trey said, wiping tears of mirth from the corners of both eyes. "He thought you were serious."

Sed chewed his lip, feeling like an ass. He had been taking it all too seriously. No wonder Trey had been so uptight. "Nah, I was just playing along with her."

"Suuuuure," Trey said, laughing even harder.

Jessica's eyes met Sed's. She smiled and winked at him. And just like that all the tension left the room. This woman, *his* woman, was amazing.

Jessica seemed to enjoy caring for Trey. Fluffing his pillow. Adjusting his bed to a more reclined position. Rubbing his wrists, which he claimed were cramping up on him. Sed was convinced Trey was making stuff up just to get her attention. Sed considered making up a few aches of his own. She was practically ignoring him and he didn't like it. At all.

A while later, Eric entered the room with a garbage bag. "It's about time you woke up, lazy ass," he said to Trey. "You think you're on vacation or something?" He crossed the room in several long-legged strides and upended the sack over Trey's lap, burying him in an avalanche of cherry suckers. "I hope they don't keep you in here longer than a day. I can't keep up with this addiction of yours."

Dave, their soundboard operator, entered with a laptop and set it on Trey's lap. "Dude, I'm tired of answering your fuckin' fan mail. Do it yourself."

"What?" Trey scrolled down a screen of messages, his fingers curled awkwardly over the touch pad.

"A thousand get-well-soon messages and counting," Dave told him. "Your fans have always been loyal."

"Not to mention crazy as hell," Eric said. "There's a whole crowd of them camped outside the hospital. Getting through security was insane."

"Awesome. I could use a little fan lovin' right now."

"Oh, there's plenty of love in there," Dave said. "Trust me."

"Any interesting pictures?"

"Slutty, you mean?" Eric said, fingering the cleft in the center of his chin.

Trey grinned his orneriest. "Obviously."

Dave, the most normal-looking roadie on the planet, sat in the chair beside the bed. "I put those in your save folder."

"I think I love you, Dave," Trey said, poking keys with one finger.

"You ready to go eat?" Sed asked Jessica. "Eric and Dave will keep an eye on Trey. And you must be starving. I know I am."

She nodded. He moved his arm to circle her shoulders and directed her toward the door. "See you later, Trey. We'll stop by again this evening."

"Later," Trey said absently, pointing at something on the computer screen and laughing with Eric. "She's right. That does make me feel better. But I don't think that bikini is legal. Not even on a nude beach."

"Dude, dude, email her back. Wait. Let me get a picture of your head staples." Eric snapped a picture of the side of Trey's head with his camera phone. "Fuckin' brutal. You are gonna get so much sympathy pussy."

Sed grinned. Yeah, Eric's antics and some fan lovin' were exactly what Trey needed. Sed was glad he'd called him.

"So, where would you like to eat?" Sed asked Jessica as they walked toward the elevator at the end of the hall.

She shrugged and snuggled closer to his side. Her hand slid discretely over his crotch on its journey to clutch the waistband of his pants. "Someplace dark. With a booth."

Hell, yeah. He was all about dark booths.

Chapter 17

JESSICA DUNKED A JUMBO shrimp in cocktail sauce and then lifted it to Sed's open mouth. He bit into it and she dropped the tail on a small plate.

"How's that?" she murmured.

He chewed and swallowed before he said, "Spicy. What is that? Horseradish?"

She kissed him, touching her tongue to his. She drew away and stared into his sky blue eyes. "I think you're right. Horseradish."

They were way underdressed for this restaurant at the Venetian hotel, but the hostess had recognized Sed and, at his request, seated them in a semi-circular booth in the far corner. As it was mid-afternoon, the place was mostly deserted and the olive-green leather backs of the booths were high to offer plenty of privacy. Both facts would serve Jessica's purposes perfectly. She hoped to take Sed's mind off things for a while.

Jessica slid her left hand beneath the white table cloth and then the cloth napkin on Sed's lap. He stiffened when her fingers brushed against his crotch. His cock stirred beneath her fingertips.

"Jess…"

She reached for another shrimp, bit off the tip and offered the second half to him. He separated the succulent meat from the ined-ible tail with his teeth. Her hand slid over the smooth leather cover-ing his thigh.

He squirmed. "Do you want to go back to the room?"

She unbuttoned his pants and slowly released his zipper. "Not at all. Do you?"

She carefully tugged his cock from his open fly, making sure to keep the large cloth napkin in place.

Sed sucked a breath between his teeth. "Kinda," he said, two octaves higher than his usual baritone pitch.

She rubbed her thumb over the head of his cock, loving how the shaft responded by twitching and thickening in her hand.

"You sure? We can have a little fun right here."

"It drives me crazy when you're naughty," he growled in her ear.

Jessica was all about driving him crazy.

Their waitress appeared, smiling brightly. "How's the shrimp?"

Sed jumped as if she'd shot him. "Good. Really good. Excellent. Yeah, excellent. I like it. It's delicious."

The waitress grinned at his over-enthusiasm and lifted a bottle of house wine in their direction. "Would you like more wine?"

Jessica stroked the silky skin of Sed's cock with her fingertips and lifted her glass with her free hand. "I'd like some more."

"Yes, more please," Sed murmured.

Their waitress refilled their glasses. "Your entrees should be ready soon."

Jessica took a sip of her wine and squeezed Sed's cock beneath the table.

"Take your time," Sed squeaked at the waitress. "We aren't in any hurry."

The young woman smiled and left them to their own devices.

Sed reached for his wine, almost knocking it over in his haste to grab it. He chugged it in three swallows.

Jessica glanced around to make sure no one was watching and then knocked the napkin off Sed's lap.

"Whoops. Let me get that for you."

She ducked under the table, hiding beneath the white table cloth. She picked up the napkin with her right hand and, at the same time, directed Sed's thick cock into her mouth with her left. She slurped him deep into the back of her throat. The china rattled as Sed grabbed the edge of the table. She pulled back, sucking hard, and bumped her head on the underside of the table. Her tongue danced over the head of his cock, stroking and teasing until Sed groaned in torment. She drew him into her throat, knowing he liked hard suction up and down his length, and she gave it to him. Repeatedly. The china rattled above her again. His feet slid across the floor as his excitement intensified and his body motions became involuntary. She sucked him faster, harder, the head of his cock bumping against the back of her throat. His hand burrowed into her hair and he held her down on his shaft. He gasped brokenly as he let go. His fluids pulsed into the back of her throat. She swallowed, sucked more of his salty offering into her mouth, and swallowed again. When she released his cock from her mouth, she blew a cool breath over his wet flesh and then covered his crotch with his napkin again. Jessica reappeared above the table and looked up at him for his reaction.

Sed had gone entirely still. She didn't think he was even breathing. Jessica nonchalantly tucked her hair behind her ears with both hands and selected another shrimp. Before Sed managed to draw a deep breath, she'd already eaten two of the tender crustaceans.

Sed released his breath in a huff. "I can't believe you did that."

She winked at him. "Yes, you can."

He tugged her closer to him in the booth, his arm around her shoulders. He nibbled on her ear. Goose bumps rose on her neck.

"You fuckin' rock, baby," he murmured.

"You rock at fuckin', baby."

He chuckled and his hand slid up her thigh beneath her skirt. She stiffened.

"Your nipples are hard," he murmured in her ear. And he would know. His gaze was trained down at her chest. "Does it excite you to be naughty in public?"

Hell yeah, it did, but she said, "The air conditioning is a little chilly."

"I could warm you up. Suck on them," he said, his eyes still trained on her beaded nipples. His hand slid further under her skirt. "And lick you." His fingers brushed over her mound. "Here." Well, that would definitely warm her up, but she doubted it would turn down her high beams.

Her flesh swelled against his fingertips, craving more than a cursory caress. His breathless words turned her on as much as his touch did. "Later," she promised. "It's still your turn."

Her hand snuck beneath his napkin again. When she touched his bare skin, his breath caught, his body convulsed. She began to stroke him, rubbing his softening cock from base to tip with a slow, gentle touch, wanting him hard again so she could give him more pleasure. Sed's fingers teased the curls between her legs, seeking bare skin. Before he could find any, their waitress appeared carrying their meal and a little stand, which she popped open to hold the tray while she served them. Sed pulled his hand from beneath Jessica's skirt and clung to the edge of the table, blushing with guilt. Jessica continued to stroke him beneath his napkin, careful to move only her wrist so the waitress didn't figure out what she was doing beneath the table. Something about the woman being there obviously excited Sed. His cock swelled rapidly in Jessica's hand.

The clueless waitress set Jessica's plate of porcini mushroom tortelloni before her. Sed held his hands out while the young woman served his plate of lasagna.

"Looks delicious," he said breathlessly.

The waitress offered him a timid smile. "Do you need anything else?"

"I'm good." Sed glanced at Jessica.

She smiled and nodded, still stroking his cock with the same slow, gentle touch.

"Yell if you need anything."

"Will do."

Jessica picked up her fork and took a bite of pasta. The exotic, earthy flavors bathed her taste buds and her eyes drifted closed in bliss. "Oh God, this is delicious." She took another bite and another.

Sed hadn't moved since their waitress had left. Jessica glanced at him and found him lost in ecstasy, but it had nothing to do with the magnificent-smelling yet untouched lasagna on his plate. His eyes were closed, lips parted, breath hitching in time with her continued slow strokes beneath the table. She shifted her hand to massage the head of his cock, rubbing and gently twisting his most sensitive flesh. Sed shuddered and emitted a low growl of torment. He used to be a lot harder to seduce. He wasn't even trying to resist her attention. He'd submitted to her power, given her complete control, and she had to admit, she liked having him at her mercy.

"Did you change your mind about the lasagna?" she asked, rubbing the slick bead of pre-cum over the skin of his cockhead with her thumb. She speared a mushroom with her fork and held it in his direction. "Want some of mine, instead? It's magnificent."

"That feels so good," he whispered breathlessly.

She leaned close to whisper in his ear. "Do you wanna come again? I'll take you there. Would you like that? To spurt your cum in my hand and watch me lick it off in front of everyone." Just talking about it had her juices dripping from her swollen, achy, hopelessly empty pussy.

He shook his head slightly. "Inside you. I wanna come inside you this time."

That was her preference too, but there was no way they could do that *here* discreetly. She should let him calm down for now and they could pick this up somewhere more private after they finished eating.

But playing with him was so much fun. She stroked him faster and kept a sharp look out for any spectators. If anyone saw the look on his face, there'd be no question of what was going on under the table. She could only imagine his expression when he'd let go in her mouth just ten minutes ago. Sed tugged her closer, plastering her body against the length of his side. His open mouth moved desperately against her throat as he tried to stifle his excited gasps against her sensitive flesh.

Those low rumbling sounds he made… Dear God, she was hot for him now. Maybe she could slip onto his lap, bury his cock deep inside her body, and no one would notice her riding him like a bucking bronco at the dinner table.

"Oh God, if you keep that up, I'm gonna come again." He grabbed her hand to hold it still. "You have to stop. This isn't fair to you." Sed sat there for a long moment collecting his breath, his rough beard stubble scratching her shoulder, his soft lips sucking gentle kisses in one tender spot on her throat as he forced himself to calm down.

"Okay," he whispered. "Okay. I think I can wait a while now."

"I don't think I can," she said and rubbed his softening cock from base to tip.

He sucked a breath through his teeth. "Please, don't. I won't be able to control myself if you get me all worked up again."

That had been controlled? What would he do if he was out of control? "Promise?"

He pulled her hand from his cock, lifted it above the table, and kissed her knuckles tenderly. "I want to do highly illegal things to you, right here, right now," he said in a sexy growl. Her nipples tingled in response. "Don't tempt me beyond reason, woman."

She could do nothing but stare at him, her heart beating erratically in her chest.

He released her hand and refastened his pants before shifting several inches away from her. He tackled his lasagna with his usual beastly flair. "You better not sit there and pick at your food for an hour," he said, taking another large bite. "We've got places to go, things to see…" He leaned close to whisper in her ear. "Your body to tease."

Jessica had never been hungrier in her life. But it wasn't food she craved. She pushed her plate aside and nudged Sed out of the booth.

While Jessica was more than ready to head for the nearest bed and get right down to business, Sed seemed to think she needed additional public foreplay. He led her to the entrance to the gondola ride that ran through the Venetian Hotel's shopping center.

He drew her wrist to his lips and placed a tender kiss over her pulse point. "It will be romantic."

Who could say no to a big, tough guy trying to be romantic? Not her.

Nestled along his side in the flat-bottomed boat, she wasn't sure which turned her on more, his deep rich voice as he sang in feigned Italian with their gondolier, or the things he was doing to her clit beneath the coat he'd spread over her lap. There was one thing she *was* sure about. Sed knew how to work her into an insatiable frenzy no matter where they were. She just wanted to get off the boat and get on the man.

Apparently, she wasn't the only one who'd been seduced by his serenade. The instant they stepped through the ride's exit, a gaggle of psycho fan chicks descended upon him. "Oh Sed *this*," and "oh Sed *that*." Jessica found herself nudged to the outskirts of the crowd while twittering females demanded autographs and photos. They had their hands all over him. *All* over him. He didn't try to stop them.

Fuming, Jessica followed the crowd—what choice did she have?—taking note of every foreign finger that touched him. Sed talked and laughed with the women as he eased his way toward the nearest exit, signing autographs without missing a step, pausing in mid-stride with a smile for a picture before continuing onward, as if this was as natural to him as breathing. His fangirls swarmed around him like an army of ants who'd discovered someone's discarded candy. Only he wasn't discarded candy. He was *Jessica's* candy and she wasn't ready to discard him. Yet.

By the time they reached the nearest taxi at the curb, and Sed managed to weasel himself into the backseat beside Jessica without the accompaniment of fans, she was downright pissed.

"Where to?" the cab driver asked.

"We should probably go back to the tour bus and get a change of clothes," he said to Jessica. "Take a shower."

"Whatever."

Sed's brow furrowed with confusion. "Are you pissed off about something?"

"Oh no. I like to be completely ignored while you're fondled by dozens of women."

He had the audacity to grin at her. With both dimples showing. The jerk!

"Where to?" the cab driver repeated.

"Mandalay Bay. There are a couple of black and gray tour buses parked behind the events center. Drop us off there."

Jessica crossed her arms over her chest. Maybe she didn't *want* to go back to the tour bus. Did he ever consider that?

"I wasn't ignoring you, baby," Sed said. "I could never ignore you."

"Well, you sure as hell weren't ignoring all those touchy-feely women."

He chuckled. "Dear God, Jess, you're actually jealous."

"Am not!"

He grabbed her and had her sprawled beneath him in the backseat within seconds. He kissed her, feasting on her mouth and stealing her senses. When he squeezed her breast, she slugged him in the shoulder. He pulled away to gaze down at her.

She glared up at him. "Do you always have to be such a beast?"

One dimple appeared as he grinned at her crookedly. "When you're pissed *and* jealous? Yes, I have to be a beast."

"Get off me."

"You wanna be on top?" He shifted her again and she found herself straddling his lap. His hands slipped beneath her skirt to stroke the bare skin of her ass. "Fine by me."

"That's not what I meant."

His mouth descended on the side of her neck. Her fingers pressed into his scalp, meaning to push him away, but he suckled that perfect spot just beneath her jaw, so she drew him closer instead. God, why couldn't her stupid body stop responding to him? It was downright annoying at times. She should be very upset with him for being so irresistible to his stupid fangirls.

The sudden lurch of her body brought her back to her senses. Well, sorta.

Sed stopped sucking and glanced out the cab window. "We're here."

Sed paid the cab driver and hauled his large frame from the backseat, dragging Jessica along with him. She wrapped her arms around his neck and let him carry her to the bus. She knew she was supposed to be mad at him about something, but kissing him as he struggled to climb the bus stairs without dropping her was much more enjoyable. She wanted this. Wanted him.

He set her on her feet near the curtained bunks and tugged his lips away from hers. Drunk with desire, she watched him remove his clothes. Her gaze drifted over his naked flesh. Shoulders broad. Hips narrow. Cock hard. Muscles bulging in all the right places. A shiver of delight snaked up her spine. When her eyes finally settled on his face, he grinned at her. "Like what you see?"

"No." She choked on her own lie.

Forcing her attention from his distracting body, her gaze landed on the dining table and the laptop sitting there beneath the stack of work she was supposed to be doing for Myrna. Jessica hadn't thought about it *once* since she'd succumbed to Sed's lovemaking the night before. She almost felt guilty. Almost. "Now that we're here, I should get some work done." She looked at him for his reaction.

Sed shrugged and then turned to enter the bathroom. Alone.

What?

She didn't really want to work right now. She wanted him to be as distracted by her as he was by him. Jessica followed him, completely under his spell.

Sed stood at the sink, lathering his face with shaving cream. She watched the play of muscles beneath the skin of his back and shoulders as he moved. Did the man have any idea how sexy he was? Yeah, probably. As he drew his razor up under his chin, Jessica moved to stand behind him. She ran a single finger down his spine. His body tensed, but he gave no other indication that he knew she was there.

She pulled off her top and tossed it into the hallway, followed by her skirt. Naked, she moved closer, pressing her breasts against his back, and wrapped her hands around his body. She wasted no time getting right down to business. She took his cock in both hands and stroked him, rubbing her thumbs over the sensitive head until he was rock hard. He had paused in his shaving routine while she'd been stroking him, but when she moved away and stepped into the shower, he continued drawing the razor over his skin. He rinsed his razor in the sink, tapped off the residue, and moved to the next section.

Why was he ignoring her now? Damn him for getting her all worked up and then playing it so cool. She could play it cool, too. She turned on the shower and wet her hair. By the time she'd finished washing it, she expected him to have joined her. With her arms suspended over her head, he had to be checking out her exposed body—the way her breasts moved and the water followed her contours. So why was she still showering alone? She glanced outside the shower door and found him clean-shaven, leaning against the sink with his arms crossed over his broad chest. He was watching her. His massive cock stood at full attention in front of him, hard as granite, yet ignored. At least by him.

"Aren't you going to join me?" she asked.

"Do you want me to?"

"Don't you think you've kept me waiting long enough?"

He stepped into the shower with her. "I'm not sure. You haven't jumped me yet."

"Is that what you're waiting for?"

"Maybe."

She moved against him, pressing her breasts into his chest, running her hands over his firm ass. "Maybe I was waiting for the same thing."

"Seems we've reached a stalemate."

"There's nothing stale about our mating."

Sed chuckled and pressed her up against the wall. He slid her back up the slick surface until she was at hip level. His cock brushed against her thigh.

He shifted his hips, seeking entrance into her body. God, she couldn't stand it. She'd waited far too long as it was. She reached between her thighs and directed him home. He slipped inside, possessing her completely with his glorious thickness. He let her slide down the wall a couple of inches to drive his huge cock unbearably deep. Yes. Finally. She gasped in delight and rocked her hips slightly to take him deeper still. *Oh Sed. Make that ache go away.*

His hands shifted to her hips to hold her steady as he started to withdraw slowly from her body. He rubbed his open mouth against her throat and murmured three syllables against her throat that she couldn't make out.

"What?"

He thrust up into her. Withdrew again.

"Nothing," he whispered.

Sed turned off the water and pulled out of her body. She groaned in protest.

He wrapped her in a towel and lifted her into his arms.

"What are you doing?" she asked.

"Nothing but missionary position," he said. "I'm a man of my word."

She laughed.

"And I shaved for you."

She freed her hand from the towel to stroke his smooth cheek. "I appreciate that."

"You're really going to appreciate it in a minute." He wriggled his tongue at her and carried her to the bedroom.

Sed opened the door and stopped short, almost dropping her. They weren't alone on the tour bus. From beside the bed, Jace glanced over his shoulder at them, his tight sculpted bod and perfect little ass in plain view. When he turned, Jessica tried to ignore his massive cock, but, well... good Lord, he put Sed to shame. Embarrassed, Jessica shifted her gaze to the woman kneeling in the center of the bed only to be even more embarrassed. Aggie was bound by her wrists to the ceiling—blindfolded and delirious with pleasure.

———

"Sorry," Sed mouthed to Jace, who displayed a confidence Sed had never recognized in him before. It must've had something to do with bringing his dominatrix to the pinnacle of pleasure and keeping her there. The woman was writhing in ecstasy, her curvaceous body begging for release. Jace slipped something into Aggie's mouth and waved Sed away impatiently. Sed closed the door quietly.

So the bedroom was out, but he wasn't anywhere close to being done with Jessica.

Her jealousy over his groupies, who he had never given a rat's ass about, had him all worked up. Maybe Jessica didn't love him. Yet. But he affected more than her body. He knew he did. And he wasn't about to alleviate his pressure on her now. Not when she was this close to giving in to her feelings. Even if he did have to garble the expression of his love by saying it against her throat.

He carried her to his bunk. Twin-sized and enclosed on all sides but the slot that faced the corridor, it wasn't conducive to their typical acrobatic love making sessions, but it could accommodate missionary position. And if he laid her body at an angle and knelt on the floor beside the bed…

He slid her beautiful body into the bunk, her head lodged near the far corner, and spread her legs to gain access to her intoxicating scent. Her taste. He kissed her there at the apex of her thighs, his lips suckling, tongue dancing over slick flesh, drawing her sweet fluids into his mouth.

She whimpered in torment, her back arching. His mouth moved to her clit. He drew the hard nub between his lips, flicking it with his tongue until she cried out.

"Don't tease me anymore, Sed," she pleaded, pulling on his ears as he moved to drive his tongue into her pussy. "Oh."

He swirled his tongue inside her, pressed deep, withdrew, and returned his attention to her clit.

"Ungh, you're driving me insane," she panted.

He sucked her clit until her body tensed with impending orgasm and then shifted his attention to her slippery pussy again. She growled with frustration. He pressed two fingers against her clit while he sucked at her swollen lips. She rocked against his fingers, seeking release. When a spasm gripped her, he moved away, holding her hips steady with both hands as he kissed a trail up her flat belly.

"No, don't stop. I didn't come yet." She pressed her hands against her eyes and shook her head desperately. "Close. So close."

He was well aware of that. He wanted to be inside her when she found release. But first, more teasing. He moved his hands up her sides, his lips to her breast. She clung to his scalp, her back arched, her taut nipple eagerly offered to his exploring mouth.

"Oh God, put it in, Sed. Now. Please. I can't stand it."

He grinned and worked his way up her body, partially joining her on the bed. One foot still on the floor, his hips settled between her thighs, his mouth suckled on her throat, his hands clung to her shoulders. When her fingers trailed down his back, his entire body stiffened. He wanted to tease her more, but he couldn't maintain his intent if she kept that up. Her nails dug into his back and she squirmed to spread her thighs further, inviting him inside. He accepted her invitation, pressing the head of his cock into her slick opening.

"Yes," she gasped.

No. Not yet. He pulled out and kissed a trail down her body again. She sucked a deep breath between her teeth. He needed more of her taste first. He slid from the bed on his knees and buried his face between her thighs. He sucked and licked at her fluids, which were flowing freely in her excitement. Feeding him. Fueling him. She squirmed and panted, her hips writhing involuntarily as her pleasure built.

When her vocalizations became desperate, he moved his lips to the inside of her thigh. She groaned in frustration, dove off the bed, and tackled him flat on his back. She straddled his belly and he let her pin his arms to the floor on either side of his head. They both knew he could out-muscle her any day, but he liked that she was hot enough for him to try to strong arm him. He'd been trying to get her to this point all afternoon.

"You've been charged with attempted murder," she said.

His eyebrows shot up in surprise. "I have?"

"Yes, if you don't stop teasing me, I'm going to die."

He chuckled at the serious expression on her face. "Are you working in my defense? I can show you my evidence." He nodded his head toward his throbbing erection.

She snorted and bit her lip to stop her laughter. She then put on her best courtroom face and shook her head. "I'm the prosecution. I've already examined your evidence. I found it unconvincing."

"Aren't I innocent until proven guilty?"

"You're talking to the victim. Also the judge. And the jury. I find you guilty, Sedric Lionheart." She slid down his body until his evidence pressed against the heat between her thighs.

"Have you determined my punishment, your honor?"

"An eye for an eye, Lionheart."

"I can take any punishment you dish out, Chase."

She grinned, one eyebrow cocked in challenge. "Oh really?"

"Try me."

He probably shouldn't have baited her. She knew every spot on his body that could work him into a frenzy, and she didn't hold back anything. She went straight for that ticklish spot at the base of his ribs, her fingers digging into his flesh. Instantly, she had him writhing around on the floor and laughing.

"No fair," he protested breathlessly.

Still tickling him without mercy, she leaned forward and clamped her mouth on that sensitive spot just under his left ear. A thrill of excitement grabbed him by the balls and he groaned. She sucked a trail down his neck and then sat upright.

"I think I need to reexamine the evidence," she said.

She shifted back and sank down on his shaft, taking him deep inside her body.

"Oh yes, this is some hard evidence you have here."

He might have gloated about winning, if it hadn't felt so amazing to be buried in her velvety heat at last. She rode him slowly, grinding her body against his, her fingers going still on his abdomen.

"I'm still not convinced," she purred.

Huh?

Jessica lifted upward until his cock fell free of her body. He gasped brokenly. Okay, he was starting to understand this attempted murder charge.

"Oh dear, I got the evidence all wet." She winked at him and slid down his body until her face was even with his wet evidence.

Her tongue darted out from between her lips as she lapped her fluids from his cock. He moved up on his elbows so he could see her, not sure why watching her clean her juices from his flesh was so fucking hot. Maybe it was those little sounds of pleasure she was making in the back of her throat. Or the tentative way her tongue danced over his flesh. Or knowing how good she tasted so she must surely be enjoying every drop.

"All dry now," she declared after way too much delectable torture.

"I think you should climb on and reexamine it."

"Don't be ridiculous. Then I'd have to dry it all over again. But I think I see some more evidence down here."

Her face disappeared between his legs and she sucked one of his balls into her mouth. His arms gave out on him and his head hit the floor with a *thunk*. "Oh God, Jess, don't do that." His protests fueled her retaliation. Her tongue worked against his flesh as she sucked gently. He couldn't stand it. If she didn't stop that, he was going to spurt cum all over his belly. His stomach clenched and pulled him up into partial sitting position. He reached between his legs and grabbed her hair.

"Stop, stop, okay, you win. I'll never tease you again."

She chuckled. "You're a liar."

"No, no, I mean it."

She sucked his other nut in her mouth.

"Jess!"

He was torn between needing her to stop and wanting her to

continue. It felt so good. He squirmed, craving her attention else-where. His cock throbbed in protest. She eventually relieved him of her pleasurable torture and lifted her head.

He sighed in relief, gulping air to try to force his impending orgasm back.

"What are you sighing about? Your punishment is far from over."

Her lips clamped over the head of his cock. She sucked him hard, her tongue writhing against his sensitive flesh. His excitement built quickly. Her name escaped his lips. "Jessica." So close. So close to letting go. And then… she stopped.

Her mouth moved to his belly and she planted tender kisses around his navel.

"Ah God, don't stop now. Suck me off. Please."

"Eye for an eye," she murmured, working her way up his body with her lips.

Unable to stand her delicate touch any longer, he rolled her onto her back and plunged into her body.

She screamed. No wait, that wasn't her. That was coming from the bedroom. Aggie's cries of ecstasy carried through the door and echoed through the entire bus. "Ah God. Yes, finally. Thank you. Jace. Jace!"

Sed glanced down into Jessica's eyes, which were wide with astonishment.

"My God, what is he doing to her?" she whispered.

Sed grinned. "I don't know, but I take it she likes it."

"Do you think you can make me scream that loud?"

He rotated his hips and drove himself deeper. Her back arched and her breath erupted in a sexy little gasp.

"I won't stop until I do."

He pulled out and lifted her off the floor.

"What are you—"

He silenced her with a kiss and set her on the kitchen counter.

He squatted between her legs, suckling her clit until she writhed against his face and clung to his scalp, mewing her pleasure in the back of her throat. Not exactly screaming. Yet.

He stood and entered her with one deep thrust. Her back arched and she banged her head on the cabinet. She didn't seem to notice. She wrapped her arms around his neck and rocked forward to meet his thrusts. When she tightened her muscles around his cock, he shuddered in delight and forced himself to pull out. He didn't want her to concentrate on his pleasure, only hers.

She opened her eyes to look at him in question. "Why'd you stop?"

He didn't answer. Instead he found her clit with two fingers and rubbed her until her mouth dropped open and she squirmed against his hand. "Mmmmm," she murmured. He gently probed her opening with his cock again, and she slipped off the edge of the counter, her pussy engulfing him in slick heat. He carefully set her back on the counter, keeping his cock buried deep. His thrusts began slow and gentle. Her cries of excitement built as he gradually increased his tempo. Her head tilted back and she ground her mound against him to intensify her pleasure. He almost had her where he wanted her. Almost. She opened her eyes to look at him and clenched her pussy around him. He pulled out slowly until his cock fell free of her body.

"No," she gasped.

He crouched down to suck at her clit again, inhaling her intoxicating scent as he drove her closer to her magical place. Even after she cried out and her body shuddered in orgasm, he continued to rub his tongue over her sensitized flesh. Her vocalizations grew louder and louder as he worked her toward climax once again.

"Are you trying to drive me crazy?" she panted.

He lifted his head and grinned at her. "Just temporarily."

"A temporary insanity defense rarely flies in a courtroom," she murmured. Her beautiful face was flushed; her eyelids heavy with desire as she gazed down at him. He loved knowing he'd created that look, but she was entirely too coherent if she could still speak.

"I'm not trying to make you fly in a courtroom."

He carried her to the sofa, set her on its edge and knelt on the floor in front of her. She grabbed his cock and shoved it into her body, shuddering in ecstasy as he filled her. He looked down to where their bodies were joined, trying not to get too excited by the sight of her pussy ebbing and flowing each time he filled her and receded. Her frame of mind still wasn't where he wanted it to be, but she was close. He lifted her legs and rested her feet against his shoulders. Rising off his knees, he thrust down into her.

"Oh," she crooned and reached between her thighs to rub her clit. She rubbed herself and rubbed and rubbed until she came with a sputtering gasp. "Oh God, Sed. Fuck me!"

He grinned to himself. He had her now.

Jessica became a creature of greedy lust, straining against him to attain another orgasm and another, completely ignoring his needs.

"More. More. Don't stop. Don't stop. Don't stop!"

"There's my girl," he murmured. "I wondered where she'd been hiding."

She shoved him off her with both feet. He fell back on the floor. For a second he thought she was angry, but she climbed on his lap in the middle of the bus aisle and took him deep inside with a cry of triumph. She rode him hard, her nails digging into his chest. She screamed in ecstasy, giving her sexual demon free rein as she sought orgasm after orgasm.

Now that she'd completely lost control, he gave himself permission to enjoy all she had to offer. She worked his cock with constricting vaginal muscles with each upward pull and each downward grind. On the verge of erupting, he called her name. He didn't want it to end yet. Not when he finally had her excited beyond reason.

He shuddered violently and lifted her off him by the hips. He tossed her on the sofa and settled his head between her thighs, sucking and licking her clit while he rammed his fingers into her. Two. And then three. The harder he shoved them into her body, the louder she screamed. She strained against him, her nails digging into his scalp as she cried out with yet another wave of release.

He kept her trembling until his own excitement abated and he crawled up her body, kissing her skin open-mouthed, his tongue dancing against her sweat-slick flesh. When they were face-to-face, he plunged into her again.

Her fingers moved to massage his back and she rotated her hips, immersing him in pleasure. He couldn't force himself to pull out this time. He was ready to join her in bliss.

"Jessica. Jessica. God, you feel like pure heaven."

Her entire body trembled with exhaustion, but still she continued to chant, "more, more, more," and he couldn't refuse.

He pulled out again and urged her into the stairwell of the bus. He pressed her back up against the door and slid between her legs. Her feet rested on the first step, while he stood on the bottom one.

He allowed his inner beast to emerge as he thrust savagely into her body. Although his strokes were entirely for his own pleasure, she apparently got off on him going primal. She bucked against him, clinging to his chest, his shoulders, his back, as if she couldn't get enough of his flesh in her hands. Her open mouth rubbed against his jaw, his chin, his throat as though she were trying to swallow him whole.

His orgasm within reach, he grabbed her wrists and crushed them into the door on either side of her head. She struggled against his hold, which fueled his need to dominate her. To fuck her harder. Harder. "This is mine," he growled into her ear. "Say it."

Harder. Harder. Oh God, he was going to come.

"Say it, Jessica. Say it."

Her word came out in a rush of air. "Y-yours."

"Yes. Mine. Don't you fuckin' ever forget it."

He rubbed his face against her throat as he let go, his entire body shuddering with release.

He backed out slightly and thrust forward again, still coming. Spurting his seed into her body. Flooding her insides with his fluids. Claiming her as his. *His.* "Ah God," he gasped. "Mine."

One more stroke was all he could take as he buried himself deep and collapsed against her, still shaking from the aftermath.

He released her wrists and she moved her hands to stroke his back. Her gentle touch kept him shuddering and twitching for several minutes.

He drew back to look at her. Maybe she'd said it because she was delirious with pleasure, but she'd said it. That she was his. He kissed her feverishly. Her lips, her face, her jaw, her neck and chest. He pressed his lips to every inch of her he could reach. She giggled at his enthusiasm.

"God, I've missed you." He touched her cheek tenderly, wanting to tell her he loved her, had never stopped, but he didn't think she was ready to hear that just yet.

She stared up at him, face flushed, eyes glassy. "You missed me... or my body?"

Before he could answer her, the bedroom door opened at the back of the bus.

"Is it safe to come out now?" Jace called from the end of the hall.

Chapter 18

SED KEPT JESSICA TUCKED securely against his side as they forced their way through the crowd surrounding the hospital. About halfway through, Jace hollered in protest, trapped in the mob. Sed backtracked and managed to keep Jessica at his hip while he untangled Jace from the arms of two overexcited fangirls. Apparently, Jace was so fucking cute, they couldn't control themselves. The first girl lodged his face between her huge breasts, squealing with excitement as he struggled for freedom. Sed rescued him before she could suffocate him. Jace wasn't accustomed to battling his way through a horde. Sed was a pro, but as much as he hated to admitted it, they needed to bring security with them.

"Any news on Trey?" someone yelled.

"Did Trey wake up yet?" asked another.

"I heard they amputated his arm. Please, tell me it's a lie."

Sinners also needed to have a press conference to stop ridiculous rumors from taking hold.

"Trey is awake and recovering just fine!" Sed shouted. "Can you give us some space here, please?"

The crowd backed up marginally.

"Are you dating Jessica exclusively now?" someone near his left arm asked.

"Of course, they're back together. You saw their video, didn't you?"

"I saw it," someone else said. "That was so fucking hot, dude."

Jessica's fingers dug into Sed's forearm. "What are they talking about?"

Sed shrugged. "Hell if I know."

They had to present ID and prove they were on Trey's guest list before they were allowed to go up to his room. The folks at the front desk looked harried and exhausted. Hospital security looked ready to break out the tear gas. While Sed, Jessica, and Jace stood waiting for the elevator, a pair of security guards escorted some fan from an open elevator car and shoved him back outside. "Sinners forever!" he screamed as he was jostled to the back of the mob.

"This is insane," Jace muttered, rubbing the silver hoop in his earlobe.

Sed chuckled. "I bet the hospital will be glad when Trey checks out."

"What video?" Jessica said, still mulling over what that fan had said outside.

"I hope Trey's in a better mood," Sed said.

Jace stared at the floor. "I haven't seen him since he woke up."

"What *video*?" Jessica grabbed Sed's arm and gave him a shake.

"I'm sure it's nothing. Calm down." Sed placed a hand on the small of her back to help her into the elevator car.

"I'm not going to calm down. That guy said, 'it was so fucking hot, dude.' What did he mean by that?"

"Maybe he was talking about the music video we released last week," Jace said. "Those scenes with Sed and that chick were pretty hot."

Jessica's nostrils flared. "What chick?"

"Yeah, someone probably thought the actress in the video was you. That's all."

Jace's brow twisted with confusion. "That woman didn't look anything like Jessica. Wasn't she Japanese?"

Work with me, Jace. "Yeah, so some of our fans are stupid and blind. Whatever."

"A music video?" Jessica wrung her hands together and took a deep, steadying breath. "I hope you're right."

Well, what else could it be?

When they entered Trey's flower-and-balloon–infested room, Trey, Eric, and Dave were squashed together in Trey's hospital bed watching the computer screen with their mouths hanging open. Some woman was vocalizing her sexual excitement on whatever porn video currently held their attention.

"What are you guys watching?" Sed asked.

Trey glanced up from the screen. His eyes moved to Jessica and widened. He slammed the laptop closed on Eric's hand.

"Ow. Fuck!" Eric jerked his hand back and then moved it to his mouth to suck on his fingertips. He reached over to slap Trey alongside the head, hesitated when confronted with a row of staples, and dropped his hand on the computer on his lap instead.

"N-nothing," Trey said.

"Well, it must've been something good. All three of you have drool on your chins." Sed was ribbing them, but the three on the bed wiped their chins on their shoulders in unison.

Dave struggled to stand. Eric gave him a push and he found his feet. "I've gotta go." And Dave darted out of the room as if Trey'd been eating too many bean burritos while they were trapped on the tour bus again.

Eric cradled the laptop against his belly and climbed from the bed as well. "Yeah, I'd say it's time to go."

"Yep," Trey said, struggling to rise from his bed. He grabbed his IV pole for leverage.

Jace grabbed his arm. "Don't hurt yourself. Get back in bed."

"All right," Sed bellowed. He glanced from Trey to Eric. "What the fuck is going on here? It's not like Jessica doesn't know you guys watch porn videos. She doesn't care and you know it. Explain."

Eric and Trey both looked at Jessica. Eric shifted the laptop down to cover the bulge in his pants.

"She'll care about this video," Trey said.

"Video?" Jessica strode over to Eric and tried to wrestle the laptop out of his hands. "Show me."

Eric shook his head vigorously. "You don't want to see it."

"Show me, Eric. Now!"

"He doesn't have to show you," Trey said, allowing Jace to stuff him back in bed. "You were there."

"Oh God, don't tell me..."

"Okay, we won't," Eric said.

Jessica yanked the laptop away from Eric and popped it open. Sed moved to look over her shoulder. He had no idea what had her so upset.

"What's the password?" she demanded.

"Uh, the password is password. Duh," Trey said.

"Jessica, don't do this to yourself." Eric squeezed her shoulder, his expression empathetic.

Jessica got the video going and the chick on screen started vocalizing again. Wait a minute. That wasn't a chick. That was Jessica. A bubble of intense rage erupted from Sed's insides. Not only was she a stripper, now she was a fuckin' porn star, too. What else was she hiding from him? And he didn't care if it was work. He'd kill the jackass she was fucking so well while clinging to some chain-link fence over the Las Vegas strip. That prick who was drilling her... Wait. Why did that jerk look so much like him?

Ohhhhh.

Sed bit his lip. That *was* him. And her. Going all out at the top of the Eiffel tower. Oh shit. She'd never forgive him for this. Not in a million years.

"Five hundred and twelve thousand views!" she bellowed. "This happened last night. How in the—I can't believe—Who posted this? And how did they get it?"

"There's some girl at the beginning of the video..." Eric attempted to take the laptop from her. "You shouldn't watch this, honey."

She slugged him in the gut. "Why not? You were."

"Yeah, but—"

"And more than five hundred thousand *other* people have."

"I think some of those are repeat viewers," Trey said. "I mean we watched it, what, five times?"

"Six, I think."

Typically, Sed found Jessica irresistibly sexy when she was pissed, but this pissed-off-Jessica wasn't sexy. This pissed-off-Jessica was terrifying. He took a step back and let Eric take the brunt of her fury.

"You watched it six times?" she screamed. "*Six* times?"

"I'm sure it was only five and a half," Trey said. "You confiscated the computer before we finished watching it that last time."

"Oh jeez, Trey, that makes me feel a lot better. Thanks." She slammed the computer on the mattress at his feet and moved the slider to the beginning of the video. "I have a pretty good idea of who filmed this and posted it online." She turned her head and pinned Sed to the floor with a glare. "One of your stupid fangirls, no doubt. The one who gave us privacy in exchange for your shirt. What do you bet?"

He lowered his gaze. "Probably." He wanted to comfort her. Knew that her anger was a front for deeper feelings, but he didn't know what to do. He couldn't take this back. Couldn't hide it. Couldn't make it go away. How could they deal with something like this?

Jessica started the video from the beginning. The attendant from the Eiffel Tower came on screen. She wore the white T-shirt Sed had given her, his signature evident across her left breast.

"I knew it," Jessica muttered.

The girl on-screen started talking to the camera. "I know there are a lot of Sedric Lionheart fans out there who hate this bitch as much as I do, so please, copy this video and distribute it as much as possible. Sed, if you see this, you are an absolute god and you can do so much better than Jessica Chase. She's such a skank." She extended her pinkie and thumb and held it to her face. "Call me, big guy. I'll treat you right. Enjoy the show, fans!"

"Skank?" Jessica sputtered. "Where does that little bitch get off calling me a skank?"

The video recording started. Grainy, but not terrible quality. The sounds. Oh dear God, the sounds. Sed couldn't help but get excited watching Jessica with her top down and her skirt up while he plunged into her eager body. And you could definitely tell it was Jessica. Their undetected audience kept zooming in on Jessica's face. And as if the title, *Sedric Lionheart Screws a Harlot Over the Vegas Strip*, wasn't bad enough, the caption at the bottom read, *Jessica Chase Orgasm Count*, and there was a rolling ticker beside it, currently at 2. When Jessica cried out and shuddered with release, the number flipped to 3. *Three?* He was sure that had been her fourth. But that was beside the point.

"God, Jess, this is bad," Sed whispered. He reached over her shoulder to pause the video. Her beautiful face stayed frozen on screen as she continued to cry out in ecstasy.

Jessica released a wounded groan though she probably couldn't even see the video through the tears in her eyes. As scary as her rage had been, the mortified look on her face was far worse. She tilted her head back to prevent her tears from falling.

"Bad? You don't say," she said, her voice surprisingly steady. Jessica crossed her arms over her chest, her jaw flexing as she worked at letting go of the anguish and recovering her anger. "Fuck it," she said. "Who cares anyway? It isn't as if I had dreams or anything. I don't need a future. Or a life."

Sed zeroed in on a link to mark the video as inappropriate. He clicked it. "There. They'll take it down," he said. "It will be okay."

"What do you mean it will be okay?" she bellowed. He winced. "Over half a million views in less than a day and that little bitch told people to copy it and distribute it. There's no telling how many copies are circulating right now."

"It's not the end of the world, Jessica. So you had sex. Big deal. Everybody does it." He grinned. "Maybe not hanging upside down over the Vegas strip with a rock star…"

Her jaw set in a hard line, she focused on the floor. "You are not making me feel better."

"It was worth a try."

He touched her chin to encourage her to look at him. She jerked her head to the side.

"We could retaliate by posting a new sex video online every day for the rest of our lives," he suggested, hoping that making light of the subject would help her cope better. Right now, she wasn't coping at all.

She scowled. Punched him in the ribs with a tiny fist. "How is that supposed to help?"

He chuckled. "It will guarantee I get well-laid on a very regular basis."

"Oh yeah, I like that plan," Trey said. "Do you take requests?"

Sed waited for her smartassed retort, but it never came. Instead, she covered her face with both hands, turned on her heel, and fled the room. Sed's eyes widened. Distraught? Jessica didn't *do* distraught. That's one of the reasons he loved her so much. He never had to deal with a hysterical female. Pissed? Yeah. Opinionated and vocal about it? Hell yeah. But not totally flipped out. Jessica usually took everything in stride. Laughed it off. For some reason, this situation was different. He honestly didn't get why it was such a big deal. She looked *amazing* on the video and he was doing his part properly. She should be proud.

Eric shoved Sed to gain his attention. "What are you waiting for? Go after her, you idiot."

Go after her. Right…

Chapter 19

JESSICA TAPPED THE DOWN elevator button like a jackhammer demolishing pavement. She needed a moment to collect herself. A ladies room, or… She turned and glanced around, looking for directional signs, but the elevator dinged behind her, and Sed (the callous jackass) was headed in her direction. She stepped onto the elevator and held the button to close the doors.

"Jessica!" Sed called, his trot increasing to a full out run. "Wait. We need to talk." The doors closed before Sed could reach them. She heard his hands slap against the outside just before the car started its descent.

Talk? She had no intention of talking to Sed. Ever again. She should have known better than to get mixed up with him in the first place.

Jessica leaned against the interior wall of the car and took several deep breaths as the elevator continued down to the lobby. A presence lurked behind her, so she couldn't allow herself to cry. Not in public. Why couldn't the rest of the world just disappear and leave her the fuck alone?

"Jessica Chase?"

Her heart thudded. She didn't know enough people in Vegas to be recognized by her real name. She turned and there stood some average-in-every-way guy she'd never seen before.

"How do you know my name?" She was almost afraid to ask.

The man hesitated and then leaned closer, his breath hot in her ear. "I saw your video today, sexy. Would you consider accompanying me to the real Eiffel Tower for a repeat performance? I'll pay your way to France. Buy you nice things. Give you cash. Whatever you want." His gray eyes took in every inch of her figure. "I just want to *fuck* that tight little body of yours."

She was too stunned to respond. Too nauseous to scream. Too humiliated to move.

"What do you say?" He grabbed her by both arms, his tongue laving her ear.

She jerked away and found herself trapped in a corner.

Instinct? She didn't know. Her knee came up and he went down.

"No," she shouted down at him. "That's what I say, you fucking jerk!"

The elevator door opened and she rushed into the lobby, leaving the jackass on the elevator floor cradling his crushed nuts and moaning in agony. She hadn't taken two steps before another man grabbed her by both shoulders and crushed her against his hard chest. She fought him, ready to deliver another groin-directed knee until she recognized her captor. *Sed?* How had he beaten the elevator fifteen floors to the lobby?

"Come on, sweetheart. I'll take you back to the hotel," he said breathlessly.

"I'm not going anywhere with you."

"I know you're upset. You probably want to hide for a while and cry. Let's get you out of here, okay?"

She gulped air. She did want to hide and cry, but not for a while. Forever.

"I'll take you to the hotel and I'll leave you alone. Or you can let me hold you. Whatever you want."

The problem was she didn't know what she wanted—being alone sounded good yet terrible, being held in Sed's strong arms sounded better yet worse—but she nodded and let him lead her to a waiting cab. She stared unseeingly out the window on the way through the city. What was she going to do? There was no way she could hide this video from her peers, her professors, her family, her friends, jerks in elevators. This kind of thing would destroy her credibility. Would it mean the end of her career? Was it over before it started? Her dreams destroyed for a few moments of bliss? It all seemed incredibly unfair.

Something hot streaked down her cheek. She dashed the tear away with the back of her hand and glanced at Sed to see if he'd noticed. When their eyes met, he smiled sadly, and then stared down at his hands, which were folded in his lap.

Another tear fell. Another. She wiped her face on the hem of her T-shirt. Damn it. This wasn't worth her tears. She was strong. She could get through this. She could always become a hermit and make pinecone wreaths in the sequoia forests. The trees wouldn't know she was a... she was a... a *skaaaank*.

Jessica took a deep breath that turned into an anguished sob. Sed touched her shoulder. That small connection was like a switch that opened the flood gates. She caught his startled expression just before she flung herself across the backseat and into his arms. He held her as if her tears would wash her away and he had no intention of allowing the raging waters to pull her from his grasp. Feeling safe, she let the humiliation wash over her. Oh God, people would see her, see her like *that*, and... and... they would think she was a slut. A whore. A tramp. A...

"It's okay, baby," Sed murmured, squeezing her tighter. "I'll fix it. I promise."

She struggled out of his embrace and glared up at him. "You can't fix this, Sed. You can't. *This* is an unfixable situation."

He cupped her face in both hands and kissed the tears from her cheeks. "I said I'll fix it and I will. Don't cry."

The cab pulled to a stop outside the Bellagio hotel and Jessica scrambled out of the car. People waiting in line for the next available taxi gawked at her as she hurried into the hotel. They'd probably seen her video. Or maybe they found the tears dripping from her jaw and her runny nose interesting. Whatever it was, she wished she had a bag to put over her head.

When they reached the room, Sed directed her to the bathroom. He turned on the taps to fill the large garden tub.

"What are you doing?"

"Pampering you. Get in the tub. I'll call room service."

"I don't want to be pampered."

"Too bad. I'm pampering."

That big tub did look inviting. And there was a complimentary bottle of bubble bath on the edge of the tub. "Okay."

Sed let out a relieved sigh. He probably thought this fixed things. Well, it didn't. Nothing would fix this.

"I'll be right back." And when he kissed her—for a fleeting moment—she started to believe that things really were going to be okay.

Less than twenty minutes later, she was already feeling more like herself. Fragrant bubbles tickling the bare skin of her shoulders, Jessica leaned forward in the tub and opened her mouth to accept the spoonful of chocolate mousse Sed offered. Her eyes rolled up in her head as she licked every decadent trace of dessert from the spoon. Smooth, sweet, and rich. She rubbed the mousse between the roof of her mouth and tongue, reluctant to swallow. Chocolate made everything better. Even *her* fucked up life.

Jessica groaned. "It's so good."

"It can't be half as good as watching you eat it." He grinned at her and scooped another spoonful from the tall parfait glass.

"Aren't you going to have any?" she asked, eagerly accepting another bite of his treat.

His grin widened and one of his adorable dimples made an appearance. "I'm saving my appetite for dessert."

"You can climb in here with me, you know." Sex with Sed was even better at taking her mind off things than chocolate. And more than anything, she longed for blank thoughts.

Sitting next to the tub, still fully clothed, Sed shook his head. "We both know where that will lead. You've had a hard day, sweetheart. I want you to relax."

She'd forgotten how sweet he could be at times. "It's hard to relax when I keep thinking about that stupid vid—"

He silenced her by stuffing a large strawberry in her mouth. She chewed, the sour tang of the fruit contrasting with the sweet chocolate still stimulating her taste buds.

"Then stop thinking about it." He reached across the expanse of lily-scented bubbles and stroked a strand of hair from her cheek.

"You are taking my mind off things."

Both dimples made an appearance this time. Her heart skipped a beat. Why couldn't he be like this all the time?

"I am?"

"Well, you and the chocolate." She opened her mouth, ready for her next bite.

He laughed. "Honest to a fault. Are you sure you want to be a lawyer?"

Her heart went from recovery to the pit of despair in one beat. "I'm not sure it's even possible now. My reputation is ruined."

"In a couple of weeks, it will be old news. No one will remember it."

"I will."

He gave her a pitying look and reached for the bottle of champagne chilling in a silver bucket near his hip. He sloshed some pale amber liquid into a flute and held it out to her. "More champagne?"

She nodded and reached for the glass.

Sed took a long swig out of the bottle. She watched his throat work as he swallowed and squeezed her thighs together to alleviate the building throb between them. She probably shouldn't want him after the day she'd had, but she did. What was it about this man that made her so stupid? And slutty? God, the whole world knew how much she liked to fuck him now—how she'd go to any lengths to please him sexually—and did that stop her from wanting him? No. Sed lowered the bottle and stuffed it back into the ice bucket, accompanied by the rattle of melting ice.

He covered his mouth with the back of his hand and chuckled. "That shit goes straight to your head."

"I don't think you're supposed to chug half the bottle." Though three glasses deep, she was working on it. She rested her wrist on the edge of the tub, her half-full flute tilted precariously. "Since you refuse to fuck me, can I have some more chocolate, please?"

"I'm not refusing. I just don't think that's what you really want right now."

"You don't know a goddamned thing about what I want." Her eyes filled with unexpected tears. "Why won't you ever listen to me?" If sex had been his idea, she'd already be on her back with him thrusting into her slutty, needy body.

He brushed a tear away with his thumb. "Shh, sweetheart, I'm not going to take advantage of you when you're this upset." He extended a spoonful of mousse toward her.

Oh yeah? Well, if he wasn't going to do as she asked, she'd just have to seduce him then. She waited until the spoon touched her bottom lip then slowly drew her tongue over it. She repeated the motion again and again, knowing what kind of thoughts she encouraged. Sed watched her lick his offering one thin layer at a time. He couldn't take his eyes off her mouth or the carefully timed strokes of her tongue. She sucked the remaining mousse from the spoon. "Mmmmm."

Sed answered her murmur of pleasure with a soft curse.

Her eyes drifted down his body, wishing he'd get naked already.

The chocolate and champagne weren't doing it for her. She could still think. Her eyes settled on the crotch of his jeans. Anything ready to tango in his pants? Getting there, but only half-mast. She could do better.

"What are you looking at?" he asked.

Her gaze lifted to his. He had one eyebrow raised at her.

"I want more."

"More what?"

"You know what I want, Sed. Give it to me." She opened her mouth for another bite.

He scooped another spoonful of mousse. "If you don't stop that, I'm going to give it to you real good here in a minute. And then you're going to get pissed at me for taking advantage of you."

"Why would I get pissed if you give me what I need?"

"Jess, you're not thinking clearly. The last thing you need right now is sex."

She completely disagreed with him. No surprise there. Jessica rubbed her mouth over the soft dessert, licking the chocolate from her coated lips in bliss. She kept her eyes closed, but she assumed he watched with undivided attention. Her tongue stroked the underside of the spoon repetitively and then dipped into the depression on top.

"I wish I was a spoon," he murmured.

After she licked all traces of dessert from the spoon, she moaned, "More, Sed. I need more."

He fed her another spoonful of mousse, and another.

"Yes, Sed. Give it to me. More."

He scraped the spoon against the sides of the glass and gave his final offering. She finished the last bite and opened her eyes.

He rattled the spoon in the glass. "It's all gone."

She glanced at the glass, noting the film of mousse on its inner surface. "There's a little left. Don't waste it."

He rubbed his index finger along the inner surface of the glass and offered it to her, his breath catching. She licked his finger from base to tip and then sucked it into her mouth. The salt of his skin mingled with the sweet, rich taste of chocolate.

"Jess," he gasped.

She sucked his finger gently, drawing her mouth back to the tip, and working her tongue along its underside, before she sucked it deep again. She released his finger and took a sip of her champagne. "Are you sure there isn't any more?" Her eyes drifted down to his lap again. His cock strained against his pants as a thick, rigid pole along the inside of his left thigh.

How was he not in the tub already?

"I can order you another."

"I think I've had enough chocolate. What else do you have to offer?" She glanced down at his lap suggestively.

He didn't seem to notice. "Champagne."

"Excellent champagne," she murmured and took another gulp of the sparkling beverage.

"Strawberries." He lifted a lid off a plate sitting beside him on the floor. The smell of beef and grease filled the air. "And a hamburger."

She chuckled. "You don't really think I'd eat that, do you?"

"I ordered it for me, but if you want some..." He took a bite. "I'll share," he said with his mouth full.

"Charming, Sed. Hand me the strawberries."

He handed her a large goblet with fresh trimmed strawberries. She drained her champagne flute in several gulps and dropped the glass on the towel next to the tub. She set the cold goblet of strawberries on her chest and bit into a berry, pretending she didn't notice the juice dripping down her chin. She could be as persistent as he was stubborn.

Sed tossed his half-eaten burger on his plate. He retrieved her discarded champagne glass and refilled it. "I think you need more champagne." He handed the full glass to her.

"You're right. I'm not drunk yet." She polished off the glass in four swallows and dropped the flute on the floor again before selecting another strawberry. "I wonder if my law professors already know about my amateur porn debut."

"You're not supposed to be thinking about that." He stuffed the final quarter of his hamburger into his mouth. He could be such a pig. She wasn't sure why it turned her on.

"This is a big deal in my life, Sed. What am I supposed to be thinking about?"

He peeled his shirt off over his head and tossed it aside. "Me."

Like she could think of anything else when he was shirtless. "You just ate, Sed. You can't come into the water for at least twenty minutes." Despite her teasing, her appreciative gaze roamed the hard contours of his naked chest and stomach. Beautiful man. About time he got down to business and gave her what she really wanted.

He took the goblet of strawberries from her and set it on the floor. "I'm not planning on swimming." He drew her body halfway around the garden tub, so that her back was to him and the edge of the tub separated their bodies. His arms wrapped around her, large hands grasping her breasts. His mouth descended to suck on her neck. "Is this what you want?"

She gasped. "Yes."

He rolled her nipples between his index fingers and thumbs, drawing a hard shudder from her body. He kissed a trail up her neck to her ear, sucking its lobe between his teeth to nibble on it. Goose bumps rose to the surface of her skin. His breath, quick and uneven in her ear, fueled her excitement.

"You drive me crazy, woman." The low rumble of his voice drove straight to her core.

"I have no idea why."

His hands slid down her rib cage. He paused, taking several deep breaths to calm his excitement. Apparently, he was still under the impression that she didn't want him to dive into the tub half-clothed, unleash his cock, and plunge into her body. He reached for the small complimentary bar of soap on the edge of the tub and unwrapped it.

"Where would you like me to wash you?" he whispered into her ear.

She grinned. "My left hand."

He lifted her hand from the water and lathered it with soap before setting the soap aside and massaging her hand with his thumbs. The pressure of his touch was perfect—firm, yet gentle.

"Clean yet?" he murmured.

"Not yet."

He continued to massage her hand. Her knuckles, the base of her fingers, palm, wrist. If this singing thing didn't work out for him, he could always become a hand masseur.

"Right hand," she murmured.

He lowered her left hand into the water and rinsed the traces of soap from it before picking up the bar of soap and lathering her right. She tried to keep her attention on the feel of his strong fingers kneading her flesh. If this didn't take her mind off things, nothing would. She didn't want to think about that stupid video and how twenty minutes of bliss might ruin her entire life, or what would happen if Trey never got better, or how much Brian despised her, or how now that Sinners weren't on tour she was sort of out of a job again, or that she had to retake Ellington's class next year, or—

"You're supposed to be relaxing," Sed murmured into her ear.

"I am relaxing."

He kissed her temple. "I can tell when your mind is churning out a million thoughts a minute."

"You'll have me thinking of nothing but you soon enough."

"I think of nothing but you most of the time. Doesn't seem fair, does it?"

She turned her head to look at him, a smile on her lips. "Bath Boy," she said in a haughty British accent, "my breasts are filthy. You are neglecting your duties."

He grinned and directed the bar of soap to the underside of her right breast and then the left. The soap slipped from his grasp and landed in the water with a splash, but he didn't take his hands from her breasts to retrieve it.

He worked the suds between their skin over her nipples. Stroking. Plucking. Kneading.

She gasped, her head falling against his shoulder.

"Find the soap," he murmured, the timbre of his voice drawing another shudder from her body.

She searched for the soap beneath the surface of the water, eventually finding it near her hip on the bottom of the tub. He accepted it from her, soaped her breasts thoroughly, and set the bar of soap on the tub's rim. His hands rubbed over her slick flesh repeatedly, driving her to madness.

"Bath Boy, I'm so dirty between my legs," she gasped.

"You are?" He nipped her earlobe.

She shuddered. "Yeah."

He took the bar of soap and slid it beneath the water's surface down her belly. She spread her legs in anticipation. He caressed her lower belly and then the insides of her thighs.

"Are you sure your back isn't dirty?" he murmured.

She wondered why he hesitated on getting right down to business. "Do you want my back to be dirty?"

"I want to help you relax."

"And I want you to ravish my body."

"I plan on it. After your bath."

She sighed in frustration. "This pampering isn't necessary, Sedric. My legs are always open to you, aren't they? We fuck. That's what we do. That's all we do. I don't need you for anything else. Get it?"

His hands moved from her body, dropping into the water. After a moment of his silence, she glanced up over her shoulder at him. His scowl almost covered his despair.

Exasperated, she asked, "What's wrong now?"

He hesitated. "Is that all I am to you? A toy for your amusement?"

"Yes, that's all you are, Sed. All you'll ever be. An amusing toy."

He closed his eyes and took a deep breath, his handsome face twisted in anguish.

He sat there for a full minute before climbing to his feet and drying his hands on a towel.

He retrieved his discarded shirt from the floor.

Left without a word.

Jessica waited for him to return, listening to sounds of him moving through the hotel suite. The outer door opened. Closed. Had he really abandoned her? Just because she'd called him a toy? Was that really all it took to hurt him? *Too easy.*

She reached for the bottle of champagne and took a long swallow. *He'll be back.*

An hour later, the champagne was gone, the bath bubbles had vanished, and the water was cold, but Sed still hadn't returned. Well, shit. What did he expect from her? They'd agreed that this "relationship" was a game. Only about sex. And now he was pissed because she wanted to stick to the terms of their agreement. Fine. Whatever. They could be done. This could be over. Why should she care? It didn't mean anything. Like she'd said, the only thing she needed him for was sex. If he had any doubt, he could ask any of the five hundred thousand people who'd witnessed her needs on video.

She pulled the plug and climbed from the tub, staggering as she reached for a towel. She wrapped it around her body and went in search of clothes. She should find Sed and apologize. Make up with him. It really wasn't his fault that she was a skank. She dashed a tear away with the back of her hand.

Her vision blurred as she left the brightly lit bathroom and entered the dim interior of the living room. She couldn't walk in a straight line. Kept drifting to the right. She'd consumed way too much champagne. She stumbled through the living area with her arms extended for balance and bumped into a side table, whacking her shin on hard wood. Eventually the pain registered.

"Ow!"

As she danced away from the offending piece of furniture, she stubbed her big toe on the sofa leg.

"Ow! Damn!" Tears of pain filled her eyes. She sat down heavily in a taupe over-stuffed chair, grabbing her smarting toe with both hands. Jessica sucked deep breaths through her teeth until the sharp pain faded to dull. Why did big toes have so many frickin' pain receptors anyway?

Comfy chair... She blinked slowly and leaned her head against the chair arm. She curled her legs under her for warmth and tugged her towel closer. *So sleepy... Sed... Please don't be mad at me... I'll find you... Sorry I hurt you... I do need you... Please, hold me... Don't leave me alone...*

Chapter 20

SED STALKED DOWN THE wide sidewalk, oblivious to the crowds milling along the Vegas strip. The throngs of people parted before him like the red sea. Apparently, his pissed-off aura preceded him and alerted them to get the fuck out of his way. He didn't even know where he was going. Back to the tour bus maybe. Or a bar. He could use a drink. And not that watered down shit they gave away at the casinos.

"Oh my God, it's Sedric Lionheart!" a feminine voice wailed.

Sed froze. He wasn't in the right state of mind to deal with rabid fans. He glanced around, looking for an escape route or a place to hide.

"It is him. Sed!" a voice said from the opposite direction. "Sed. Sed. Sed! I love you."

He spun on his heel, wincing at the large group of young women racing toward him. His only means of escape was the busy street beyond the sidewalk. He headed in that direction, but hesitated on the curb. Cars zoomed past.

Several bodies careened into him and he stumbled, one foot landing in the road. A car blared its horn as it swerved, barely missing him.

His fangirls wouldn't push him to his death, though. Several hands grabbed his T-shirt and pulled him back onto the sidewalk.

Fabric tore along his back. While he'd regained his balance, within seconds, he'd lost his shirt. Again. Why did they always have to rip his shirt off? Christ. There was a reason he kept his hair short and didn't wear jewelry. If they could grab it, they considered it fair game for their collections.

Hands, belonging to various females in the growing mob, touched, caressed, squeezed, poked, and prodded any bare skin they could get their hands on.

A few of the more bold ladies copped a feel of his ass beneath his jeans.

Another grabbed his crotch. "So that video wasn't enhanced," someone murmured into his ear from behind. "You are a monster."

He pulled a hand away, only to have it replaced with another. Camera flashes were going off all around him. The excited twitters of high-pitched voices made his head swim.

Normally, it didn't bother him to be fondled and groped by appreciative female fans, but he'd had enough of being used for one day. Jessica thought of him as a toy, and all these chicks just saw him as an object for their amusement.

No one gave a shit about him. Not the real him. He tried to be a good guy. To treat Jess right and she reminded him of how little he really meant to her? Fuck her. He didn't need her. He didn't need anyone.

"Back off!" he bellowed.

Everyone froze.

Hesitated a few seconds.

Continued their game of who can touch Sed in the most invasive manner.

"Sed!" a familiar masculine (thank you, God) voice called from just outside his circle of admirers.

An engine revved loudly and girls dashed aside as a Harley Davidson bumped over the curb and onto the sidewalk. The bike stopped next to Sed and its driver slid forward on the seat.

Jace. Bassist. Savior.

"Get on," Jace said, jerking his helmeted head toward the back of the bike.

Sed peeled his fangirls' leech-like hands from his body and climbed onto the motorcycle behind Jace.

"Can I have your autograph, please?" a young woman asked, her grip like iron on his wrist. "Please!"

"Some other time."

Sed tugged free of her hold. The motorcycle shot forward, hopped the curb and entered traffic. Several horns blared as Jace cut across three lanes.

"Man, you saved my life. Did you just happen to be driving past?"

"I saw the chaotic crowd of females. Figured it was you in the middle of it. Or Brad Pitt."

Sed chuckled. "I thought you were visiting Trey."

"Eric doesn't want me around." The bike rumbled loudly as Jace accelerated, whipping between cars in the heavy traffic. The guy was a maniac. Sed's heart raced after the first near fatality. By the third, he just wanted off the fuckin' bike.

"Hey, slow down. Shit, man, are you trying to kill us?"

"Just don't want to be seen riding with a half-naked dude on the back of my bike."

Sed laughed so hard he almost fell off the motorcycle. He wrapped his arms around Jace's waist, the cool, smooth leather of Jace's jacket against his bare chest. Sed rested his chin on Jace's shoulder. "Is this better, snookums?"

"Ack!" Jace scooted forward, but Sed tightened his arms to keep him from shifting onto the shiny red gas tank. "Get back."

Sed snorted. "Slow down and I'll let go."

Jace slowed and carefully moved to the lane closest to the sidewalk. As promised, Sed released him and scooted to the back of the seat. A moment later, they turned into the parking lot where the tour buses were still parked.

"Home sweet home," Sed murmured as Jace pulled to a stop next to the front bus.

"Did you want to go somewhere else?"

"In this outfit?" Sed climbed off the back of the bike and let himself into the empty bus. Jace followed.

Sed found a spare shirt in the bedroom that didn't smell like stale sweat. He donned it and returned to the common area.

Jace, who was seated at the dining table, watched Sed pass as if he wanted to talk. Rare for Jace. Better humor him.

Sed slid into the bench across from him.

"So what have you been up to lately?" Sed asked. "Haven't seen you around much. You're always taking off on your bike."

Jace shrugged, rubbing the small hoop earring in his lobe between his thumb and the side of his index finger. "Stuff."

"You're probably just sick of Eric harassing you all the time."

He shrugged again. "Eric's cool. He was here first."

"Eric can be real a douche bag, you know? Don't let him get to you."

"No, really, he's cool. You should cut him some slack."

"Me?"

"The dude idolizes you and you cut him down all the time. He just laughs it off, but..." Jace shrugged again.

The quiet ones always surprised him with their insight. Was he too hard on Eric? Sed scratched his forehead, scowling in thought. He did cut Eric down, but Eric needed that to keep him on an even keel. Didn't he? Yeah, as an outsider, Jace just didn't understand their dynamic.

And why did he just think of Jace as an outsider? He was a part of the band just like the other guys. Just because he'd only been with the band two years...

"Do we make you feel like an outsider?" Sed asked.

Jace dropped his gaze to the table. After a long moment, he said, "Not exactly."

"If there's anything I can do—"

"Where's your girlfriend?" he interrupted.

"I left her back at the hotel. She pissed me off." Actually, she'd hurt him, but it pissed him off that she could do it so easily.

"You want a ride back?"

Sed sighed, annoyed by his own weakness. He should just stay away from her. It would make things easier. He knew she'd lashed out at him because she was hurting. He wasn't sure how to take that hurt away, but he had to try. "Yeah, if you don't mind, but I need to do something first."

He pulled his lyrics journal from under the cushion of the bench seat and started to write. It would help to get these feelings out of his head, where they churned incessantly.

He labeled the page: "Used."

He then scrawled beneath the title, in barely legible script:

You don't see me.

Blind to the real me.

I'm not who you think I should be.

But I can't be someone I'm not.

He paused, chewing on the end of his pen.

I'll try to be who you need,

what you need,

I fail again

tear me, cut me, make me bleed

if it opens your heart to me.

Just don't leave me with nothing.

Less than nothing.

Like the last time.

Use me.

It's better than existing without you.

He closed the notebook and shoved it back under the seat.

"Are you writing lyrics?" In his enthusiasm, Jace looked younger than his twenty-four years. Brown eyes wide with eagerness, his typical cool veneer slipped aside for at least three seconds.

"Just a few lines as inspiration strikes." Sed slid out of the bench. "Are you ready to go?"

"Huh? Oh yeah. So do we have enough for an entire new song yet?"

"Several, actually. I've got most of the lyrics down, but I'll need Eric to get the arrangements worked out."

"Eric?"

"Fucking gifted with arrangements. He's got a golden ear. He can take a bunch of disjointed riffs, solos and lyrics, and like magic churn out a song, complete with one of his amazing drum tracks. Have you ever seen him compose?"

Wide-eyed, Jace shook his head and followed Sed off the bus.

"He and Jon Mallory used to work well together. They'd disappear for a weekend with a stack of music—Brian's guitar work, my lyrics—and return with fifteen or twenty new songs, ready for the recording studio. They wrote the entire last album that way. Not sure how he'll do now that Jon is gone." Sed scowled. That might turn out to be a problem, actually. It hadn't occurred to him until that moment. "Eric will just have to compose with me this time. And you."

"Me?" Jace sputtered. "I don't know a thing about writing music."

Sed laughed. "Me neither, but that won't stop me."

Jace grinned. "I'll try to stay out of Eric's way, but I would like to see him work."

Sed had never recognized it before, but Jace admired Eric. Even though Eric treated him like a kid and continually picked on him about his size. Weird.

Without warning, a blinding light hit Sed in the face and a microphone appeared under his chin. "Sed Lionheart, every music fan out there wants to know, is this the end of Sinners?" Bright flashbulbs went off all around him. Damned paparazzi. How did they know he was here?

Sed lifted a hand to block the glare from his eyes. "What?"

"With Trey Mills out of commission, will the band break up?" the reporter shouted.

"What? No. Trey will be fine. Jesus, give him a few days to recover before you start talking about the band breaking up."

"I see. And do you often engage in public sex with prostitutes and then post the videos online?"

"Prostitutes?" Sed was too stunned to do anything at first. His next instinct was to kick some ass. "Jessica isn't a prostitute, you asshole. She's... she's..." What was she to him exactly? He wasn't sure, but he did know what he wanted her to be. "She's my fiancée!" Sed tried to take a swing at the prick, but Jace grabbed him from behind and pinned his arms to his sides.

"Don't make this worse, Sed," Jace said. "Let's get out of here."

"If you write anything bad about her, I'll fucking kill you, do you hear me?" Sed yelled at the journalist as Jace forced him to move in the general direction of his motorcycle. Several roadies and the head of Sinners' security came out of the pigsty bus. They quickly diverted the journalist and gang of photographers so he and Jace could make their escape.

Jace climbed onto the Harley and started the ignition. It roared to life between his thighs. "Let's go."

Sed preferred to go kick that reporter's ass for referring to Jessica as a *prostitute*, but somehow he pulled it together enough to climb on the motorcycle behind Jace and not fall off as they sped away.

As the surge of testosterone and adrenaline in his blood stream began to wane, he realized he'd told the reporter that Jessica was his fiancée. That would fix a few things, wouldn't it? God, he hoped so.

"You okay back there?" Jace asked.

"Yeah. Just get me to the Bellagio."

They took some less-traveled road that ran parallel to the Vegas strip and Sed found himself standing behind the hotel within minutes. "Thanks for the ride. Are you going to go see Aggie again?"

"Maybe." Jace shrugged. He drove off before Sed could blink.

Sed had planned to ask Jace if he wanted to have a drink with him while he avoided returning to the hotel room. He wondered how pissed Jessica would be because he'd left without saying a word. If he had to guess, he'd go with excessively pissed. He stopped at a blackjack table on his way through the casino. Played a few hands. Drank one watered down Jack and Coke after another. He still wasn't ready to return to the room. He wasn't in the mood to get yelled at, and he wasn't nearly drunk enough to stop caring. By the time he was drunk enough, it was close to two a.m. He cashed in his chips, surprised to find he was a couple grand ahead, and took the elevator back to their floor.

He hesitated at the door. She'd probably left immediately after he had. The room would be empty. Lonely. He'd probably never see her again.

No sense in wasting a comfortable bed though. He didn't want to go back to the bus and sit there by himself. Or potentially get harassed by some stupid journalist again. He could go play a few more hands of cards. The dealers would keep him company.

Coward, a little voice inside his head accused. Yeah. So?

He took a deep breath, slid the keycard into the lock, and pushed the door open. The bathroom light and the lamp near the bed were still on. Together they gave off just enough light to reveal Jessica sleeping in the chair wearing nothing but a towel and a slack expression. Had she fallen asleep while waiting for him?

He put out the 'Do Not Disturb' sign, closed the door, engaged the dead bolt, and crossed the room to stand beside the chair. He watched her sleep for several moments. Her face was squashed against the chair arm and drool trickled from the corner of her mouth. Attractive? No, not really. Endearing? Completely.

He leaned forward and touched her bare shoulder. Her skin was cold as ice. How long had she been passed out in the chair?

"Jess, let me put you to bed."

She opened her eyes and grinned sleepily when she recognized him. "Sed," she murmured. "I was looking for you." Her words were slurred as she spoke.

He grinned. "In the chair?"

"I hurt my toe. Sorry." As if that explained anything.

"Why are you sorry?" he asked, scooping her into his arms and carrying her toward the bed.

"For calling you an amusing toy."

He grinned down at her as he carried her. An apology? Good enough for him. "I'm not amusing?"

"No." She shook her head and then giggled. "I mean, yes, you are amusing. You're not..." She sighed, her expression vacant. Her arms wrapped around his neck and she snuggled against him. "You know what I mean. I like you." She kissed his collarbone through his T-shirt. "I like you. You."

Well, it was a start. A far cry better than hate. "You, Ms. Chase, are very drunk."

"Yes I am," she agreed loudly and burst into delighted peals of laughter.

He grinned and laid her down across the bed. He tugged her towel loose and opened it, leaving her naked to his eager gaze.

"Whatchoo lookin' at, Sedric?" she said. Giggled. Snorted. Covered her mouth with her hand and laughed again.

"The most beautiful woman in existence."

He crawled up onto the bed and stretched out on his side beside her. He bent his elbow and rested his head on his hand, trailing the fingertips of his free hand over her belly. She shivered.

"Are you going to ravish me now, Mr. Lionheart?" she asked, her voice husky.

"Every inch of you," he murmured and kissed her shoulder tenderly. "It's about time!"

She giggled again, but her smile faded as his fingertips moved along the side of her belly to the protrusion of her hipbone. He stroked the ridge there—back and forth, back and forth, watching gooseflesh rise over her skin and her nipples harden with need. He leaned forward and kissed her waiting lips. She tasted of champagne and strawberries.

He enjoyed exploring every inch of her. He used his lips, his hands, fingernails, the smooth inner surface of his forearm, his teeth, his tongue, all the various textures of his body to stimulate her skin. He began with her forehead and worked his way down to the tips of her toes. She made no protest when he turned her onto her stomach and started the process again, moving up her body from the soles of her feet to the tender spot on the back of her neck.

He paused, noticing she'd stopped moving and sighing with pleasure. He brushed her hair back from her face and found her eyes were closed.

"Jess?" He shook her shoulder and she started, snorting as she regained consciousness. "You aren't into this, are you?"

"Feels so good I fell asleep," she murmured. "Tired."

"You never could hold your liquor."

He pulled back the covers and shifted her body over to the sheet. He covered her and tucked the blanket under her chin. She snuggled into the covers and immediately went slack. The least she could have done was use him for her amusement before she passed out in a drunken stupor. Well, there was only one thing to do when faced with this level of sexual frustration.

Sed stood, stripped off his T-shirt, and dropped to the floor.

Push-ups.

Chapter 21

THE NEXT MORNING, AFTER indulging in a vigorous naked yoga session to ease her mind and lure Sed between her thighs where he belonged, Jessica accompanied Sed to visit Trey in the hospital. Trey had been moved to a new room, but he wasn't taking it lying down. He was in a heated debate with a local physician who'd taken over his care.

"There is no reason for me to stay here," Trey told the physician. "The CT scan showed no swelling, no bleeding. I've already proven I can walk, use the bathroom, eat solid foods. What more do you want?" He crossed his arms over his chest. He had yet to notice them standing just inside the doorway, witnessing his tantrum; but Jessica doubted that would have altered his behavior.

"I want you to calm down, Mister Mills," the physician said in a heavy Indian accent. "It is still quite possible for your wound to reopen and cause more internal bleeding. This is a very serious condition for you to have. You must continue with your medical care for at least three more days. Absolute minimum."

"Three more days?" Trey banged his head back against his pillow. "I'll die of boredom by then. I'm fine. Why won't you believe me?" He thought for a moment, got an "aha" look on his face, and then reached for the cell phone resting on his bed tray. "I'm going to call my father. We'll see what he says."

Trey concentrated very hard on extending his index finger and poked several buttons before lifting the phone to his ear with an "I'll show you" expression.

Jessica grinned to herself. The guy was totally endearing. Like the little brother everyone wanted, but was glad they didn't have.

While Trey was manipulating his father on the phone, he noticed Jessica and Sed in the doorway. He smiled brightly and waved them into the room.

The doctor turned toward them, looking frazzled and flustered. "I hope you have come to talk some sense into your friend."

"He didn't have any sense to start with," Sed said in his rumbling baritone.

"I heard that, Lionheart," Trey said. Looking all gloaty, he said into his phone, "Yeah, okay, Dad. Whatever it takes to get me out of this place. The doctors here are quacks."

His physician shook his head and left the room.

Jessica couldn't believe how great Trey looked. His color was back. That spark of orneriness had returned to his emerald eyes. If it weren't for the staples in the side of his head and the awkward way he held his hands, she could almost imagine he'd never been injured at all.

"So is your dad going to get you out of here?" Sed asked, sinking into the chair next to Trey's bed. He tugged Jessica down to sit on his knee.

"Yeah. Thank God."

"You look better today," Jessica said. "How are you feeling?"

"Not bad. My head is sore."

"You've always been a sorehead," Sed quipped.

"Fuck you."

"See what I mean?" Sed chuckled. "How are your hands?"

Jessica elbowed Sed in the ribs.

Trey tucked his hands under the covers self-consciously, his smile fading into a scowl. "They're getting better, I think."

"That's good. We need to get back on the road as soon as possible."

Jessica elbowed Sed in the ribs again. The man was so oblivious of his insensitivity at times.

Sed scrunched his brows together. "What?"

She ignored him. She didn't want to make Trey feel worse by spelling out Sed's stupidity.

"Are you going to stay with your parents while you recover?" Jessica asked, hoping to change the subject.

Trey wrinkled his nose. "It's the only way I could get Dad to agree to get me out of here. At least they have a pool."

"I guess we can work in the studio while we're waiting for you to get better," Sed said, off in his own little future-planning world. "We can probably get everything recorded in a couple of weeks. Except your parts, Trey. Unless you want Brian to record the rhythm guitar sections for you."

Trey looked like someone had ripped his still-beating heart from his chest, tossed it on the linoleum, and stomped on it.

"He doesn't mean that, Trey." Jessica climbed off Sed's knee and grabbed his nipple, twisting and pulling hard to coax him to his feet.

"Ouch! Jesus Christ, woman. What are you doing?" Sed protested as he rose from the chair.

"I need to speak to you in the hall for a moment," she said between clenched teeth. "Now!" She released his nipple and stalked toward the door.

"What did I do?" Sed asked, trailing after her.

When they were out of earshot of Trey's open door, she turned to confront him. "How can you be so callous, Sed? Did you see the look on his face?"

Sed's expression read clueless. "Huh?"

"Trey, you idiot. You hurt him. He's been conscious for a day and you already have Brian taking over his work as rhythm guitarist on the new album. What are you thinking?"

"I didn't mean permanently. Just for the recording."

"The album will wait until he's better."

"So we're just supposed to sit around and twiddle our thumbs while he recovers? We can't tour without him." He got a reflective look on his face. "Unless we can find someone to fill in for him."

Jessica punched him in the chest. "I can*not* believe you just said that!"

"It's nothing personal against Trey. If we stop now, we'll lose our momentum. We're finally where we want to be as a band, and wham, this happens."

She knew she couldn't talk down his drive to succeed, so she changed tactics. "Do you really think Brian will agree to play without Trey? You know they work as a unit. Are you going to replace Brian, too?"

He sighed loudly. "I'm sorry I hurt him. I'm just worried. A lot of people depend on us for a paycheck, you know?"

So he wasn't just thinking of himself as she'd first suspected. Now she felt bad for yelling at him. "It will work out. I guarantee it."

He grinned. "Can I get that in writing?"

"Sure. Why not?"

He lifted his shirt, revealing red marks around his left nipple. "And I think you owe this guy an apology."

She rolled her eyes at him and walked towards Trey's room.

"Jessica," he called. "Can I book an appointment for make-up sex in two hours?"

Several people walking the corridor stopped to gawk at them.

She paused and glanced over her shoulder at him, her eyebrows drawn together in an angry scowl. "Sedric!"

"What?" He shrugged and started after her.

"You don't need an appointment."

He laughed and wrapped his arms around her waist as he careened into her. He lifted her feet off the ground and carried her into Trey's room. They found him in a frustrated rage, repeatedly smashing his under-responsive hand with the television remote control.

Chapter 22

JESSICA GLANCED UP FROM the computer screen at Brian. Myrna had just dumped a huge backlog of data on her lap and Jessica was eagerly entering it, ready to prove she was worth her inflated salary.

"Where's Sed?" Brian asked. "We're supposed to be leaving for L.A. right now."

Trey had left with his parents in their BMW the day before. The other tour bus and equipment truck were already on the road. As soon as Sed turned up, they could leave too.

"He said he had to go do something real quick. I thought he'd be back by now."

"He didn't tell you where he was going?"

Jessica shook her head. "I'm not his lord and master."

"Heh. Could've fooled me." Brian rolled his eyes and started to walk away, but Jessica grabbed his arm.

"Honestly, Brian, I don't understand why you have such a problem with me. You didn't used to be so hurtful."

"Maybe it has something to do with what you did to Sed."

"What I did to Sed? What exactly do you think I did to him?"

"You destroyed him when you left him for no reason."

"No reason? You have no idea why I left him, do you?"

"He told us all about it. You left because he couldn't afford to put you through law school."

Jessica's jaw dropped.

"You're just a gold-digging—"

"That's what he told you?" she sputtered.

"Are you going to deny it?"

Brian thought she was a gold-digger like her mother? Like her *mother*? Jessica couldn't breathe, much less speak in her own defense.

"That's what I thought." He jerked his arm out of her grasp and headed toward the bathroom.

"No! That's not why I left." She stood and trailed after him. Brian paused outside the bathroom door. "I left because he said he wouldn't marry me if I went to law school. *I* was paying for it, but he forbade me to go. That's why I left. I didn't want him to control my life. He had no right to make me choose between what I love and who I love."

Brian turned and stared at her reflectively until she began to fidget under his intense brown-eyed gaze. "Now that, I believe. He did the exact same thing to Eric twelve years ago."

"Not the exact same thing," Eric said from his bunk, where he was lounging reading a titty magazine. "I could have left the band. Switching to drums wasn't so bad. I like them." He scratched behind his ear. "I mean, *now* I do. Back then? Not so much."

"Sed thinks he knows what's best for everyone," Brian said.

"The infuriating thing is, he usually does," Eric said.

"Sorry I judged you so harshly, Jessica," Brian said. "I'm glad you stood up to him. I'm not sure why you're giving him this second chance. He probably doesn't deserve it. But he'll change for you. Do anything to make things right. He loves you that much."

Sed *loved* her? She didn't believe that. Maybe he loved the way she looked. Or the way she gave his body pleasure and took pleasure from his. But who she was on the inside? She doubted he could pick her out in a police lineup if it came to identifying her by who she really was.

"Go!" Sed's voice boomed outside the bus.

"I don't want to." There was something familiar about that whiny female voice. Jessica was sure she'd heard it in a recent nightmare.

"Either you go inside and do it or you can do it in front of everyone out here in the parking lot."

Jessica's brow furrowed. He'd gone to pick up some groupie? What exactly was he forcing the poor woman to do? Jessica started toward the bus steps to intervene.

"Fine." The young woman trudged up the stairs with Sed behind her.

Jessica paused in mid-step the instant she recognized Sed's companion. It was the attendant from the Eiffel Tower. What was he thinking, bringing the little video-taping bitch here? Did he want her murder on his hands? Jessica was definitely ready to commit the crime.

"Go ahead," Sed prompted.

"I'm sorry," she mumbled at Jessica's feet.

"I don't think she heard you," Sed said. "And look at her when you say it."

The girl lifted her head. Her face was streaked with tears. "I'm sorry, okay. I'm sorry. I only did it because I was jealous. Because I want him. And all he wants is you. All he ever wants is you. You don't deserve him." Her hands clenched into fists. "But I am sorry I recorded that video. And I am sorry I posted it. I'm sorry because he'll always think of me as the bitch who hurt you. I really wish you would drop dead, you fucking whore."

Well, that was the worst apology Jessica had ever received, but it was an apology. She lifted her gaze to Sed. He looked entirely perplexed by his fangirl's tirade.

"You hunted her down and brought her here to apologize to me?" Jessica asked.

"She wasn't supposed to say it like that." He nudged the girl on the shoulder. "You weren't supposed to say it like that. We rehearsed—"

The young woman covered her face with both hands, her body quaking with sobs. "Don't make me say it again. Please."

Sed nudged her again. "Hey, you promised me."

"It's okay, Sed," Jessica said. "She doesn't have to apologize if she doesn't want to. I'm satisfied knowing I have something she wants but will never have. She'll always wonder if things might have turned out differently if she hadn't been such a vindictive little bitch."

"I was picturing more groveling and begging for your forgiveness, but if you're satisfied..." Sed shrugged. He took the girl by the elbow and led her toward the exit. "Out you go."

"Wait, Sed. Please, don't hate me. I can't stand thinking that you hate me. Please, Sed. Please. I'm so sorry." The young woman continued to wail all the way down the stairs.

"That's the kind of apology you owe Jessica, not me."

But Jessica didn't need the girl's apology. Sed had gone out of his way to try to make her feel better. It was a truly nice thing for him to do. She was touched despite herself.

"His methods are completely unorthodox," Myrna said, "but you know he means well, don't you?"

Jessica smiled and nodded. He was trying to fix things. It was what he did.

Sed slammed the door. "Let's go, Dave," he shouted, "before she tries to cling to the side of the bus."

Dave started the bus and eased forward, while Sed peered anxiously out a tinted window.

Jessica stepped behind him and wrapped her arms around his waist. "Thank you."

He glanced over his shoulder to look at her. "I thought maybe if she apologized, you'd feel better. I mean, I know it doesn't fix much, but—"

She lifted her hand to cover his lips. "It helped. I do feel better."

Both dimples showed as he grinned against her fingertips. "Then it was worth Brian's favorite guitar."

"What?" Brian bellowed. "You gave her my guitar?"

Sed laughed. "Kidding." He turned to face Jessica, his expression turning serious. "You're going to stay with me in L.A., aren't you?"

She hadn't really considered what she'd do once they got back to L.A. "Are you sure the guys won't mind?"

He glanced at his band mates in confusion. "Why would they care?"

"It's pretty crowded, isn't it?"

"Why would it be crowded?"

"The loft over that dry-cleaning business isn't very big."

"Oh God, you don't really think we all still live there, do you? That was unbearable. I have a condo on the beach now."

"Nice," she murmured. He'd managed to become rich since the last time they'd shared living quarters. She scowled at the thought. "I could stay with my parents." Her scowl deepened. Beth, who stayed with her family in the summer, wouldn't be back in town yet, and Myrna hadn't paid Jessica yet, so her options were limited.

"You don't want to stay with me?" Sed asked.

"I don't want to be a pest. Or a mooch."

"You wouldn't be a pest or a mooch. I want you to stay with me." He lowered his head to whisper in her ear. "Lots of privacy plus plenty of space equals loads of sensational sex."

She grinned. "Well, if that's what you have in mind, I'll have to say yes, I'd like to stay with you in L.A. Well, until Trey recovers and we go back on tour."

Staying at Sed's apartment was just temporary, so that didn't mean they were living together. Right? Yeah. Temporary. She added rent money to the growing tab she owed him.

"Excellent." He hugged her and kissed the top of her head. "I can't wait until you see the place. You'll love it."

"Don't get the wrong idea, Sed. This isn't going to change our relationship. It doesn't mean we're serious."

"Being engaged isn't serious?" Jace asked.

Jessica turned to look at him. "What are you talking about?"

Jace glanced at Sed and then lowered his gaze to the floor. "Never mind."

"Why would you think we're engaged, Jace?"

"Sed told that journalist—"

Sed grunted in warning.

"Nothing," Jace said.

"What journalist?" Jessica looked up at Sed. "What did you do, Sed? You didn't lie about our relationship, did you?"

"I didn't mean to, it just popped out. I couldn't let him think that you were really a prostitute."

"A prostitute? Someone thought I was a prostitute?"

"Yeah, I fixed it though. I told him you were my fiancée to protect you."

"You told him *what*?"

"You're yelling."

"Of course I'm yelling! You lied about something that seriously affects my life. This story will get around and people will believe it, no matter how ridiculous it is."

"Ridiculous?"

"How could you tell him I was your fiancée? Like I'd ever consider marrying you."

"Well, what did you want me to say, Jessica, that you're just some chick I like to bang? That you're nothing more to me than a good lay? That would have done nothing to fix your reputation."

"And who destroyed it in the first place? Oh, that's right. You did." Jessica grabbed a stack of data sheets and the laptop from the dining table. She tucked it all under one arm. "I can't work with that idiot around," she said to Myrna, who raised both brows at her but said nothing. "Email me if you need anything." Jessica stomped up the corridor. "Stop the bus!" she yelled.

Dave slammed on the brakes. Jessica grabbed the pole beside the driver's seat so she didn't fall on her face.

"Jesus, don't scare me like that," Dave muttered.

Jessica slung her purse over her shoulder and headed for the exit. "Let me out," she growled at Dave.

He scrambled to obey her and the bus door swung open.

Sed followed her down the steps. "Where are you going? I thought you were staying with me until we go back on tour."

She was so pissed she couldn't see straight. "I would rather... I would rather... stay at my *mother's* house." Which was about the worst thing she could think of. She stalked off toward the Mandalay Bay parking garage and her piece of shit Nissan Sentra still parked there.

"Jessica?" Sed called after her.

"I am sick of you fucking up my life, Sed! Give me a call when the band goes back on tour. Until then I don't want to hear from you or see you or even know you're alive."

"Yeah? Well, next time someone calls you a prostitute, I won't correct them," he yelled.

"That's better than the world thinking I'm engaged to a self-centered son-of-a-bitch like you."

―⁓―

Sed watched Jessica walk away with his heart lodged in his throat. Was there anything worse than watching her leave him? No. He headed after her, but Myrna grabbed his arm.

"Let her go," she said.

He shook his head vigorously. "I can't."

"You have to, Sed. She needs to figure out who you are. Why you do the things you do. She doesn't get it. She thinks you're trying to control her life. Until she figures out that's not your intention, you're just going to drive her crazy. Give her time to understand *why* you did what you did. A few minutes to miss you, sweetie." She patted his cheek sympathetically. "She will, you know."

"But she's *leaving*." He pointed a hand at Jessica's shrinking figure as if that explained all his inner turmoil. "She'll be back. She said to call her when the band goes back on tour. If she really never wanted to see you again, she wouldn't have given herself that out."

"That's just her need for money talking."

Myrna snorted. "I can't believe you think that. I give her three days—tops—before she's on your doorstep wanting you back. Just trust me on this, okay? I know you love her. That's why you try so hard to fix things for her. She hasn't figured that out, yet. You've got the poor girl so confused she's never going to see it. And no matter how much you want to, you can't *make* her see it. She has to figure it out on her own."

Jessica disappeared from view, taking the heart previously lodged in Sed's throat with her.

"Promise you won't go after her, Sed. That you'll be patient. Give her a couple of days to catch her breath."

"I'll try."

"Sed?" Myrna said reproachfully.

"Fine. Whatever. Psychologist knows best."

Before the bus even merged onto the highway, Sed had already thought of three reasons he needed to contact Jessica as soon as they reached L.A. She'd left her suitcase on the bus. She had left several piles of Myrna's data behind. And he missed her. Already.

Chapter 23

STARING AT THE INNOCUOUS cadet-blue bungalow, Jessica sat in her mother's driveway filled with dread. She couldn't do this. Could not stay in that house. Sure, her mother was a pain in the ass and made her crazy with the constant harping, but her stepfather, Ed... Just thinking about him made her skin crawl.

A five-hour drive, mostly through the Mojave Desert, had done a lot to put things into perspective. It was astonishing how much better her brain worked when a certain man wasn't stirring her emotions like a blender on liquefy. She felt kind of bad for going off on Sed just because he'd reacted badly to the press. In the same situation, she wasn't sure what she would have said. She definitely wouldn't have claimed to be his fiancée. More likely, she'd have gotten physically violent. In his stupid, macho way, Sed had been trying to make things better. He hadn't succeeded. Not by a long shot. But it had been his intention. Sometimes that was more important than the outcome. Wasn't it? She didn't know.

Jessica pulled her cell phone out of her pocket and stared at it for a good ten minutes before dialing Sed's number.

"Jessica?" Sed answered breathlessly.

"Hi."

"Hi."

Silence for a long minute.

"Did you need something?" he asked finally.

She glanced up at her mother's house and then at the dashboard. "A place to stay," she said in a mousy squeak.

Another long silence. "Do you want to stay with me?"

She nodded, her chest tight. Why did she feel like crying?

"Jessica?"

She realized he hadn't heard the marbles rattling around in her head when she'd nodded. "Yes. If you don't mind."

"I don't mind."

"I'm sorry I went off on you in Vegas. I know you were just trying to fix things."

"Sometimes I say some pretty stupid shit."

"Sometimes?" She laughed. It felt good. She didn't understand why it bothered her so much to fight with him. She didn't like the idea that she had started to care about him again in such a short time. Or maybe she'd never stopped caring. She didn't know. She just wanted to be with him. Even if that meant she had to swallow her pride, call him, and ask for a place to stay. *Stupid, Jessica. So stupid.*

"Do you know where I live? Or do you want me to pick you up?"

"Give me your address. I'll find it."

While she was writing his address on a receipt she'd found in her purse, the front door opened and Ed stepped out on the porch. His bulbous eyes brightened when he noticed her sitting in the driveway. She lodged the phone between the side of her head and her shoulder, put the car in reverse, and headed back to Sed. The lesser of two evils, she told herself, which in no way explained the buoyancy in her heart.

Chapter 24

SED OPENED THE FRONT door to his condominium and there stood Jessica on his threshold. Myrna had given Jessica three days and she hadn't lasted six hours. He forced himself not to gloat. She cared. She did, or she wouldn't be there. He would pretend like he hadn't been in his car on his way to her mother's house when she'd called.

"Come in," he said, beckoning Jessica inside. She glanced around as she entered, carrying one of the bags from her car. Her eyes opened wide in disbelief.

"This place is huge!" Her voice echoed slightly in the two-story foyer.

"I got a great deal on it. It was in foreclosure. I paid about half what it's really worth."

She continued into the condo, glancing around at the tasteful decor. Most of his furniture was white, the pillows, rugs, accent pieces, and artwork red and black. "I assume you hired a decorator."

He scratched his head. Not exactly. Tanya had taken her payment in sexual favors. Over a week's worth of them. But that had been a year ago. "Uh… A friend took care of it for me."

Jessica gave him a reproachful look, but didn't press for details. "Where's the guest room?"

Yeah, like he was going to put her in there. "My bedroom is up on the second floor."

She followed him up the cast-iron spiral staircase to the second floor. There was an open loft area at the top of the stairs—his man cave and entertainment mecca. Massaging recliners, home theater, stereo, video games, dartboard, pool table, wet bar, and, through a set of French doors, an enormous rooftop balcony complete with hot tub, BBQ pit, and a spectacular view of the ocean.

Jessica glanced around, her mouth still agape. "This is a bachelor's wet dream."

"You don't like it?"

"It's wonderful, Sed. How do you stand living on the tour bus when you have this waiting for you at home?"

"You know I love to be on tour. I live for it. But if I can't be on the road, this keeps me entertained for a couple of days." He took her bag from her and tossed it over his shoulder before grasping her hand. "Let me show you the bedroom." He wanted some make-up sex. Like, immediately.

He led her through the expansive loft area to a set of white double doors along the far wall. He pushed the handle down and the door swung open. Jessica's breath caught. The furniture was all heavy and mahogany, except for the small love seat in the corner of the room, which was upholstered in cream-colored fabric. His king-sized four-poster bed dominated the room. The thick navy and chocolate brown bedding looked inviting, but Sed had no plans to take a nap.

Jessica walked around the bed and gazed at the fireplace. He'd never understood why he needed a fireplace in Southern California, but Tanya had insisted upon it. And when Jessica knelt on the thick rug and leaned toward it for a closer inspection, he sent a silent word of thanks to the insatiable interior decorator.

"Careful." He reached for a remote on the dresser. "I'll turn it on."

She started when the autopilot lit the gas logs in the grate.

"Cool." She sat back on her heels. "I've never had a fireplace before, but I've always wanted one. It's kind of competing with the air conditioning, though."

Like he cared. He set her bag on the floor and the remote on the dresser. He crossed the room and sat beside her on the rug. It had thick padding beneath it and was softer than most beds he'd slept on. Perfect for… "Do you want to make love?" he asked, gazing into her jade-green eyes. The light of the fire made her skin glow like honey.

"Do you?"

He shrugged. "Not really." He leaned closer and kissed her hungrily.

She tugged his T-shirt off over his head, interrupting their kiss, and placed her small, warm hands on his chest, exploring his eager skin with her palms. "Me neither," she murmured, and lowered her head to kiss his neck. "But we can make *out* for a couple of hours."

"You read my mind."

For once, they had all the time in the world to enjoy each other. No worries. No interruptions. Complete privacy. Sed leaned back into the soft rug and closed his eyes, allowing her to kiss, stroke, and suckle his bare skin as much as she wanted. Attentive to every inch of his torso, Jessica couldn't seem to get enough of touching him. He couldn't tell which of them was enjoying it more. When she urged him to turn over and lie on his stomach, he knew their hours of making out would soon end with frenzied sex. She knew what touching his back did to him.

She gently scratched every inch of his back. Every muscle of his body went taut with excitement. His nipples hardened into tight beads. He rubbed his chest against the soft faux fur of the rug, trying to calm himself down. No good.

"You're so tense, baby," she whispered, kissing his shoulder.

Tense? He'd show her tense, but before he could drag her beneath him, she straddled his thighs and began to knead the muscles of his back with a firm, but gentle, massage. She soon had worked him over from shoulders to lower back, turning him into a puddle of flesh, his muscles like melted butter. His dick, squashed beneath him, protested its neglect by throbbing incessantly. God, he was hard, but her hands felt so good he didn't want her to stop.

She leaned over him, her long hair tickling the skin along his spine. She kissed and suckled paths over his back. He twitched and groaned, unsure how much more he could take.

When she'd kissed her way to his neck, she whispered into his ear, "Do you want to make love?"

He rolled over and tugged her on top of him, seeking her mouth for a feverish kiss. His hands moved to her ass, pressing her pelvis against his so she could feel for herself exactly how much he wanted to make love.

She broke the kiss and looked down at him, grinning. "Is that an anaconda in your pocket or are you just happy to see me?"

"Why don't you check it out?"

She slid down his body and reached for his belt. "If this turns out to be a big, thick snake, I'm going to be very upset."

She freed his cock from its confines and planted a gentle kiss on its head. It twitched, desiring more rigorous attention. She wrapped a hand around its base and sucked the rest into her mouth. Her hand gently stroked upward while her mouth moved down to meet her hand. When the head of his cock lodged in the back of her throat, she swallowed.

His breath caught.

She pulled her head back, her hand sliding down at the same time. It felt strange to have his cock worked in two directions at once. Strange and wonderful. He tried to keep his body still and his gasps of delight at a minimum as she continued to work him in the same maddening fashion. He didn't want her to realize how close he was to letting go. He wanted his cum in her mouth. Wanted her to swallow it.

His lack of obvious enthusiasm spurred her competitive spirit and she stroked him faster, sucked him harder, swallowed him deeper.

Eyes squeezed shut, he bit his knuckles and held onto the rug with his free hand. He couldn't stop the involuntary arch in his spine though. She jerked his pants down his thighs and her free hand moved to gently massage his balls, while her mouth and hand moved together, separated, moved together again over his cock.

It built, the need to flood her mouth with his seed.

He lifted his head and pried his eyes open to watch her suck him. *Ah God!*

It burst. He dropped his head back on the floor as a hard spasm gripped the base of his cock. Jessica gasped in surprise as his first spurt filled her mouth. She swallowed and sucked harder, accepting more of him, drawing his offering deep into her throat. Even after he'd completely spent himself, she continued to suck him to prolong his pleasure until he couldn't take any more.

"Ah Jess, stop, please."

"Uh-uhn," she murmured, shaking her head slightly, his cock still in her mouth.

He shuddered, slowly growing softer and softer in her mouth. Pausing only to remove their clothes, she didn't relent until she had him rock hard again. When she released him from her mouth, he opened his eyes, but his vision was so blurred he had to close them again. She crouched over him, her feet planted near his hips, and sank down, taking him into her dripping wet pussy.

"Sit up," she urged.

Still in a stupor of spent desire, he forced himself upright, resting his weight on his hands to hold himself in a seated position. She held onto his shoulders as she lifted up, rocking onto her toes, and then drove down onto him hard.

"I need it. I'm so hot, Sed."

He could feel her molten heat and her juices dripping down to bathe his crotch. "Take it."

She took it. Lifting up and plunging down on him so hard it had to hurt her tender flesh, but she was relentless. As she slid up, she twisted her hips and then slammed down on him again, rotating her pelvis to drive him deeper, deeper. She continued as such until her legs gave way and she had to drop to one knee. She leaned to one side and drove her body down on his at an angle. "Take it, Jess. All of it."

She rode him harder, faster, until her other leg lost its strength and she had to ride him while perched on both knees. She worked her internal muscles then, squeezing as she drew upward. Damn, if she didn't stop that, she'd make him come again, and he knew she'd yet to let go. He opened his eyes to watch her. She looked half frustrated, half exasperated and her energy was quickly waning.

He wrapped his arms around her and flipped her over onto her back. She gasped in surprise.

"You need it hard and deep?"

She nodded miserably. He pulled out.

"No," she protested.

He picked her up off the floor and carried her to the bed. He pulled her to the mattress's edge and opened her legs wide. His gaze settled on the beauty of her feminine folds. Open to him like silky flower petals. Inviting. The flesh swollen, flushed, and slick. He lowered his head and lapped at her juices. So sweet. And her smell? Damn.

He grabbed his cock in one hand, attempting to calm himself as he relished her taste, her scent, her warmth. He plunged his tongue into her tight hole and she moaned in torment.

"Sed," she gasped, her fingers digging into his scalp. The sound of his name on her lips sent ripples of pleasure down his spine. "Sed, I want you. Inside. Please." Her fingers moved between her legs and she stroked her clit, trembling with unfulfilled desire. He leaned away to watch her rub herself. She worked that tiny bud of flesh with two fingers, grinding it in a circular motion, up and down, back and forth. Circles again. Her hips moved with her fingers. "Mmm. Mmm. Mmm," she panted as she sought release.

He stroked his cock as he watched her, not wanting to interrupt her attempt to get off because it was so fucking sexy to watch. She shuddered and rubbed faster, harder, her back arching off the bed. Her pussy was so swollen, so hot, so wet, so ridiculously empty.

Sed stood, grabbed her hips in both hands, and plunged into her. Her back arched until only her shoulders touched the mattress.

"Oh God, Sed. Yes," she cried. "Fuck it hard."

His fingers dug into her ass to hold her still so he could pound into her.

"Yes," she screamed. "Yes. Yes. Yes!"

He fucked her harder. Harder. She pulled her hand away from her clit and her body quaked as she finally found that elusive orgasm. He thrust into her harder. Yes, harder. *Take it, Jess. Feel it inside you. I'm part of you. Part of you. Feel it.* She strained against him as he continued to thrust into her like a man possessed. As her tremors began to subside, he reached between their bodies and stroked her clit, mimicking the technique he'd watched her use. Her pussy convulsed around his cock with renewed excitement. When she whimpered from overstimulation, he urged her onto her side without breaking the connection between their bodies and found a steady rhythm inside her.

He stroked her full breast with one hand, her smooth back with the other. She trembled before him, her eyes closed, lips parted, head tilted back with mindless pleasure. He wondered how many times he could make her come before he let himself find release again. He did love a good competition, even if it was with himself.

Still resting on her side, she moved her knees together, making herself delightfully tight inside. But this wasn't for his delight, it was for hers. He eased her top leg up over his arm to open her wide. He thrust deep and gyrated his hips to stretch her in multiple directions.

"Oh," she gasped.

He concentrated on his motions, withdrawing until but an inch was inside her and then thrust steady and deep before gyrating, gyrating, gyrating and withdrawing again.

"That feels wonderful, baby," she whispered.

He repeated this motion countless times, slowly and methodically exciting her to the brink of insanity. She met his deep thrusts now, gyrated her hips with his, whimpered when he withdrew, gasped when he thrust deep. Giving her a vaginal orgasm took a lot of work and concentration. He knew she'd sputter with release if he so much as tapped her clit, so he was incredibly careful to keep her pleasure focused inside. Finally, her hips buckled. "Sed, Sed, what's happening?"

"Bear down on my cock, baby. Try to push me out."

Every muscle inside her contracted around his cock as she tried to force it from her body. She gasped in surprise, involuntary spasms rocking her core. He felt her orgasm throughout his entire cock. "Oh my God, Sed. Oh. Oh." Her vocalizations grew increasingly high pitched and louder as she came. He thrust in and out slowly, prolonging her pleasure, until her entire body writhed involuntarily.

"What was that?" she murmured, in a stupor. "I've never felt anything like it."

"That was two."

"Two?"

He pulled out and rolled her onto her belly, before urging her up onto her knees. "Are you ready for three?"

He joined her on the bed, kneeling behind her between her knees.

"Three what?"

He answered her by surging forward and filling her again. Her arms trembled and she lowered her upper body to the bed. He grabbed a handful of her hair and jerked her body back upward.

She cried out, a sound of mixed pain and pleasure. He hesitated. Had he gone too far?

"Don't stop. Pull my hair. Hurt me, Sed."

He yanked her hair again, even harder this time. Her neck jerked back at a vicious angle.

She laughed huskily. "Yeah, now fuck your dirty bitch like a dog. Fuck her good and hard like she wants it."

He almost came right then. She didn't give him time to collect his wits. She rocked forward and back, urging him into motion. He met her strokes, thrusting hard, pulling her hair with each penetration. He leaned forward and grabbed the globe of her breast in his free hand, pinching her nipple hard between his thumb and the side of his index finger, rolling it back and forth and then soothing the ache by massaging with the palm of his hand.

"Yes," she gasped.

He ran his hand from her breast down to her clit, pinching it between thumb and fingertips, stroking it front and back. He thrust his cock into her with the same rhythm and tugged on her hair. She sputtered as she came for the third time. He released her hair and she collapsed onto her face, still shuddering in the aftermath of her quick and dirty release. He pulled out and pushed her down flat on her stomach. He slid her body forward across the smooth chocolate-brown comforter until she spilled over the edge of the bed.

"What are you doing?" she asked, catching her fall with her hands on the floor.

"Preparing you for number four."

"Number four?"

He entered her from behind again, his hands on her thighs to keep her from falling off the bed. Keeping her hanging upside down over the edge of the bed without sending her toppling to the floor took extreme concentration, but he loved rubbing his balls against her clit with each penetration. She held still, just taking him. Taking him. Allowing him inside her body. Accepting his possession. His domination.

His balls tightened. Not yet, he thought.

He refused to let go until he made her come ten times. Ten times in a row. He had to hold back. He buried himself deep and held still, rocking slightly, letting the spasms of pleasure take him, but squeezing the muscles at the base of his cock as his seed tried to erupt in spurts. No, not yet. Not yet. Ungh.

Jessica held perfectly still, letting him regain control. When he'd forced it back, he began to move inside her again.

"I think I'm going to pass out," Jessica said. "I'm getting dizzy."

"Then you better come quick."

"Sing to me."

He grinned, grinding his balls against her again before withdrawing. "Do you have a request?"

"Something romantic."

"Then nothing Sinners," he said, laughing. He continued to possess her with a consistent and relentless tempo.

"'G-good-bye Is Not Forever' is…oh, oh, I'm getting close again. Harder, Sed."

"Nope. This is all you get." He sang to her though as he kept the same slow pace, his balls rubbing her clit, his cock filling her deep.

"*Tomorrow was my second chance to make things right but it never came. I'm sorry I never treasured the time we had for those regrets I take the blame. You gave everything you had. I took without giving back.*" Sed paused in his song, feeling ridiculous for singing it to her while they made love. "Baby, you realize this song is about Trey's dead dog, don't you?"

"I don't care. Sing it. I'm so close. I can picture you up on stage. You're so hot when you command an audience of ten thousand."

"Fifteen thousand," he corrected.

"Yeah. Don't stop singing. Sing something else if you'd like."

Actually, he'd written a song just for her a couple of years ago. Dare he put his heart on the line and sing it to her now? Why not? "*When I first realized that—*"

"Oh Sed, put your finger in my ass, please. I feel so empty there."

"If I let go of your legs, you'll fall on your head."

She shifted, supporting her entire weight on one hand so she could rub her finger over her anus in a circular motion. "Ungh, I'm gonna come. I'm gonna…" He watched her slide her finger deep inside her back entrance and almost followed her into orgasm as she cried out. She thrust her finger in and out of her ass while her pussy clenched around his cock.

"Damn that's sexy, baby. Does it feel good?"

Her answer was a hoarse cry. She wriggled her finger inside until she stopped shuddering and then pulled it out, redistributing her weight on both hands again. He eased out of her body and she did a somersault off the bed, landing gracefully on her back on the carpeted floor.

He climbed from the bed and tumbled her beneath him, kissing her skin tenderly from her lips to her breast. He drew her nipple into his mouth and sucked gently. She sighed, her fingers stroking his hair.

He loved her so much. Was she ready to hear it yet? He feared she'd leave if he brought it up.

"I'm completely satisfied," she murmured. "You can let go inside me."

He lifted his head to look down at her. "You sure?"

She nodded and spread her legs for him. He slid inside her again with no intention of letting go. This one would make five. She had six more orgasms to go. She worked him as he thrust into her, using those amazing muscles inside her body that thrilled his cock like nothing else. She succumbed to the maddening delight first, however, and shuddered beneath him sometime later.

"You're still holding back?" she whispered, her eyelids heavy with spent desire.

"I'm not trying to," he lied. "Let's try the love seat."

He bent her over the back of the piece of furniture and thrust his fingers into her ass as he pounded his cock into her pussy. She didn't last five minutes that way. As her sixth orgasm rippled through her, Sed grinned to himself. God, he loved this woman.

"You still didn't come?" she gasped, as he led her out of the bedroom and into the loft.

"Maybe with you on top." He settled into his wide and comfortable recliner and she climbed on his lap. She turned on the chair's vibration, which felt wonderful on his tired muscles. Fucking her properly was hard work, but the rewards were well worth the effort. She sank down on his cock.

He'd never felt her work so hard at pleasing him. Her pussy tugged at him relentlessly as she concentrated on making him come. Since she was in charge, he could lean back and count backwards from a thousand. He kept losing his place and gasping in bliss. The woman was determined to succeed. He slid a hand between their bodies and stroked her clit while she rose and fell.

"You're going to make me come again," she complained.

"We should come together," he murmured.

"Yeah," she agreed. "You'll know when."

But when she shuddered with release, he still held back.

"I don't understand," she whispered, almost in tears. "Doesn't it feel good, Sed? Don't you like it?"

He hadn't meant to upset her. "That was seven," he told her, stroking her hair from her face. "You get ten before I get one."

"Don't be ridiculous. I'm exhausted."

"Then just lie there."

"Where?"

"On the pool table."

He used his fingers and mouth to drive her to her eighth orgasm as she writhed on the green felt of his pool table. He then led her out onto the balcony.

"Someone will see," she protested as he pressed her naked body up against the railing.

"We're on the top floor. No one can see us."

He cuddled up against her back and entered her from behind. He suckled her neck and rubbed his hands over her perfect breasts, her flat belly, the flair of her hips. They watched the sun set into the ocean as they mated to the rhythm of the waves. It was twilight before she found release again.

"One more?" she whispered, obviously exhausted.

"Yeah. The hot tub should be nice and warm." He was glad he'd thought to turn it on before she'd arrived.

They entered the huge tub and she climbed on his lap, facing him. His dick felt so abused at this point he wasn't sure if he could come at all. She found energy somewhere and rose and fell over his lap, tightening around him, relaxing. He let himself feel it this time. Let the urgency build. No holding back. Well, a little.

"Are you close again, baby?" he asked, forcing his eyes open marginally.

She was utterly stunning, her skin wet and rosy, her breasts rising above and sinking below the water as she rode him. "Yeah. I'm gonna come again." She bit her lip and twisted her hips. His entire cock throbbed from swollen head to parts unseen within his body.

"Good. Good. Oh." Release caught him by surprise, his seed erupting from him like a raging volcano. It pumped into her body, the spasms intense, the pleasure incredible. He gasped, still spurting, still filling her body, still blinded by bliss. "Jessica. Oh God, Jessica." He couldn't breathe. Could only come and come and come. Even after his cum was spent, his muscles continued to contract at the base of his cock. He grabbed her ass and held her down, groaning in some abyss between ecstasy and agony. When it finally subsided, he took a deep breath and collapsed against the edge of the hot tub.

"Did you come again?" he asked her. He'd been too caught up in his own pleasure to pay attention to her reactions.

"Nine orgasms is plenty, Sed," she murmured, cuddling against his chest.

He wrapped an arm around her loosely, drawing her closer. He draped his other arm over his eyes. "Well, next time then."

"Yeah, next time." Beneath the water, her fingers gently stroked the skin over his ribs. She kissed his collarbone. If she was half as exhausted as he was, she simply lacked the energy to find his mouth. They sat there for a long time, their bodies still intertwined in the roiling hot water, trying to regain their bearings.

"Did you miss me, baby? Is that why you called begging for a place to stay?" Sed murmured, his brain obviously not functioning.

Jessica stiffened, moved from his lap, and started to climb from the hot tub.

He opened his eyes to look at her. "Jess, where are you going?"

The look she gave him might just freeze the steaming water around him.

"I didn't call *begging* for a place to stay," she sputtered.

Her slick, wet skin begged for his touch as she hauled herself out of the hot tub and darted into the apartment through the open glass doors. He sighed loudly and forced himself to stand, water pouring from his body in torrents. He hadn't meant it that way. Would he ever get this right with her? He honestly didn't know how and it frustrated him to no end.

Sed stumbled his way back into the house. When he found her in the bedroom, she was already halfway dressed. Her clothes clung to her wet body, but she couldn't seem to get away fast enough.

"Jess, don't go. I didn't mean you actually begged. It came out wrong. I'm glad you're here." He had to convince her to stay. Whatever it took. The was no way in hell he was letting her walk away from him twice in one day.

"I'm going to my mother's." She slipped into her sandals and slung her bag over her shoulder.

"You'd rather stay with sicko Ed than here with me?" He couldn't believe she was willing to go anywhere near her perverted stepfather.

The blood drained from Jessica's face and she covered her stomach with one hand. "Don't do that to me," she said. "Don't make me feel trapped here."

If that's what it took, he'd do it. "Your mother is still married to the guy, isn't she?"

Jessica nodded, her bag sliding from her shoulder to the crook of her elbow.

"I bet he climbs into your bed naked while you're not there. Rubs his body between your sheets. Makes out with your pillow. Plays with himself while he thinks of you and comes all over your mattress."

"Shut up!"

"Enjoy your family reunion." He headed to the bathroom for a towel.

She followed him. "You're such an asshole. You'll do anything to get your way, won't you?"

"I'm not sure why you're leaving. I said I didn't mean it that way. But go ahead. Leave." He wasn't sure what he'd do if she actually left. Groveling came to mind. So did physical restraint. "I'm sure I can find someone to keep me entertained until the band goes back on tour." Lying worked okay sometimes, but he knew her reluctance to go home was his best bet. "And I know your mom and *Ed* will be happy to see you."

Her bag dropped to the floor. She looked physically ill. "I'll stay, but I'm sleeping in your guest room and as soon as Myrna pays me, I'll have rent money for you."

Heh, I win. "I don't want your money, Jessica. If you insist on compensating me, just suck my cock twice a day," he teased.

He reached for her, but she took a step back. She lifted an

eyebrow at him, her nostrils flared. "Just when I start to think you're *not* the biggest asshole on the planet, you go and ruin it by opening your mouth."

Well, shit. Now what had he said wrong?

Chapter 25

Sed clasped Eric's hand and clapped him on the back. "Did you bring it?"

"Yep." Eric handed Sed a huge stack of guitar music. Music Brian had written while making love to Myrna. The sheer quantity was overwhelming. The quality? Perfection.

"Awesome," Sed said. "I invited Jace, by the way."

Eric rolled his eyes. "Why?"

"Uh, he's our bassist." Sed shifted the stack of music under one arm and stepped further into the condo, ushering Eric inside. "He's already in the studio."

"If he annoys me, you have to send him home. I can't compose when I'm annoyed."

"He won't annoy you. Gush all over you? Maybe."

Eric followed Sed to the spare bedroom he'd had converted into a studio. This would be the first time they'd had a chance to use it. "Got beer?" Eric asked.

"I always have beer."

"And lyrics?"

"Some. I'll show you what I have. We'll probably need to add to them."

"I brought a couple of ideas." Eric fished a tiny wirebound notebook out of his inner vest pocket.

"We'll take a look."

Eric entered the studio, checking out the soundboard, recording equipment, and various instruments. They didn't plan to actually record here, but if they ever decided to drop their record label, it was equipped for it. Eric sat in the chair across the square coffee table from Jace. "Hey, little man. Been keeping busy?"

Jace rubbed his earring between his thumb and forefinger. "No. I'm ready to get back on the road."

"Yeah, no kidding. I hope Trey gets better soon."

"He won't get better until he starts trying. Lazing around by his parents' pool all day isn't helping," Sed said, scowling. "I guess I'll have to go straighten him out."

"That's probably a good job for Brian. Put him on it," Eric said.

"That would require Brian leaving Myrna's bed for more than five minutes. Ain't gonna happen."

"Speaking of women in bed, where's Jess?"

"She went to a yoga class and then to go pick up her mail from her mother's house. She's sure to be in a foul mood when she returns, so let's get busy." It had taken her a week to get up the nerve to go visit her mother and she'd only agreed to it because Ed was away on business.

"This should be cool." Jace sat up straighter so he could see all the scraps of music on the coffee table.

Sed and Jace watched Eric riffle through the stack of guitar music.

"I looked at some of this last night," Eric said. "Lots of good stuff here." He sorted the music into about twenty piles spread from one corner of the large square coffee table to the other. He held his hand out to Sed. "Lyrics?"

Sed handed him his lyrics notebook. He experienced strange jolts of nervousness in his belly as Eric read through the pages.

Eric tore a page out and set it on a stack of music in the center of the table. "You been tormented lately, Sed?" Eric asked. "Lots of angst in here."

Sed shrugged, feeling self-conscious. His lyrics were always highly personal. It was like exposing his soul to the world.

"The fans will love this." Eric ripped out another page and handed it to Jace. "Read that."

Hands on his thighs, Sed gripped the fabric of his jeans to keep himself from snatching the page out of Jace's hands. This was a hell of a lot easier when he didn't participate. In the past, he'd just supplied some lyrics and saw the finished products as songs.

"Awesome," Jace said. "What's it about?"

Sed took the page from him and read the title. "Sever." He'd written this after he'd seen a captain go down with his ship in a movie. He'd thought the guy was an idiot. "Cutting ties."

"Let's start with that one," Eric said, setting the notebook aside. "I know just the music for it. Hard and heavy." He scanned the sets of music on the table, lifted a stack, and set it on his knee. "Here it is. Jace, hand me a guitar. I need to hear it."

Jace glanced around the room and spotted the acoustic sitting on a stand in the corner. He retrieved it and handed it to Eric. Eric tuned the guitar in Brian's typical drop D, and then played a few bars of the riff. He didn't have Brian's innate soloing skill, but Eric could play. "Yep," he said, shifting that score to his other knee. He read from the next score and played a few bars of a solo at half tempo. "We'll make this the bridge."

"A solo for a bridge?" Jace asked.

"It will work. Brian will love adding embellishments between stanzas. You know how he is." Eric pulled a pen out of his pocket and scratched out a few lines of music, adding a couple of notes in their place.

"Yeah." Jace looked awestruck.

Eric rearranged the sections several times and then nodded. "Okay, I've got the guitar music worked out. Now we need the bass line." He glanced at Jace.

Jace jumped to his feet and pulled his bass out of the case behind the leather sofa. Eric pulled two sets of drumsticks out of his pockets. Sed wondered if he had a drum kit in that pocket, too. Eric tapped a rhythm on the table with his sticks. "Match it."

Jace plugged his bass into a practice amp and strummed a line distinctly Sinners. Yet, more. How had he managed to improve perfection? It struck Sed that they were about to take their music to the next level. With their bassist, of all people.

He glanced at Eric to see if he recognized it too.

"Not bad," Eric said, nodding in appreciation. Didn't Eric hear him? The guy was a phenomenon. His sound was so much richer than Jon's had been, it was as if they didn't even play the same instrument. They had to exploit the hell out of Jace's talent on the new album. Eric glanced at Sed. "You ready to sing?"

Off in progressing-our-fame land, Sed started. "Oh yeah. I'm ready." He cleared his throat. Even though it had been weeks since that bouncer had grabbed him at the strip club, his throat still bothered him. Not so bad that it affected his voice. It just felt different. Achy. Especially when he screamed.

"Like this," Eric said. He sang the chorus lyrics as he envisioned them.

"Sever it, never let it take you down.
Sever it, before it takes you under.
Sever it, tied, gagged and bound.
Sever it, no sense in going under.
Let.
It.
Go."* Eric carried the last note for several measures and stopped tapping the table with drumsticks. "How does that sound?"

"Perfect," Sed told him.

"Now you sing it."

"I can't sing in that octave. You sing it."

"I'm the drummer, not the singer."

"You used to be. So sing that chorus and in the background, I'll scream like this:

Sever.

Severrrrrrrrr.

Severrrrrrrrrrrrrr." Sed let each roar increase in length and volume.

"Sing it together," Jace requested, leaning toward them, his bass guitar drooping to around knee level.

"I'm not singing," Eric insisted. "Helloooo." He pointed to himself. "Drummer. Drum-*mer*."

"Humor him," Sed said.

Eric rolled his eyes. "I feel like an ass."

"You are an ass," Sed insisted with a grin, "but you have the perfect pitch for this chorus. Sing."

Eric sighed heavily and then sang the chorus, just like before. Sed entered his rumbling screams throughout Eric's more melodic vocals. When they stopped, they stared at each other in surprise.

"That. Was. Awesome," Jace said. "Holy shit. Do it again."

"I can't sing, Sed," Eric said.

"You just did."

"I don't have the right stage presence to be a vocalist."

Sed remembered telling him something like that twelve years ago. You'd think the guy would have gotten over it by now.

"Dude, I'm not handing lead vocals over to you. But there's no reason you can't sing that chorus from behind your drums. It sounded excellent."

"Yeah, excellent," Jace agreed. "My God, Eric. You're amazing."

Sed glanced at Jace. "You've got something on your nose." Sed rubbed his own nose with the side of his finger. "Right there."

Jace mimicked his motion. "Did I get it?"

"Nope, it's permanently brown."

Jace laughed and shook his head. "Jackass."

Sed glanced at Eric, who had gone unnaturally silent. "Don't think too hard," Sed said. "You might hurt yourself."

"Do you really want me to sing that chorus? I don't want to infringe upon your territory or anything."

"As if that's even a possibility."

Eric chuckled. "True, that. Okay, I've been thinking."

"Now we're in serious trouble," Sed whispered at Jace out of the corner of his mouth.

"No, hear me out," Eric said. "You used to play violin, right?"

Sed's nose crinkled. "Yeah, when I was a kid."

"We should get you an electric violin to add to a couple of songs."

"What have you been smoking? Must've been some good shit."

"Just try it. I'll be trying something different. You should too."

"Do I get to try something different?" Jace asked eagerly.

"No," Eric said.

Jace scowled.

Before Sed could call Eric a freakin' retard for not recognizing Jace's skill, Eric said, "Well, maybe. You should add more embellishments to the bass lines to complement Brian. You're a better bassist than Jon was. I think you need to push your skill level on the new album. You must be bored as fuck playing that repetitive shit Jon composed before you signed on."

Jace beamed and glanced from Eric to Sed and back to Eric. "Okay."

"Don't get a swollen head, little man," Eric said with a thinly veiled grin. "You'll tip over."

"Hey, I've got muscle and a great center of gravity. Unlike a certain bony drummer."

Eric laughed, reached across the table, and punched Jace in the shoulder. Sed was glad he'd thought to invite Jace. His drummer and bassist needed to work as a unit. And his rhythm guitarist, currently putting no effort into his recovery, was necessary to bridge lead guitar with percussion and bass.

"I'm going to go call Trey," Sed said. "He needs to be here a lot more than I do. Lyrics last. Carry on. I'll be right back."

"Hey, I can't wait around here all day. I've got shit to do," Eric said.

Sed left the studio and picked up the phone in the entryway. Before he could dial the number, Jessica came through the door. When she saw him standing there, she paused and then burst into tears.

He hung up the phone and drew her into his arms. "What's wrong?"

Jessica stuffed a piece of paper in his hand. "I lost my scholarship."

"What? Why?" His first thought was they'd found out about their little sex video. He gazed down at the crumpled paper in his hand and read the first few lines. "Academic probation? Why are you on academic probation?"

"Because Ellington failed me on my final paper, I got a C in Legal Research and Writing last year. A C *minus*." She gulped air and sniffed her nose. "To keep my scholarship I can't get a grade below a B. They usually give the student a chance to retake the class before they strip them of their scholarship award. Especially someone who has A's in every other class."

"They aren't gonna give you another chance?"

She shook her head. "According to this, they had a meeting of the deans and because they had no way to contact me, they took the word of the instructor. She despises me, Sed. No telling what she told them."

"Why didn't they just call your cell phone?"

"They still have my old number." She lifted a hand at him. "Yeah, duh, I know."

He shrugged. "So, you go talk to the deans and try to get their decision reversed."

"They won't listen to me. Dr. Ellington is one of the most respected professors at the university. She carries the dean's balls around in her pocket."

"I'm not going to let you give up that easily, Jessica."

Her eyes narrowed. "You're not going to *let* me?"

"Nope." He took her by the arm. "Let's go. I'll drive you to the college right now."

She jerked her arm out of his grasp. "This is the exact reason why I broke off our engagement. You can't tell me what to do, Sed."

"I am telling you what to do. Get in the car."

"I'm not going anywhere with you."

"Get in the car, Jessica."

"Or you'll do what?"

He knew exactly what would piss her off most. "I'll write a check for your tuition and send the receipt to your mother."

Her jaw dropped. "You wouldn't!"

"Wouldn't I?" He lifted an eyebrow at her.

"I hate you sometimes," she sputtered.

"Only sometimes? We're making progress."

"I know what you're trying to do. You can't fix this for me, okay? So just butt out of my business."

"I wasn't planning on fixing it for you. I was just going to give you a ride to the college and wait outside while *you* fix it."

She stared at him as if he'd grown a third eye.

"I can't fix this," she said finally. "And I can't afford another twenty thousand dollars a year for school if I lose my scholarship." But her expression had turned thoughtful.

"If?" he prodded.

"Maybe if I show the dean my term paper, he'll recognize that Dr. Ellington graded me unfairly. I didn't deserve to fail that paper. I *know* I didn't." She scowled, crossing her arms across her chest. She was entirely adorable when she threw tantrums. He doubted she wanted to hear that at the moment, however.

"Good. And if that doesn't work?"

She sighed loudly. "I'll take out loans."

"That's my girl." He touched her cheek gently and she glanced up at him.

"You really are an overbearing prick sometimes, you know that?"

"Yeah, I know. I have your best interest at heart, so you forgive me. Right?"

"Heh. Hardly."

"Yo, Sed, what's taking so long?" Eric called from the end of the hallway. "Is Trey coming over or what?"

Sed had completely forgotten that he was supposed to call Trey. "Change of plans, dude. I have to go do something with Jessica real quick."

Eric rolled his eyes and made a sound of annoyance. "You know bands break up because of their singers' girlfriends for a reason."

If Eric had been within range, Sed would have decked him.

"Just stay here and finish your session with the guys," Jessica said. "I'll go by myself."

"I said I'd drive you."

"I can drive, you know."

"I want to be there. In the unlikely event that you need me."

She hesitated, then turned on her heel and stalked out to the car. She even let him drive and didn't pull away when he reached over to take her hand and pressed her knuckles to his lips.

Chapter 26

JESSICA SANK INTO THE leather-upholstered chair across from the dean. She was glad she'd changed into a neat skirt and sweater set when she'd stopped by her mother's house to pick up her term paper. She needed the self-confidence boost.

Dr. Taylor set his elbows on his desk and folded his hands in front of his chin, assessing her with piercing blue eyes beneath arched gray eyebrows. She imagined he'd been a very attractive man in his youth. Still was in that distinguished older gentleman way.

"How can I help you, Ms. Chase?"

"I received this letter in the mail while I was… out of town. It says the council of deans decided to revoke my scholarship for the upcoming semester."

"That's right. Dr. Ellington made it clear that you're undeserving of such a prodigious award."

Jessica figured it had been something like that. Why did Dr. Ellington have it out for her? "The rest of my grades are exemplary," Jessica said. "I'd like the chance to prove myself."

"What kind of a chance?"

"I'll retake her class."

"Dr. Ellington doesn't want you in her class."

So she wasn't just imagining things. "Why not?"

"Maybe she doesn't think you're living up to your potential."

"So she fails me on a final paper worth fifty percent of my grade? That doesn't make sense." She pulled the graded paper out of her folio. The huge red F emblazoned on the coversheet made her wince. "Read it. Tell me if you think it deserves a failing grade."

"I don't question the grading methods of my professors. If she thought you deserved a failing grade, then you did."

"Can I take the course independent study? Or is there another instructor who teaches it?"

"No and no," Dr. Taylor said.

She was beginning to think coming here was a waste of time. Maybe she could appeal to his sense of justice. He was a law professor first, a dean second. "Other students in my position are given a semester to bring up their grades before their scholarships are revoked. Why doesn't that provision apply in my case?"

"Other students attend their probation hearings."

"I didn't know about it. I would have attended if I'd known."

His gaze moved from her eyes to her neck and settled on her chest. He cocked his head at her. "Did you enjoy your time working in Las Vegas?" His gaze shifted back to her face.

Her eyes widened. "How did you know…" She reminded herself that she hadn't been doing anything wrong. "I was there for a summer job."

"An internship at a law firm, I'm assuming."

She lowered her gaze, her cheeks hot. "Well, no. I needed to make money and internships don't pay. But I'm not working in Vegas anymore. I'm doing research for a psychology professor."

"What kind of research?"

Her cheeks flamed hotter. She couldn't bring herself to meet his eyes. "Uh… well, she's studying promiscuity in band groupies." Why did her voice sound so squeaky? "Sir."

"Interesting. Are you a test subject? That guy you did at the top of the Eiffel Tower is in a band, isn't he? Are you one of his groupies?"

Bile rose to the back of Jessica's throat. Dean Taylor knew about the video? Now would be a great time for a black hole to open up beside her and suck her into oblivion.

"How much do you want this scholarship?"

She looked up. A second chance? "I'd do anything."

"Anything? Would you, say…" He shrugged nonchalantly. "…suck me off?"

She must have heard him wrong. "What?"

"I can overturn this decision with one signature. I just require the proper motivation."

She could not believe this. Jaw set, teeth clenched, she growled, "I'm sure you're aware that there are laws against sexual harassment."

He sat up straighter in his chair and chuckled uncomfortably. "That was just a hypothetical question, Ms. Chase. I needed to know how serious you are about continuing your studies."

"Not that serious." She climbed to her feet and stuffed her failed term paper back into her folio.

"Leave that paper on my desk and I'll get back to you with my decision."

She paused. Should she swallow her pride and hand over the paper? Screw that. He'd think he'd won. "I'd rather inform the other deans what you just said to me. And the campus president. And your wife."

"I've just given you your one chance, Jessica. Don't be stubborn." He smirked. "They've all seen your video. Don't refuse your one opportunity to change everything. We can pretend your brilliant paper changed my mind."

His hand disappeared beneath his desk and she heard his fly unzip.

"A twenty thousand dollar scholarship for five minutes, Ms. Chase."

The skin on her back tried to crawl off her body. "I'm going to report you for this."

He chuckled. "It's your word against mine. Who do you think

they'll believe? A prestigious law professor with a spotless record or a stripper sex-kitten from the wrong side of town?"

"Fuck off."

He shrugged nonchalantly again. "If you'd rather fuck than suck, I wouldn't object."

Her folio flew out of her hand of its own accord. Okay, so maybe she hurled it at him. Unfortunately, he ducked and it hit the back of his chair instead of his smug face. She spun on her heel, flung open his office door and stalked through the outer office, glaring at the startled secretary as she left.

Jessica found Sed outside at the curb, leaning against the front fender of his Mercedes on the passenger side. Some petite Asian chick with pink highlights in her hair stood before him, giggling like an idiot. When Sed noticed Jessica marching in his direction, he smiled brightly. It faltered when he caught her expression.

"I assume that didn't go well."

She climbed into the passenger side of the car, shooting eye-daggers at his giddy young companion, while he walked around the car and slid behind the wheel.

"You okay?"

"Drive," she bellowed, fighting angry tears.

"Jess?"

"Just drive, okay? Drive!"

He started the car and pulled into traffic. "Where am I driving?"

"I don't care. Just not here." She hit the dashboard with both fists. "That ass. That unbelievable ass. How dare he? How *dare* he?"

Sed squeezed her knee. "What happened?"

She couldn't tell him. She just couldn't. "Nothing."

"Something happened. Do you have any chance of getting your scholarship back?"

"Not anymore." Her head started swimming. She knew she was hyperventilating, but she couldn't calm down.

"Why not?"

"Because I refused to suck the dean's cock, that's why not!" She drew in a deep breath, hoping to retrieve the words she'd unthinkingly spewed.

Sed slammed on the brakes. The seat belt dug into Jessica's shoulder and then she banged her head on the headrest. Angry horns blared as cars swerved around them.

"*What?*"

Sed did a U-turn into oncoming traffic. More horns blared.

"Are you trying to kill us?" Jessica screamed, gripping the door handle with both hands, her eyes squeezed shut.

"I do have murder on my mind at the moment. Yes."

"Sed, don't do this."

"Do what?"

He pulled to a halt in front of the building Jessica had recently vacated, illegally parked in the middle of the street with two tires on the center median, and opened his door. Jessica grabbed his arm before he could climb from the car.

"Don't make it worse. I took care of it, okay? He won't bother me again. I told him to fuck off." *Oh my God, I told the dean to fuck off. I'm so screwed.*

"I just want to make sure your rejection sinks in. I think my fist will do the trick." He cracked his knuckles, the muscles in his forearms straining against his skin.

"Sed, you can't."

"Why not? The prick has it coming to him."

"Maybe he does—"

"Thank you."

"—but I don't want you to fight my battles. When you brought me here and let me go in by myself, I thought you finally understood. But you don't understand at all."

"What I really don't understand is why men think they can talk to you like that."

"He knew I was stripping in Vegas," she said. "And he saw our video, Sed. Oh God. They've all seen it." She couldn't catch her breath.

"That shouldn't matter." He slammed his door and shifted into first gear. The tires squealed as the car shot forward.

"Why are you driving like a maniac?"

"Because I'm pissed and you won't let me hit anyone."

"I shouldn't have said anything," she murmured. "You always overreact."

"Do you really think I'm overreacting?" Sed slammed both palms into the steering wheel. "Some sonuvabitch tells my girlfriend to suck his dick and I'm overreacting!"

"Except I'm not your girlfriend."

He growled, his eyes narrow, jaw taut. "Of course you aren't. How could I forget?"

Chapter 27

SED WAITED FOR THE first commercial to interrupt the ball game before he took the beer out of Trey's hand and set it on the side table. Trey took his eyes off the TV to gape at Sed.

"How long has it been since you picked up your guitar?" Sed asked.

Trey shrugged. "Doesn't matter. Can't play it anyway."

"You're never going to play again if you don't try. Do you expect to wake up one morning and be back to one hundred percent with no effort?"

"Lay off, Sed. I thought you invited me over for a beer and to watch a ball game, not to bitch at me."

"Someone has to bitch at you. Lots of people rely on us for a paycheck. How are we going to pay them if we keep canceling shows? And how long do you think our fans will back us if we keep turning them away?"

"Our fans are awesome, Sed. Loyal 'til the end." He grabbed his beer and chugged it in several swallows.

"If we keep canceling tour dates, the end is going to come a lot sooner than you think. No concerts. No new album. Do you want this to end? We worked our fucking asses off to get this far. You gonna let it go without a fight?"

"I am fighting."

"I don't see you fighting. I see you pussing out."

Jessica wandered out of the bathroom, drying her hair with her towel. Her one towel. "Are we going out tonight? Or can I lounge around in shorts?"

"I vote for that outfit," Trey said.

Jessica peeked out from under her towel. "Shit," she muttered and wrapped the towel around her naked body.

"No worries. I've seen it before. Me and a couple million other people."

Jessica shook her head at him. "Screw you, Trey."

"If you insist."

"Did I forget to mention that I invited Trey over?" Sed scratched his head as he looked up at Jessica from his recliner.

"Yeah, you forgot to mention that." She headed for the bedroom. "I'm going to go slip into something more... more."

Unable to take his eyes off her slim thighs, Sed watched her until she disappeared in his bedroom and then turned his attention back to Trey. What had they been talking about? Oh yeah. "You know I wouldn't push you if I didn't think you could handle it."

"Bullshit."

Okay, he would. Someone had to. "Have you even been going to physical therapy?"

Trey scowled. "I go."

"Let me guess how that goes. You flirt with your therapist for an hour and then you go home."

He looked at the ceiling and grinned. "Maybe."

"It's obvious that you don't care about the band anymore. What do you think I should do about that?"

Trey's recently acquired tan lightened a shade. "What's that supposed to mean?"

"What do you think it means?"

"Are you considering replacing me?"

"I didn't say that."

"But you thought it." Trey pressed the leg rest of the recliner down and stood.

"How long are we supposed to wait for you, Trey? You tell me."

Trey headed for the stairs. Sed launched himself from his chair and took off after him.

"Don't run away," Sed demanded. "I need to know if you're done. By the amount of effort you're putting into your recovery, I'd say you don't think the band is worth it."

Trey turned and shoved Sed with all his strength. Sed stumbled backward and hit his lower back against the pool table. He pulled himself upright, giving Trey a wide berth.

"You know I don't think that!" Trey yelled. "The band means everything to me. Everything."

"Prove it."

Trey shook his head slightly, turned and took the stairs two at a time. He stormed out of the condo and slammed the front door behind him. Sed took a deep breath and rubbed his face with both hands.

Jessica appeared at his elbow. "Did I hear yelling? Where did Trey go?"

"He had to go practice his guitar or something."

"You didn't bully him, did you?" Jessica's eyes narrowed suspiciously.

"Me?" He tried on his best innocent expression. "Of course not."

Chapter 28

BACKSTAGE A WEEK LATER, Sed clamped a hand over Trey's shoulder. "Are you sure you're ready for this?"

"Kind of late to change my mind now, isn't it?" Trey adjusted his guitar strap into a more comfortable position on his shoulder and then stared at the pick in his left hand. He hadn't been able to grip it for more than a few days, but he'd called their manager, Jerry, to reschedule tour dates despite everyone's insistence that he needed more time to recover.

Now they had this sold out show to contend with. A packed venue of fifteen thousand. So Trey was correct, it was too late to change his mind.

"I feel a little rusty," Brian said. "I hope I remember the set. It's been almost three weeks since we set foot on a stage and we didn't have time to rehearse this afternoon."

"Like falling off a bike," Sed assured him.

"Embarrassing and painful?"

"Exactly."

Doing the sound check onstage, Jake strummed Brian's guitar and played an intricate riff to ensure the instrument was tuned and responding to the amplifier. He earned a few cheers from the waiting crowd. Roadies loved to play rock star.

Sed looked over his shoulder to where Jessica promised she'd stand and watch the performance. She smiled at him and waved. He waved back. The groupies who'd gotten backstage passes from the roadies glared at her.

Sed glanced at Trey, who was limbering up his fingers. He still didn't have full mobility, but he could play chords. Brian watched him, wincing when Trey attempted part of one of their dueling solos and missed every note. "If you can't keep up tonight, just let me carry all the solos."

"I'm not a fucking invalid." Trey scowled.

"No one said that," Brian said. "You're pushing yourself too hard."

Trey glanced at Sed, who dropped his gaze to the floor. Yeah, that was mostly Sed's fault and he knew it, but fans only remained loyal for so long, and while most everyone understood why they'd cancelled tour dates and refunded tickets, it didn't make them happy.

"I'll be fine," Trey said.

Jake signaled them into position. Sed stuck his earpiece in his right ear and a sound-muffling earplug in his left. He'd be able to hear the band and instructions from the sound crew from the earpiece. Now he heard mostly, "Check. Check. Check." He gave Dave a thumbs up to let him know he could hear him just fine.

Brian and Jace settled their instruments into place and moved to the side of the stage. A slightly green Trey followed them. Eric stood just behind the drum kit, ready to take his stool as soon as the lights went out. Someone thrust a microphone into Sed's hand. The adrenaline rush hit him like the most powerful stimulant on the planet.

He lived for this shit. The music. The crowd's adulation. Their energy. He owned it and it owned him.

The stadium lights went down and the crowd cheered. Another rush, more powerful than the first, kicked Sed's heart rate up another notch.

The three guitarists trotted across the stage in the dark. The beat of the bass drum thrummed through Sed's chest. A low blue light illuminated the floor, lighting the stage enough for Brian and Trey to find the foot pedals that switched out their various amps, and for Sed to find the set instructions taped to the floor. The musical intro to the first song was rather long, giving Sed time to hum and warm up his vocal cords for that first scream. Like Brian, he felt a little rusty. His voice a little coarse.

Trey did fine shredding chords in the intro and the crowd cheered. Though good, Trey's playing was more reserved than usual. Thready.

With too little rhythm guitar to balance it, Jace's bass riff sounded more pronounced. But when Brian entered with his signature finger-burning note progressions, fans wouldn't notice Trey's playing lacked his usual skill.

At the end of Brian's intro, Sed raced across the stage, his low growl increasing in volume until it broke into a loud battle cry. The crowd screamed when the lights suddenly went bright and they recognized he'd entered the stage. God, he loved these people. All fifteen thousand of them.

Sed sang with his usual enthusiasm, stalking from one end of the stage to the other, raising his hands to encourage the crowd to participate. All the while, the music playing in his ear sounded off. Not terrible, just sort of weak. He glanced at Trey, who'd already broken into a sweat. Not normal for him. He usually rocked on his heels and strummed each chord with gusto. Tonight he had a hard time keeping up.

Shit. Shouldn't have pushed him so hard. Sed knew he was responsible for this entire fiasco. He'd made Trey feel guilty and uncertain of his place in the band. Sed had just been trying to encourage him, not force him into taking a step he wasn't ready to take. But they had a show to finish. He hoped Trey could hang in there for nine more songs. No one expected him to be as good as he usually was. Just there. Singing his occasional back up vocal. Strumming chords the best he could.

Brian finished his solo, and the segment where Trey usually accompanied him sounded entirely hollow. Sed glanced across the stage to see Trey staring at his hands as if they were on fire. Brian noticed as well. He quickly made his way from stage left to stage right and talked to Trey out of hearing range of the microphone. Trey shook his head. Brian said something else and Trey nodded. Trey pulled a guitar pick off the tape on his microphone stand and picked up on the series of chords that made up the majority of the rhythm guitar section. He managed to play it consistently until the end.

"How are we doing tonight, Salt Lake City?" Sed called into his microphone. He held the mic toward the crowd and put his hand to his ear.

The crowd responded with loud cheers.

"Are you ready to get crazy?"

More cheers. He glanced at Trey, who liked to talk to the crowd. He and Brian were in deep conversation near the drum kit. Trey looked upset. Brian, ever Trey's rock, just kept talking him down.

"As you've probably heard, we've had to cancel ten shows over the past few weeks, but Sinners is back to rock Salt Lake. How do you all feel about that?"

More cheers.

"Hey, Trey, why don't you come say something to the fans? I think they've been worried about you."

Trey gave him a scathing look and stepped up to the microphone. "Hey."

The roar from the crowd was deafening.

"He's still not back to his usual bad-ass self, but he said he couldn't stand to miss another show. Is that what you said, Trey?"

"Yeah," he said quietly.

Brian wrapped an arm around Trey's shoulders and spoke into the microphone. "He's feeling kind of slow these days. I think they sucked half his brain out through this hole in his head." Brian pointed to the ugly scar that ran a semi-circle around the side of his head. At least the staples were gone now.

Trey didn't respond to the barb. Yeah, something wasn't right. Best leave him alone. They might as well continue and get this over with.

"You know what I think?" Sed said into the mic. "I think it's time to climb the gates of hell."

Brian raced to his side of the stage to stomp a foot pedal that changed his amplifier settings. Eric tapped on a cymbal behind them. The intro to "Gates of Hell" was insane, and while Brian performed with his usual spectacular flare, Trey missed an entire progression and his guitar fell silent. There was a horrifically loud bang followed by screeching feedback in Sed's ear. Sed winced, covering his earpiece with one hand. He turned to see Trey stalk offstage. Trey's favorite guitar lay in pieces in the middle of the stage, its neck snapped near the yellow and black body.

Brian stopped playing and ran after him. Sed turned his attention back to the crowd. "We'll be right back, folks. Don't go anywhere." He handed his mic to Jace as he headed after the two guitarists. "Entertain the crowd until I get back."

Jace did a very good impression of a fish out of water, but Sed didn't have time to worry about Jace's ability to speak to the crowd. Trey had just trashed a $6,000 guitar and stormed offstage. Things were not boding well for their comeback show.

Brian had Trey by the shoulders backstage.

"Hey, it's okay," Brian said. "We'll just call off the show—"

"We're not calling off the show," Sed said.

Trey turned his attention to Sed. "You heard me out there. I can't play."

"You were doing fine."

"Were you listening at all? I sound like shit."

"Brian can take up some of your slack. Just do the best you can. And get back onstage." When Trey didn't move, Sed added, "Now." Pointing toward the audience.

"I'm not going back," he said. "I can't even hold on to my fucking pick."

"You said you were ready for this, so get back out there and play some music. I really don't care how much you suck."

"Sed," Brian protested.

"What? Are you going to baby him some more? He needs to man up and do his best. If you keep letting him get away with this crap, he's never going to get better."

"Hello, I'm standing right here," Trey said. "I can hear everything you're saying."

Sed looked at Trey. "Am I right?"

Trey dropped his gaze. "I just need more time to get stronger."

"We all tried to tell you that, but you wouldn't listen. You made your choice and now you're going to stick to it, even if I have to drag you kicking and screaming back onstage."

"Trey you don't have to do this," Brian said. "Honestly, the fans will understand if we send them home."

"You couldn't be more wrong, Sinclair," Sed said. "I'm going back out there now. Even if it means singing a cappella into a megaphone."

Sed turned and stalked back toward the stage. He found Jace standing center stage, his face the color of cranberries, telling knock-knock jokes. Surprisingly, the crowd seemed to be enjoying his extreme discomfort. Especially the young women, who were practically swooning over his uncharacteristic interaction.

"Knock knock," Jace whispered into the mic.

"Who's there?" the crowd yelled.

Jace noticed Sed crossing the stage. "Oh thank God, Sed's back." Jace passed Sed the microphone and made a beeline toward the drum kit to hide.

"Oh thank God, Sed's back who?" the crowd yelled.

"Oh thank God, Sed's back to kick this show into high gear. Are you people ready to rock?"

The crowd yelled.

"Sorry about that unscheduled break, folks. Trey thinks he sucks too much to play for you wonderful people. If you agree, stay quiet, but if you think he should get his severely injured self out here and do the best he can, you should let him know it."

Eric started a repetitive beat on the bass drum and the crowd rose up to the challenge. "Mills, Mills, Mills," they chanted.

Within a minute, Brian came back onstage, followed by Trey, who looked incredibly sheepish. Trey stepped up to his microphone stand. "I'm not sure what I've done to deserve such great fans, but I'll try to get through this, if you pretend you can't hear all those triplets I can't finger."

"You can finger me, Trey!" some chick screamed in the audience.

Trey laughed. "I probably wouldn't be very good at that either, honey, but I'd be more than happy to give it a go."

Sed grinned. There's Trey. He was wondering where he'd wandered off to.

Trey continued, "Also, I sorta demolished my favorite guitar, so even if I could play, nothing would sound right."

"You have a spare," Brian said into his microphone.

"Hardly broke in."

Jake dashed across the stage and handed Trey his red and white Schecter. The roadie then picked up the pieces of the destroyed yellow and black.

Sed heard Dave in his earpiece, "'Gates of Hell' from the top, guys. Trey, just improvise. Play a fuckin' open E chord the entire song if you need to. Something. Brian, double up on your outro and try to fill in on the solo. Can you handle that?"

Trey and Brian gave Dave a thumbs-up. Eric tapped his cymbal to start the song again. Sed took a deep breath and growled into his microphone.

The next four songs sounded pretty much as bad as the first, but they made it through. The crowd seemed to delight in Trey's struggle rather than be critical of it. Sed even caught Trey smiling once.

When it was time for their break, they left Brian onstage by himself to play some new solos for the crowd, while the rest of the band headed backstage. Eric, red in the face and drenched in sweat from head to foot, upended several bottles of water over his head. A roadie handed him a fresh shirt and he changed into it.

Sed grabbed a towel and wiped the sweat from the side of his face. He waved at Jessica standing just in view next to the stage while he chomped down several pieces of red licorice to lubricate his vocal cords. His throat was really bothering him tonight. Must be from not using it for several weeks. Singing wasn't a problem, but his usual screams hurt.

Jessica grinned and waved back. Some red-headed chick next to her said something and Jessica gave her a look that would freeze the Caribbean Sea. Jessica blew Sed a kiss which incited the woman to flip Jessica off behind her back. The woman spun on her heel and stomped away. Myrna whispered something to Jessica and she laughed.

Sed smiled to himself. He wasn't sure why he worried about Jessica so much. She could obviously take care of herself. His dad had always insisted a man's job was to protect the women he loved— whether mother, sister, wife, or treasured lover. Dad had lived that rule and enforced it by example, so it wasn't something Sed could easily shake. It was ingrained and he didn't want to abandon it, necessarily. But he wanted Jessica and to keep her, he realized he had to let her take care of her own problems. Occasionally.

Jace and Trey had gone off to a corner and were talking to each other in quiet tones. Sed approached them, hoping to offer Trey encouragement. Or piss him off again. Whatever worked.

"It doesn't sound the same without a pick," Trey said to Jace.

"I know, but you could play. Try it."

Trey clamped his pick between his teeth, freeing the fingers of his left hand. He tried strumming with his index finger and thumb. "It feels weird."

"It's not permanent," Jace said. "Just 'til you can hang on to your pick."

"It sounds weird, too."

"Maybe we can get you a banjo pick," Jace suggested.

"A banjo pick?"

"Yeah, they slip over the tip of your finger. You don't have to hold them."

Trey sighed. "Fuuuuck, this sucks." He shook his head. "I suck."

Sed clapped him on the back vigorously. "We should have conked you on the head years ago. The fans love it."

"The fans love that I suck?"

Sed shook his hand. "The fans love your devotion. They know you're out there for them."

"He's out there for you, you idiot," Eric said. Sed's brow furrowed, but before he could ask for clarification, Eric changed the subject. "Brian seems more tired than usual from doing all that improvised solo and riff fill. We should head back and let him off the hook." Eric wrapped an arm around Trey and squeezed his shoulder. "You ready?"

"You could take my place." Trey looked ill at the thought of returning to the stage.

"I could. But then who's going to play drums?"

Trey took a deep breath and let it out in a huff. "Okay, let's get this over with."

Eric directed Trey back toward the stage, his arm still around him. "I hope you're in the mood for female booty tonight. You don't mind if I watch, do you? Of course you don't."

"Actually, I'm not in the mood for any booty tonight."

Eric's arm tightened around Trey's neck and he covered Trey's forehead with his large hand. "Oh my God, you must be dying. Doesn't feel like you have a fever." He grabbed Trey's chin. "Say ahhhhh."

Trey laughed and opened his mouth. "Ahhhhh."

Eric tilted his head to look in Trey's mouth. "Tonsils appear normal. Don't tell me…" Eric looked gravely serious. Sed couldn't help but snigger at his antics.

"Don't tell you what?" Trey asked.

"They performed the wrong surgery. You've had…" Eric closed his eyes as if the thought was too difficult to bear. "…a vaginoplasty."

Trey scowled and flipped him off. "Aw, fuck you, Eric."

"Not me, I don't swing that way, but I've heard if you get Brian drunk enough…"

Trey's eyes widened to the size of saucers. "Where'd you hear that?"

"Don't get your hopes up. Myrna doesn't share well with others."

"Sometimes she does." Trey winked.

Eric and Jace exchanged surprised glances.

"Did you all have a threesome?" Eric asked.

"Maybe."

"You lucky son-of-a-bitch."

Sed stared up at the rigging above the stage, pretending he didn't care. Brian let Trey *do* Myrna? How the fuck had Trey managed that? Sed just had to come within three feet of the woman and Brian completely freaked out.

"I want all the details later." Eric released Trey's shoulder at the edge of the stage and headed behind the drum kit.

When Sed reappeared onstage, Brian looked relieved to see him. Sed took the microphone off its stand and headed toward the audience. "Master Sinclair!" he announced, a hand extended in Brian's direction.

The crowd whistled, applauded, or yelled their appreciation of Brian's skill. Brian nodded his head in a slight bow and went to check on Trey.

"Anyone think Master Sinclair looks a little worn out?" Sed asked.

"I think he does," Jace said into Trey's microphone.

"Sinclair, are you feeling tired lately?"

"Uh, no, Sed, not really," Brian said, also into Trey's microphone.

"Feeling a little low in the back?"

"Nope."

"Left ring finger cramping up on you?"

Brian chuckled. "Oh, I get what you're doing."

Sed smiled his most shark-like grin.

Brian held up his left hand to the audience, showing off his thick platinum wedding band. "I got married about a month ago."

"Sorry, ladies," Trey said, ruffling Brian's hair. "He's taken."

"Yes, I am," Brian agreed, his eyes shifting backstage to where Myrna stood watching the show next to Jessica. Myrna blew Brian a kiss.

The news prompted mostly cheering from the crowd, but some female booing as well. Sed hoped getting some of the attention off Trey would help him deal with his situation a little better. He wasn't sure what else to do for him.

"What about you, Sed?" someone at the front of the audience yelled. "You still engaged to that hot piece of ass from Vegas? When do we get another video of you fucking her?"

Sed's head swiveled toward the audience, his heart thudding, his blood hot. "Who said that?"

The people surrounding the big-mouthed jackass backed away slightly, leaving a circle of empty space around him.

"I'm gonna kick your fucking ass," Sed bellowed. Before he could dive off the stage and beat the ever-lovin' shit out of the douche bag, someone grabbed the back of his shirt.

Brian shook his head at him. "Don't lose your cool, dude."

Too late. He was tired of everyone treating Jessica like a piece of meat. She was so much more than her perfect outer shell. Jessica appeared at his elbow and pulled the microphone out of his hand. He looked at her in surprise.

"You know what would be nice?" she said into the microphone, looking up at Sed. Instantly, he found himself lost in her wide jade-green eyes. "If all these limp dicks would find a woman of their own and get laid occasionally. Maybe then they'd have less time to jack off to our sexual adventures."

She kissed his jaw and handed the microphone back to him before returning to her place beside the stage. Sed chuckled and rubbed his forehead. She sure handled things better than he did. "Best lay on the planet, and she's smart, too," he murmured into the microphone. He glanced over his shoulder at Trey, who was smiling broadly. "You ready?" he called to the band.

Trey managed to keep up now that he'd given up on his pick and stuck to riffs and shredding. Not their best performance, but the fans had a great time, and that's all that mattered. During the wicked musical outro of "Twisted," Sed let himself get caught up in the moment and dove into the crowd.

With their hands in the air, a group of about twenty fans caught Sed above their heads. Hand over hand they passed him around the crowd and eventually toward the stage. When he was within reach of the barrier fence, one of the security guards pulled him free of their clutches. He hadn't crowd surfed in ages. He'd forgotten how fun it was. With the security guard's help, Sed found his footing on the concrete floor and stood with his belly against the metal barrier fence facing the crowd. He thrust both hands in the air, allowing the first rows of the general admission pit to touch, grab, and hug him enthusiastically. He slapped high fives with dozens of fans, squeezing each hand before moving to the next.

The security guard kept trying to tug Sed away from the crowd by the back of his shirt. He was perfectly fine. He might have a few bruises to show for his brazen interactions with the crowd, but it was well worth the adrenaline rush served by their adulation and excitement.

Brian's voice came over the speaker system. "Uh, Sed? The song is over."

He honestly hadn't noticed. "Get me a mic," he said to the security guard.

A minute later, a mic was thrust into his hand. "How are we feeling tonight, Salt Lake? Are you having a good time?"

The nearby noise of the crowd came through the loud speaker. "You know, my throat has been bothering me all night and I'm feeling pretty lazy. Do any of you dudes know our song 'Reformation'?"

The chorus of the song spread across the crowd as the majority of them started singing. Of course, everyone knew "Reformation." It had topped the rock charts for over a month last winter.

"Maybe one of you can help me sing it up on stage."

The entire barrier fence surged forward in their excitement to join him.

"Not just anyone. If you want on my stage, you have to audition first." He turned his head to look at the band, who watched him warily. "Intro to 'Reformation.' Just until the end of that first scream."

In his earpiece, Dave said, "What are you doing, Sed? This isn't part of the show."

Tonight it is, he thought. "You," he said to the spike-haired guy directly in front of him. "You want to audition?"

"Fuck yeah!"

Sed signaled the band and they started the song. He held the mic to Spike's mouth and he screamed the intro. Sed winced after about five seconds of the guy's blood-curdling screech and pulled the mic away. "Cut. Cut. Cut." The band stopped playing mid-note. "Dude, did you swallow a dying cat? What the fuck was that sound that just came out of your mouth?"

The guy laughed with no hard feelings.

"Next," Sed said and moved to another audience member. He continued down the barrier, letting five or six guys try their voices, until he found a guy who could produce a sound that didn't make him want to shove pencils through his eardrums. "That's more like it. What's your name?"

"Justin."

"Justin, you're hired."

"Yes! Do I get paid?"

"What's your going rate?"

He hesitated. "Can I get a kiss from your woman?"

"Next!" Sed called.

Justin grabbed his wrist. "Just kidding. Jeez!"

"Sed has no sense of humor as far as Jessica is concerned," Brian said into a microphone.

Sed tilted his head reflectively and nodded. "You're absolutely right, Brian. Next!"

Sed helped the next auditioner over the barrier. He didn't sound half as good as that Justin jerk, but Sed wasn't in the mood to tolerate bullshit about Jessica, even in jest. He and his helper, named Lance of all things, took the stage. The crowd absolutely loved Lance as he made a total ass of himself by singing like a tone deaf drunk at a karaoke bar. Trey stopped playing half way through the song, but not out of frustration. He was laughing so hard he couldn't find his fret board.

At the end of the song, Sed shook hands with Lance. Lance gushed over his guitar hero, Master Sinclair, for a full minute before heading off the stage. He waved at the crowd.

"Let's hear it for Lance," Sed called into his microphone, raising his hand in the air. The crowd cheered on cue. "Get him a backstage pass, Jake. He makes Trey laugh."

Trey wiped the tears from the corners of his eyes. "Yeah, he does."

After their set, Sed handed his microphone and earpiece to a roadie on his way offstage. Jessica met him at the bottom of the steps and wrapped her arms around him.

"You were wonderful, baby," she murmured.

"Thanks." He smiled and stroked away the moisture he'd left on her bare arms. He loved when she wore sexy little dresses with spaghetti straps. And she looked sensational in green. Hell, she always looked sensational. "I'm sweating all over you."

"Not *all* over me," she murmured, "but I hope that's about to change."

He bent his head and kissed her passionately, his tongue caressing her upper lip. Dozens of camera flashes went off in unison. Jessica stiffened and pulled away.

"I'll meet you on the bus," he murmured into her ear.

She scowled, but nodded. Sed removed his shirt, wiped the sweat off his face with it, and threw it into the crowd of onlookers in stadium seats above. A scuffle broke out between two chicks and the guy who'd caught it. By the time Sed left the side of the stage, security was breaking up a full out brawl in the stands.

Sed wandered past the dressing room, ignoring the after party the opening bands were enjoying. He was on his way to the bus and his woman. He hoped she was ready to roll, because he was ready to rock her world.

———

After leaving the backstage area, Jessica strode down the wide corridor that led outside. A raucous laugh caught her attention as she passed the open door to one of the dressing rooms. Some chick had her dress up over her head, showing her black panties and lack of bra to anyone who cared to pay her any attention. One of the opening band members poured a beer down her front and she squealed, holding still as he licked the alcohol from her breasts and belly.

Jessica wondered if Sed partied like that when she wasn't around. She was certain he did. He'd probably be glad when she left so he could get back to—

Something slammed Jessica in the face. Pain streaked through her right cheek and eye. She stumbled into the wall, her arm raised defensively. Someone grabbed two handfuls of her hair and slammed her into the wall, then dragged her face down to the floor.

"Ain't so high and mighty *now*, are you, bitch?" a female growled at her.

Jessica swept her legs to the side, catching her attacker's ankles and sending her flying. Unfortunately, she still had a strong hold on Jessica's hair. Jessica cried out and grabbed the woman's wrists, squeezing until she finally released her hair. Jessica shoved her away and climbed to her feet. Her face throbbed in pain, but she was too pissed to care.

"What is *wrong* with you?" Jessica bellowed. It was the same woman who had bragged that she was going to fuck Sedric Lionheart after the concert. Jessica had already put the stupid bitch in her place once. When the tramp had stormed off, Jessica had assumed that would be the end of it.

"I sucked that roadie's cock for nothing," the woman said, launching herself from the floor in Jessica's direction.

Racing down the hall, Sed caught the woman around the waist just before she careened into Jessica. "What in the hell is going on here?" he asked, his eyes searching Jessica's face. "What happened to your cheek?"

"She sucker punched me. I didn't even see it coming." Jessica felt pretty ridiculous, actually. If she hadn't been so worried about Sed partying like a rock star, she might have blocked her attack.

The lead singer of the opening band, Kickstart, staggered out into the hall from the dressing room. "Whaz... whaz goin' on out here." He blinked hard and opened his eyes wide when he noticed

Sed. "Ah, it's bloody Sed. Right-o. Only got yerself two honeys tonight? I got a couple… *hic!*… a couple to spare if yuh need s'more." He leaned against the wall and let his dark eyes drift up and down Jessica's body. "I'll trade you ten of mine for this one 'ere, though." He belched and scratched his balls.

As if!

Sed rolled his eyes at Jessica. "Could you get someone from security?" he asked the guy who had metal studs pierced through every imaginable location on his face and neck.

"Security? Is there a problem?" a second rocker asked, peeking into the hall. Jessica recognized the lead guitarist, or maybe he was the bassist, of Kickstart. At least he wasn't falling down drunk. He stroked his long braided beard with one hand while he looked from one person to the next.

"This chick attacked my girlfr—" His gaze shifted to Jessica's face again. "Erm…"

"Your dick warmer," Jessica supplied.

Sed laughed. "If I said that, I'd be pulling a knife from between my ribs as soon as I fell asleep tonight."

Jessica shrugged.

"I'll take her off your hands," the bearded guy said.

"I don't want you. I want Sed," the woman insisted.

Jessica noticed that the woman had become complacent putty in Sed's hands.

Jessica nostrils flared. She hated groupies. Absolutely hated them.

"Look, bitch, I already told you, Sed fucks me and only me until we call it quits. I don't put up with infidelity bullshit and he knows it. Now if he really wants to fuck you, all he has to do is say so, and he can do whatever he wants. Of course, I'll never let him touch me again." Her gaze shifted to Sed's face, wondering how he was going to react to her posturing. She was as bad as he was when it came to staking her claim. "So, who's it going to be?"

He hesitated. She couldn't believe he hesitated. He shoved the girl into the drunken singer's arms, took two steps and grabbed Jessica. She squeaked in surprise when he grabbed her ass and pressed her mound against his thick cock.

"I love it when you're possessive," he growled at her. "It makes me so fuckin' hard."

Her pussy throbbed in response. Nipples tightened. Goose bumps rose along the surface of her skin. He rubbed his hands down her arms, shifting every nerve ending in her body to full throttle.

Her fingers curled into his naked chest. "Then why don't you do something about it?"

He lifted her off the ground by her ass and she wrapped her legs around his waist, her arms around his neck. She stroked his silky, soft hair and kissed him while he carried her down the corridor and out into the warm night air behind the stadium. She was vaguely aware of camera flashes going off on their way to the bus, but she didn't really care at the moment. She just wanted her man to take her. The sooner the better.

He carried her up the bus steps and dumped her on the sofa, reaching under her dress to rip her soaking wet panties from her body. Eyes closed, she leaned back and found her head on someone's thigh.

She looked up to find Trey smiling drowsily at her. "Don't mind me," he murmured.

Sed thrust into her and she cried out, her eyes closing, back arching. He held her hips as he pounded into her, already gasping excitedly. He grunted and groaned, chanting her name as he lost control. Trey's hand brushed the spaghetti strap from her shoulder and pushed down the fabric of her bodice. When Trey stroked the underside of her breast with the gentlest of touches, Jessica gasped.

She forced her eyes open and looked up at Sed. Did he know what Trey was doing? Did he even realize Trey was sitting on the end of the sofa? Sed had his eyes closed, concentrating fully on working her pussy into a frenzy. He was doing a damn fine job. Jessica squeezed his cock inside her and he shuddered. "Yeah, baby. Squeeze me. Ungh."

She held him tight while he thrust into her with a relentless rhythm.

Trey's hand cupped her breast, his thumb brushing over her nipple. She tilted her head back to look at him. His tired gaze was focused on her breast. He stroked her nipple repeatedly, until it budded to his satisfaction. "Lovely," he whispered.

His head dropped back on the sofa and he closed his eyes. She noticed the prescription medication bottle in his free hand. His painkillers always made him tired, but she couldn't believe he could fall asleep with a girl getting fucked on his lap. What the hell kind of meds was he taking anyway?

Chapter 29

SED WATCHED TREY STEP out of the bathroom and stumble his way to the front of the bus. Trey said something to Dave, who was driving them through a mountain pass on their way into the Midwest.

Sed could barely hear Dave's response over the engine noise as it climbed the steep grade road. "We're kind of in the middle of nowhere, man, but I'll try to find some place to stop."

"Thanks, buddy," Trey said.

Trey made his way back to the sofa and plopped down next to Brian.

Sed watched Jessica across the table for a moment as she typed data from the night before into Myrna's laptop. Jessica had finally caught up on the data backlog and she refused to get behind again. Sed touched her wrist to gain her attention and she glanced up. Sed nodded toward Trey, their conversation about him the night before at the forefront of his mind. She shrugged, not getting his silent message.

"Hey Trey, why do we need to stop?" Sed called to him.

Trey started and then smiled broadly. "I'm almost out of medicine."

"Again? Didn't you just get a refill a couple of days ago?" Sed asked.

Trey avoided his gaze. "I spilled about half the bottle down the sink. I'm such a klutz since my surgery." He ran his fingertips along the scar under his hair. You couldn't even see it now unless he pushed his hair up.

"You're a terrible liar."

"I'm not lying."

"Sed, get off his case. Why would he lie about being a klutz?" Brian handed Trey several pieces of music. "What do you think of this? Do you think you can handle it? It's got a lot of triplets, and I know those are still hard for you."

Trey frowned as he read over the lines of notes. "I'll get through it somehow. I'm getting better."

"Yeah, I know." Brian patted Trey on the thigh. "Do you want to practice for a while?"

"Yeah, okay. Get my guitar out. I'll be back in a minute. I need to use the bathroom." He climbed to his feet and headed toward the back of the bus.

Sed glanced at Jessica again. She nodded, her expression sad as she watched Trey amble past and slip into the bathroom again.

"We've got to do something, Jess," he murmured.

"I think so too," she whispered so only he could hear, "but what do we do?"

"Let me talk to the other guys first. See how they want to handle this."

She nodded. "I'll help any way I can."

He reached across the table and squeezed her hand. "Thanks."

Sed slid from the booth and sat next to Brian, who was tuning Trey's acoustic guitar on the sofa. "We need to do something about Trey."

"He's doing the best he can, Sed. His fingers are getting stronger every day. Don't be so hard on him."

"I'm not talking about his guitar playing. I'm talking about his painkiller addiction."

Brian's fingers stopped moving over the strings and he looked up at Sed. "What do you mean?"

"You're his best friend. How can you not notice? He's in the bathroom right now poppin' another pill or three. He's going to end up killing himself."

"He's just using the bathroom, Sed. No need to call in the Feds."

"He just went to the bathroom ten minutes ago. And do you really buy that story about him spilling his pills down the sink? Come on, Brian, look at the signs. We saw this happen to Jon and we ignored it until it was too late. I'm not going to let it destroy Trey too."

"In case you've forgotten, Trey has a prescription and he needs his meds. Jon was abusing illegal drugs."

"Addiction is addiction. Percocet is a narcotic. He was only supposed to be on it for two weeks and it's been over a month. How does he keep getting refills? Something is not right here."

"If it will make you feel better, I'll ask him about it."

Sed didn't think Brian was taking him very seriously. The bathroom door slid open and Trey emerged. He paused next to Sed, unsteady on his feet.

"You okay there, bud?" Sed asked.

"Just a little dizzy. I need to sit down."

Trey nudged Sed closer to Brian and sat heavily on the sofa beside him. "So does Jessica help you write songs, like Myrna helps Brian? I guess not, since you haven't finished a song all summer. Have you run out of things to say or what?"

Trey obviously wasn't thinking clearly. "Actually, as you should know, we've written several songs for the new album. Are you sure you're feeling okay?"

"I feel fantastic. Brian, hand me my guitar. Let's see if my stupid fingers want to cooperate today."

"See, Sed. I told you he was fine." Brian handed Trey his guitar.

Trey glared at Sed. "Are you talking about me behind my back?"

"I think you need to stop taking those painkillers."

Trey ducked his head. "I can't play without them."

"How would you know? You haven't tried. Your head doesn't hurt anymore, does it?"

"It doesn't hurt because I'm taking my pills."

"How many have you had today?"

"Two."

"Today, Trey, not in the past ten minutes."

"Get off my case, Sed. If it weren't for the pills, I wouldn't be able to play at all. If I can't play, you'll kick me out of the band."

"If you get messed up on drugs, *then* I'll kick you out of the band."

"I'm not messed up on drugs!"

Jessica appeared before Sed and took his hand. "I've got an itch only you can scratch, stud."

"I'm sort of busy at the moment." He couldn't believe she'd just barge in the middle of his conversation with Trey.

She glanced pointedly at the bedroom. "I really want to get you alone." She pulled on his arm until he relented and climbed to his feet.

"Jessica, now is not the time—"

She covered his mouth with her hand. "Come with me."

Sed tugged her hand from his mouth. "I'm not going to let this rest, Trey," Sed assured him as he allowed Jessica to pull him to the bedroom.

She closed the door behind them.

"I hope you didn't bring me back here for sex," Sed said.

"Of course not." She moved to the bed and shook Myrna's shoulder. "Myrna, are you awake? We need to talk to you."

Myrna took a deep breath and opened her eyes. "Jessica?"

"Yeah, and Sed."

She blinked heavily and sat up, holding the sheet over her naked breasts. What in the hell was Brian doing to her that left her in such a state of exhaustion?

"What's up?"

"We were hoping you could talk some sense into Brian," Jessica said.

Myrna looked entirely confused. "Huh?"

Sed sat on the bed next to her. "We think Trey is abusing his pain meds. Brian doesn't seem to recognize it."

"Abusing? Do you have proof?"

Jessica hesitated. "He keeps getting refills."

"And he needs a prescription for those refills, so he obviously needs them."

"Something doesn't add up, Myrna."

Myrna collapsed back on the mattress and covered her head with a pillow. "Did you already accuse him, Sed? Jesus, what are you thinking?"

"I'm not going to let him throw his life away on drugs."

"He's having a really rough time. You letting him know you don't trust him will make it worse."

"You've got to be kidding me," Sed grumbled. "You don't see this as a problem either? I thought you, of all people, would recognize the slippery slope he's sliding down."

"Sed, he has a prescription. I don't know why you're equating this with a problem."

"He's taking more than he's supposed to. A lot more."

"Where's your proof?" She slid the pillow from her face and looked up at him. "You have a tendency to jump to conclusions and assume you're always right. Maybe you're wrong. And you know what I see? I see Trey getting back to normal. The way he used to be. You don't see that?"

"All I see is him heading to the bathroom to secretly take another pill when anything bothers him. Even little things. He's not dealing with his problems. He's trying to cover them up."

"You've seen him in the bathroom taking pills?"

Sed sighed in frustration. "Not directly. No."

"Maybe he just needs a moment to himself."

"Maybe." He knew that wasn't the case, but Myrna wasn't going to listen to him. She'd already decided he was off base. He'd been counting on her support to get Brian in his corner, because Trey would listen to Brian. Now what was Sed going to do?

"Myrna," Jessica said, "I think Trey's abusing his painkillers too. The longer we wait, the more addicted he'll become."

"His prescription will run out eventually and then you won't have anything to worry about. Can I go back to sleep now?"

"Yeah, fine. Whatever." Sed stood, took Jessica's hand, and headed for the door. At least Jessica was on his side. It made him feel a little better about doing what he knew he had to do. No one was going to like it. Least of all Trey.

Jessica closed the bedroom door behind her and grabbed Sed's arm, hoping no one could overhear their conversation in the main cabin. Trey and Brian were quietly strumming their guitars while Jace and Eric listened to them play. The bus slowed as it entered the exit ramp to a midsized town.

"I'll go inside the pharmacy with Trey," Jessica whispered. "He'll be less suspicious of me."

Sed nodded. "Yeah, we need to be careful or he's going to become better at hiding it from us, which will make it harder to help him."

She touched his face. He really did care deeply about people. She didn't know why she hadn't seen it before. Jessica leaned against him, resting her face against his chest and murmured, "You're a good man."

He chuckled. "Nosy, you mean."

She smiled. "That's one way to put it. Righteous is another."

"Self-righteous?"

She laughed. "That's not what I meant, but yeah, sometimes."

"I really don't know if you're insulting me or complimenting me."

She leaned back to look up at him. "I like it when you do what you think is right, even if you have to go it alone. It shows your strength."

He stared down into her eyes and lifted his hand to brush a lock of hair behind her ear. She tilted her head back to accept his kiss, but the bus pulled to a stop. Jessica braced herself so she didn't topple over from the momentum. "I'll try to see if I can find out how he's getting all these refills."

"Don't blow your cover." He kissed her forehead and slipped through the bathroom door, closing it behind him.

Trey set his guitar aside and climbed to his feet. "I'll be right back. Anyone need anything?"

"I do." Jessica stepped forward. "Just a few feminine products. Tampons, maxi pads (the overnight ones), panty liners, a disposable douche, body wax. You guys will probably appreciate me having some Midol on hand and—"

Trey winced. "I'm not going to buy all that girl stuff for you. Get it yourself."

Jessica huffed with annoyance. "Fine. I don't see what the big deal is. It's not like the clerk is going to think it's for you."

He opened the bus door and Jessica followed him. "I'd end up getting the wrong thing and you'd send me back in there for more." He shuddered.

She laughed. "Probably." Well, now she had a legitimate reason to be in the store with him. She just hoped the aisles were arranged properly for eavesdropping. She walked beside him across the parking lot, trying to think of something to say that might get him to reveal something. "I was listening to you play back on the bus. You sound great."

He stroked his eyebrow with the side of his finger. "You think so? I still can't get my middle finger to go where I want it, but the rest are back to normal. Mostly."

"Just think where you were a month ago. None of your fingers would go where you wanted them."

He smiled slightly. "I guess so. Maybe I'm getting better faster than I think."

"You're doing great, sweetie." She rubbed his back encouragingly. "I'm amazed by how hard you've been working. I don't know where you find the will to carry on. It must be frustrating."

He looked away. She caught a flash of guilt on his face before he smiled. "Yeah, well, I know the guys are counting on me. And the crew... The opening bands... The fans... The record label..."

"That's an awful lot of pressure." When he started fidgeting with the chain dangling at his hip, she decided to drop the subject.

They entered the chain drugstore through a pair of sliding doors. Trey examined the layout of the establishment and located the pharmacy counter at the back.

"You don't have to wait for me," he said. "If you just want to get your stuff and go, that's fine."

She nodded, deciding it would look suspicious if she dawdled while he waited on his prescription. While she pretended to shop for vitamins near the prescription counter, she kept an eye on Trey out of the corner of her eye.

He opened his wallet and presented a prescription slip to the technician at the counter. "I need to have this filled."

The technician read the prescription. Her eyes widened and she looked up at Trey.

"Head injury," he said, pushing back his hair to show her the wicked scar that curved across the side of his head. "I need those quick. I ran out of my last prescription a few hours ago and I am supposed to take my next dose in a few minutes."

"You need to be careful about running out of these things. I hear the withdrawal symptoms are horrible."

"Yeah. I was going to wait until Monday, but my doctor told me to find the nearest pharmacy and get it filled."

"Do you have an insurance card?"

Trey made a big deal about riffling through his wallet several times. "Shit. I seem to have lost it." He sighed and buried his forehead in his hand. "What am I supposed to do now?"

"If you have a credit card—"

Trey looked through his wallet again. "I'm sure I have enough cash, I just hate to see my insurance company get out of footing their part of the bill." He grinned at her. "Leeches."

She smiled. "Maybe if you keep your receipt they'll reimburse you. Or you could call them and get your prescription card number."

He sighed. "I think they're closed on the weekends, but you're a real sweetheart for helping me out." He pinned her with those sultry eyes of his and Jessica knew the sweet thang behind the counter didn't know what hit her.

The technician blushed. "I'll just call your physician to make sure this is legit and put it in with the pharmacist."

Trey's face fell. "I *know* my doctor doesn't work Saturdays. Is there any way around that? I kind of need this now."

"It's company policy." She shifted from foot to foot.

Trey brushed his hair back from his scar. A move that seemed inadvertent, but Jessica knew better.

Staring at the side of his head, the young woman clutched the prescription slip to her chest and winced with empathy. "I know you're in a bind. I'll take care of it." She typed something into a computer and winked at him.

His smile of gratitude probably set her socks on fire. "Thanks. You're a doll."

Biting his lower lip, Trey tapped the counter with his fingertips and pushed off its edge with both hands. He turned and his gaze landed on Jessica. She started and knocked half a dozen bottles of vitamins off the shelf. She squatted to pick them up.

Trey's hand came into her line of sight as he retrieved one of the bottles. "For prostate health," he read off the bottle. "Either you're the best transvestite I've ever seen or you're spying on me, Jessica Chase. Did Sed put you up to this?"

She snatched the bottle out of his hand. "No, I was just… just looking for the… uh… iron supplements. I get sort of anemic this time of the month." She glanced up at him and smiled. "Blood loss. You know how it is."

He paled and cringed. "No, actually, I don't. Thank God." He stood and scanned the shelf. He quickly found the iron supplements, plucked a bottle off the shelf, and put it in her hand. "There you go. Now go find the rest of your girly stuff and head back to the bus."

Jessica bought all the stuff she'd told Trey she needed. She tried to see what he was up to while she stood in the checkout line, but her line of sight was blocked by a display of cheap stuffed animals.

Sed was waiting for her outside the bus when she left the store. "Well? What did you find out?"

She sighed. "Not much. He had a new prescription slip and he didn't have his insurance card with him so he paid cash. He somehow talked that poor girl into not calling his physician for verification. She'll probably get fired."

"He had a new prescription slip? He didn't try to get a refill or trick them with that bullshit story about him spilling his pills down the sink?"

"Nope. He handed the pharmacy tech a new prescription slip."

Sed looked thoughtful for a moment. "I wonder how many of those he has."

"Sed, I feel sort of bad sneaking around trying to catch him doing something wrong. He's been through a lot."

"Yeah, I know. But if he's using, I'm going to put him through a hell of a lot more."

Chapter 30

SED DUMPED THE LITTLE peach-colored pills from the prescription bottle into his palm and counted them. Thirty-six. Yesterday, there had been fifty-two. The label clearly said one to two tablets every six hours, not to exceed eight tablets per day. Though math wasn't Sed's thing, he knew Trey was taking more than double the proper dosage. Would this be enough evidence to get the rest of the band to make a stand against him? Sed didn't want to waste any more time. He knew in his gut that Trey needed help and he wasn't going to wait until they found him overdosed in his bunk as the final sign that they should do something.

Sed carefully returned the remaining pills to the bottle, secured the lid, and tucked the amber container into his pocket. He let himself out of the bathroom and settled on the sofa beside Trey. Trey had dozed off again, his head leaning at an odd angle against the back of the sofa. He never did much more than sleep these days.

"Tired, Trey?" Sed asked and nudged him in the side to wake him.

"Let him sleep," said Brian, who sat on Trey's other side watching TV. "The concerts are really wearing him out."

Sed snorted. "Yeah, the *concerts* have really been knocking him on his ass lately." Sed shook Trey's shoulder. "Hey, sleepyhead, wake up."

Trey groaned and covered his eyes with both hands. "Fuck, man, leave me alone."

"Why don't you just go to bed? You don't look very comfortable sleeping like that."

Trey sat there for a long moment as if he were physically incapable of lifting his head off the back of the couch. He finally hauled himself to his feet and headed directly for the bathroom. The bottle of pills in Sed's pocket suddenly felt very conspicuous.

A lot of loud rattling and swearing came from the bathroom. Trey opened the bathroom door. "Has anyone seen my pills?"

"Did you check your bloodstream?" Sed asked, scratching behind his ear.

Trey was instantly in his face. "You took them, didn't you?"

"Maybe."

"Jesus, Sed, give him his pills. What is wrong with you?" Brian said.

"There's nothing wrong with me." He locked gazes with Trey. "Why don't you tell Brian how many pills you took today?"

"Give me my fuckin' pills, Sed."

Sed lifted his hips off the sofa and pulled the bottle from his pocket. Trey tried to snatch it from his hand, but Sed held it firmly. "This label says you're supposed to take four pills a day. A maximum of eight. How many have you taken since last night, Trey? Do you even know?"

Trey grabbed Sed's wrist and tried to wrestle the bottle out of his hand. When that didn't work, he took Sed's little finger and bent it back viciously. "Ow, damn. Take the fuckin' things then." Sed released the bottle into Trey's custody.

"That wasn't funny." Trey took several shuddering breaths through his nose as he tried to regain his composure. "You don't understand my pain. You don't understand."

Sed's heart twisted. He knew Trey was hurting, but it wasn't the kind of pain that Percocet would help. "How many pills have you taken today, Trey?"

"I don't know," he yelled, "six or seven."

"Six?" Sed shook his head. "Try sixteen."

Trey scowled. "How would you know?"

"I counted them last night and again just a moment ago."

"I dropped some. I can't… I can't hold on to things… and I… they…"

He spun on his heel and headed to the bedroom. He slammed the door, but it did nothing to buffer the sound of his frustrated scream.

"Jesus Christ, Sed, you are such an ass." Brian stood from the sofa and walked to the end of the hall. Myrna watched her husband pass the dining table, obviously dumbfounded by the entire scene. Jessica sat across from Myrna, wiping stray tears from her eyes with the back of her hand.

Brian knocked on the bedroom door.

"Go away!" Trey yelled.

"Trey, it's Brian. Let me in." He waited patiently for several minutes. Eventually, the door opened and Brian slipped inside.

"Why are you so hard on him, Sed?" Myrna asked. "Don't you think he's suffering enough?"

Sed took a deep breath. Did they think he liked having to always be the asshole of the group? He'd love to turn a blind eye and pretend like everything was just fine, but he simply didn't have it in him. Not when someone he cared about was on a path of self-destruction.

Chapter 31

LOUNGING ON THE BED in the back bedroom, Sed trailed his fingertips up and down Jessica's bare shoulder. After a concert, he usually
satisfied his lust and fell directly asleep, but tonight his mind was too
full. They'd played ten consecutive shows in a little less than three
weeks, each one better than the last. Sed's throat still bothered him
(he sang through the pain), but Trey's improvement was nothing
short of miraculous. Sed was convinced that was the reason the rest
of the band refused to see what was going on right under their noses.
But Sed saw it and he couldn't let it go.

"We've got to figure out how he's getting new prescriptions,"
Sed said. "He should have run out of slips by now. How many of the
damned things did his dad give him, anyway?"

"He keeps them in his wallet," Jessica said drowsily.

Sed shifted her from his chest and sat up.

"Where are you going?" she asked.

"I'm going to get to the bottom of this tonight."

He climbed from the bed and slipped into a pair of shorts. He
let himself out of the bedroom and crept to Trey's bunk. Ordinarily,
Trey would be partying with the roadies or fucking some lucky
groupie on the other bus, but now he slept too much to participate
in his usual fun. Sed slid the curtain back as quietly as possible. As
he'd expected, Trey was out cold and still fully dressed. Sed eased
Trey onto his side and retrieved the wallet from his back pocket. He
opened Trey's wallet, feeling like a total ass until he saw the sheer

number of prescription slips nestled inside. They were blank, except for his father's signature at the bottom.

Rage boiled through Sed's veins. How could Dr. Mills just give him a free pass to the world's prescription medicine cabinet? Trey's parents had always given him everything his heart desired, but this was going too far.

"That stupid bastard."

Trey rolled over and opened his eyes. "What are you doing?"

"I found your secret stash of prescription slips." Sed pulled one offending slip from Trey's wallet and tossed it at him, then another and another. "I wondered how you kept getting more of that shit. What do you have to say for yourself?"

Trey's eyes narrowed. "Get the fuck out of my business, Sed."

"I'm in your business, Trey. I'm so far in your business, your grandchildren will call me partner."

Trey growled and flung himself from his bunk, tackling Sed to the floor. Sed let Trey punch him several times, hoping that releasing some of his pain and anger would let him admit he needed help.

"Why can't you just leave me alone? Why?" Trey punched Sed again. And again. "Why? Why?"

Sed wrestled him face down on the floor and leaned his weight into his back until he stopped struggling. "Why? Because you're the only Trey Mills I have and I'm not going to let you follow the same path Jon took. I'm not going to let drugs destroy you the way they destroyed him."

"I'm not taking any drugs," he squeaked, panting heavily.

"You are, Trey. It doesn't matter that they're prescription. You're addicted to them. You have to admit it to yourself before I can help you."

"I'm not addicted. I need them to play. Without them… I can't… I just can't…"

"How do you know if you can play without them? Have you tried?"

Trey's body began to shake. Even though the bus's corridor was dimly lit, Sed knew he was crying. Sed moved to sit on the floor beside him, giving Trey a moment to collect himself.

After several long minutes, Trey picked himself off the floor, sat beside Sed, and leaned against the bunk. Sed averted his gaze while Trey wiped his tears on the hem of his shirt.

"I don't want to need them, Sed, but I can't think of anything other than the feeling they give me right after I take one. The feeling that everything is all right. Everything is fine." He shook his head. "I know everything's not fine, but for a few minutes it feels like it is. It doesn't last near long enough, and then…" Trey took a deep breath. "I need another one."

"So you realize the drugs aren't helping you."

He nodded slightly.

"And you want to stop taking them."

He hesitated, and then nodded again.

"There's a rehab center—"

"No."

Sed's eyebrows lifted. "No?"

"I'm not going to rehab. I don't want the press in my business. I don't want anyone to know. Okay?"

Sed stared at him for a long moment. He could only imagine how Trey was feeling, but he could understand not wanting the press and the fans to know what was going on. Sometimes being a celebrity sucked.

"Okay. So what are you going to do, then? I don't think you can just quit these things cold turkey."

"I feel horrible when I just sleep through the night without taking them."

"Maybe your dad can tell us what to do."

Trey grabbed Sed's forearm with surprising strength. "No, don't tell my dad."

"He's the one who gave you an unlimited prescription. He had to know what could happen. Fuck, Trey, everyone knows you have an addictive personality."

Trey ducked his head. "My dad didn't give those to me. I took them from his office. He doesn't know."

Sed's heart sank with disappointment. "Wow, Trey. I don't even know what to say to that."

Trey stared at the floor between his feet. "Don't tell Brian I've been lying to him," he whispered.

"You can't keep this from the people close to you. You need their support."

"Let's just go. Go somewhere away from everyone and get me off the pills. You're the only one who can help me, anyway."

"I don't know what to do, Trey. I'm not a doctor. I don't think you can quit this shit just like that." Sed snapped his fingers. "We can check you into rehab under a fake name. They'd know how to help you. It's not that I don't want to help you. I don't know how." Sed squeezed Trey's shoulder. "I'm sorry."

"I'm not going to rehab. If you don't want to help, then fine." He brushed Sed's hand aside, climbed to his feet, and headed for the bathroom.

Sed grasped his forehead in one hand. What should he do? Maybe Jessica had an idea. He returned to the bedroom and found her dressed and packing a suitcase.

"What are you doing?" he asked.

"We're going to take Trey and help him before he changes his mind."

"You heard everything?"

"Yeah, I was listening. Call his father."

"He doesn't want his father to know."

Jessica put her hands on her hips. "Either he calls him, you call him, or I'm calling him. Our only other option is to check him into rehab."

"I'll call him," Trey said behind Sed, "but not here. I need to get away as soon as possible."

Jessica pushed Sed aside and grabbed Trey in a tight embrace. "I'm proud of you, sweetie. We're going to get you through this. Okay?"

Trey nodded, clinging to her like a frightened child. "You two make a good team. You'll have me kicked into shape in no time."

Team? Sed liked the sound of that.

Chapter 32

JESSICA CRAWLED UP ON the bed behind Sed and hugged him around the waist, kissing the side of his neck just behind his ear.

"I know this is hard, baby," she whispered. Trey had finally fallen asleep after a horrendous morning of suffering through withdrawal symptoms. "But you're the only one strong enough to be there for him."

He covered her hands with his. "I'm only strong when you're beside me."

She hugged him harder. "I don't believe that. You're always strong. That's why everyone depends on you so much."

"You've never been around me when I'm not with you."

Her brow knotted with concentration. "I suppose that's true, but…"

He shifted to the side and tugged her onto his lap. "Without you, I'm nothing. Don't you understand that?"

He kissed her before she could protest. When he drew away, he touched her cheek. "Let's go to bed before Trey wakes up again."

She liked this time together. The last few days had been so tough. Wearying. They scarcely had a moment alone together. Technically, they weren't alone now. She glanced at the other hotel bed. Trey was out cold. The tremors of this morning had stilled. Dr. Mills had been correct about the treatment. It just didn't seem fair that Sed had to be the one to administer it. She could only imagine how bad Trey suffered, and he'd probably blame Sed for that pain for the rest of his life.

She looked up at Sed and smiled, tracing weary lines around his eyes with her fingertips. "Kiss me again first."

She could tell he was exhausted, but he gave in to her wishes and kissed her. A deep kiss that made her toes curl. When he drew away, he set her on the edge of the bed and stood. He stripped down to his birthday suit, giving her a glorious eyeful of broad shoulders, narrow hips, and bulging muscles, and slid between the sheets. "Come keep me warm."

She climbed into bed with him and pulled the covers up to her neck.

"What's with all the clothes?" he asked, rubbing his hands over her soft cotton nightshirt.

"Um…"

He stripped her nightgown over her head and stuffed it under the pillow.

"I thought we were going to bed."

"We are in bed." He rubbed his lips over her jaw. "I need this, sweetheart. Don't you want to?"

She did and she couldn't argue with his logic. Well, she could, actually. She turned her head and watched Trey sleep for several moments. "Trey might wake up."

"We'll be quiet. He'll sleep right through it. And if not, well… I'm not shy. Are you?"

"Maybe."

He stripped her panties down her legs and stuffed them under the pillow as well. "Slow and quiet."

They'd never done anything slow and quiet in all their time together. Might be an interesting change of pace. If it was even possible.

"Slow and quiet." She ran a gentle hand over his hard pecs, pausing to stroke the tiny bead of one nipple.

"This will be a challenge," he whispered. "Do you realize I haven't had you for 68 hours?"

She chuckled. He knew how long it had been to the hour? "How many minutes is that?"

"Too damned many."

He rolled on top of her. She tensed. "Wait, I'm not ready yet."

"Shhhh. No more words."

He buried his hands in her hair and tilted her head back, exposing her neck to his questing lips. She sighed and closed her eyes, relaxing beneath him. She should've known he wouldn't just shove it inside without any consideration for her pleasure. This was Sed. Not a selfish bone in his body. Well, on most occasions.

She opened her eyes, staring at the ceiling, her chest filling with emotion. She'd been so very wrong about him for so long. How would she ever make amends to him? He caressed her skin gently and shifted upward to look her in the eye.

"Bored?"

It probably did look that way. Her staring off into space while he worked at exciting her body. "Never." She pulled her hand from under the covers to touch his face. "Sed?"

"Look, if you're not into this—"

She silenced him by pressing a finger to his lips. "I don't want this to just be about sex anymore. I want…" What did she want? "I want you to make love to me."

"Isn't that just sex?"

She shook her head. "No, it's not. It's so much more."

"Jess, I'm exhausted, I'm not sure I can live up to your expectations."

He didn't get what she meant. And she was too afraid to clarify. Maybe she'd work up the courage to bring it up again at a later time. She just couldn't force her pride down enough to put her mistakes about him to words. *I was wrong, Sed. So wrong.* Why couldn't she say it? She felt it. Remorse for hurting him. Regret for time lost between them.

"That's okay," she said. "I'm sure whatever you have in mind will be wonderful."

His fingers moved between her thighs, stroking her to excitement quickly.

"I just want to be inside you," he whispered. "Where I belong."

She reached for his cock, gently stroking its length up and down. Touching him fueled her excitement. His fingers dipped inside her, testing her readiness. She opened her legs for him and urged him to settle his hips between her thighs. Resting on his elbows, he looked down at her in the lamplight. "Help me find you, Jess."

Why did she feel like those words held more than one meaning?

She guided him into her body and he slid into her slowly, never taking his eyes from hers. He captured her wrists and pinned them to the bed on either side of her head. Why did he do that? She didn't like him to overpower her.

"Don't hold me down."

"I'm not holding you down, I'm holding myself up." He released her wrists and kissed her temple. "How do you want me to hold you?"

"I don't know. Equal." *Equal?* Even she wasn't sure what she meant by that.

He stretched her arms above her head and linked his fingers with her. "Is that okay?"

He withdrew slightly from her body and pressed deeper. Her back arched. "That's wonderful."

They stared into each other's eyes as Sed found an agonizingly slow rhythm. She couldn't decide if it was the connection between their bodies or the one between their souls that gave her greater pleasure. She couldn't look away from his gaze. And she didn't want sexual release. She just wanted to be with him. Forever, like this. Together.

"I always want to be a part of you," he whispered.

Her eyes filled with tears. She couldn't help it. "You always are a part of me, Sed. Even when we're apart."

"Yeah. I feel like that, too."

She struggled to free her hands from his, and reached up to grab the back of his neck. She lifted her head and kissed him passionately. When she drew away, he grinned at her crookedly. "Are you trying to get me excited now?"

"You weren't excited before?"

He looked like someone caught in a lie. "Well…"

She chuckled. "I'm sorry, I'll stop trying to get you excited."

"I'm excited in a whole different place," he said. "Well, yeah, there." He swiveled his eyes pointedly in the direction their bodies were joined. "That's always excited when you're near. But other things are excited, too."

She tightened her sheath around him and wriggled her hips, massaging him inside her.

He gasped and his eyes drifted closed. "Ah, okay, mostly just that part now."

His thrusts into her body didn't intensify however.

"If it's okay with you," he said, "I'd just like to concentrate on feeling you around me. Knowing I'm a part of you."

"That's perfectly okay with me." She liked this closeness. It greatly differed from their usual need for excitement and intense pleasure, yet satisfied her in a way she couldn't explain.

Jessica lost track of time, but it must have been at least an hour later when they finally sought release together. Her pleasure had built slowly, so when it finally unleashed, her entire body writhed beneath him in ecstasy. She somehow kept herself from screaming, but couldn't quiet her excited gasps. He let go a moment later, not his usual growling, cursing display of insanity. His mouth fell open in wonder, his head tilted back. He held his breath and stared into her eyes as he spent himself inside her.

He drew her against him and kissed her temple. "I love you," he whispered. "I can't keep it inside any longer. I know you don't feel the same—I can live with that—but it doesn't change how I feel. I love you so much I can't breathe sometimes."

She hugged him, her heart too full to repeat the words. She'd say them as soon as she could find air. She tried to relax, but her entire body remained tense in his arms for several moments. She didn't think she was ready for this. She did care about him. She did. But she still didn't feel his equal and it was something she needed to be happy. She wanted a partner, not a dictator.

An agonized moan came from the next bed. Trey sounded more wounded animal than human. Sed jumped out of bed and into his pants. He forced Trey to take a drink of water. Trey slurped from the glass, gripping Sed's wrist.

"Oh God, kill me, Sed. Even my bones hurt. Please, just kill me."

"Can't do that, buddy," Sed told him. "I need you. And we both know this is all about me."

He glanced over his shoulder at Jessica and winked.

Okay, she couldn't try to deny it any more. She loved him. So much. She needed to tell him. Wanted to tell him. But she didn't. She would. When the moment was right. And it wasn't right. They needed to get Trey better first, so they could decide what to do about these feelings.

Trey covered his mouth with the back of his wrist. "I'm gonna throw up."

Sed hauled Trey out of bed and got him as far as the bathroom threshold before he vomited all over the floor. Jessica slid into her nightgown and climbed out of bed to help.

"Sorry. Sorry," Trey groaned and got sick again. In the toilet this time.

"Nothing to be sorry about, man."

Sed pulled a towel from the rack above the toilet and Jessica took it from him. "I've got it."

He smiled his gratitude and she bent to clean up Trey's mess.

"Don't make her clean that up. I'll get it," Trey whispered. He threw up again.

"It's not a big deal, Trey," Jessica assured him. He hadn't eaten anything all day so it really wasn't a big deal. She rinsed the towel out in the sink and made another pass over the floor. "I'm just glad you missed the carpet."

"Do you want another drink of water?" Sed asked.

Trey's eyes widened and he shook his head vigorously. "That's what made me puke." Sitting on the floor, he leaned against the tub and rested his forehead on his bent knees. "Can I have another pill yet?"

"Half a dose," Sed reminded him. He glanced through the bathroom doorway at the clock radio on the nightstand. "And not for two more hours."

"I'll die by then," he whispered and then went quiet.

Jessica watched Trey with concern. He didn't move a muscle. Almost as if he really had died. "Is he asleep?"

"I think so." The two of them stared at him for several minutes. He'd gone so still, Jessica wasn't sure he was still breathing.

She worried her bottom lip with her teeth until she couldn't stand idly in the doorway any longer. She grabbed Sed's elbow. "Sed, check him."

Sed leaned over and shook Trey's shoulder. "Trey. If you're going to sleep, go back to bed."

Trey took a deep breath and lifted his head. "Yeah, okay," he murmured.

Sed helped him to his feet and Jessica stepped aside as they moved out of the bathroom toward one of the queen-sized beds. Sed dumped Trey onto the bed. Jessica wet a washcloth in the sink and wrung out the excess water before going to sit on the edge of Trey's bed. He started when she touched the folded washcloth to the back of his neck.

"This used to make me feel better when I was sick," she said. "If it bothers you, I'll leave you alone."

He relaxed slightly. "It's fine."

She left the cloth on the back of his neck and lightly rubbed her hand back and forth over the soft T-shirt along his back. He blinked his eyes wearily. "Feels nice," he murmured, his eyes drifting closed.

She glanced up at Sed, who was watching over them like a mother hen.

"Save some of that for me," he said, grinning.

She nodded, still rubbing Trey's back. "I won't be able to keep yours platonic though."

"I can probably live with that."

"When's he supposed to start feeling better?"

"His dad said as long as a week, so at least a couple more days. I should probably call the guys. I'm sure they're worried."

"Yeah. We did sort of kidnap him and disappear."

"If we hadn't, they'd have caved and given him more meds. I mean look at him. He's a mess. And he's always been very good at getting his way."

"Because he's a sweetie." Jessica brushed his long bangs out of Trey's face with her free hand. He hadn't shaved in days. Scruffy wasn't a good look for him.

"And I'm an asshole, so I get stuck with all these crappy jobs."

"I already told you. You get stuck with this kind of stuff because you're strong, Sed. Dependable."

"Nope, he's an asshole," Trey murmured. "He's trying to kill me and he gets off on it."

Jessica swatted Trey on the butt. "You behave."

Trey squirmed beside her and curled into a fetal position. "Rub back," he requested in an exhausted, yet impish voice.

She rolled her eyes at him, but rubbed his back gently. His body slowly relaxed again. She turned the washcloth to the cool side and looked up at Sed. He was watching them with his cell phone in his hand and a puzzled expression on his face.

"Something wrong?" she asked.

He shook his head as if to clear it of cobwebs. "No. I'll be back in a few."

Jessica watched Sed leave the hotel room, wondering what had him so introspective.

Chapter 33

SED STOOD ON THE landing outside the hotel room and stared out at the parking lot. What did Jessica want from him? He couldn't figure her out. Didn't she hate his overbearing nature? The way he took charge without even considering what anyone wanted? She'd said that was the entire reason she'd left him. But when he exerted his will over Trey, she praised him for it. Like it was a good quality to have. How could she praise him for it and hate him for it at the same time?

He sighed and wiped a hand over his face. If there were a Jessica Chase instruction manual, it would be written backwards in Arabic Pig Latin and twelve thousand pages long with random pages missing. Sometimes he wished she wasn't so damned complex. He couldn't puzzle this out right now; he needed to call Brian and get reamed for snatching Trey from under his nose.

He checked his phone. He'd had it turned off for a reason. Twenty-three missed calls. Ten voice mails. Sixteen text messages. All from Brian and Myrna. Even a couple from Eric. He dialed Brian.

"Where the fuck are you?" Brian answered on the first ring.

"Nice greeting," Sed murmured.

"Is Trey with you?"

"Yeah, I've got him. We're weaning him off his pain meds. If it works, you might actually recognize him the next time you see him."

"What do you think you're doing? You can't just take someone off narcotic painkillers without medical consultation. Myrna said he'll go through all sorts of horrible withdrawal symptoms."

"I consulted his father. Dr. Mills entrusted his son to me and told me how to do this properly. Trey doesn't want the media to find out about his little addiction, so we're discreetly taking care of it on our own. If anything goes wrong, I'll say to hell with what he wants and check him into a hospital, but for now, we're trying this."

"Let me talk to him."

"No. He'll have you over here doling out Percocet like its jelly-beans in ten minutes flat. I just called to let you know he's safe with me and Jessica. I'll call you in a couple of days with an update."

"Don't turn off your fuckin' phone again, Sed."

"Have a nice day."

"Sed!"

Sed ended the call, turned off his phone, and tucked it back in his pocket. He supposed the next time he saw Brian, Brian would punch him in the face. Eh, he probably deserved it. Pissing people off was Sed's forte.

Now what was he going to do about Jessica? He thought she'd freak out when he told her that he loved her, but she'd frozen up on him. Her body had gone all stiff and she hadn't said a word. That couldn't be good, could it? He shouldn't have told her how he felt, but it was too late to take it back now. Maybe she'd forget about it.

Not fuckin' likely. If Trey hadn't cried out in pain right after he'd said it, she'd probably have already dumped him.

"Why am I such an idiot?" he asked aloud before returning to the hotel room. Their friends with benefits relationship worked just fine and he had to go and mess it up with a love confession. *Dumb, Sedric. Real dumb.*

Jessica still sat beside Trey on the bed, rubbing his back with a soothing touch. Sed almost wished he were sick so she'd take care of him like that. He loved this tender, caring side of her. It was such an important part of who she was and she worked so hard to cover it up. As if it were a weakness instead of one of her greatest strengths.

Sed closed the door and crossed the room to sit facing Jessica on the free bed.

"Well, we can add Brian to the list of people who think I'm an asshole."

"That's not a list, Sed. It's called a phone book," Trey quipped, his eyes still closed.

"Apparently, you're feeling better," Sed said.

"I've never felt worse in my entire life, but Jessica has a magic touch."

Sed grinned crookedly at Jessica, who blushed. "I am very aware of that."

"A little lower, please," Trey murmured.

Jessica shifted her hand to his lower back.

"Lower."

Just below the waistband of his jeans.

"Lower."

"Trey!"

"Now move your hand around to the front and rub," he said, sounding like he was on death's door. "Rub."

She spanked him instead. "You are so naughty, Trey Mills."

"Oh yeah, spank me, baby. I'm naughty." He scowled suddenly and emitted a pained whine. His body curled into a tighter fetal position. He gasped as he tried to breathe through the pain, his fists clenched. "Please, Sed. I need... I need... You don't know what this feels like. Please, give me a pill. Half a dose. Whatever. Just make it stop hurting."

"You've got an hour and a half to go," Sed reminded him, though he knew he wouldn't be able to watch Trey suffer for that long.

"I can't wait. Please. I feel like I'm dying. Like someone is hammering nails into my bones. I can't... Can't..."

Jessica took the cloth from the back of Trey's neck and mopped the sweat from his face. She looked like she might burst into tears at any moment.

"How long can you wait?" Sed slid his hand into his pocket

where he had half dosage pills in a small envelope. Dr. Mills had told him never to cut Percocet in half, because they would dissolve too quickly and might cause a fatal overdose. So he'd called in a low dose prescription for his son and they were supposed to space them apart until Trey didn't need them anymore.

"I can't wait at all. I need it now," Trey insisted.

"Thirty minutes."

"Give me a fuckin' pill, Sed."

"Maybe we should give him one now," Jessica said.

"Thank you!" Trey said.

"Fifteen minutes."

"You're so goddamned stubborn," she said, scowling at Sed.

Stubborn? He'd compromised. Why did that make him stubborn?

She rubbed Trey's back. "He'll give you a pill in fifteen minutes," she said. "That's not very long. You can make it. You're a tough guy."

Trey snorted. "Tough guy? What tipped you off? Was it the whining or the crying?"

"It was the wailing."

He grinned, and then shifted to his back, his hands over his eyes. Into fetal position again. Onto his stomach. Back to fetal position. Pale and sweating. Panting. Clutching his abdomen. Absolutely miserable.

Sed checked the clock. Only five minutes had passed. He fished an oval-shaped, pink pill out of the envelope and handed it to Jessica. "Here. Go ahead and give it to him."

"He's got ten more minutes." She handed the pill back to Sed.

"Yeah, ten more minutes," Trey gasped. "I can make it."

"Since when did I become the softest one in the room?" Sed asked.

"Since you told Jessica you love her so much you can't breathe sometimes." Trey chuckled halfheartedly.

Sed frowned. "You heard that, huh?"

Jessica hit Trey with a pillow. "Just how long have you been awake?"

He grinned sheepishly. "I haven't slept in over two days."

"You ass." Sed shook his head in disbelief. Trey had heard a hell of a lot more than a love confession then.

"Is my ten minutes over yet?"

"You still have an hour and ten minutes," Sed told him, tucking the pill back into the envelope.

"Don't joke around like that, man."

"Who's joking?"

Chapter 34

"Do you feel like going out for dinner tonight?" Sed asked Trey.

"Why don't you take Jessica out? You have to be sick of looking at me."

To be honest, Sed would like to spend some time alone with Jessica, but Trey had only been drug free for forty-eight hours. Sed wasn't sure they should leave him by himself just yet.

"We could order a pizza," Jessica said from the table where she'd settled down with the laptop to edit the research journal article Myrna had emailed her.

"We're going back tomorrow, right?" Trey asked.

"Are you ready to go back?" Sed asked.

"Hell yeah. I miss Bri… my guitar. I'll be fine here by myself. You guys get out of here. Seriously. Bring me a doggie bag or something. I'll watch a movie. Take a nap."

"Check your email," Sed added.

Trey glanced at Jessica who'd been hogging the laptop for two days. He grinned impishly. "Okay, you're on to me. I need to check on my internet love interests."

"All twenty of them," Sed teased.

"Give or take."

"You sure you're okay with this?" Sed gave him one last time to change his mind before he swept Jessica off her feet.

"Do I need to kick you out of the room and lock the door?"

Sed leaned over and messed up his hair. "I'm glad you're back to yourself."

It surprised Sed to see tears in Trey's emerald green eyes. "Thank you, Sed. You saved me. I won't ever forget that."

Sed punched him in the shoulder before they both turned into blubbering messes.

Trey hit him back. "Get out of here, asshole."

Sed chuckled. "I could be a real asshole and make you wait in the bathroom while I take out my sexual frustration on my woman for a couple of hours."

"Don't talk to me about sexual frustration," Trey said. "If I had any energy I'd go hunt some tail of my own. Maybe tomorrow."

And only then would Sed believe that Trey was actually back to normal.

Sed moved to stand behind Jessica's chair and rested his hands on her shoulders.

She looked up at him. "I've got to get this done for Myrna."

"It will still be there tomorrow."

"I don't have anything to wear."

His eyes skimmed over her sexy bare feet, baggy pink sweats, gray T-shirt, and haphazard ponytail. "You look beautiful."

She rolled her eyes at him. "If you think I look beautiful, then you *must* be sexually frustrated. It's causing hallucinations."

"You're always beautiful." He leaned over to kiss her temple, his hands moving from her shoulders to wrap around her waist. "Are you ready to go then?"

She covered his hands with hers and smiled. "That depends. Where are we going?"

"I don't care. Anywhere. Nothing fancy. Just... out." He kissed her temple again. "Get your shoes."

"Do flip-flops count as shoes?"

"They do to me." He released her and went to the dresser to retrieve his ball cap. He put it on backwards and added his sunglasses. He did not want anyone to recognize him tonight. He just wanted to be a regular Joe out with his girl. He slipped his wallet into his back pocket and fastened the chain to the belt loop of his jeans.

He turned to find Trey and Jessica grappling over the laptop. "I have to save this file," she insisted.

"It's my turn."

She poked Trey in the ribs and he twisted sideways, but didn't release the edge of the screen. "You're going to break it," she said. "I'm almost finished. Calm down."

Trey released the laptop and sighed with over-exaggerated exasperation. Sed caught the mischievous gleam in his eye and knew he was just messing with her. Sed smiled to himself. Yeah, Trey was back. Maybe Brian would forgive him now.

While she saved her file, Jessica hummed the Final Jeopardy jingle under her breath. She was as ornery as Trey was. God, he loved her. She still hadn't said anything about his love confession. He'd expected her to dump him, which might have been easier to deal with than her not saying a goddamned word about it for three days.

Her smiling face appeared in his unfocused line of sight. "Let's go eat and have some fun." She planted a playful kiss on his chin.

"What kind of fun?"

"I'm sure we'll think of something."

He took her hand and headed for the door. The faster he got some food in her, the faster they could move on to the fun. "Later, Trey."

"Don't do anything I wouldn't do."

"Well, that leaves open a world of possibilities," Jessica quipped.

"You know it," Trey said.

Sed tugged Jessica from the hotel room and closed the door behind them. He drew her into his arms and stared down at her in the glaring yellow of the streetlight in the parking lot. "Alone at last." He lowered his head and kissed her deeply. He expected her to protest, but her arms stole around his back and she pressed her tight little body against the length of him. All senses set to go, his hands shifted to the curve of her ass and pressed her closer.

She gasped and tore her mouth from his. "Food first, fun later."

Luckily, there was a chain restaurant across the street.

—∞—

Jessica picked at her salad, watching Sed through her lashes. When should she tell him she loved him?

Now?

Her heart fluttered.

No, not now. Maybe later.

"What's wrong? You're really quiet." Sed tossed an empty rib bone on his plate.

"Nothing," she lied. "Are we going straight back to the motel room after we eat?"

"Trey's expecting some dinner. But knowing him, he's ordered himself some takeout and has seduced the delivery driver by now."

Jessica wiped her damp hands on her pants. "Maybe we should tour the city."

Sed paused with a rib halfway to his mouth. "I figured you'd never want to do that again after what happened the last time."

She scowled. Why'd he have to bring Vegas up now? "Yeah, well, it wasn't the end of the world. Not an experience I'd like to repeat, however."

"It wasn't good for you?"

She looked up at him, catching his knowing grin. "Oh don't get me wrong, the sex was fabulous, but the video quality was shoddy."

"I know a great film crew. They do all of Sinners' music videos. Maybe we can add some special effects to our next public encounter. Heavy metal sound track. Giant robots. Explosions in the background when I come inside you. Stuff like that."

She picked up one of his French fries and tossed it at him. It hit him on the cheek and landed on the table. "We just have to be more careful."

Nodding, he devoured his barbecued rib. "Eat faster," he insisted, his mouth full.

She grinned and pushed her salad around her plate.

"Slight problem," she said. "I don't have a skirt on."

"It's dark out," he said, stuffing French fries in his mouth ten at a time. "No one will see a thing."

"And there isn't really anything worth seeing around here."

"So we hop in a cab and drive around until we find someplace interesting."

She stole one of his French fries and nibbled on it.

"You aren't eating faster," he pointed out.

She tried to eat faster, but she was nervous around him tonight. Ever since he told her he loved her, things felt different. Confusing. "Can I ask you something?"

"What kind of something?" he asked suspiciously.

"Why do you let Eric watch you have sex with your groupies?"

He leaned away from the table and rubbed a hand over his backward ball cap. "You know about that, huh?"

"Yeah, I know. Will you tell me why?"

He gazed out the dark window beside them. "You don't want to ask me that."

"I just thought… I thought if you like it that much, I wouldn't mind Eric watching us together. If you wanted him to." She felt the heat rise up her neck to her cheeks, but forced herself to not duck her head, so he'd know she was serious.

His gaze swiveled back to her. "Really?" After a moment, he shook his head. "I don't need him to watch us."

Her brow furrowed. Need him? Sed needed Eric to watch? This entire time, she thought it was Eric who needed that kind of voyeuristic stimulation. "What do you mean, you don't need him?"

"I don't have any problem getting off with you, Jessica. Something about him watching me do boring chicks helps me get off. Without him there, I just can't... get excited enough." He stared at her for a moment and then lowered his gaze. "See, I told you that you didn't want to ask me that."

"You can't get off with other women?" She was so stunned by the idea that her head started to spin.

"Why do you think I do two or three of them at a time?"

She winced. Okay, she didn't need that reminder.

"Since you left me, I have a hard time, you know." He glanced at her pointedly.

"I have no clue."

"Finding satisfaction." He hesitated. "Will you just finish your salad, already?"

She grinned, feeling strangely validated. "I'm the only girl who gets you off?" she pressed.

He scowled at her. "Do you know how horrible that is for someone who loves sex as much as I do? I went two years like that. Sex was a chore to find ten seconds of relief. Sometimes I thought I'd do better being celibate."

"Poor baby." She didn't feel one bit sorry for him, though. Just happy for herself. "I'll make it up to you in a few minutes."

"You'd better," he growled. "This thing with Trey has made things impossible. You're always there, but it would be wrong to pounce on you every couple of hours."

She grinned. "Why is that wrong?"

He groaned. "Will you just eat faster?"

Chapter 35

"Let us out here," Sed told the cab driver.

The cab pulled to a stop along the curb and let them out. Jessica glanced around, a confused expression on her face. On the other side of a chain-link fence, brightly colored slides sloped and twisted around deep pools. A fake volcano spewed orange-lit water into the air. People shouted and laughed throughout the attraction.

"A water park?" she asked. "This place will be packed."

Actually, as it was after dark, the parking lot was almost empty. "I thought you were feeling adventurous."

"I am, but I didn't bring a swimsuit."

"I'm sure they sell them."

"We have to be discreet, Sed. No repeats of Vegas."

"Agreed."

As they walked hand in hand toward the entrance, Jessica still seemed uneasy.

"Something's bothering you," he said.

"This is like a family place. There will be little kids all over the place."

"No one will know what we're doing." He spotted a sign next to the cash register. *No one under 16 admitted after dark.* He pointed at the sign. "Does that make you feel better?"

"A little."

"Two, please," he said to the cashier and reached for his wallet.

"We close in an hour," the attendant told him.

Only an hour? Well, he was with Jessica. An hour should be plenty of time. "That's fine."

They went to the gift store first. Jessica sorted through a rack of swimsuits in her size. He pulled a white string bikini off the bar and handed it to her.

"Try this one," he growled into her ear.

She lifted it to eye level. "It's kind of… re*veal*ing."

He growled against her neck. She shuddered and headed for the dressing room with the bikini in hand. He grabbed the nearest pair of swim shorts in his size and went to stand outside the curtained dressing rooms at the back of the store to wait for Jessica. He heard the rustle of her clothes as she removed them on the other side of the curtain. He glanced up at the security camera and shifted his merchandise in front of his raging hard-on. God, he couldn't wait to sink into her warm flesh.

"How does it look?" he asked gruffly. If it weren't for the damned security camera, he'd have already joined her to see for himself.

"Skimpy."

"Let me see."

She slid the curtain back and he dropped his swim shorts on the floor. "Whoa," he said, eyes skimming the rounded tops of her breasts spilling from the scraps of fabric, her belly, the triangle of white fabric concealing… He forced his gaze to her thighs. *Thighs.*

She turned around and watched him over her shoulder. His gaze moved down her sexy back, the lower curve of both ass cheeks peeking from beneath the swimsuit, her thighs. God, her thighs. And her slender calves. Thighs. Ass. And her… "Ungh."

"Well?" she asked. She turned to face him again, looking down at her body uncertainly. She brushed her hands over the flare of her hips. "Do you like it?"

She wanted him to form actual words? "Nice," he managed. *Nice?* She looked fucking amazing. *Say it, Sed. Before she closes the curtain.*

Too late.

He stared at the red gingham curtain that concealed her from his eager gaze. His brain slowly started to function again. "It looks great, babe. Perfect. You look perfect in it. I think you should get it. I mean, it looks really, really good on you. Awesome. Did I mention sexy?"

She chuckled and called to him through the curtain, "I saw the look on your face, sweetheart. Of course I'm going to get it."

Yes!

"Did you find anything?"

Who cares? "Yeah." He glanced around, wondering what had happened to the swim shorts he'd been holding. He noticed them on the floor and stooped down to retrieve them.

Back in her sweats and T-shirt, she let herself out of the dressing room. Now that she'd reminded him what was under those baggy clothes, he couldn't wait to get his hands all over her. Those thoughts did make walking normally a challenge, however.

He bought her swimsuit and his, as well as a couple of beach towels. They left the shop and made their way to the locker rooms near the Olympic-sized swimming pool. He pinned her to the wall near a glowing torch and kissed her deeply. After a moment, he pulled his mouth away and gazed down at her. His dick strained against his pants as he pressed it against her lower belly.

"Do you have any ideas on how to get this hard-on into the pool without the whole world noticing my tented shorts?"

"Towel around the waist? That's how I plan to conceal the juices dripping down the inside of my thighs."

He growled in torment, drawing a shudder of anticipation from her. "You're deliciously evil."

She chuckled.

"But mostly delicious." He dug her scrap of bikini and one of the beach towels out of the sack and handed them to her. "Meet you on the other side," he murmured. "Don't dawdle."

"No chance."

He watched her enter the women's dressing area, and then went into the men's. He successfully got into his swim shorts, locked his belongings in a rented locker, and wrapped his towel around his waist. It did make his tented shorts less noticeable, especially if he bent at the waist slightly. At least, that's what he told himself.

He waited impatiently outside the women's dressing rooms. Ignoring the appreciative stares of nearby women, he crossed his arms over his chest and scanned the attractions looking for something that would offer them discretion, but not diminish the excitement of their overt naughtiness. Wave pool. Definitely the wave pool. The sound of the rhythmically lapping waters had *his* lap at full attention.

Jessica stepped out of the dressing room looking hotter than the sun. She'd let her hair down and, as she'd planned, had her towel wrapped around her waist. It hid her thighs from view but didn't prevent him from thinking of her juices and how much he wanted to taste them.

"Wave pool?" he asked, extending his hand toward her. She grasped it a little tighter than usual.

They gazed across the expanse of concrete, pools, and fountains to the wave pool. The attraction was tucked in the farthest corner of the park and only had a few people surfing amongst the waves on inner tubes and body boards. Except for the glow of the occasional torch stuck in the sand, the entire right half of the pool was bathed in darkness. Plenty of shadows for discretion.

"Wave pool," she agreed breathlessly.

He led her to the shadowed side of the pool. Male heads turned as she passed. The fact that she was with Sed didn't seem to phase them.

When they reached the five-foot marker on the side of the wave pool, Sed tossed his towel on the ground and jumped into the water feet first. He moved toward the deep end until the water sloshed against the tops of his shoulders and held his hands out to catch

Jessica. She dropped her towel, took his hands, and slid into the water in front of him. She released his hands and shifted them to his shoulders.

"My feet don't touch the ground here." Her legs brushed against his as she treaded water to stay afloat.

"Just hold on to me," he murmured. "There is no height disadvantage in the water."

They were eye-to-eye for a change and got lost in each other's gazes as they stared at one another.

"I'm glad you took off your sunglasses," she murmured, lifting her wet hand to touch his cheek. "When you wear them, I miss looking into your gorgeous blue eyes."

"I hope no one recognizes me. I should have bought some swim goggles to replace my disguise."

She laughed. "That would have been *so* sexy, baby."

Thirty minutes until the park closes, a loud speaker announced.

Sed nuzzled Jessica's neck. "I need to be inside you."

She shifted closer, tightening her arms around his neck and wrapping her legs around his waist. "I need you inside me."

He reached between their bodies and pushed the front of his shorts down. His dick sprang free, hard as stone and ready for action. He carefully brushed the crotch of her bikini bottoms to one side and guided himself into her body. Her mew of pleasure, as she sank down to take him deep, grabbed him by the balls. He shuddered, his eyes drifting closed, his mouth open. Her warmth surrounded him, so soft and inviting. His pleasure was intense. His need overwhelming.

His hands shifted to the slick skin of her ass, drawing her closer, pressing himself deeper. Water sloshed over her face as the waves built. There was a height difference now that their bodies were joined. He inched toward shallower water. She leaned back, her fingertips gripping his shoulders. She locked her shins into his sides and drew her hips away, before taking him deep again.

He watched her as she took charge of their joining. She seemed totally oblivious to anything but the feel of his body filling her, receding, filling her again. He let her ride him, relishing her obvious pleasure, but forcing his attention to their surroundings occasionally. He had to keep a lookout for anyone who might be paying attention. He didn't want to risk her getting hurt by some idiot with a video camera again.

He'd rather watch her getting off on him, however—her head tilted back in reckless abandon, her hair trailing in the water behind her. Her eyes were closed, but her lips remained parted as she gasped and groaned and gasped and groaned.

Yeah, baby. Feel me. I'm part of you.

"Sed." The crashing waves drowned out most of her plea. "Touch me. Touch me. Please. Oh."

She was definitely about to come. He shifted his hands to her breasts, his thumbs working their way under her tiny bikini top and brushing against the hard pebbles of her nipples. She shuddered, her silky sheath gripping his cock as she wriggled her hips impatiently. He groaned.

"Touch me there," she insisted.

"Where, baby?" he murmured, rubbing his lips against her throat. "Where do you want me to touch you?"

"My clit. Please. I need. I need to…"

He moved his hand between her thighs and stroked her fast with his middle finger. She shuddered, and came with a loud cry. Her pussy clenched spasmodically around him as she strained against him. She'd completely lost track of where she was. Sed kissed her deeply, drawing her shouts of pleasure into his throat.

Jessica trembled with aftershocks of release for several minutes and then her body stiffened with panic as she regained her sense of place. She turned her head, breaking their mouths apart and glanced around.

"Did anyone see?"

"Do I care?"

The waves had died down now and the pool was relatively quiet. After Jessica had taken in their surroundings, and recognized that no one was paying attention to them, she turned her gaze to his.

"God, you made me come so hard," she groaned, her eyes rolling into the back of her head. "Nothing is hotter than doing you in public."

"My turn now."

"Yeah, it is," she agreed, amusement in her tone.

"Can you unclench your legs? I'm going to have some major bruises on my ribs tomorrow."

Her pretty jade-green eyes widened and she loosened her legs. "Oh God, I'm sorry, sweetheart. I didn't know I was hurting you."

"Well worth it. Now just relax. Except do that tightening thing you do inside. I love that."

She squeezed him inside her. Tighter. Tighter. Relaxed. The pleasure in his groin was almost unbearable. His eyelids fluttered.

"Like that?" she asked, a knowing grin on her face.

"Oh yeah, just like that."

He held her hips still with both hands and thrust into her, pulled out, thrust in, keeping all the action beneath the surface of the water. Within her body, she squeezed him as he pulled out, relaxed when he thrust forward. His balls were so full and tight, he knew he wouldn't last much longer. He fought impending release though, clenching muscles at the base of his cock that were insistent on involuntarily expelling his seed inside her. He groaned against her throat, finding it difficult to relish that first orgasm without letting go. The spasms of pleasure subsided after a long moment and he started to thrust inside her again, working at building himself up once more.

"You're the only man I know who can do that," she whispered, nibbling on his ear, her breath warm against the wet skin along his neck, her fingers stroking the sensitive skin on either side of his spine.

"Do what?"

"Come without ejaculating."

He leaned back and grinned at her. "You noticed that, huh? It takes a lot of concentration. And Kegel exercises."

"Same kind I do so I can do this?" She squeezed him inside her even harder than before and he shuddered.

"Yeah, that Kegel guy was a genius. But can we not talk about this right now?"

"Sorry," she murmured.

Fifteen minutes until the park closes. Please make sure you've collected all of your belongings before you leave, a loud speaker announced.

"Damn it. They'll be kicking us out soon." He shouldn't have held back the last time.

Jessica's hands moved to his chest, her fingers trailing down over his skin. "Just press me up against the wall and fuck me like an animal, Sed. I know you want to."

Actually, it hadn't entered his thoughts, but that *would* do the trick quickly. "You don't mind?"

She cocked an eyebrow at him. "Would I have mentioned it if I minded?"

God, he loved this woman. And not only because she was his sexual equal. But right now? Mostly for that reason. He walked closer to the wall and pinned her back to its textured surface.

"Let me know if I hurt you and I'll try to settle down."

She nodded, the trust in her gaze absolute. She wrapped her legs around his waist loosely, to give him plenty of room to move and keep her hips tilted for easy penetration.

He gave lust free rein.

He thrust into her. She took all of him, wriggling her hips and squeezing his cock inside her to increase his pleasure. His perfect goddess. *Jessica.* He found a rapid tempo. Thrusting deep, withdrawing. The intensity built with each stroke. His need to possess her, to claim her, brand her, drove him to madness.

"Mine," he growled against her throat, sucking her flesh into his mouth to leave his mark upon her skin.

"Yes, Sed. Yours. Take it."

He fucked her harder. He wanted her to feel him. Know him. Be one with him. Be all his. Only his.

"Jessica," he groaned. Already close to exploding inside her, he had to know, "Do you feel me?"

"Yes. I feel you. Do you feel me?"

"Yes. It's mine. Tell me it's mine."

"It's ours."

"Ours," he sighed in agreement and shuddered as he lost himself and spilled his seed inside her, the pleasure intense, the emotions overwhelming. "Take it, Jessica," he cried, still coming, still filling her with more of himself. "Take it all. Take everything I am."

"I've got you," she whispered, wrapping her arms around him and pulling him against her. She kissed his temple tenderly. "I love you, Sed." She rubbed her nose against his cheek. "I love you."

He gasped and took a deep shuddering breath, his chest full to bursting, his vision blurred with tears. "I love you," he whispered around the lump in his throat and hugged her closer. He struggled to contain his tears, but could not stop them from falling. Hopefully, she'd think those were droplets of pool water dripping from his jaw and striking her shoulder.

Chapter 36

SED PULLED THE TOUR bus door open and hefted a suitcase up the stairs. Before he could set it down, Brian shoved him into the partition that separated the driver's area from the main cabin.

"You son-of-a-bitch, you always think you know what's best and just do whatever the hell you want without any consideration—"

Trey grabbed Brian around the waist and pulled him out of Sed's face. "Leave Sed alone," he said. "I owe him my life."

"Trey!" Brian hugged him with both arms. Their little bromance disturbed Sed sometimes, especially now that Brian was married. "How do you feel?"

"How do I look like I feel?" Trey struggled from Brian's stranglehold of an embrace.

Brian looked him over. "You look… great."

Jessica wandered up the stairs, carrying the laptop case and her mammoth-sized purse. "Yeah, he does."

Myrna pushed her husband aside and hugged Trey. "We missed you, sweetie. I'll go make you a cherry pie. How does that sound?"

Trey rolled his eyes in bliss. "Wonderful. Sed tried to starve me to death last night."

"You do look thin," Myrna said disapprovingly. She went to the kitchen, opened a cabinet, and started pulling out ingredients.

"We thought you'd call for take out," Jessica said, looking guilty.

Sed felt no guilt for abandoning Trey for a night. Just happiness. Jessica loved him. Nothing else mattered.

—m—

Jessica glanced up from the final draft of Myrna's journal article. Sed handed his cell phone to her. "It's your mother."

Jessica's heart skipped a beat. Her mother had been forbidden to call unless it was an emergency. Jessica grabbed the phone. "Mother? What's wrong? Did something happen?"

"I thought you'd like to know that you got a letter from the University today. From the dean's office."

"Did you open it?"

"After the chewing out you gave me last time, of course I opened it."

Jessica winced. "Well?"

Something inside her wanted the letter to refuse her the chance to win her scholarship back. She just wasn't sure she even wanted to *be* a lawyer anymore. Mostly because she'd have to be away from Sed again, but also because failure did not sit well with her and the thought of being at the same institution as Dean Taylor made her skin crawl.

"Your probation stands," her mother said, "but if you pass that class you failed—"

"I didn't fail it, Mother."

"If you get an A when you retake it, you'll get to keep your scholarship."

Jessica didn't know if she should be elated or disappointed. Well, she knew she *should* be elated, but now she had a tough decision to make. She looked up at Sed who stood watching her as anxiously as Sed was capable of being. Could she leave him again? Even temporarily?

"I thought you'd be happy," Mother said.

"I am." She wasn't. "Does it say what I have to do?"

"In addition to your regular third-year classes, you have to take the failed class, too."

"Anything else?"

"You have to pay for the extra class out of your own pocket. It's not covered by your scholarship. You don't expect me to foot the bill, do you? You know I can't afford—"

"No, Mother. Don't worry about it. I can come up with some money. Thanks for calling and letting me know."

"Is your boyfriend going to pay for it?"

Jessica scowled. "No. What do you think I've been doing all summer? I've been working."

"If you'd just marry that rich rock star guy, you'd never have to work. Then you wouldn't have to worry about all this going to school nonsense."

Jessica rolled her eyes. How many times had they had this conversation? A thousand times? A million? "Good-bye, Mother."

"Take care," she said brightly.

Jessica ended the call and handed the phone to Sed.

He hugged her. "I'm sorry you didn't get your scholarship back."

"Oh, I got it back. I just have to pay for that class I have to retake."

"You got it back?" Sed tugged her back by her shoulders to look down at her face. "Why aren't you dancing in celebration?"

She shrugged. The semester started in two weeks and her time with Sed would come to an end. Myrna's project was ending too, and she'd be heading back to Kansas City for the start of fall semester. There was no reason for Jessica to stay. No reason, except her feelings for Sed.

"I love you," she whispered around the knot in her throat.

He grinned, both dimples in full view. "I love you."

She kissed him deeply, wanting him to make her forget all her worries for a couple of hours and immerse herself in him. He took her hand and led her to the back bedroom, incapable of disappointing her.

Chapter 37

JESSICA WORRIED HER LIP as she and Myrna waited in the deserted dressing room for the guys to take the stage in Dallas, Texas. Myrna was no longer collecting data, so they'd watched every performance this week. Tomorrow, Myrna would catch a plane back to Kansas City, and the next day… Jessica didn't want to think about it.

"What's bothering you?" Myrna asked.

Jessica glanced up. "I'm not ready for this summer to end."

Myrna nodded. "I know the feeling. But don't worry, Sed will come see you when the band takes a break."

"Yeah, every couple of months."

Myrna's brows drew together. "That is so gonna suck. I need to find a new vocation."

"I know the feeling."

"That's not the only thing bothering you, is it?"

Jessica shrugged. "I'm usually excited when a new semester starts. But now, I'm not even sure I want to be a lawyer anymore."

"I've always had a hard time picturing you as a lawyer. You're too…" Myrna looked reflective for a long moment. "…good."

"Don't we need good lawyers?"

"Of course. You just don't fit the greedy, corrupt stereotype."

"I've been pegged into a stereotype since I grew breasts. No one takes me seriously. They judge me as…" She didn't know how to explain it. Men ogled her. Women hated her at first sight.

"Too sexy."

Jessica shrugged. "Yeah, I guess. Do you think it's the way I dress or what?"

"Jess, you spend most of your days in sweats and flip-flops. It's not the way you dress, you just look sexy. Your body. Your face. The way you carry yourself. Don't be ashamed of it. Women pay plastic surgeons a lot of money to attain your natural assets."

"I'm not ashamed, but I do get tired of being treated like a commodity. I thought becoming a lawyer might finally earn me some respect."

"That's why you want to be a lawyer? Honey, I don't think there are many professions that are less respected than lawyers."

"Respect is part of it. I really just want to help people. Protect them from all the bad things that happen in the world."

Myrna chuckled. "You're more like Sed than I realized."

Jessica pulled a face. "Really? I don't see it."

"There are a lot of careers that help people. No one said you have to become a lawyer. You are allowed to change your mind."

Jessica's shoulders suddenly felt lighter. She hadn't realized how much the thought of going back to that school was weighing her down. "I am?"

"Why not?"

Yeah, why not?

"The guys are set to go onstage in a few minutes. Are you ready to go?"

Jessica smiled at Myrna and nodded vigorously. Just the thought of seeing Sed onstage had her heart throbbing in her chest. Especially now that she knew she could stay with him. He'd be thrilled. Wouldn't he?

Chapter 38

JESSICA STILL HADN'T TOLD Sed that she wanted to drop out of law school. And she didn't have any idea how Sed would react to her proposition. She hoped he understood where she was coming from and didn't think she was trying to trap him or giving up on her dream (it simply wasn't her dream anymore). She loved him. She wasn't ready to leave him to work toward something she no longer wanted. Not when she had everything she desired right here.

The bus eased to a stop outside the airport terminal. Sed opened the bedroom door. She took a deep breath.

"Are you all packed?"

"I'm not going."

His brow furrowed. "What?"

She climbed from the bed that was covered with all her belongings and her open, yet unpacked, suitcase. She wrapped her arms around him and looked up into his tired eyes. He hadn't been sleeping well the past few nights. She kept finding him sitting at the dining table in the dark, drinking beer alone.

"I'm not going back. I don't want to go to law school anymore. I want to stay on tour with you for a while and then—"

"No," he said firmly. He peeled her arms from his body and shoved her aside.

She paused, his words a slash to her heart. He just didn't know what she meant. She needed to explain herself better. "Will you let me finish?"

"This isn't our deal, Jessica. Our two months are up and now you're supposed to leave."

Deal?

Leave? But...

"You don't *want* me?" Her voice cracked as her throat squeezed shut with emotion.

"The game is over now. Go back to school, Jessica."

Over?

No. She couldn't accept that. Couldn't. No. He... He was...

"I don't want to go back to school. Will you listen to me, Sed?" Tears blurred her vision. Stupid tears. They never worked with Sed. They pissed him off and she knew it. She dabbed at her eyes with her fingertips. "Sed, please. Just listen."

He started to shove her belongings into the open suitcase on the bed. "No, I'm not listening. You are not chickening out. You're going back."

"You don't understand. That isn't why..."

He slammed her suitcase shut and pressed it into her chest. "Good-bye."

"I'm not finished talking to you." She slammed the suitcase down on the floor, her nostrils flaring and eyes narrowing.

"I'm finished talking to you. Get out!"

"Sed... You don't understand. Will you just listen?" Frustrated, she hit him in the shoulder. "Listen to me!"

He picked up her suitcase, took her by the arm, and pulled her toward the front of the bus. He tossed her suitcase out the open door. Her luggage sprang open, scattering her clothes across the wide sidewalk next to the terminal.

"Sed, don't—"

He grabbed her and hugged her against him until she thought her ribs would crack. She hugged him back, her lungs aching with unshed tears.

He'd changed his mind. Thank God. She couldn't walk away from him again. She just… couldn't…

He released her abruptly and then pushed her out of the door. She stumbled over her open suitcase and struggled to regain her balance. Her purse landed on the ground next to her feet. The bus door swung shut and then the vehicle eased away from the curb, leaving Jessica alone.

Utterly.

Chapter 39

BETH GRABBED JESSICA IN a bear hug the moment she stepped into the terminal. "I missed you," Beth said breathlessly. "Tell me all about your summer. Did you make good money stripping before you got fired?"

"No," Jessica said.

"Are you and Sed back together?"

"No."

"No? What do you mean, no? I thought things were going well. What happened?"

"We'll talk at home. I'm tired." Jessica *was* tired, and didn't think she could handle talking about Sed at the moment. His rejection was still too fresh. Too... *raw*. She'd thought they were finally working as a team instead of butting heads in constant opposition and then *this*.

Jessica stomped through the terminal toward baggage claim. "We need to make an ice cream and chocolate run," Jessica said to Beth over her shoulder.

By the time they got to their shared apartment, Jessica was no longer in the mood for ice cream or chocolate. She really just wanted to curl up in a ball on her bed and cry herself to sleep. Beth wouldn't hear of it. She brought two enormous servings of cookie dough ice cream into Jessica's room and interrupted her unpacking.

"Tell me everything." Beth slurped a bite of dessert into her mouth. So Jessica told her everything. Well, almost everything. From

Sed finding her in Vegas to him kicking her off the bus that morning. She conveniently left out some self-incriminating tales.

"Why do you put up with him? He's such an asshole. Seriously, Jess, you can do better. You deserve to be happy."

"I love him, Beth. It's not something I can help. I tried to tell him why I want to drop out of law school—"

"What?" Beth's spoon slipped from her grip and rattled in her bowl. "You're dropping out of law school? Why would you do that?"

"I told you I was on academic probation."

"But you got your scholarship back."

"I was thinking of becoming—don't laugh—a nurse."

Beth's brown eyes enlarged until Jessica feared they'd pop out of her head, and then she fell over on the bed laughing. "You had me going there for a minute, Jess."

"I'm serious. I can take most of the classes online—"

"Have you lost your mind? What a horrible, thankless job."

Jessica scowled. "I don't think so. I can't think of a more admirable job."

"All that time around that drug addict—"

"His name is Trey."

"All that time around… *Trey*… must have addled your brains and given you some ridiculous Florence Nightingale syndrome. You're going to be a great lawyer, Jess. You're so smart, and you're really good at arguing points logically."

Jessica snorted derisively. It was apparent that Beth had never seen her when she was around Sed. There was nothing logical about her interactions with the man.

Beth patted her hand. "You've had a tough day. Sleep on it. I'm sure you'll see that continuing with law school is what's best for you."

"I'm really tired of everyone thinking they know what's best for me. This is my life and I should be able to do whatever I want with it."

"Just sleep on it, okay? And promise you'll go to the first day of classes. For your bestest best friend." Beth offered an exaggerated pout.

"Yeah, fine, whatever. Now get out of my room and take your nightmare-inducing midnight snack with you."

Jessica would go to the first day of classes, but just to prove to herself that law school wasn't for her. It had nothing to do with Sed. The big jerk.

God, she missed him already.

Chapter 40

JESSICA FOUND A SEAT near the front of the lecture hall. Old habits died hard. Because she was taking Ellington's class with students a year behind her, she didn't know anyone. That was okay. She wasn't there to socialize, she was there to decide if she was dropping out or working her ass off to get this grade up to an A. As if. There was no way Ellington would ever give her an A. Jessica knew she was setting herself up for failure. That idea settled in the pit of her stomach and started churning out one hell of an ulcer. It just seemed a shame to waste all her hard work. And all that money. Just to… fail. She took a deep breath. *You can do this, Jessica. You can. You are not a failure.* But she felt like one. It took a great deal of fortitude just to stay in her seat. If she hadn't just attended an inspiring Criminal Law seminar with one of her favorite professors, who had reminded Jessica how much she loved studying law, she'd have already been out the door.

An attractive young man sat down beside her. "Hello," he said, "I'm Curtis. Are you in this class?"

Jessica nodded, not wanting to talk to Curtis. She wasn't too fond of men, especially attractive men, at the moment. Soon, another young man sat on her opposite side.

"Is Curt bothering you?"

"Not really." She pulled her laptop out of her backpack and booted it up. She had a sinking suspicion that the reason Dr. Ellington hated her so much was exactly this. Excessive masculine attention. She didn't ask the guys in the class to surround her, lean toward her, try to initiate her in conversation, but they always did. Always had. Probably always would. She considered getting up and moving to a vacant corner, but doubted that would keep them at bay.

"Would you like to grab a coffee with me after class?" Curt asked.

"No, thank you," Jessica said.

"But you want to go with me, right?" the guy on her other side said.

"No. I have a boyfriend." She'd *had* a boyfriend. She swallowed the lump in her throat. "A big, muscular boyfriend who gets very jealous." *And dumped me for no good reason.*

The guy chuckled. "I can see why."

The young man sitting behind Jessica leaned forward and touched her shoulder. "I think the three of us can take him."

Dr. Ellington entered the lecture hall, her presence demanding instant attention. The young men surrounding Jessica sat up straighter in their seats. Jessica forced herself not to hide under her chair.

Dr. Ellington glanced around the room. When her eyes fell on Jessica, she smiled coldly. "Good morning, class," she said. "I hope you're ready to work hard. I don't put up with any nonsense in my class." She pulled her laptop out of its case and hooked it up to a projector. "I assume you're all well rested after lazing about all summer."

No one said a word. Already intimidated, just as Dr. Ellington liked them.

"How was your summer, Ms. Chase?" Dr. Ellington asked, her blue eyes hard and punishing as she stared Jessica down.

"Fine. Thank you for asking."

"Just fine? I think it was probably better than fine. Seems to me you had a rather adventuresome summer. A screen debut of sorts. Would you care to share your internet notoriety with your classmates? I'm sure they'd be interested in how Jessica Chase spent her summer."

Jessica's soul drifted toward the ceiling. This was not happening. "No. I'd rather not."

"Well, I'm sure they'll look it up online after class." Ellington turned her back and started to write on the dry erase board.

While the professor's attention was elsewhere, every person in class popped open their laptop.

They're just getting ready to take notes for class, Jessica tried to tell herself.

After a moment's delay, stunned gasps echoed around the tiered seating.

Why wasn't there any air in this room?

"Now class, this is not the place to view that kind of seedy material," Ellington said with a cruel smile.

Jessica took a deep breath. She realized she had to deal with this stuff—she had come to terms with that—but not like this. This was too much. Why would Ellington purposefully draw their attention to it?

Jessica caught the video on the computer screen beside her. Sed was thrusting in her body over the Vegas strip. Her vocalizations of pleasure grew louder as Curt turned up the volume. He groaned in torment. "Oh my God. That is the hottest thing I've ever seen in my life."

Jessica slammed her laptop closed and rammed it into her backpack. She shot from her seat.

Curt grabbed her arm. "Hey, baby, we could skip the coffee and go straight to the action, if you'd prefer."

Jessica jerked her arm out of his grasp and ran from the room. She managed to keep the tears in check until she collapsed into the driver's seat of her piece of shit Nissan Sentra. It never failed. Even when absent, Sed *always* fucked up her life.

Chapter 41

ON THE TOUR BUS, Sed sat at the dining table staring down at Jessica's picture. God, he missed her. He knew that their breakup was for the best. She deserved to make a life for herself and he wasn't helping in that regard. Maybe someday they'd make it work. After she finished school and had her career going in the direction she wanted and deserved. He clung to that hope.

Brian took a seat in the booth across from him. "Hey, you okay?"

Sed nodded. "It's still a little raw, but I'll live."

"Need to talk about it?"

"Nope. How are you holding up now that Myrna's back at work?"

"Can't stand it."

They stared at the table in cooperative misery.

"Is it time to head to the stage?" Sed asked.

"We have a few minutes. Did Jerry get the studio reserved for next week?"

"Yeah, we're all set to record the first few tracks. He wants to get the new single on the shelves."

"Are we going to add it to the show, then?"

"Don't know. Probably should. It would help sales." Rehearsing a new song didn't hold the appeal it should, however.

Eric wandered out of the bathroom. "Why are we all hiding on the bus?"

Sed chuckled. "Brian and I are avoiding groupies. Don't know what the rest of you are doing."

"It's been a fucking drag around here for the last three days," Eric said.

"Sorry to ruin your fun, Sticks," Sed said.

Sed tucked Jessica's picture into his pocket and headed off the bus toward the concert venue. The small group of fans standing behind the bus erupted into cheers. Normally, Sed would go talk to them, but he wasn't in the right frame of mind. Brian took up his slack and headed for the fans, while Sed was let into the backstage area of the stadium. He found the dressing room labeled Sinners and went inside.

"There you are," a gorgeous brunette in an impossibly short skirt said. "I've been waiting for quite a while."

She looked familiar. Sed was certain he'd fucked her a couple of times, but couldn't remember her name. "I could use a beer."

"No problem."

She returned less than a minute later with a cold beer and a warm smile. "You don't remember me, do you?"

"Yeah, I remember you. I'm not good with names, though."

"Jillian."

He nodded, still not able to place her, and took a long draw from the beer bottle. "I'm going to go get warmed up now."

"Can I help you with that?"

"Not unless you plan on making me scream for twenty minutes."

"That was my plan, actually."

Sed paused, considering her offer. He knew he'd be back to his old ways eventually. Trying to bury the pain of Jessica's absence by putting his dick in any warm female recess that would accommodate it, but not yet. The thought of fucking another woman left him cold.

"Not tonight, Jillian."

He chugged his beer and ate a few pieces of red licorice. The glycerol helped keep his vocal cords lubricated and they seemed to need it a lot recently. He warmed up. First with low growls and then worked his way up the octaves to get his voice ready for the punishment of singing a live show. His cords were getting tired. He needed a couple of days off. He could really feel the difference in his voice after doing several concerts in a row. Tonight was their last show for a week, but he'd be in the studio for several days and the repeated takes brutally punished his throat. He needed to stop screaming so much and sing more, but the fans had come to expect his style.

Before long, the rest of the band arrived and then a roadie called them to the stage. Sed tried to get excited enough to perform, but he felt mostly numb. He hoped Jessica's first day of class had been better than his miserable, lonely day.

Chapter 42

JESSICA STOOD OUTSIDE THE concert venue, wondering why she'd driven over three hours to see a man who didn't want her. She still wanted him. She couldn't explain why.

Jake, one of Sinners' roadies, raced past the barrier and climbed into the truck that held the band's equipment. He emerged seconds later with a length of cord. He glanced up and caught sight of Jessica. His eyes widened with surprise. "What are you doing here?"

"I'm not sure."

"Do you want to come inside?"

She nodded.

Jake drew her around the barrier, talked their way through security, and left her in the corridor that led to the stage. She could hear Sed singing onstage in the stadium. The shouts of the crowd and the band's music were just background noise. God, she loved him. Missed him. She had to see him. Even if he didn't want to see her. She'd stay out of sight and just watch him. It would be enough.

She crept behind the stage and squatted next to the drum kit. Eric stumbled over a beat. She glanced up to find Eric staring down at her in confusion. She pressed a finger to her lips. She just wanted to see Sed. She didn't even want him to know she was there.

Eric shrugged slightly and continued to pound his drums and cymbals with his typical enthusiastic flair.

Jessica couldn't take her eyes off Sed as he paced the front of the stage, singing, screaming, growling, raising his hands in the air to encourage the crowd.

Why can't I let him go? He doesn't want me.

She wiped her suddenly leaky eyes on her shoulder and sniffed her nose. What could she have done differently? She wasn't prepared to live without him in her life. She'd thought things were going so well between them and then like flipping a switch, he'd declared their relationship over. Why? Why would he do that? Had he lied about loving her? To hurt her, maybe? Like she'd planned to hurt him originally. Had the whole thing been a game to him? He was a much better player than she was.

Brian moved to the front of the stage and climbed on the ego riser to play his solo. Sed moved to the back of the stage to grab a drink of water. He chugged half a bottle and set it down near the drum kit. His eyes fell on Jessica. They widened. He froze. When Brian's solo ended and Sed was supposed to continue singing, he didn't move. Jace shoved him and he snapped out of his trance. Sed turned and entered the song mid-chorus. The crowd had been singing the lyrics anyway. They didn't seem to mind his lapse.

When the song ended, he handed his mic to Trey and launched himself over the drum kit platform to Jessica's hiding place. She stumbled backwards over a collection of cords, but Sed grabbed her by her upper arms before she could flee.

"What are you doing here?"

She couldn't answer his question, because she didn't know. She shook her head, tears streaming down both cheeks.

"I don't want to see you," he bellowed. "Don't you get it? Go away!"

She shook her head harder, tears flying from her cheeks. "No, I *don't* get it. I don't get it at all! What changed, Sed? What… I don't understand… Please, Sed. Please."

"You're gonna beg, Jess? Beg like one of my groupie whores? Go ahead. Beg. Beg me to take you back. It won't change anything."

"I love you." She couldn't see his expression because his face was blurred behind her tears. "I *love* you."

"You and fifty thousand other women."

He released her and she sat down hard on the stage. She drew her knees to her chest, wrapped her arms around her shins, buried her face against her knees, and sobbed.

Sed's voice came through the speaker a moment later. "What do you say, Fresno? Are you ready to climb the gates of Hell?"

Chapter 43

SED HAD BEEN UNPREPARED to see Jessica that soon after their breakup. He felt guilty for being so hard on her, but he didn't think she'd leave otherwise. He refused to be her excuse for giving up on law school and her dreams. Things would never be right between them if that happened. But after the cruel things he'd just said, things would probably never be right between them again anyway.

God, he couldn't breathe.

Which made it exceedingly difficult to sing.

But not as hard as it was to keep his attention from the back of the stage where he'd left the only woman he'd ever loved sobbing on the floor.

Somehow, he got through "Gates of Hell" and "Good-bye Is Not Forever." He allowed himself a quick glance behind the drum kit. Jessica was gone. A gaping hole filled the place where his heart had been a few days ago. This was what was best for her. He had to believe that, because it sure as hell wasn't what was best for him.

When the band went on break, leaving Master Sinclair to dazzle the crowd with his solos, Sed grabbed a licorice rope and stared at the floor, chewing slowly and trying not to think much. He could not allow himself to hunt for Jessica, apologize, grovel for acting like an ass. He had to stick to his guns.

"Where's Eric?" Jace asked.

Sed glanced up. Usually, Eric would be drenching himself in water and changing from his sweat-saturated shirt into a dry one, but he was conspicuously absent. Sed rounded the back of the drum kit and found Eric trying to coax Jessica out from between two empty equipment cases. How had she managed to cram herself into such a tiny space? Sed hesitated. He couldn't stand to see her like that, especially knowing he was responsible. Why had she come back? She obviously wasn't thinking clearly. He'd given her a perfect out.

Fuck.

Sed nudged Eric aside and extended a hand toward Jessica. "Come on out of there."

"Get away from me, you asshole!" she shouted. "I fucking hate you."

So they were back to this. He'd thought it would make it easier, but no. "It's okay to hate me, just do it somewhere safer."

"Why do you care?"

He reached into the space and grabbed her ankle, trying to tug her out of her hiding spot.

"Don't touch me." She kicked at him. The stack of cases wobbled. He released her leg and stepped back.

"All right, I'll leave you alone. Come out for Eric, though. He'll be worried about you under there."

"Yep." Eric peeled his sopping wet T-shirt off over his head. "And if you don't, I'll throw my sweaty shirt in there with you."

Sed stalked off around the drum kit and once out of sight, paused to watch Jessica squirm from between the equipment cases. When he was sure she was safe, he headed back to the stage. He clapped Brian on the shoulder and encouraged the crowded to cheer their guitar hero's amazing compositions. He then extended a hand toward Trey, who'd joined Brian in the middle of his last solo and sounded better than ever. A second round of cheering for Trey now.

Sed paused halfway through the next song to get another drink of water. His throat felt raw, his vocal cords strained. He hadn't consumed enough glycerol during their break, but it shouldn't have made this much of a difference. On his next carried note, he broke off in the middle with a ragged cough. Maybe he was coming down with a cold. He finished the song, keeping his volume down to alleviate the burning sensation in his throat, and left Trey in charge of the crowd while he headed offstage to chew more red licorice.

Travis, one of their long-time roadies, patted him on the arm. "You okay, Sed?"

He nodded. "Sore throat." He glanced around, not meaning to look for Jessica, but unable to help himself.

"Do you want me to get you some numbing spray?"

"Yeah, that would help. I'll be back after 'Twisted.'" He returned to the stage to find Trey and Jace fighting over a pair of panties that some chick had thrown onstage.

"Did I miss something?" Sed asked.

"Those are for me," Jace insisted.

"Aw, Trey, let the kid have his panties," Sed teased.

Trey tossed them over Jace's head to Brian, who caught them in one hand and dangled them from a finger.

"Ah, fine, whatever," Jace grumbled and headed to the back of the stage to hang out by the drum kit.

Brian rolled his eyes. "I guess Jace doesn't want your phone number, sweetie," he said to the girl who'd tossed them onstage. "Try a bra next time. They fly farther."

Sed chuckled, but even that hurt. He cleared his throat. "Who out there is feeling a little twisted tonight?"

The crowd cheered in response, knowing it meant Sinners was about to treat them to their most energetic anthem, "Twisted." Eric thudded his bass drum with the introductory beats of the song. Sed roared through the first measure. When he screamed the first note, something thick and hot poured down the back of his throat. He choked on the liquid, covering his mouth with one hand.

When he drew his hand away, it was covered in blood.

Blood?

He stared at his fingers in disbelief. They blurred out of focus. The stage rose up to meet him as he blacked out.

Chapter 44

JESSICA STOOD OUTSIDE SINNERS' dressing room, leaning against the wall. She'd finally calmed down enough to stop crying, but she wasn't leaving until she saw Sed. She wanted to tell him what an asshole he was and that she never wanted to see him again. Yeah. That's exactly why she wanted to see him. So she could tell him off.

The music blaring from the stadium stopped. Strange. They'd just started the next song. A moment later, a roadie sprinted down the corridor, talking frantically into a cell phone. Jessica's heart rate kicked up a notch when the wail of an ambulance stopped just outside the back doors. Paramedics flew by with a gurney.

A fan? A roadie? Had something happened to Trey? He'd seemed fine the last time she saw him. Concerned, she headed after the paramedics. When she reached the edge of the stage, she froze. Trey had blood all over his hands, but it wasn't his.

"Sed!"

She launched herself across the stage. Brian caught her around the waist, but she fought him until he released her. She landed on her knees next to Sed. Blood. Blood everywhere. And it was coming from Sed's mouth.

"Do we intubate?" one of the paramedics asked another.

"God, I don't know. Where's all the blood coming from? He's going to drown in it."

They rolled Sed onto his side, and a pool of blood spread across the stage from his mouth.

"Help him!" Jessica insisted.

"Stand back, ma'am." One of the paramedics examined the inside of Sed's throat with a tiny flashlight. "His trachea isn't collapsed, but he's blown a blood vessel in his throat. Keep him on his side and let's get him to the hospital. We can't fix this here."

They lifted him onto the gurney. No one else moved. The entire stadium stood silent. Several roadies helped the paramedics lower the gurney to the floor and then they were racing toward the ambulance with Jessica on their heels.

She could hear a crowd of people following behind her, but she could only see Sed. Unconscious. Shallow breathing. Pale. Blood trickling from the corner of his mouth. So pale.

Oh God, please let him be okay.

Jessica waited for the paramedics to load Sed into the back of the ambulance and then climbed inside without hesitation.

"Ma'am?"

"I'm his wife," she lied.

She sat near Sed's feet and held on to his shin while the paramedics tried to get the bleeding to stop the entire long ride to the hospital.

At the hospital, Jessica was the only one there to impress upon the emergency room doctor the importance of treating Sed's throat carefully.

"He sings professionally. Please keep that in mind when you work on his throat."

"Do you want him to sing or live?"

"I want him to live, obviously. I'm trying to think about what *he* would want."

While they worked on him, Jessica stood just outside the curtain wringing her hands. How had this happened? Her thoughts kept returning to that night at the strip club when Sed's throat had been injured by that bouncer. Surely, that injury would have healed by now, but maybe all the screaming he did onstage had prevented full recovery.

A nurse ushered Jessica to the waiting area. The place was packed with familiar faces.

Trey grabbed her by both arms. "Is he going to be all right?"

"I think so. They got the bleeding stopped, but I'm not sure they were careful with his vocal cords."

What would Sed do if he couldn't sing? Singing was his life.

They waited for word from the doctor for over an hour. When he finally came to report Sed's status, he approached Jessica.

"Your husband lost a lot of blood, but he's going to be just fine. As soon as he wakes up, you can go see him."

"How's his throat?" Trey asked. "Will he be able to sing again?"

"There will be a long healing process and there might be some scar tissue. We won't know for sure until the swelling goes down. Right now he has a tube down his windpipe to keep his airway open."

"I'm sure he'll be fine," Eric said. "This is Sed we're talking about here. He won't let anything stand in his way or put up with any bullshit. Not even from his own body."

Sed was moved to a room upstairs and the crowd of band members and roadies headed to a waiting room on that floor.

"Can I sit with him while he sleeps?" Jessica asked the nurse.

"It's past visiting hours. You should all come back in the morning."

"He is going to freak out when he wakes up and doesn't know where he is."

"I know you're worried about him, honey, but rules are rules."

"When do visiting hours begin?"

"Eight a.m."

Unacceptable. She couldn't go seven hours without seeing him. Without touching him.

"What room is he in?"

The nurse eyed her warily.

"So I know where to go in the morning."

The nurse consulted her computer. "Room 2117. Now head

on home and get some rest. I'm sure he'll be really happy to see you in the morning."

Jessica smiled wearily and nodded. She told the guys waiting at the end of the hall what the nurse had told her.

"I fuckin' hate hospitals anyway," Trey said. "How long are they going to keep him in here?"

"At least until they can take the tube out of his throat."

"He has a tube in his throat?" Brian whispered, paling under his stage makeup.

"I'm going to sneak into his room and stay with him while he sleeps," Jessica told them. "Will one of you distract the nurse for me?"

"Is she hot?" Trey asked.

"I don't know," Jessica said, exasperated.

"That would be a no," Trey said. "But I'll do it for Sed, because he needs you, Jess, no matter what stupid shit he told you."

Jessica smiled in appreciation. She wasn't sure if Trey was correct, but she wasn't going to let Sed get away that easily.

And now that he'd be unable to talk, he'd have to listen to her for once.

Trey went to schmooze the nurse. He could charm the pants off a rattlesnake, and probably had more than once. While the nurse's head was ducked, Jessica crept through the partially open door of Sed's hospital room.

The only light came from the private bathroom. When her eyes adjusted, she quietly pulled a chair up beside his bed and sat next to him. She couldn't believe such a big, commanding guy could look so frail. She took his hand, the one without an IV, and touched it to her cheek.

"I'm here, Sed. Everything's going to be okay."

He didn't respond. Not even with a twitch, but that was okay. They were together. That's all that mattered to her.

Chapter 45

SED FELT LIKE HE'D been run over by a train. He peeled his eyes open, but everything was blurry, so he closed them again. He tried to remember what had happened. He remembered being onstage, the pain in his throat, and choking on blood, but nothing after that.

He lifted his hand and winced as something tugged at a vein in the back of his hand. He tried his other hand, but someone was clinging to it. His throat felt strange. He couldn't even swallow properly and he couldn't close his mouth.

Panicked, his heart thudded in his chest like a jack hammer. He jerked his hand away from his unknown visitor's and reached for his throat. Someone stopped his progress.

Jessica whispered, "Sed, it's Jessica. You're in the hospital. Can you hear me?"

He tried to form words, but nothing came out. Not a solitary sound.

"Don't panic. There's a tube in your throat to keep your airway open. As soon as the swelling goes down, they'll take it out. How are you feeling?"

He rolled his eyes toward her and she smiled at him, her fingers stroking his hair. He tried to convey his level of displeasure with a look, but she seemed oblivious. What was she doing here? She was supposed to be in school.

"You're getting your color back already," she said. "I couldn't believe how much you bled. They had to give you a transfusion."

He freed his hand from hers and lifted it to his neck, wanting her to tell him about the injury. He hoped she knew Sed sign language, because he had a lot of questions.

"Everything's going to be okay," she promised. "You blew a vessel inside your throat. It's not near your vocal cords or anything, but you've got to let it heal. That means no singing and no talking for at least a week."

He mouthed the word "What?" to the best of his ability.

"It won't be so bad. I'll take care of you."

He gave her a stern look and pointed to the door.

"I'm not leaving, Sed. And you can't tell me what do, because you can't talk." She offered him a self-satisfied grin. "I'm dropping out of school to take care of you."

He shook his head vigorously, but had to stop because it sent waves of pain down his throat.

"We need to talk. Well, I need to talk and you need to listen."

"Jess…" he tried to say, but her name came out as a huff of air.

"I'm never going to pass Dr. Ellington's class. Let me tell you why." As she told him how her professor had *nonchalantly* revealed their video to her classmates, Sed's fist clenched tighter and tighter. Why did people always treat her so unfairly? Didn't they see how wonderful she was? He couldn't stand the thought of her giving up her dreams because someone else thought she should. He wrapped an arm around her and urged her head down on his shoulder so he could rub her back and stroke her hair with his free hand.

"So I guess it didn't matter that I got a chance to earn my scholarship back."

Sed couldn't believe how calm she was about the situation. Shouldn't she be fighting that Dr. Ellington bitch tooth and nail? He supposed a person could only take so much abuse and humiliation, but Jessica wasn't the type to take injustice lying down. That was one of the things he loved so much about her.

A nurse entered the room. "Good to see you're awake, Mr.

Lionheart," she said. "Are you comfortable? One blink for yes, two for no."

Was he comfortable? He had a fucking tube down his throat. Did she really need an answer to that question? He blinked once though.

"Later, we're going to take that tube out and see if you can swallow, but you have to promise me that you won't try to talk. You have a lot of damage in there and if you don't completely rest your voice, there's a chance you could lose it permanently. Do you understand what I'm saying to you?"

He blinked once, but knew it would be damn near impossible not to talk. Especially when Jessica was making one of the stupidest decisions of her life.

Jessica leaned back and looked down into his eyes. "You're not going to chase me away again," she said. "I don't care how much of an asshole you pretend to be. I know better."

He rolled his eyes at her and she smiled.

"I'll make sure he doesn't speak," Jessica said to the nurse. "Even if I have to keep his mouth shut with duct tape."

The nurse grinned. "Good, because I get the feeling that this one doesn't follow instructions."

Sed tried to protest, but realized it was no use.

"The doctor will stop by soon to explain your condition better."

Sed gave her a weary thumbs up. When she stepped out of the room, Jessica climbed to sit on the edge of the bed with him.

"I've got our entire situation figured out," she said. "This is how things are going to be between us."

Oh really? He was interested to know how she'd figured out an impossible situation.

"First, we're dating exclusively. No more games on either end. Are you in agreement? One blink for yes. I'm not taking no for an answer."

He tried grinning around the piece of plastic between his teeth, but it hurt his mouth, so he blinked. Once. A beautiful smile lit her face.

"Great. I'm moving into your condo while I finish school…"

One blink.

"…but I'm paying rent."

Two blinks.

"You are not allowed to argue with me, Sedric. I'm calling all the shots here. Also, I'm dropping out of law school."

But she'd just said she was finishing school.

"I've decided it's not what I want to do. I still want to help people, that's why I was going to become a lawyer, but I think I want to become," she flushed, "a nurse. Don't laugh."

He couldn't have laughed if he tried. And he wouldn't have tried anyway. She'd make a wonderful nurse. She was gentle and caring, yet tough enough to be perfect for the job. But none of that mattered. Suddenly giving up on her lifelong dreams had nothing to do with a change in interest and everything to do with the people at that school who had power over her. And when Sed was back on his feet, he would be exerting *his* power over them, even if it meant Jessica would never forgive him.

"I am going to file an official grievance against the dean and Dr. Ellington. I don't want anyone to think they chased me away and I gave up."

Sed squeezed her hand. But she *was* giving up. Didn't she realize that? And he couldn't stand to see her this way. Defeated. He knew what he should do. Support her in her decision. Stand back and let her do what she thought she needed to do. Even though he was incapacitated in a hospital bed, it wasn't in him to just take these things lying down. And normally it wasn't in her, either. What was she so afraid of?

"I do think I'll go to class tomorrow though. I really need to tell that bitch off. Publicly."

There's my girl. He welcomed that spark of fight in her.

"Even if I report them, I doubt anything will happen to either one," she murmured. She glanced up at him. "Dean Taylor was right. I don't have any credibility."

Sed scowled. When had the dick told her that?

"Do you think it's worth it? Should I even bother filing a grievance?"

Sed blinked emphatically. Or at least he hoped it look emphatic and didn't look like he had bleach in his eyes.

"You're right. I'll go. I'll never feel right about it if I don't at least try to set things right."

He smiled and blinked in agreement.

"I kind of like you this way," Jessica said. "All placid and compliant."

Don't get used to it.

"I should leave you alone so you can rest."

He blinked twice. Under no circumstance did he want her out of his sight. Now that they were officially a couple, he planned to take full advantage of her company.

Jessica scooted closer to him on the bed and stroked his stubble-rough cheek with the back of her hand. She leaned over and brushed her lips against his temple. His jaw.

"I can't wait to take you home and pamper you. In every imaginable way."

He was definitely up for some pampering and was already imagining every way.

Someone cleared their throat and Sed looked up to a gray-haired man in a white coat. His doctor, he presumed.

Jessica turned her head to glance at the doctor and then smiled down at Sed. "We'll talk more later. Or rather, I will."

Sed decided he liked it when she talked. He'd try to make an effort to listen more often. She kissed the tip of his nose and then moved away from the bed.

The doctor stepped closer to the bed. "I'm Dr. Jarvis—ear, nose, and throat specialist. I'll just cut to the chase here. Mr. Lionheart, you can't keep punishing your throat. All that growling and screaming has frayed your vocal cords and damaged the lining of your throat so badly that you tore an artery. An artery, Mr. Lionheart. I've never seen an injury like it. If I didn't know better, I'd think you'd been swallowing swords for a living. I'm putting you on a voice restriction order for a week. No talking, no singing, and definitely no screaming. After that week, you need to see a specialist again and hope there's significant improvement. If you don't give yourself time to heal, you might never sing again. Do you understand what I'm saying?"

Sed couldn't breathe. He hadn't realized how serious his condition was. He choked on the tube as panic squeezed his throat.

"Do you understand?" Dr. Jarvis repeated.

Gasping for air, Sed blinked once.

"We'll take that tube out now and see what we have to work with."

A nurse stepped up on the other side of the bed. She placed a hand on Sed's forehead to ease his head back. "Relax, Mr. Lionheart. This won't be pleasant, but it will be over quick."

He tried to relax, but it wasn't easy. As the tube was pulled free, it felt as if his throat was being turned wrong side out. And then it was gone. His throat felt tight and sore, but at least he could bend his neck. His first instinct was to try his voice, but the doctor already had a tongue depressor on his tongue.

"Open."

The nurse scribbled notes while the doctor described what he could see. Didn't sound good.

"I want him scoped this afternoon," Dr. Jarvis said. "We need to take a better look at those cords."

"Yes, doctor," the nurse said.

The doctor met Sed's eyes. "It looks better than I expected. Can you swallow?"

Sed swallowed, but it brought tears to his eyes.

"Take it easy. No talking. And soft foods only."

Sed nodded. The doctor took the chart from the nurse, scribbled some additional notes, and then left the room.

Jessica moved to stand beside him and kissed his forehead. "He said it looked better than expected. That's good news, right?"

He closed his eyes and nodded slightly. How could Sinners record their album next week if their lead vocalist couldn't sing?

Chapter 46

Sed's eyes eased open to Eric's concerned expression.

"Ah good, you're awake," Eric said.

How was he supposed to sleep with Eric staring down at him so creepily?

"Let's get out of here, buddy," Eric said. "I've got your wheelchair oiled and ready to roll."

His throat was on fire, but he didn't need a fuckin' wheelchair. "Wha—"

Eric's hand blocked his words. "No talking. Jessica put me in charge."

Where *was* Jessica? She'd still been there when they'd given him that sedative the night before.

"She said she'll meet you at home. She went to do something at the University."

Good. He hoped she clawed that professor's eyes out. Sed used Eric's arm to sit up in bed and then stood on wobbly legs.

"I hope you're up to stopping by the studio," Eric said, while Sed slipped into his clothes. "Brian and Trey are recording today."

Sed's heart skipped a beat. They were recording without him?

"We figured we better get some recording done before something else happens. Every time we try to work on the new album, one of us gets injured. First, Myrna's ex-husband smashes Brian's fingers, then Trey's head injury, now you've gone and blown your throat out. Jace and I are afraid to get out of bed. I think the new album is cursed."

Sed grinned. "Superstitious much?" The raspy sound of his voice surprised him.

"Hey, no talking."

"My throat doesn't feel too bad." It hurt to talk, but wasn't unbearable. As for screaming and singing, Sed had no plans to do that today. Perhaps tomorrow.

Eric pulled a roll of duct tape from the bottomless pocket inside his leather vest. He peeled back a piece of gray tape, tore it off with his teeth, and stuck it over Sed's mouth. "Jess said I'd probably need this. I promised her I wouldn't let you talk."

Sed yanked off the tape, along with some beard stubble, and crushed it into Eric's hair.

"Now that was totally uncalled for." Eric ripped the tape out of his hair with a grimace. "Look at this shit." He showed Sed the tape covered with black hairs of various lengths.

Sed pointed to where his whiskers had once been.

"Let's get you out of this place," Eric said.

After they secured his release, Sed followed Eric to the parking garage. Eric jumped over the driver's side door into his convertible '68 Corvette Sting Ray. A nice looking car, painted a deep emerald green, but its interior was trashed and the engine needed a total rebuild. Eric had been trying to get this car fixed up for over a decade. Problem was, he insisted on doing all the work himself. What he lacked in time, he equally lacked in skill as a mechanic.

"You got her started?" Sed asked quietly as he let himself into the passenger side.

"Isn't she sweeeeet?"

"I doubt she'll make it back to L.A."

"He didn't mean that, baby," Eric said to his car, stroking the steering wheel lovingly. He scowled at Sed. "And you aren't supposed to be talking, Mister Jerkface von Pessimist."

Eric turned the key and the engine whined. It whirred several times, but didn't catch. "Come on, baby. I'll buy you a new intake manifold." He pumped the gas pedal and cranked her over again. The engine sputtered, caught, backfired, and then died again. "Sounds like you'd rather have new plugs."

Sed covered his mouth with the back of his hand and muttered, "Dude, your car is a piece of—"

Eric reached into his pocket and retrieved the duct tape. "Don't make me use this."

"Maybe you should wrap some around the engine. Couldn't hurt."

"Shut up." Eric hit the steering wheel with frustration and turned the key again. She started right up. "I guess she wanted it rough."

They headed southwest out of Fresno. The sun beat down on them mercilessly, but the convertible top was shredded, so there was no use in putting it up.

"So are you going to give that violin playing idea a try?" Eric asked, the wind riffling his already wild black hair into something bordering on profane. "You could replace some screaming with that."

Sed hadn't given it much thought since their brief song writing session over a month before, but he nodded. He didn't really want to give up his signature style, but he wasn't sure he had a choice.

"Trust me. It will be cool!" Eric glanced at him out of the corner of his eye. "I've also added some piano pieces to a couple of the songs. Did you know Jace plays the piano?"

Sed shook his head. Beyond Jace's bassist skills, Sed didn't know much about him at all.

"He played some stuff for me back at your studio. He's amazing. We need to fully utilize his talent. He seems to think he's still auditioning for the band. Doesn't want to step on any toes."

Sed scowled. Why would Jace think that? His trial period was long over.

With no warning, Eric hit the brakes and the Corvette skidded into a parking lot. Sed grabbed the dashboard and prayed that the axle didn't snap as they went airborne over a speed bump.

"Want some ice cream?"

At risk of his life? No. But since they were already in the drive-thru line, ice cream sounded wonderful.

Eric ordered an ice cream cone, a couple of burgers, fries, and a Coke.

Thank God. Sed was starving.

At the drive-thru window, Eric handed the soft-serve ice cream cone to Sed. Eric popped a straw in his drink, set the coke between his legs, and placed the entire bag of food between his hip and the driver's side door.

Sed licked his vanilla ice cream. He winced every time he swallowed, but despite the threat of pain, he couldn't wait to bite into a big juicy hamburger. His stomach rumbled loudly in agreement. Eric reached into the bag and stuffed several fries into his mouth as he turned back into traffic.

"Pass that over here," Sed insisted.

Eric swallowed and took a slurp of his drink. "Pass what over there?"

"My burger. I'm starving."

"No burger for you, bro. You're on a soft food diet. Or have you forgotten?"

"Bullshit."

He reached across Eric and got his hand on the bag before taking a sharp elbow to the ribs.

"Back off, dude. Jessica said only soft foods for you."

"Since when do you listen to Jessica?"

"Uh, since always. She said if you started acting like a baby to remind you that you need to heal for your concert next week."

"Like a baby?"

"And if you're a good boy, she said she'll have a surprise for you."

Surprise? He liked the sound of that.

"Now, shut up. You're on voice restriction." Eric grinned wickedly and unwrapped a deluxe hamburger with one hand, while effortlessly merging onto the freeway. "And *I'm* trying to eat here."

Sed sighed loudly and lapped at his ice cream. Though he hated to admit it, Eric was right. He needed to be careful with his throat and give it a chance to heal. He vowed not to talk for the rest of the day. No matter how much he wanted to cuss Eric out.

Eric moaned in bliss. "This is the best damned burger I've ever had."

And it smelled like heaven on a bun.

"Wanna bite?" Eric swayed the burger back and forth beneath Sed's nose. "Can't have one." He drew it away and took another bite. "Mmmm. Good."

Sed punched the soda cup between Eric's thighs. It exploded in Eric's lap, drenching his crotch, the seat, and the dashboard.

"You ass!"

Sed wiped his wet hand on Eric's shoulder and then slurped some melting ice cream into his mouth. Jessica's surprise had better be spectacular. Leaving him in Eric's care. What was she thinking?

Eric stuffed a wad of napkins between his legs to absorb the puddle of soda. His hamburger now rested somewhere on the floorboard. "If you weren't injured, I'd kick your ass for that."

Sed lifted an unconvinced eyebrow at him.

"You'd better watch your back, Lionheart."

Sed pretended to shudder with fear.

"And I'm telling Jessica."

Sed took what was left of his cone and stuck it upside down on Eric's shoulder.

"Dude, knock it off. I'm trying to fuckin' drive!"

Heh, I win.

Halfway to Los Angeles, Sed leaned his head against the back of the seat and closed his eyes. The rumble of the engine, with its consistent knock, must have lured him to sleep, because the next thing he knew, they were sputtering to a stop inside a parking garage near the recording studio. The engine coughed, then died.

"Nice nap, douche bag?" Eric asked, drawing his lean body over the driver's side door and leaving a sticky puddle behind in the driver's seat.

Sed nodded drowsily. He supposed he was still a pint or two low on blood, and that half an ice cream cone hadn't been exactly filling.

Rubbing his eyes, Sed followed Eric into the building and the appropriate recording booth. Brian and Trey were in the studio wailing on their guitars. Without a doubt, the new album was going to be their best yet.

Assuming Sed's voice returned.

"Where's Jace?" Sed asked, noting one member of the group was absent.

"No telling," Eric said. "I swear he's an international spy. He just comes and goes as he pleases. No one can keep track of him. He's probably off with his dominatrix chick again. Or smuggling tomatoes across the Mexican border."

Oh yes, Jace Seymour, international tomato smuggler.

Sed sat next to the soundboard operator. He leaned with rapt attention toward the glass that separated him from his guitarists, suddenly in awe that he worked with these talented motherfuckers. When the current take came to an end, Trey waved at the window.

"Perfect. We got it," the operator said into a microphone. "Why don't you guys take a little break? Your fingers must be exhausted."

Trey and Brian removed their guitars and left the studio to enter the booth.

"They let you out of prison already?" Trey said. "I was stuck in there for days and days."

"My injury wasn't as serious as yours."

"Looked pretty fuckin' serious to me," Trey said. "What did the doctor say?"

Eric reached into his vest and produced a roll of duct tape. "I'll tell them. You keep quiet."

Sed nodded.

"He needs to check with a specialist in a few days and get the all clear before he'll be allowed to sing. He might be okay before our next tour date, but if not, we're cancelling the show."

"No, we are not cancelling any shows. I'll be fine. I guarantee it."

Eric ripped a piece of tape off the roll and waved it in Sed's face. "Quiet, vocal one."

Sed rolled his eyes at Eric and glanced at Trey and Brian. "Sorry to mess up the recording schedule."

Eric stuck the tape over Sed's mouth. "I warned you."

"Don't worry about recording right now," Trey said. "We can wait a while to record vocals. We'll get Eric in here next."

"And then Jace," Brian added. "Seriously, don't worry about it, Sed."

Sed peeled the tape off his mouth, wadded it into a ball, and threw it at Eric.

Trey's brow furrowed as his gaze followed the trajectory of the tape ball. "Did you piss your pants, Eric?"

"Sed did it."

"Sed pissed your pants?" Trey shook his head slightly. "Man, that takes pissed off to a whole new level."

"I think that's pissed on, not off," Brian said.

"Yeah, and I'm telling Jessica. She'll probably break up with you for this, Sed."

"Not likely."

Brian and Trey exchanged glances.

"Does this mean you two are together now?" Brian asked.

Sed lowered his gaze. Brian wasn't too fond of Jessica. He probably wouldn't appreciate that they'd solidified their relationship.

"They're pretty serious," Eric said, in full-out gloat-mode.

"How serious?" Brian asked.

"Exclusive," Sed murmured.

Trey beamed. "Congratulations, man!"

Sed smiled a thanks and then turned his attention to Brian. Brian's intense gaze didn't waver from his face. "So when are you going to ask her to marry you?" Brian asked. "Soon, I hope."

Sed gaped at him.

Brian grinned crookedly. "I mean, you love her, right?"

"Yeah, of course I love her."

"Will you just blink, goddammit?" Eric bellowed.

"Blink?" Brian asked.

"That's how he's supposed to say yes, instead of talking." Eric peeled another piece of duct tape from the roll.

Sed flipped him off. "This is how I say fuck you, instead of talking." He seized the tape from Eric's hand.

"Jessica will definitely cancel your surprise over this."

If Sed hadn't been so curious about this surprise of Jessica's, he would have punched Eric in the forehead and given him a real reason to tattle.

"So are you going to ask her?" Brian pressed. "Soon?"

Sed hesitated, glanced sidelong at Eric, sighed, and then blinked.

"Awesome," Trey said with an unusual level of enthusiasm and a smug look sent in Eric's direction. Sed wondered why they were acting so weird about it. "How did you ask Myrna to marry you?" Trey asked Brian.

Brian chuckled. "Which time?"

"I was there the first time," Eric said.

"That's right, you were."

"He got rejected."

"Thanks for the reminder, Sticks. I eventually wore her down."

Trey thumped Brian on the back. "Of course you did, stud."

"You know, Sed," Brian said, "if Jessica hadn't broken your

heart, you wouldn't have been interested in my girlfriends, they wouldn't have cheated on me, and then I might have never met Myrna. Things happen for a reason."

Sed chuckled. "Strange bit of logic there, Brian. Sorry about all that crap I put you through."

Brian shrugged. "It all turned out for the best."

Brian was such a great guy. Understanding. Forgiving. Sed wanted him to be the best man at his wedding.

Brian grinned. "Myrna's going to injure me severely for telling you guys this, but we're trying to get pregnant."

"Already? Jeez, the honeymoon isn't even over yet," Eric said.

"She says she isn't getting any younger. It's now or never."

Sed smiled his congratulations until he saw the look on Trey's face. Happy for Brian? Not even close. Trey looked physically ill.

"Is she going to quit that sex professor job of hers, then?" Eric asked.

Brian sighed. "She wants to finish this year first. We're trying to time her pregnancy so she'll deliver at the end of next May. She wants to write nonfiction books for a while and might move out to LA while the baby is small. Maybe, she said. The woman is stubborn. You know?"

Eric laughed. "You think?"

Brian glanced over his shoulder at Trey, who quickly covered his horror-struck look with an indulgent grin. "Don't plan on me babysitting while you and Myrna disappear into the bedroom for hours at a time."

"You aren't planning on living with us, are you?"

Trey's face fell. He swallowed his horror and then laughed. "Of course not. Hard to party when a baby is crying all hours of the day and night." Trey nodded toward the studio. "Ready to record the next track?"

"Yeah. Let's do this. If we get done early, I can go visit Myrna in

Kansas City for a couple of days." He balled his fists, bit his lip, and demonstrated his pelvic thrusts. "Practice my baby-making techniques."

"Practice makes perfect," Eric said and nudged Brian in the ribs with his elbow.

"I think he's had enough practice," Trey grumbled. "Let's just get back in the studio."

Brian clasped Trey's shoulder and followed him into the booth. "You're a fuckin' slave driver since you got full mobility back in your fingers."

Eric took the seat next to Sed, acting a bit too nonchalant for sincerity. "I think you should wait a while before you ask Jessica, man. Don't rush it. Do you even have a ring?"

Sed reached into his pocket and pulled out a folded scrap of paper. He unfolded it and dumped Jessica's ring in his hand. He pinched it between his thumb and forefinger and held it up for Eric to see.

"Kind of small, don't you think?"

Sed scowled. True. But it was hers and it belonged on her finger. Eric snatched the tattered paper out of Sed's hand. "What's this?"

"Nothing."

Eric turned his back on Sed and held the paper up above his head so he could read the lines of scarcely legible scrawl.

"Is this a song? Did *you* write it?"

Sed yanked the paper out of his hand and stuffed it and Jessica's ring into the front pocket of his jeans.

"I didn't know you could write sappy love lyrics, Lionheart."

"Shut up," Sed said, hoping Eric would forget about his stupid, mushy song. He didn't know why he was still carrying it around. At least Eric didn't know that he and Brian had recorded an acoustic version of it two years before. He'd never live that one down.

Eric rested his elbows on the soundboard with its hundreds of equalizer sliders and knobs. "She'd like it, you know."

Sed pretended to be deaf.

"Even though it's obvious that a pussy wrote it."

Ignore him.

"You should record it for her when you get your voice back."

That was a good idea, actually.

"So how do you plan to get that ring on her finger? Come on. You can tell me." He nudged Sed in the ribs a couple of times with his elbow.

Why did Eric care so much all of a sudden? Had Jessica put him up to this?

"Very carefully," Sed said and covered his mouth with a piece of tape so he wouldn't have to talk about this embarrassing shit with Eric anymore.

Chapter 47

Jessica took a seat directly in front of the instructor's podium so Dr. Ellington wouldn't be able to miss her. Curtis, the guy who had hit on her last class, sat beside her and leaned close. Jessica's instinct was to draw away, but she forced herself to remain where she was, even when his fingers brushed her wrist.

"I'm surprised you returned," he said.

She turned to find his eyes trained on the swell of her bustline. Typical jerk. He chomped his gum, his fingers stroking her skin now. When she didn't respond, he lifted his gaze to hers.

"Why are you surprised?"

He shrugged. "Most girls would be too ashamed to show their face after being seen in such a compromising position. Or in your case... positions."

"I'm not most girls."

"I'll say." His gaze moved back to her chest.

"Would you mind giving me some breathing room? There's this thing called personal space and you're invading mine. Big time."

He leaned back a couple of inches, but grinned at her suggestively. "I was wondering if you do private parties."

Her brow furrowed. "What?"

"You're a stripper, too, right? Me and my friends can come up with a couple grand to pay you. You interested?"

Her jaw set in a hard line, she folded her desk back and moved over a seat. Curtis stood to slide next to her again. Before he could sit down, a young woman hopped over the back of the chair and sank into the seat. "I'm sitting here."

Curtis scowled and moved to take the vacant seat to Jessica's right. Another young woman shoved him aside and sat down.

The chairs surrounding Jessica filled with other women. Curtis rolled his eyes and stood directly in front of Jessica. "So, are you interested?"

"Get lost, jerk."

He curled his lip at her. "Slut." Curtis crammed his hands in the pockets of his khakis and took a seat on the other side of the room.

The young woman who'd hopped over the chair back touched Jessica's sleeve. "I'm glad you came back. What Dr. Ellington did to you the other day was wrong. All the women in the class think so."

"Most of the men, too," the woman seated directly behind Jessica said. They all turned their heads to glare at Curtis. "With a few slimy exceptions."

Jessica could barely speak through the lump in her throat. "You don't think badly of me?"

"For sleeping with Sed Lionheart? Eh, no. A bit jealous, maybe."

She couldn't believe they weren't all pointing fingers and calling her names. She was suddenly glad she'd decided to come back to class, even though it meant entrusting Sed's care to Eric when she'd left that morning.

"You're not in our year, are you?" the first girl said.

"No, I'm a third year. Ellington failed me on my final paper last year, so I'm supposed to retake the class."

"Are you really engaged to Sedric Lionheart?"

Jessica flushed. "Engaged? Not exactly. Maybe someday soon." If she could find the courage to ask him. "We're dating. Um. Exclusively."

"No kidding? Wow, what a babe. He's the reason God gave women eyes."

The door at the front of the room opened and Dr. Ellington

stepped up to the podium. She looked haggard and tired, not at all like her usual, polished-ice self. She glanced around the room suspiciously. "Do we have an experiment on gender segregation going on here, or what?" Her gaze landed on Jessica. "Oh, I see. Class is dismissed. Work on your midterm paper. First draft due Monday."

The entire class gasped in horror.

Dr. Ellington turned on her heel and strode from the room.

Jessica sat there dumbfounded for a few seconds and then rose from her chair and headed after the woman. Trotting several yards behind her down the corridor, Jessica followed Dr. Ellington to the dean's office. By the time Jessica stopped at the receptionist's desk, Ellington was already inside Dr. Taylor's personal office.

"I need to talk to the dean," Jessica said.

"He's busy at the moment. Do you have an appointment?"

"No, but I'll wait until he's free."

"Take a seat."

Jessica sat next to his closed door. She could hear Dr. Ellington yelling in the office and she watched the shadows of her pacing feet under the crack of the door. "I want her out of my class. She's nothing but trouble. A stupid little whore who has no right to continue at this institution."

The dean's voice was muffled by distance. Jessica strained to hear his reply. "Mary, you know we can't expel her. She hasn't done anything wrong."

"Either she goes or I go!"

"Do you know how many students were in my office complaining about you yesterday?" Taylor said. "More than twenty. What you did was way out of line. To save my reputation, you should be the one to go."

"What? You're siding with her? How can you even consider such a thing, Harold?"

"You know I want you to stay, baby. Come here."

Jessica heard Dr. Ellington sniff her nose. The dean's chair creaked. "That's better."

"You're not really considering firing me, are you?" Dr. Ellington's voice sounded needy.

"I am. But you know how to change my mind, don't you?"

The chair creaked again. Jessica heard… a zipper being released? She leaned closer to the door.

"That's my girl. Suck it how you know I like it. That's it… Jessica."

Jessica? Ellington's name wasn't Jessica. Why would he call her—Oh…

Jessica's eyes widened. *Oh!* She jumped to her feet, her focus darting around the room. She met the receptionist's gaze and the woman shrugged as if to say this kind of thing happened all the time.

Jessica moved to stand before the receptionist's desk. "I don't think I need to talk to the dean after all."

The secretary nodded, her uncomfortable gaze trained on her desk. As Dean Taylor's vocalizations grew increasingly enthusiastic, his receptionist's cheeks grew increasingly pink.

"How does listening to that make you feel?" Jessica nodded toward the closed door.

The receptionist hesitated and then spoke in a whisper, not meeting Jessica's eyes. "Physically ill. I've been looking for another job, but haven't found one yet. And I can't afford to just quit."

"You need to file a sexual harassment suit against him."

The secretary's eyes widened and met Jessica's directly. "Oh, he's never touched me. A couple of students. Dr. Ellington. And—"

"He doesn't have to touch you. The fact that you're being forced to listen to that while you're trying to work is enough to win a sexual harassment case. And working here, I'm sure you can find a good lawyer."

"I can't afford a lawyer."

The sounds of Dr. Taylor getting off came through the door. "Yeah, yeah, suck me, Jessica. Oh God. Swallow it. Swallow it. Yes!"

While Taylor shouted in triumph, Ellington choked. Gagged. Then all was quiet. Jessica held her breath. She didn't want Taylor and Ellington to realize she was out there listening.

"Why are you crying, Mary?" Taylor asked, his voice muffled through the door. "You're getting what you want. Your job is safe. I'll make sure of it."

Jessica's heart twanged with empathy. For Dr. Ellington. She didn't really know why. The woman had treated her like garbage. The ice queen was probably getting exactly what she deserved. "You should take this straight to human resources," Jessica whispered to the receptionist. "They're required by law to investigate."

"That's how his last receptionist got fired," she whispered. "*False* accusations. Dean Taylor has too much clout at this institution. They'll never do anything about him."

Well, maybe *they* wouldn't do anything about the pig, but *she* would.

"I don't have my degree yet," Jessica said, meeting the receptionist's dark brown eyes and holding her gaze, "but I'm sure I can find someone to represent you in court. For free. It's time to take him down a peg or two."

"You'd do that?" the receptionist said. "Go against the dean? For me?"

"For you," she said. "And for me. And every other woman he's ever harassed. Including Dr. Ellington."

Chapter 48

WHEN JESSICA HEARD THE front door open, she hurriedly lit the candles she'd arranged on the dining room table to set the mood. She leaned to the side so she could watch Sed approach around the two-story high pillar in the foyer, but stayed in her chair and waited for him to join her. That had been a close call. Jace had left less than ten minutes ago. If Sed would have caught him here, she knew it would have gotten ugly. And ruined Friday's surprise.

"What's all this?" Sed murmured.

"I thought you'd be hungry."

When he noticed she sat waiting for him in the tiniest of pink lace negligees, he growled in appreciation. She indicated the seat to her left. "Have a seat, sweetheart."

Sed kissed her temple and then sat beside her. "Is this my surprise? You look beautiful."

She flushed with pleasure. "Part of it. And thank you. How's your throat feeling?"

"Not bad. I heal quickly. I can talk okay now."

"No, you can't." She reached under the table and retrieved the gift bag she'd stashed at her feet. "Your surprise is in here. Have you been good for Eric today?"

He hesitated, looking at the ceiling in deep concentration, and then nodded.

Somehow she doubted he was being sincere, but she handed the gift bag to him.

"What is—"

She covered his mouth with her hand. "No talking, Sed."

He reached into the gift bag and pulled out a small dry-erase board and marker. He didn't even try to hide his disappointment. "I thought you'd get me something sexy."

"If you use that to communicate instead of talking, I have another surprise for you."

"Yeah?"

"You'll probably like this one better."

He uncapped the marker and wrote *OK* on the board.

She reached up and cupped his face in her hand. His cheek was rough with a day's beard growth and she took a moment to enjoy the texture against her fingertips. She then kissed him tenderly. "If you're a good boy, I'll be a very naughty girl."

VERY naughty? he wrote.

"Very, very naughty," she murmured and kissed him again.

His gaze caressed her skin in a most distracting fashion. She was determined to get through this meal without pouncing on him, but now that he was here, she doubted they'd make it all the way to dessert. He'd be lucky if she let him finish his appetizer. Or start it.

School? he wrote.

"I've decided to finish law school—I have important work to do—but I'll tell you about that later. Right now, you need to eat. Are you hungry?"

He nodded earnestly.

She removed lids from the containers of food scattered across the table. "I tried to think of things that wouldn't hurt your throat."

He watched her reveal one dish after another. *You cooked all this?*

She read his message and laughed. "No, sweetheart, it's take out. I wanted you to enjoy it, not have to choke it down and pretend I'm not poisoning you."

He took her hand and kissed her knuckles.

"So what are you hungry for?"

You, he wrote.

"That's dessert."

Let's start with dessert.

"Don't tempt me. I'm trying to take care of you. Help you build up your strength for your concert next week. And our little side trip on Friday." The one Jace had helped her plan while Eric kept Sed distracted in the recording studio.

His eyebrows shot up. *Trip?* he wrote.

"You didn't think I was going to be very, very naughty in the privacy of our own home, did you?"

He grabbed her off her chair and pulled her onto his lap. "How naughty?" he murmured against her throat.

"Unbelievably naughty. But only if you follow doctor's orders to the letter. No more talking, okay?"

He blinked—meaning yes—and opened his mouth wide.

"You want me to feed you?"

He blinked again.

She reached for the bowl of macaroni and cheese. She turned to straddle his lap on the chair, holding the bowl between their bodies, and offered him a bite from the plastic serving spoon. While he chewed, she took a bite herself. Since she was feeding him, his hands were free to explore her body.

He seemed to like her new pink nightie. He traced the top of the frilled bodice, which was cut so low it barely covered her nipples. And with an expert flick of Sed's thumbs, it no longer did.

He stroked both nipples in maddening circles while she fed him another bite of overcooked mac and cheese.

After he swallowed, she leaned closer and claimed his mouth in a passionate kiss. "I love you," she said against his lips. It felt good to say it. Without hesitation. Without regret.

"I—"

"Shhh. Don't talk. You don't have to say anything. I feel it."

He shifted his hips and she really felt it then. Hard, attentive, and pressing against her mound. And since they weren't in a restaurant, she could ride him at the dinner table like a bronco all night if she felt like it. Jessica fed him another bite and rocked her hips to rub herself against him.

Sed stared into her eyes, his gaze so intense it made her heart throb. "I need to tell you something."

"Write it down." She tried to feed him another bite, but he turned his head to one side.

"You need to hear it."

"Sed, don't make me resort to duct tape."

"I haven't kissed another woman since I met you."

She snorted with laughter. "Yeah right."

"It's true."

"Sed, I caught you naked with three girls the night we got back together. I'm not stupid."

"I didn't say I didn't have sex with other women, I said I haven't *kissed* another woman."

"Oh." Her gaze dropped to his chin. Why did he think that was so important? "Why not?"

"I only kiss women I love."

Her brow knotted with confusion. "But you kissed me that first night in the strip club and then again when you said you hated me on the tour bus." And pretty much constantly ever since.

"I only kiss women I love." He cupped her cheek in one hand and pressed his lips to hers. "Only you."

She supposed that was his way of being true to her. She wondered why he'd waited so long to tell her. "I'm glad," she whispered.

"Have you?"

When she opened her mouth to speak, he covered her lips with two fingers. "Never mind."

"You act like you know what I'm going to say."

"It's none of my business."

She captured his wrist with her free hand and pulled his hand away from her lips. "I *have* kissed a couple of men." Jessica held his gaze so he'd know she was being serious.

He winced and she was pretty sure it wasn't due to throat pain.

"But I didn't enjoy it. There was no passion. Not like with you. Not even close." She smiled at him gently, as both of his dimples made an appearance. And while she was making confessions… "For the record…" She took a deep breath. "I haven't had sex with anyone since we broke up."

"*No one?*"

Unable to meet his eyes, she shook her head. It was kind of embarrassing to admit how much he'd affected her. How he'd ruled certain parts of her life, even in his absence.

"Not once in two years?"

Her nostrils flared. "No! I said I haven't. What? You don't believe me?"

He took the bowl from her and set it on the table before wrapping both arms around her and hugging her against his chest.

"I should have never let you go, Jess. I should have gone after you. I should have fixed it. Whatever I had to do, I should have—"

She pulled back to look into his eyes. His watery gaze drifted to the ceiling as he tried to get a handle on his emotions.

"I have plenty of regrets of my own, Sed, but I've decided to let them go. You should too. We can't change the past, but we can move forward."

"So much wasted time."

She shook her head. "No regrets." She grabbed his chin to gain his attention and gave him a stern look. "And you're talking way too much. If you say one more word, I'm cancelling our trip next week."

That shut him up, but it didn't stop him from expressing his feelings with his hands and lips. He suckled the pulse point beneath her ear and she gasped, her body instantly igniting with need.

"Before you get me too worked up, I should warn you that I have the first draft of a paper to write this weekend, so you're going to have to entertain yourself while I hit the books."

He pulled back to look at her, scowling.

"You're the one who insisted I go back to school. Remember?"

He sighed and nodded.

"But tonight, I'm yours."

He grinned and reached for the dry erase board. *You don't want to be a nurse anymore?* he wrote.

She flushed and shook her head. "I was just afraid to go back to law school. The way Dean Taylor made me feel and that whole failure thing... I'm over it." She grinned at him. "But I can still be *your* nurse. Tell me how I can make you more comfortable, Mr. Lionheart." She ran a finger down the center of his chest.

Feed me, he wrote. Not the request she'd had in mind, but okay.

"What would you like? Mashed potatoes? Cheese soup?"

Something cold.

"Your throat's really bothering you, isn't it?"

He nodded. She shouldn't have let him talk as much as she had. She would be a more attentive nurse from this point forward.

She scanned the table for something cold and soothing. "Gelatin? Or I can get a Popsicle out of the freezer."

His hand tightened on her hip, telling her he didn't want her to get up.

Jell-O is fine.

She claimed the bowl of orange gelatin cubes and fed them to him with her fingers.

Tell me about school today, he wrote and set the dry erase board aside.

"Um, okay. I found out I'm not the only one the dean has propositioned sexually. I also found out how Dr. Ellington gets her way and the reason she probably hates me in the first place."

Sed lifted an eyebrow in interest, his tongue teasing her fingertips as he accepted her offering of gelatin.

"Ellington sucks the dean's cock in his office. And I'm pretty sure it pisses her off that he calls my name while she does it. I heard him."

Sed choked on the jiggly orange cube he'd just slurped down his throat. Before he could vocalize a protest, Jessica covered his lips with her fingers.

"He's no threat to you, sweetheart. And now that I know what a slime ball he is, I'm no longer intimidated by him. I've dealt with his kind before. He can't get to me. I won't give him that power ever again."

She could tell Sed was struggling with his strong protective instincts. He probably wanted to pound Dean Taylor into the ground which, honestly, she wouldn't mind watching. After several deep breaths, Sed nodded at her to continue. She smiled and offered him another cube of gelatin.

"So I'm building a sexual harassment case against him. A big one. You might call it huge. His secretary knows all kinds of things that go on behind closed doors and she was happy to share information. She told me about a student who graduated a few years ago who is now a practicing lawyer. Apparently, Taylor harassed a friend of hers until she dropped out of school. Sound familiar?"

Sed cupped her cheek, sympathy in his blue eyes.

"Anyway, I went and talked to her lawyer friend this afternoon. She agreed to take on the case *pro bono*. I'll be doing a lot of the leg work—building the case, contacting witnesses and stuff—because she's so busy with her current case load, but I cannot *wait* to get to work on this. Taylor is not going to get away with that kind of behavior anymore. I wish I was done with school so I could cross-examine that bastard on the stand. One more year and I can put slime balls like him in their place. I had planned to become a defense attorney, but this is what I want to do. Protect women from jackasses who use their positions of power to sexually harass them. It pisses me off to no end."

Sed surprised her by kissing her until she was breathless. When he pulled away, he gazed into her eyes with a new awareness.

"You get off on this shit," he murmured.

She laughed. "Well, yeah, I guess so."

"I get it now." She could practically see the light bulb go on over his head. "God, baby, I'm sorry I ever asked you to give it up."

He kissed her again, starving for her mouth. And she didn't have to wonder if he kissed other women like this. He didn't kiss other women at all. Only her. The bowl of gelatin slipped from her grip and landed with a ploppy-clatter somewhere on the marble floor. She didn't care. She had to keep kissing him. Kissing him and holding his handsome face while she sucked at his lips.

She rocked her hips against him, rubbing her mound against the hard bulge in his pants. Too many clothes. Too many. She needed him. Inside. Desperately. Now.

Thank God he was a mind reader.

Sed reached between them, unfastened his pants, and released his cock. She cried out against his lips, unwilling to separate their mouths even when he slid the crotch of her panties aside and directed his rigid member into her throbbing flesh. She sank down, shuddering with delight as he filled her. Her feet found the rails under the chair and she used them for leverage to rise and fall over him. Faster, she rode him. Faster. Fueling her need. Still kissing him.

His cock, hard and thick, rubbed her in exactly the right spot each time it plunged into her body. He felt so good inside her. Perfect. Her pleasure built quickly to its climax. Pulsations of sheer delight rippled through her insides. She cried out into his mouth and shuddered against him.

Jessica stopped, unable to move. After a moment, Sed wrapped an arm around her waist and lifted her onto the edge of the table. She cried out in protest as his cock fell free from her body and their mouths separated. He stood and pushed his pants down to his knees. She slid her hands beneath his shirt and lifted it to expose his tight abs.

"Nine more?" he murmured as he directed his jutting cock back into her eager body.

She wrapped her legs loosely around his hips. "I think I can handle five more. Tops."

He grinned at her and slowly pulled out. Slowly. Slowly. In complete control. His fingers sought her clit. A spasm gripped her body and she shuddered.

"Only five?"

She chuckled. "Don't wear yourself out. You have to go to the studio tomorrow." Her hands shifted from his belly to his back and he shuddered. He surged forward, burying himself deep. Her back arched in ecstasy.

"Why?" he said breathlessly. "I can't sing anyway."

"You are too much of a distraction and I have to write my paper. I *have* to pass that class." And she would pass. Failure was not an option. But she had other reasons to send him off to the studio. She had to make plans for Friday. The day she was going to ask Sed to marry her.

Chapter 49

SED AWOKE KNOWING TODAY would be the day. The day he would ask Jessica to marry him. Which would be a challenge since he wasn't supposed to talk. She wouldn't have a hard time convincing him to remain silent today. Yesterday, his throat had hurt. This morning, it burned and ached so bad he hesitated to breathe. But he could tolerate the pain. What he couldn't tolerate was the idea that she might refuse to marry him. He couldn't really blame her if she did. He'd been a selfish ass the last time they'd tried forever, but that didn't change how much he wanted her to be his wife.

He watched her sleep for a moment, struck by her beauty and reveling in the knowledge that she slept in his bed—*their* bed—and she'd be there every morning for the rest of their lives. They would make it. Failure was not an option.

Sed leaned out of bed and scooped his pants off the floor. He removed her engagement ring from his pocket and held it up to the limited light filtering through the curtains. He didn't have a plan. He just wanted the ring back in her possession as soon as possible. Like, right now.

He lifted her left hand and started to slip the ring onto her ring finger. She gasped and flung her hand to her forehead as she regained consciousness. The ring went flying.

He heard a tiny ping on the opposite side of the room before she said, "Why is the sun up? What time is it?" She lifted her head from the pillow to check the clock on the nightstand. Her eyes widened and she jumped out of bed. "Oh crap, it's late. Why didn't the alarm go off?"

Well, they hadn't exactly been thinking about alarm clocks when they'd finally made their way up to bed the night before. An amused smile on his lips, he watched her dart around the room.

"Sed, get up. I'm going to hop in the shower."

"I'm up." At least that's what he meant to say. His words sounded more like a bunch of rusty nails rattling around in a tin can. Sucking dry air all night? Yeah, not so good for the healing process.

Jessica climbed up on the bed to kneel beside him. She kissed his forehead tenderly. "Oh sweetheart, your poor throat."

He remembered a time when he wished he were injured so she'd show him the affection he craved. He was rethinking that wish right about now.

She kissed his eyelids. The tip of his nose. "I know the guys need your input to record, but maybe you should stay home and rest."

He reached for the dry erase board on the nightstand. He'd used it the night before to give her instructions on his care. He erased *Lick my back*, and replaced it with *Keep me company?*

She pouted. "I want to, sweetheart, but I can't. I have to get to the library."

Well, he didn't want to stay home by himself all day. *Drop me off at the studio, then.*

"You sure?"

He blinked, meaning yes. She kissed him. Just the motion of his lips as he returned her kiss sent pain shooting through his throat. He produced a pained whine, which prompted Jessica to cup his face in both hands.

"I'll be right back," she murmured against his lips, drew away, and headed out of the bedroom, not towards the bathroom.

He puzzled over where she was going for a moment and then remembered her ring now lay somewhere on the other side of the room. He climbed from the bed and searched for it on his hands and knees. His fingers brushed over the plush carpet in a widening circle as he made his way toward the far wall. He couldn't find it. His heart thudded with panic. He didn't even realize Jessica had returned to the room until she straddled him and sat on his back. The heat between her thighs against his lower back sent his senses spiraling out of control.

"Are we going to play cowgirl and stallion?" she asked, rocking slightly and making him even more aware of the endless delights at the apex of her legs. "Can I take you for a little ride?"

He glanced at her over his shoulder. "I'll give you—" Pain cut his teasing reply short. He winced. Jessica leaned over his back and shoved an orange Popsicle in his mouth.

He damn near had an orgasm as he slurped the cold liquid down his burning throat.

She kissed his shoulder and climbed off his back. "Better?"

He nodded, still slurping in bliss.

"As much as I'd like to take you out for a morning ride, I've got to get in the shower. You need to get ready too. Okay? The guys will be waiting for you and I've got to get to the library before it closes."

He blinked, finding it hurt less than nodding, and waited for her to go into the bathroom before continuing his search for her ring, his dwindling Popsicle lodged in the back of his throat. He finally found the ring resting against the baseboard behind the floor-length curtains. He'd just climbed to his feet when Jessica exited the bathroom drying her hair with a towel. Her one towel. God, he'd never get tired of that beautiful sight.

She pointed toward the bathroom and he went to do her bidding, the ring concealed in the palm of his hand.

After his shower, Sed got dressed and then leaned against the bathroom sink. He stared down at the engagement ring he held pinched between his thumb and forefinger. Maybe he should buy her something bigger before he asked her. Something more like the ring Brian had bought for Myrna. Some countries had a smaller gross national product than what that ring had cost Brian. This cheap thing Sed had bought for Jessica in his starving-musician days bordered on pathetic. Insignificant in size and quality, true, but it did hold special meaning. At least it did to him. He'd carried it around with him for two years, hoping one day to return it to her. He was determined that today be that day.

"Are you almost finished in there?" Jessica called from the bedroom. "I need to do my hair and we're already running late."

He'd try the passive approach. A tad less passive than trying to stick it on her finger while she slept, but he couldn't talk, so this method would make sense. He wasn't being a coward. She'd find this simple action romantic. Right? Of course she would.

He set the ring on the edge of the sink where she was sure to find it and, heart thudding with a mixture of excitement and anxiety, left the master bathroom clean-shaven and ready to face a day of being silent in the studio. After Jess found the ring and they made love for a couple of hours to celebrate, that is.

Sed stepped up behind Jessica and planted a kiss on the side of her neck. Just thinking about that ring on her finger had him more randy than a teen who'd just touched his first real boob. Her shorts hindering skin on skin contact, Sed's hands slid over the ridges of her hipbones and down between her thighs.

"Mmmm," she murmured, "if you don't stop that, we're never going to make it out of here." She glanced up at him over her shoulder. "You okay? You look a little pale."

He nodded at her curtly.

"Your throat hurts, doesn't it? Go eat another Popsicle. I'll hurry."

Another Popsicle did sound heavenly—and so did removing these shorts and bending her over the end of the bed for a quickie—but what he wanted most was to hear her reaction when she found her ring on the sink. He wondered if she'd even recognize it. He directed her toward the bathroom and gave her rounded bottom a playful swat.

She laughed and headed for the steamy room beyond the open door. He waited for the sounds of her excitement. And waited. The hair dryer switched on, but no other sounds came from the bathroom. Had she missed seeing it? How could she miss it? He'd set it right there in plain view.

Sed crossed the bedroom and peered through the bathroom door. Her engagement ring still sat untouched on the edge of the sink next to her hip. Any minute now, she'd notice it.

Any minute now.

Any minute now she'd... bump the ring with her belly? Shit! The ring skittered around the basin before plunging down the drain.

Sed darted across the room, nudged Jessica to one side, and stuck his fingers down the drain hole. Nothing but air and a bit of sludge. That's what he got for being too cowardly to present the ring to her properly in the first place. And for not having a plug in the damn sink drain.

Jessica gave him an odd look. "What are you doing?" she called over the whir of the hair dryer. "Did you lose something?"

He shook his head and went to the kitchen in search of tools. He was sure he had a pipe wrench somewhere. He just hoped the ring had gotten caught in the trap and was not on its way to the sewage treatment plant. While he was in the kitchen, he grabbed a grape Popsicle from the freezer and stuck it in his mouth, allowing the cool liquid to bathe his burning throat. He then returned to the bedroom to wait for Jessica to vacate the bathroom.

Jessica joined him a few moments later, looking so stunning in her little green tank top with her hair just right, her lashes thickened with mascara, and her lips shiny with gloss that he temporarily forgot how to breathe. Thinking? Thinking was totally out of the question. She pressed her body against his and wrapped her arms around him, her hands sliding down his lower back toward the heavy weight pressing against his butt. He came to his senses just in time to catch her hands before she discovered the wrench in the back pocket of his jeans.

She smiled at him. "Are you ready?"

He lifted a finger at her to tell her he needed a minute and then closed himself in the bathroom, locking the door behind him. He didn't want her to know he'd faithfully carried her ring around for such a long time only to lose it down the sink the first time it left his possession for more than five seconds.

He had one side of the trap loosened beneath the sink when she started knocking impatiently.

"Are you all right in there?"

"Fine," he said, though he doubted she could hear him croaking beneath the sink.

He unscrewed the other side of the trap, trying to limit the amount of clanking he produced, and pulled the pipe loose. He rescued the ring from the sticky goo in the trap and rinsed it in the sink. It took him a moment to register why water started pouring from beneath the cabinet onto his boots.

Dammit! He shut off the water and reached for a towel to soak up the puddle spreading across the floor. Perhaps he should go back to bed and start over. Tucking Jessica's ring back in his pocket, he took a deep breath before climbing under the sink to reattach the trap. If his throat never healed properly and he had to give up singing, he could mark plumber off his list of potential careers.

"Baby?" Jessica called, the concern in her voice evident even through the door.

He tightened the pipe on both ends, washed his hands, and threw the wet towel from the floor in an inconspicuous corner.

He opened the door to her anxious face. He eased out of the bathroom and closed the door against his back, pulling a face of disgust. "You do *not* want to go in there," he said, his throat protesting every word.

She touched his forehead with her fingertips. "You're all sweaty. Are you sick?"

He shook his head.

"I'm okay," he rasped, cupping her lovely face in both hands.

"You'd be better if you'd *stop* talking." She grinned and stuck something over his lips. He checked the mirror over the dresser. A pink smiley face sticker? Was she fucking kidding him? From her chortle of amusement, he decided she was. She handed the dry erase board to him. "You're supposed to be using this, remember?"

He nodded obediently, removed the sticker from his mouth, and stuck it to the luscious curve of her breast above the neckline of her tank top. And then it occurred to him. He could ask her by writing it on the board.

Where my ring? he wrote and handed the board to her.

She read it and handed it back to him. Not exactly the excited, tearful reaction he'd been hoping for.

"What ring? I don't know where it is, Sed. We'll have to find it when we get back."

He glanced at his message and realized he'd spelled "wear" wrong. Damn it. He erased the message with his wrist.

WEAR, he wrote.

She glanced at the message and patted him on the back. "You look gorgeous, sweetheart. It doesn't matter what you wear."

"Jessica."

She flashed a sheet of smiley face stickers at him. "No talking, Sed."

Funny how smiley face stickers were far more threatening than a roll of duct tape. Well, now what?

He followed her to the car, lost in thought. Maybe he wasn't supposed to ask her to marry him today. Maybe the universe kept standing in his way for a reason. He climbed into the passenger side of the Mercedes and Jessica climbed behind the wheel. He gazed at her left ring finger, which was entirely too naked for his tastes. As far as he was concerned, the rest of her could stay permanently naked, but not that finger. That finger needed something material that proved to the world she was his. Eternally. Maybe he could get the ring on her while she drove, but her hand was all the way over *there*.

"I'd ask you what has you all introspective again," Jessica said, glancing at him as she waited for the community's security gate to open, "but you're not supposed to talk. Will you write it?"

It's just. He paused for a long moment, wondering what he should write. *I love you.*

She lifted his hand and pressed his knuckles to her lips. "And I love you."

He grinned. Music to his ears.

Music.

That's it. Her song. She needed to hear her song before he proposed. *That's* what the universe was trying to tell him.

"And I love those dimples."

He hated the damn things, but if they made her happy, he'd be sure to smile like a dipshit more often.

She dropped him off at the recording studio on her way to the library. "Do you want me to pick you up, or can one of the guys give you a ride home? I'm not sure how late I'll be."

I'll get a ride, he wrote obediently.

She leaned across the car and kissed him. "I can't wait until Friday. You better behave so I won't have to cancel."

He knew she was manipulating him, but when she slid her hand between his thighs, he didn't much care. He couldn't wait until Friday either.

When he entered the studio about thirty minutes later—he and Jessica had gotten a *bit* carried away in their good-bye kisses—Eric greeted him.

"I wasn't sure you were going to show up." He nodded at the dry erase board in Sed's hand. "What's that for?"

Talking, he wrote.

"You don't need to talk to play violin."

Eric picked up a case from the floor and opened it. A jet black electric violin sat nestled in its confines.

"I'm not—" Sed's throat protested and he winced. He switched to writing again. *I'm not playing violin, Eric. Forget it.*

"You know it's all the screaming you do that destroyed your throat."

"So?" he croaked. Some lackey thrust a bottle of water into his hand. He opened it and took a soothing/painful swallow. He was really wishing he'd stayed in bed with a supply of Popsicles and his personal nurse beside him.

"We need something to replace it."

Sed blinked twice—no.

"Temporarily, at least. Even if you can sing, you know you're not going to be able to scream for a while. And I know you don't want to be the reason we have to cancel a bunch more shows."

Did everyone know how to manipulate him? First Jess. Now Eric. Eric's slim black brows arched over his piercing blue eyes. "Try it?"

Fine.

Sed lifted a hand to block the sparkling white gleam produced by Eric's wide smile, the gloater.

"Here," Eric said, thrusting a stack of music at Sed. "I was up all night finding the exact pitch for every scream in our set."

Every scream? That must have taken him hours. Sed nodded in appreciation, looking over the pages of music and the new additions to their songs in red ink. Well, at least he had something to do while the rest of them recorded. He'd need a lot of practice to pull this off onstage in a week. He'd kind of forgotten to mention that his violin playing sounded like distorted saw blades wrenching through scrap metal.

Brian poked his head out of the recording booth and beckoned Sed over with a wave. When Eric tried to follow Sed into the booth, Brian shoved him out and closed the door.

"Trey and I got to talking last night and we think you should propose to Jessica this Saturday onstage in San Francisco. During the break, you can sing that song you wrote for her. Trey and I have some great acoustic guitar music worked out for it."

Sed scratched his head in confusion. Why was Brian so insistent on him proposing to Jessica?

I do want to sing her the song, but why do I need to do it onstage?

Brian read the message and smiled. "She'll love it. Remember how happy she was the first time you proposed publicly? And you didn't even sing to her that time."

"Come on, Sed," Trey said, leaning against the door to keep Eric, who was banging into it repeatedly outside the booth.

I'll think about it. The "slip the ring on her finger while she wasn't looking" idea was still his favorite option.

"Well, don't take too long to decide. We've only got a week to prepare."

Yeah, okay, whatever.

"*Yeah?*"

"Yeah, I'll do it," Sed rasped, his annoyance level increasing enough to prompt speech. Why had he refused pain meds again? It's not like he'd fall into Trey's pattern of addiction. And he could really use a reprieve from this agony.

"Don't mention it to Eric," Brian whispered. "You know he can't keep a secret."

Sed nodded. That was true.

"Will you just let me in?" Eric yelled.

Trey moved away from the door and Eric burst into the booth.

"Oh," Trey said, "were you trying to get in?"

"What are you guys doing in here?" Eric asked suspiciously.

"Nothing that you need to worry about," Brian said with a wicked smile.

Chapter 50

EVEN THOUGH SED'S DOCTOR had given him the okay to talk normally and to sing at Sinners' concert the next night, Jessica insisted he keep writing on his dry erase board to save his voice for the concert. His throat was perfectly fine. Mostly.

They were in the car on their way to her surprise destination and she was still threatening him with canceling their trip. He continued to obey her, but once they were there, all bets were off. He was tired of writing on this stupid fucking board.

Where are we going? Sed wrote on the board.

"It's a surprise."

Fifteen minutes later they pulled into the unfamiliar driveway of a vast estate. At the gate, she gave both their names. The gate swung open and she drove up the lane.

What are we doing here?

She was too busy finding her way to the airstrip behind the modern-styled mansion to read his message.

"Jess?" he grabbed her arm.

"Relax, sweetheart. Flying will get us there faster."

"Flying?"

"Shh. Dare said we could borrow his jet. And his pilot. Good thing. I don't know how to fly. Do you?"

"His jet?"

"Well, it actually belongs to Exodus End, but they park it on Dare's airstrip. Since they're touring by bus this month, it's not getting much airtime. He said we could use it."

"Since when does Dare have an airstrip?"

"I dunno. Jace suggested it."

"Jace?" Had Jessica ever even spoken to Jace?

"Yes, Jace. Apparently, Jace and Dare are pretty close friends. And your band mates have some kind of bet going. I'm not sure where Dare fits into their scheme."

Sed's brow furrowed. *Bet?* "What bet?"

She grinned. "Like I'd tell you that. I wouldn't want Brian and Trey to win." She winked at him and parked the car near the hangar. A black jet with Exodus End's band logo painted on the side awaited their arrival. What in the hell was his woman up to?

Jessica sat in the beige leather airplane seat and stowed her purse under her feet. She knew she was gawking, but couldn't help it. The six luxurious seats in the cabin were arranged so that each pair faced its partner. There was a sofa. A wide screen TV. Was that a wet bar? Her gaze darted from one extravagance to the next.

Sed took the seat across from her and fastened his seat belt. The pilot, dressed in ripped black jeans and an Exodus End T-shirt, looked less like a pilot and more like a roadie. Or a fan. He wandered through the cabin to speak to them. "It's a short flight. We should be there in less than an hour and a half. The restroom is aft." He grinned at their clueless expressions. "Meaning to the back."

Jessica spotted a door in a gleaming wood panel at the back of the plane.

"The galley is only partially stocked," the pilot continued, "but there's beer in the fridge. Maybe some pretzels and nuts in the cabinet. I dunno."

"Ice?" Sed asked hoarsely.

Jessica scowled. She still didn't think his voice was up to doing an entire live show. He should be in bed. Resting. Not gallivanting around San Francisco so she could surprise him with some over-the-top marriage proposal.

"Yeah, there's crushed ice in the freezer. Dude, I heard about what happened to you onstage last week. Is your voice okay?"

Sed nodded resolutely.

"I'll get you some ice." Jessica stood and moved to the galley area near the front of the jet. It had marble countertops, for crying out loud. Apparently, Exodus End was doing very well. Jessica dispensed some ice chips into a clear plastic cup, which had their band logo on the side (for crying out loud), and returned to Sed's side.

He smiled in gratitude when she handed him the cup, and then he shook some ice into his mouth. His eyes drifted closed in bliss.

Poor baby.

"...so they decided if they're going to tour the world next year, they might as well buy a jet. Plus Dare is dating some chick in Hawaii. Like there aren't enough gorgeous women in California for him to bone. So we're in the air whenever he stops by home and Max keeps getting pissed off 'cause Dare's using the jet for his personal entertainment," the roadie/pilot jabbered. "I never thought I'd be flying a jet for Exodus End. And now for *the* Sed Lionheart. Fuckin' sweet!"

"Is Max going to be pissed that Dare let us borrow the band's jet?" Jessica asked. It felt kind of strange talking about the lead singer of Exodus End like she knew him. She didn't. Like most people on the planet she knew *of* Maximilian Richardson, but that wasn't the same thing.

"Dare won't give a shit. It's Dare." The pilot spread his arms wide as if that explained everything. He burst into laughter, which eventually ended in a snort. "Besides, vocalists and lead guitarists always butt heads. It's some unspoken rule. I think it has something to do with their enormous egos." The guy's eyes widened and he glanced down at Sed. "I didn't mean you and Sinclair."

Sed shrugged and shook more ice into his mouth. "We butt heads on occasion."

The dude checked his watch. "Time to hit the road, or the sky, I suppose," he said. "Where the fuck is Jordan? You can't fly a plane without a pilot."

"I thought you were our pilot," Jessica said.

"Copilot. I don't have enough flight hours. No worries. Jordan is awesome. She used to fly a Harrier in the Royal Navy."

She used to fly a Harrier?

An attractive blonde dressed like a pilot (thank God) in a trim blue skirt suit and doofusey pill-shaped hat entered the plane and poked the copilot in the shoulder. "Did you do the safety check, Lee?" She spoke with a strong British accent.

"Yep, this bird is ready to fly."

"Good." Her eyes met Sed's and then Jessica's. Her brusqueness vanished as she smiled warmly. "Sit back and relax, friends. We'll have you to your destination shortly."

Jordan turned and strode to the cockpit at the front of the plane. Jessica returned to her seat and fastened her seat belt.

"I'll close off the cockpit and give you two a little privacy." Lee winked at Sed and offered his palm for five. "Mile high club, baby."

Sed indulged the guy by slapping his hand and then shook more ice into his mouth.

"You'll need to keep your seat belts fastened during takeoff," Lee informed them and then headed for the cockpit. He slid a wooden panel shut, sealing the cabin from the front of the plane.

"Is the ice helping?" Jessica asked Sed.

He blinked.

"Are you up for this?"

He checked his crotch, adjusting his jeans to allow room for expansion. "Give me a couple of minutes and I'll be all the way up."

She shook her head at him. "I meant this day trip. You should probably be resting up for your concert tomorrow. I feel guilty."

"You feel guilty for fulfilling all my fantasies?"

"Yes. Please rest your voice."

He picked up his dry erase board. *U R 2 far away.*

She stretched out one leg and could just reach his toes. "I agree."

The engines roared to life at the back of the plane.

Sofa? he wrote and cocked his head toward the sofa.

She didn't know if it was the safest place to be during a takeoff, but it had seat belts, so it must be okay. She unfastened her seat belt and darted across the aisle just as the plane began to taxi. She secured herself to the sofa and Sed settled beside her, his cup of ice in one hand, dry erase board in the other. She fastened his seat belt for him and snuggled up against his side, finding his solid warmth comforting, yet unsettling. He set his board aside and wrapped an arm around her shoulders. Yes, this was much better. She wondered if Jace and Eric were on their way to the Golden Gate Bridge yet. A flutter of nerves danced through her belly. She mustn't let herself think about what was in the works for sunset. She and Sed still had an entire day to enjoy together and she refused to be distracted by something that wouldn't take place for another ten hours.

Oh, who was she kidding? She was a wreck. What if Sed wasn't ready to get engaged again?

"Please make sure your cell phone is turned off through the entire duration of the flight," Jordan announced over the intercom.

Sed dug his cell phone out of his pocket and flipped it open, then pointed to the screen, showing Jessica that he had a message.

"It will wait until we get to San Francisco."

So that's where we're going, Sed wrote.

Sed turned off his phone, shoved it back into his pocket, and drew her closer. He kissed her hungrily, his mouth cold from the ice. She clung to his collarbone, her entire body hot from the man.

Before the plane even left the ground, he had her dress half off and her senses fully ignited. She checked to make sure the door concealing the cockpit was still closed and then unfastened his pants. As promised, he was all the way up.

"I've never done it on a plane," he whispered in her ear, his eyes glassy with excitement, his face flushed.

"Until now."

Her fingers trailed lightly down the length of his cock. He sucked a breath between his teeth.

"Tell us to take off our seat belts," he chanted. "Tell us to take off our seat belts."

Jessica continued to tease him while his hand kneaded one bare breast gently. His fingertips plucked at her nipple. More kneading. More plucking. Not nearly enough fucking. She groaned.

"Ah God, Sed, hurry. I need you." She grabbed his cock to show him how much.

"Jess. Jess."

As the plane gained altitude, her ears popped. The plane dipped as they hit a pocket of turbulence.

"Hold tight, folks," the pilot said over the intercom, "and please remain seated through this rough patch here."

Sed's hand moved to Jessica's other breast. He tossed more ice chips in his mouth and sucked a cool trail along the side of her neck.

His hand moved to the hem of her dress and slid it upward to reveal her mound. She spread her legs and closed her eyes. She wouldn't be able to handle watching his hand bringing her pleasure. His fingertips separated her swollen flesh and slid over her clit. She shuddered violently. Or maybe that was the plane hitting turbulence again. He quickly sent her senses spiraling high above the earth and it had nothing to do with the miracle of flight.

"Ah God, Sed, I can't stand it."

"We are now at cruising altitude," Jordan said over the intercom, "feel free to move about the cabin..." The rest of her words didn't register.

Sed released both their seat belts, flattened Jessica on her back upon the sofa, and plunged into her body with a groan of torment. Jessica cried out as her body strained against his, taking its pleasure instantly in a deep, pulsating orgasm. His hard, quick strokes carried him to join her seconds later. He held her hips while he erupted inside her, his cock buried as deeply as possible, his face contorted in ecstasy. He took a gasping breath and collapsed on top of her, cradling her body in his arms.

He chuckled, his body quaking above her. "Sorry about that, sweetheart. I didn't realize you had me that worked up."

She cupped his face to get him to look at her. "I liked it. It was exciting." As she stared into his sky blue eyes, she knew he never got that worked up over any other woman. Just her.

"You want to try again?"

"Many, many times," she said, "but later. While we're sightseeing."

His cock twitched inside her. "If I didn't already love you, Jessica Chase, I'd fall in love with you all over again, every minute of every day."

She kissed him, emotions stealing her breath. She gazed up at him, brushing her thumb along his cheekbone. "You can be so sweet sometimes."

He rolled his eyes. "That secret dies with you. Promise me."

"I promise."

He grinned, both dimples making an appearance. "So what are we going to do today in San Francisco?"

She wiggled her eyebrows suggestively. "What aren't we going to do?"

Chapter 51

SED'S WOMAN WAS AWESOME. They'd enjoyed a soft-food lunch in Chinatown followed by hot, uninhibited sex against a wall in some back alley. She'd taken him to the top of Coit Tower in all its phallic glory and they'd gazed out over magnificent views of San Francisco with his cock buried inside her from behind. His black leather duster was undoubtedly the best clothing investment he'd ever made. After hiking up several hills from hell and getting "lost" in some bushes for about an hour, they'd gone to an art museum. He didn't remember much of what they'd seen there. The most interesting and beautiful thing in the place had been the woman with him. And how was he supposed to concentrate on art and culture and refinement and all that bullshit when she kept rubbing her succulent ass against his ever-attentive cock? She'd driven him so mad with lust, he'd eventually pulled her into a supply closet and she'd given him the best blow job of his life.

He had no idea where the limo was taking them now, but realized he enjoyed letting Jessica run the show. She was damn good at it.

"Are you tired?" she asked.

Exhausted, but he'd never admit that to her. "I'm fine."

"We can relax on the boat."

His interest perked. "Boat?"

"A romantic dinner and sunset on the bay."

"Sounds wonderful. Why did you go to all this trouble?"

"Because I love you."

"And how did you afford it?" Not that he was unwilling to pay for it. If she put it on his credit card, he was perfectly okay with that. He just wondered.

"Myrna paid me. And I got my scholarship back, so I had some extra cash to blow."

He stared at her in disbelief. "You were irresponsible with money for me?"

She scowled, that wonderful hair trigger temper of hers exploding. "I wouldn't call it irrespons—"

He cut off her words with a hungry kiss. When she went limp and compliant in his arms, he pulled away and stared into her lovely jade-green eyes. "The best day of my life used to be the day I asked you to marry me onstage in Pittsburgh, but as memorable as that was, today has been even better."

She smiled at him. "It's not over yet."

"It can't possibly improve."

"I'll consider that a challenge."

Oh yes, please do. His cock stirred in his pants again. Before he could make good use of his excitement, the limo let them out at Fisherman's Wharf. The crowd buzzed with curiosity in their wake. He didn't know if it was because people recognized them or because they'd been riding in a limousine, but no one approached. Jessica took his hand and led him to a large sailboat near the end of a dock. The captain greeted them, handed Jessica a picnic basket, and within minutes they were on their way across the water. He needed to call Brian to tell him he was already in San Francisco. They wouldn't be riding to the venue together as they'd planned.

"I need to use the restroom," he told her and kissed her gently.

She glanced out at the western horizon anxiously. "Hurry back," she said and started removing things from the picnic basket, carefully arranging them on the small round table on the deck.

In the bathroom, Sed turned on his cell phone and it beeped. New message. Three of them. All from Brian.

The first message said, "Sed, you need to stay home today. Eric and Jace are up to something. Call me."

Eric and Jace?

And the second, "Dare told us you're on your way to San Francisco with Jessica. I hope you check your messages soon. I have something important to tell you. Call me. Immediately."

The final message, "Sed, whatever you do, don't get on that boat!"

Sed's heart sank to his toes. Too late for that. He was already on the boat. Was Jessica planning to kill him and then dump his body overboard before sailing off into the sunset with his drummer and bassist? And how did Brian know about their plan? Was he in on it or trying to save Sed's life? Palms sweating, Sed dialed Brian and waited for him to answer.

"Finally. I've been waiting for you to call me back all day."

"What the fuck is going on, Brian?"

"Please tell me you're not on the boat."

"I'm on the boat."

"Shit!" Brian then spoke to someone on his end, "He's already on the boat."

"Shit!" Trey said in the background.

Brian spoke into his phone again, "Okay, moving on to plan B."

Sed scratched his head behind his ear. "Plan B. What was Plan A?"

"You've got to do it today, buddy. Like, right now."

Sed was not following him. Like, at all. "Do what?"

"Propose to Jessica."

"Yeah, tomorrow during the concert. We already planned the whole thing."

"You can't wait. Go do it right now."

"Now? What's going on, Brian?"

Brian hesitated and then sighed loudly. "I can't say."

"Tell him," Trey said loud enough for Sed to hear.

"It's not a fair win if we tell him. It won't count."

"I'm not getting the tattoo of Eric's choice on my ass because you're being some honorable douche bag," Trey said. "Give me the damn phone. I'm telling him."

Sed held the device away from his ear as his two guitarists wrestled over Brian's phone. Loudly. Apparently, Brian won.

"You have to ask her to marry you before sunset. Okay?" Brian said breathlessly. "Just trust me on this. You know I wouldn't steer you wrong."

"I'm not asking her until she hears her song. It's the only reason I haven't proposed yet." Well, that, and he was nervous. Also putting the ring on her finger in her sleep hadn't worked out so well.

"So sing it to her."

"Without music? Don't be stupid, Brian. You and Trey have been rehearsing her song all week."

"What about the recording you guys made a couple years ago?" Sed heard Trey say in the background.

"Yes! I forgot about the recording. Perfect! Sed, if I play the song for her over the phone, will you ask her? We can still play it for her live at the concert tomorrow." Brian made a sound of desperation—half whine, half groan. "*Please.*"

Brian never asked Sed for much and he owed the guy a lot. Sed sighed in annoyance, knowing he couldn't refuse. "If you send me the song, I guess so."

Brian released a sigh of relief. "Thank God. I hope I still have it. I'll check my files and call you back A.S.A.F.P."

"Fine," Sed said. "You know, if you crazy bastards would quit making stupid bets…"

"You've made your share of stupid bets."

Sed couldn't deny it.

"I'll try to find it," Brian continued, "but if for some reason I can't, promise you'll ask her anyway. Before sunset."

What was the big deal with sunset? Was she going to turn into an ogre or something?

"I'll ask her. When I'm ready."

Trey was hollering, "What did he say? Is he going to save our asses? I mean literally. Brian?" when Sed disconnected.

Sed still didn't completely understand the bet or what Eric and Jace had to do with anything. Maybe Jessica could explain it. He set his phone on vibrate and stuffed it back in his pocket. Before returning to deck, he used the bathroom facilities and washed up in the little sink. He no longer thought Jessica planned to kill him (well, probably not), but he was a bit leery of her intentions now that he knew she was in on some stupid bet his band mates had devised. No telling what he was in for.

On deck, he took the chair across from her and she smiled sweetly, the sinking sun making her strawberry blonde hair glow a pale gold.

"Canned peaches? They should be easy on your throat."

His throat really wasn't bothering him at all, but he nodded, unlikely to ever refuse her coddling. "What happens at sunset?"

She dropped her fork in the big container of peaches. "The sun goes down."

He shook his head at her. "Smartass," he murmured with a crooked grin. After she retrieved the fork, he watched her lick peach syrup off her fingers.

"Why did you ask me that?" she asked suspiciously.

"I just talked to Brian on the phone. He seemed to think something significant was going to happen at sunset. Something involving Eric and Jace. You aren't planning to murder me, are you?"

Her initial stunned expression quickly turned to uneasy laughter. "Murder you? Eh, no, not exactly."

"Then what exactly are you planning on doing?"

"It's a surprise. A good one. I promise." She offered him a peach with her fork. "Just relax, okay? You're making me nervous."

He slurped the peach down his throat. "Making *you* nervous?"

"Look," she said, pointing at something over his shoulder. "There's Alcatraz."

Why was she pointing out one of the most horrible prisons in existence? Maybe she was just trying to distract him. They were sailing away from Alcatraz and closer to the Golden Gate Bridge over her shoulder.

"And there's the Golden Gate Bridge."

She glanced behind her and turned a sickly shade of green. "Already?"

The closer they got to the bridge, the greener she looked.

"Are you okay?" he asked.

She nodded slightly. Fed him another peach.

Sed's phone vibrated in his pocket. His heart skipped a beat. He hoped it meant Brian had found the music file. At the same time, nerves were getting the better of him. They should just wait until tomorrow.

The sun sank lower, appearing as a glowing red-orange ball on the horizon.

His phone vibrated again. He took a deep breath and pulled his phone from his pocket. It was Brian.

"I need to take this, sweetheart. Excuse me." He turned his back on her and answered, "What?"

"I found it. Put Jessica on the phone and I'll play it for her."

Sed took a deep breath and handed her the phone. This was it.

She gave him an odd look as she took the phone from his hand.

"Brian has something you need to listen to."

She glanced at the bridge behind her. It loomed larger and larger with each passing moment. "Can it wait?"

"Please."

She held the phone up to her ear. "Brian?"

He said something to her, Sed could only guess what. Her expression changed from curiosity to wonder, and then her eyes filled with unexpected tears.

"Oh no, don't do that," Sed said.

"You wrote this song?" She covered her lips with trembling fingers. "For me?" she asked, her voice cracking.

"Yes, I wanted you to hear it before—"

"It's beautiful."

The time was right. Certainty replaced his nervousness in an instant. He removed her ring from his pocket and went down on one knee before her. "Jessica," he said, his heart full to bursting, "will you mar—"

Her eyes widened. "No. No, don't do that. Not now. You'll ruin everything." She dropped his phone, stood, and pulled him to his feet by his shirt.

Her verbal slash to his heart stole his breath.

No? She'd said no. How could she say no?

Jessica turned and waved vigorously at the bridge overhead with both arms. She took Sed's hands in hers. He felt it. He saw it. Her love. It was there in her eyes. So clear he could reach out and touch it. Why had she refused him?

Why?

The ring. It was too small. She deserved better. What had she said when she'd thrown it at him two years ago? Hock that cheap piece of shit. But even if that was her reasoning, he could not accept it. Would not. She loved him. He knew she did. So why? Why had she said no? What could he have done differently? He couldn't let her go again. He just couldn't. She had to—

"Sed, sweetheart. Look up at the bridge."

Sed obeyed, too stunned to argue. He could barely hear the roar of a motorcycle on the bridge far above and then an enormous white banner unfurled over the edge of San Francisco's most famous landmark. *Will* was written on the banner in huge red letters. A few seconds later a second banner opened. *you.* And then a third. *marry.* Someone (Jace?) was riding a motorcycle across the pedestrian walk of the bridge and opening the banners one by one. *me.* And the final banner fluttered open: *p²S.*

"Pez?"

"Oh no, they got the last banner upside down." Jessica laughed and then looked up at Sed. "It's supposed to say Will you marry me, *Sed*?" She smiled anxiously. "Well? Will you?"

Her beautiful face blurred as ridiculous, sentimental tears filled his eyes. He wiped at them with the heels of his hands. She was asking him? For real? *Yes, yes, God yes.* He lifted her left hand, pressed it to his trembling lips, and then, at long last, slid her ring on her finger.

She glanced down at it and gasped. "This is my ring. The one you gave me in Pittsburgh."

He nodded, incapable of speech. His heart clogged his throat.

"You kept it? You didn't hock it to fix your tour bus?"

"It never left my pocket. It's yours, Jessica. Always has been, always will be," he said breathlessly. "And now it's back where it belongs. On your finger."

"Oh, sweetheart, I can't even tell you how much this means to me." She clutched her hand to her chest, pressing the ring against her heart. Now *her* eyes were filling with ridiculous, sentimental tears. But they looked good on her. Sed cupped her cheek and kissed her tenderly, glad that insignificant trinket meant the world to her as it always had to him. After a long moment, she drew away from his caressing kiss.

"You never answered me," she whispered. "Will you marry me, Sed?"

Unable to catch his breath, much less form words, he did the only thing a singer without a voice could do: he blinked.

"I'll take that as a yes." Jessica grinned and tackled him to the deck. She made short work of his shirt and feverishly pressed her lips along the hard ridge between his pecs, down his quivering belly to his belt buckle. "I'm feeling incredibly naughty, Sedric. How about we consummate this engagement, right here, right now?"

He smiled, knowing both his damned dimples were showing, but he was too giddy to care. "I accept your terms, counsel."

She straddled his hips and pulled her dress off over her head. Her naked skin glowed like honey in the final rays of sunset. He covered her breasts with both hands and her eyes drifted closed in bliss. Dear God, this woman was awesome. His woman. His heart. His Jessica. *His.*

Sed was the happiest man on the planet. Life could not have been more perfect.

Acknowledgments

If it weren't for music, my world would exist in a constant shade of grey. So thanks to the hundreds of musicians who have inspired my creative work and added color to my life. Keep on rocking, so I can keep rolling.

I'd like to thank my family for being understanding and patient when I'm in the writing zone and for never giving up on me. Their unending support and faith in my ability means more than they'll ever know. Sean, you rock!

I'd like to thank my second readers—Sherilyn Winrose, Beth Hill, Judi Fennell, Lisa Brackmann, and Jill Lynn Anderson—for offering their excellent professional opinions and advice on this work. They helped make Sed sing and Jessica worthy of his devotion.

I'd also like to thank my online writing group, The Writin' Wombats. I wouldn't be where I am today without their knowledge, help, support, and occasional (okay, *regular*) kicks in the pants.

Major thanks to my agent Jennifer Schober, who gets me through the business side of this with most of my hair still attached to my scalp.

Finally, I'd like to thank my awesome editor, Deb Werksman, who totally rocks, her ever-helpful associate, Susie Benton, and all the folks at Sourcebooks who believed in an unknown writer enough to give her an incredible opportunity.

About the Author

Raised on hard rock music from the cradle, Olivia Cunning attended her first Styx concert at age six and fell instantly in love with live music. She's been known to travel over a thousand miles just to see a favorite band in concert. She discovered her second love, romantic fiction, as a teen—first voraciously reading steamy romance novels and then penning her own. She currently lives in Nebraska.

Read on for an excerpt from

Backstage Pass

SINNERS ON TOUR

OLIVIA CUNNING

A STACK OF HANDOUTS tumbled from Myrna's laptop case to the floral-patterned carpet. Un-freakin'-believable. She'd forgotten to zip the compartment in her haste to flee the seminar room. With a loud sigh, she bent to gather the scattered papers. Could this day suck a little more, please?

A chorus of "chug, chug, chug, chug," followed by enthusiastic cheers came from across the lobby near the elevators. Well, someone was having a good time tonight. It certainly wasn't her.

She crammed the papers inside her bag and jerked the zipper closed before continuing through the overdone hotel lobby on her way to her sixth-floor room. A long, hot bath sounded like heaven. How had she let her associate dean talk her into presenting at this stupid conference in the first place? What a total waste of time. The other professors in her field wouldn't know an innovative idea if it stood on its head and sang "The Star-Spangled Banner." And why did she care what her colleagues thought of her methods anyway? Students loved her classes. They were always full. She had waiting lists for—

Steps echoed hers. The hairs on the back of her neck stood on end. She paused—her heart racing, palms damp.

Whoever followed stopped several steps behind her. She could hear him breathing.

Jeremy?

No. It couldn't be her ex-husband. He didn't know how to find her. Right? Tell that to the cold sweat trickling between her breasts.

She clutched the handle of her laptop case, prepared to clobber whoever was dumb enough to sneak up on her.

"You gave a great seminar, Dr. Evans," an unfamiliar voice said to her back.

Not Jeremy. Thank God. She took a deep, shaky breath and glanced over her shoulder.

A lanky, fortyish man extended his hand in her direction. "Who would ever think to use guitar riffs in discussions of human psychology? Not me. I mean, I'm sold on the method. I'm just not sure I can pull it off with your level of, uh…" He cleared his throat. "…*enthusiasm*." He grinned, gaze dropping to the neckline of her tailored, gray suit.

Her heart still hammering in her chest, Myrna suppressed the urge to throttle him and extended her free hand to accept his handshake. "Thank you, Mister uh…"

When his fingers wrapped around hers, his smile spread ear-to-ear. "Doctor. Doctor Frank Elroy from Stanford. Abnormal Psych. Head of the department, actually."

Ah, Doctor Ass. Doctor Pompous Ass. I've met you before. Thousands of times.

She nodded and plastered a weary smile to her face. "Nice to meet you, Doctor Elroy."

"Say, would you like to have a drink with me?" He nodded toward the cocktail lounge to her left, his thumb stroking the back of her hand.

Myrna cringed inwardly while maintaining her smile. This guy was the antithesis of her type. Boring. No, thanks. Her present aversion to boring existed at a visceral level. "I'm sorry, but I'll have to pass. I was heading up to my room to crash. Maybe some other time."

He deflated like a punctured balloon. "Sure. I understand. You must be exhausted after that lively…" He grinned again. "…discussion."

Discussion? Had he been there? "Bloodbath" seemed a more fitting description and she felt particularly anemic at the moment.

"Yeah," she muttered, eyes narrowing. She yanked her hand from his, spun on her heel, and continued toward the elevator, walking around the edge of the hotel's bar and skirting several bushy, potted plants.

A loud round of laughter drew her attention to the cocktail lounge. Four men sat in a semi-circular booth, laughing at a fifth man who was lying on his back in the center of their table. The table, covered with glasses containing various amounts of amber liquid, tilted precariously under the man's weight as he leaned to one side. His companions scrambled to rescue their beers from certain demise.

"Tell the room to stop spinning," the lounging man shouted at the knock-off Tiffany lamp above the table.

"No more beer for you, Brian," one of his friends said.

Brian held up a finger. "One more." He lifted another finger, "or two," another finger, "mmmmmaybe four."

Myrna grinned. The five of them didn't exactly "blend" with the conference attendees, mostly professors, scattered throughout the lounge and lobby. The unconventional crew in the booth drew more than their fair share of animosity and stares. Was it the tattoos? The various piercings and spiked jewelry? The dyed hair, strange haircuts and black clothing? Whatever. They were just guys being guys. And not a boring one in the bunch, she'd wager.

Myrna took a hesitant step toward the elevator. She'd love to go hang out with them for a while. She could use a little fun—something other than stimulating conversation with an intellectual. She got enough of that at work.

Brian, still lounging in the center of the table, vocalized a riff, while playing masterful air guitar on his back. Myrna recognized the series of notes at once. She used it in her class discussion on male sensuality, because no one on earth played a guitar more sensually than Master Sinclair. Hold the phone! Could that be...? Nah, what would the rock group Sinners be doing at a college teaching conference? They were probably just fans of the band, though the name Brian made her lead guitarist senses tingle. Wasn't Sinners' lead guitarist named Brian Sinclair?

One of the men seated in the booth turned his head to scratch his chin with his shoulder. Despite his mirrored sunglasses, she instantly recognized vocalist Sedric Lionheart. Her heart rate kicked up a couple notches. It *was* Sinners.

"I am so fucking drunk!" Brian yelled. He rolled off the table, knocking over several empty beer glasses, and landed on the laps of two of his companions. They dumped him unceremoniously on the floor.

Myrna snorted and then glanced around to make sure no one had witnessed her produce such an unladylike sound. She *had* to go talk to them. She could pretend she wanted to meet them because of her seminar. In truth, she loved their music. They weren't too hard on the eyes either. The definition of exactly her type. Wild. Yes, please. Guaranteed to give her exactly what she needed after the day she'd had.

Abandoning her plan to hide in her room, Myrna skirted the low wall that separated the lounge area from the corridor. She paused in front of Brian, who was struggling to crawl to his hands and knees. She set her lumpy laptop case on the floor and bent to help him to his feet. The instant she touched his arm, her heart skipped a beat and then began to race.

Animal magnetism. He had it. *Hello, Mr. Welcome Diversion.*

His gaze drifted up her legs and body, his face slowly tilting into view. He had features a sculptor would love: strong jaw, pointed chin, high cheekbones. Would it be presumptuous of her to examine the contours of his face with her fingertips? Her lips? She forced her attention to her hand, which gripped his well-muscled upper arm.

"Be careful with this arm," she said. "So few guitarists have your skill."

He used her support to stagger to his feet. When he stumbled against her, she caught his scent and inhaled deeply, her eyes drifting closed. Primal desire bombarded her senses. Did she just growl aloud?

His strong hands gripped her shoulders as he steadied himself. Every nerve ending in her body shifted into high alert. She couldn't remember that last time she'd been instantaneously attracted to a man.

Brian released her and leaned against the back of the booth for support. He blinked hard, as if trying to focus his intense, brown eyes on her face. "You know who I am?" he asked, his voice slurred.

She smiled and nodded eagerly. "Who doesn't?"

He waved a hand around theatrically, which set him even further off balance. "Every stuffed-shirt geek in the whole damned place, that's who."

He snarled at a gray-haired woman in a heavy cardigan who sat openly gaping at him. The woman gasped and turned her attention to her ocean blue cocktail, slurping the blended beverage through a tiny, red straw as nonchalantly as possible.

"Brian, don't start shit," Sed, the group's lead singer, said.

The acidic look Brian shot at Sed could peel paint. "What? I'm not starting anything. These people all have *fuck*-king staring problems!"

True. They were staring. Most of them at Myrna now. Probably wondering how to best rescue her from *enemy* territory.

"Do you mind if I sit with you for a while?" Myrna asked, hoping to become less noticeable by sitting. She tucked the lock of hair that had escaped her hairclip behind her ear and smiled at Brian hopefully. He stroked his eyebrow with his index finger as he contemplated her request. She knew what he must be thinking. Why would a stuffy-looking chick in a business suit request to sit with five rock stars?

Sed scooted over in the semi-circular booth and patted the empty expanse of forest green vinyl beside him. She tugged her gaze from Brian to look at Sed. Sed's boy-next-door good looks contrasted his bad-boy, womanizing reputation. She didn't follow the personal lives of the bands she admired, but even she knew Sed's rep. His smile, complete with dimples, could ice a cake, which was likely why he covered it so rapidly with a scowl. A quick veil of indifference returned his cool status. Those darling dimples didn't quite fit his image.

Myrna slid into the booth next to Sed, wiping her sweaty palms on her skirt as she settled beside him. *Okay, I'm in. Now what?*

"Are you some kind of business woman or something?" Sed leaned back to examine her professional attire.

Myrna didn't mind his twice over. "Or something. Actually, I'm a stuffed-shirt geek. A college professor here at the conference."

"No shit?" She recognized the speaker, who sat across from her, as Eric Sticks, the band's drummer. "If I'd have known college professors were hot, I might have considered an education."

Myrna laughed. She glanced up at Brian who still leaned against the booth next to Eric's right shoulder. Her heart gave a painful throb. God, he was gorgeous. "Would you like to sit down, Brian?"

Myrna scooted closer to Sed, her knee settling against his beneath the table. Brian collapsed on the seat beside her, lodging her between two of the sexiest and most talented musicians in the business. She'd died and gone to heaven. *Play it cool, Myrna. If you start spazzing out like a fan girl, they'll tell you to get lost.* And she certainly didn't want that.

Brian leaned forward and rested his forehead on the table with a groan. It took all of Myrna's concentration not to offer a soothing touch. She knew who he was, but he didn't know her from Adam. Well, hopefully, he could tell her from *Adam*, but, uh...

She took a deep breath to collect her scattered thoughts and forced her attention to Eric. She could look at him without getting all giddy, but found she couldn't stop staring at his insane hairstyle—half-long, a center strip of short spikes, the rest various lengths and just plain strange. A crimson, finger-thick lock curled around the side of his neck. *Rock star hair.* She stifled an excited giggle.

"So what do you teach?" Eric took a sip of his beer, his pale blue eyes never leaving her face. Well, maybe he checked out her chest a little, but he mostly kept his gaze above her neck.

Myrna winced at his question and lowered her eyes to the table. Any chance of her earning their respect would evaporate the moment she revealed what subject she taught. "Do I have to say?"

"Come on."

She sighed heavily. "Human Sexuality."

Eric sputtered in his beer. He wiped his mouth with the back of his hand. "Fuck me."

"Well, yeah, I guess that is my subject matter," Myrna said, with a crooked grin.

The guys laughed. Except for Brian. Unmoving, his head still rested on the table in front of him. Had he lost consciousness? *Wasted* didn't come close to describing his current condition.

"Is he okay?" Myrna asked.

"Yeah, he's just a little fucked up," Eric said.

"He's a lot fucked up," said Trey Mills, the band's rhythm guitarist, who lounged in the booth next to Eric.

"Shut up," Brian murmured. He turned his head to look up at Myrna. He held one eye closed as he tried to focus on her. She had an inexplicable urge to straighten his tousled, jet-black hair, which fell just below collar-length and stuck out at odd angles all over his head. "What's your name, Professor Sex?"

She smiled. Maybe he was interested. "Myrna."

Backstage Pass

SINNERS ON TOUR

By Olivia Cunning

*"Olivia Cunning's erotic romance
debt is phenomenal."*
—LOVE ROMANCE PASSION

• •

FOR HIM, LIFE IS ALL MUSIC AND NO PLAY...
When Brian Sinclair, lead songwriter and guitarist of the
hottest metal band on the scene, loses his creative spark, it
will take nights of downright sinful passion to release his
pent-up genius...

SHE'S THE ONE TO CALL THE TUNE...
When sexy psychologist Myrna Evans goes on tour with the
Sinners, every boy in the band tries to woo her into his bed.
But Brian is the only one she wants to get her hands on...

Then the two lovers' wildly shocking behavior sparks the whole
band to new heights of glory... and sin...

• •

*"These guys are so sensual, sexual, and yummy.
[T]his series... will give readers another wild ride,
and I can't wait!"*
—NIGHT OWL REVIEWS
5/5 STARS
REVIEWER TOP PIC

978-1-4022-4442-1 • $14.99 U.S./$17.99 CAN/£9.99 UK